THE IRON MAIDEN

14206-ANTH

THE IRON MAIDEN

Bio of a Space Tyrant #6

Piers Anthony

14206-ANTH

To order additional copies of this book, contact:
Xlibris Corporation
1-888-7-XLIBRIS
www.Xlibris.com
Orders@Xlibris.com

CONTENTS

Editorial Preface *7*

Finger Whip 9

Bubble 20

Empty Hand 29

Children 44

Woman 58

Hidden Flower 75

Gerald 102

Betrayal 123

Second Love 156

Secret 176

Hopie 196

Campaign 219

Tyrant 245

Tyrancy 269

Shelia 290

Saturn 307

Planets 323

Affair 344

Fifteen Women 366

Dream 385

Author's Note *403*

There have been many biographies of the Tyrant of Jupiter, Hope Hubris, and five volumes of his private memoirs, of a more personal nature. He surely lived a life worthy of them. But he functioned throughout his tenure with the substantial support of his younger sister, Spirit. She was a more private and less expressive person, seldom seeking the center stage, and so she is comparatively unknown. But she was arguably as important to the Tyrancy as was her brother. Certainly it would never have come to pass without her. Therefore she is worthy of her own biography. This is that narrative.

Spirit wrote no autobiographical material; it was not, she said, her way. She was persuaded only with reluctance to tell her story, in fragments, with many promptings. She pleaded the urgency of the business she had to accomplish, and indeed she was a busy person, but it was more than that. It was as if she hardly saw herself as a person in her own right, but rather as an adjunct to her brother and to the Tyrancy. But she did have a personal life, and she did have feelings, for all that she was known by many as the Iron Maiden. Much of what she accomplished is a matter of voluminous record, often credited to her brother. Her feelings are to a degree extrapolated here, because of her aversion to their open expression. She declined even to comment on the portions of this narrative when shown for her approval or correction. "It will do," was all she said.

It will have to do.

HMH

CHAPTER 1

FINGER WHIP

Spirit struggled with herself before approaching her brother. She did not want to bother him, but there was no other person she could truly trust. He had a special awareness that gave him an almost supernatural rapport with others, and that enabled him to relate to her as no other person could. But by similar token, she was more than a little in awe of him. Finally she thought of a way: she would make him a deal. Then it would be even, and she could get what she wanted.

He was in his room, studying. He was not impressive physically at age fourteen; he was thin, not tall, with brown hair and the swarthy Hispanic complexion. But he was very understanding, and that was perhaps what she liked best about him. He never laughed at her, in contrast to big sister Faith, and he never betrayed her confidences. Thus he was her model for social behavior; before she did anything different, she would ask herself whether Hope would do it, and if the answer was no, then she would not.

"Hope?" she inquired tentatively.

He looked up. "Spirit," he said, smiling. That encouraged her; there was something about him, a warmth that the smile enhanced. It wasn't her imagination, because she had seen others react positively to his presence; he was popular among classmates. Some kind of personal magnetism that radiated invisibly out from him and reflected from others. He could be a student leader if he wanted to be; so far he hadn't sought it.

"Hope, I want to make a deal."

He focused more alertly on her. "You don't have to do that, little sister. Just tell me what you want."

"No, this is something you maybe won't want to do, so I have to trade you for it. What do you want?"

He knew her well enough not to argue. "I want a good grade on this paper I'm studying for. I don't think you can help me there." He wasn't teasing her; he never did that unkindly. He had the courtesy to take her seriously, and she truly appreciated that. "Maybe if you tell me what you want, I can figure out a price for it."

"Okay. I want a finger whip."

"A what?"

"A finger whip. It's a little thing, sort of an invisible thread about a meter long with a bit of a weight on the end. It hooks to the middle finger, and you can flick it out so it stings someone."

"That's an odd toy."

"It's not a toy, it's a weapon. It really stings. A few of the kids have them, and I've got the marks to prove it." She showed two small welts on her left arm, that she had used to protect her body or face. "So if some tough boy comes, I can stop him."

Hope frowned. "If some tough boy comes, maybe you had better tell me, so I can intercede. I'm supposed to do that for Faith, now that's she's beautiful."

"I know. She needs protection. I don't have that problem, because I'm not pretty. I just don't like getting pushed around."

He gazed at her with that uncanny perception he had, as if seeing through her face and into her mind. It was another aspect of his gift; he could read people, and know their nature, and whether they were lying. It kept him out of a lot of trouble. Their parents were aware of this, which was probably why they had assigned him to protect Faith. Faith was so pretty she scintillated, and boys clustered around her, but she wasn't smart. Not the way Hope was. So Hope had to watch out for her, and she was under orders to heed him, which truly rankled her. To Faith, the only thing lowlier than a little brother was a little sister.

"You don't have that problem yet," Hope said. "But you will."

"Sure," she agreed derisively. Did he think she had never looked in a mirror?

"And I can't be with you all the time, so maybe you're right: you need to be able to defend yourself. I'll help you get the finger whip."

"Great!" she exclaimed, relieved, because he could have said no, and it would have been reasonable for him to do so. Hope was eminently reasonable, except when he wasn't. "What do you want in return?"

"Nothing, Spirit. You're my sister, and you have a reasonable need; that's enough."

"That's not a deal. I want it to be a fair exchange, so I don't owe you anything."

He smiled. "I think your gratitude will do."

"No it won't! You got that anyway."

"Then I'll take your support, at such time as I need it."

"You got it." He had that already, also, but now it was a legal commitment. If he ever needed her help, she would give it without limit.

"But I must debate something you said. Will you listen?"

That meant it was serious. She braced herself, ready for a lecture on the caution and responsibility any weapon required, even a finger whip. "Sure."

"You aren't not pretty."

This tumbled her brace, coming as it did from an unexpected direction. "I'm not what?"

"Faith is beautiful. You said that you are not pretty. You feel inferior to her because of that. You are mistaken."

He had scored, as he always did. But she had learned to listen to his words carefully, because sometimes he spoke so precisely that it was deceptive. "I'm mistaken? I'm not not-pretty—but that doesn't mean I'm pretty. What's my mistake?"

"Remember, you said you would listen."

He was going to explain in some detail. In the past she had not always had patience with his explanations, because Hope was as smart as Faith was pretty, and Spirit was about as far behind him in that respect as she was behind Faith in looks. But this time she really wanted to have it, because he had touched a nerve. "My feet are anchored to the planet and my ears are locked open."

He reached out and patted her shoulder. Some might have thought this to be a condescending gesture, but it was as though an electrical charge passed from his hand to her body, providing a momentary thrill. She liked his touch, because he didn't touch unless he cared. "You are not pretty now, but that does not mean you are locked down. Faith was much the same, at your age, eleven, but in the following two years she changed significantly. Suddenly the boys were noticing her, and as she caught on and began prettifying herself, it got worse. The key was puberty. You are about to grow breasts and all the rest, and then you will perhaps be as pretty as Faith, if you wish to work at it as she does."

This was hard to believe. "Work at it?"

"I think half of Faith's beauty is her body. The other half is the way she arranges her hair, applies makeup, the clothing she chooses, and her attitude. She makes a science of prettiness. I think you will have a similar body, but maybe not care to make a similar effort. You're not ugly or even plain, you're merely unfinished, and if you did your hair and face and clothing as she does, you would be pretty now—and beautiful in two years."

"You're fooling!" But he wasn't, and she knew it. She trusted his judgment; if he said she would be beautiful, then she would be. She felt an internal melting and shifting, for he had just taken down her biggest liability and granted her the potential for what she had feared would be forever beyond her reach.

Hope merely shook his head, gently, waiting for her acceptance to form and solidify. Then he spoke again. "Neither are you stupid. You are as smart as I am, only in a different way."

"But you can read and move people! I can't do that."

"You can organize, you have nerve, and you have a tough core. You learn rapidly and well. Those are good qualities."

He had addressed her unspoken concern: that she wasn't smart. Now she had two legs to stand on.

She felt herself brimming. "Oh, big brother, I—I'm going to—would you—?"

He spread his arms, and she turned and plumped into his lap, hugging against him. Then the tears came, while he held her firmly and patted her back with his fingers. Spirit seldom cried; in fact this was the first time in months. But her life had changed, by the power of his insight, and she couldn't handle it immediately.

After a time she sat up straight, still on his lap, and fished for a handkerchief. He found one and carefully wiped her face for her.

"Don't tell," she said.

He nodded, agreeing not to tell anyone that she had cried.

"I love you, big brother."

"And I love you, little sister."

"I'm going to kiss you. Don't tell."

He nodded again, and held still for her kiss. She planted her damp mouth against his and pressed close, suddenly taken by passion. The kiss endured, becoming ardent. The pleasure she had felt before at his touch spread through her body, fulfilling it in a fashion she did not understand but nevertheless reveled in. She had said she loved him; she had understated the case, if that was possible. He was, for this timeless moment, her world.

But she had to end it, because she had started it and it was thus her province to define the experience. Reluctantly she lifted her head back. Then, somehow ashamed, she got off his lap and ran from the room.

She had come for a deal for a finger whip, but gotten so much more, she just had to be alone for a while. She had to reassemble her psyche, orienting on the prospect of becoming lovely instead of plain. Of being halfway smart instead of dull. Two years—that wasn't much time to wait. To be even a little like Faith, and like Hope: now she dared dream.

They had exchanged professions of love, but while his had been familial, hers had been romantic. She did know the difference. She not only loved her brother, she desired him—and knew that that was out of line. Fortunately he was innocent in this respect, seeing her not only as his sister, but as an eleven year old girl, not realizing that her emotion preceded her body by a year or two. So she could hide the illicit nature of her feeling, even from him. *Especially* from him. She could conceal it because she had to. It was her second level secret.

Still, he *had* kissed back. So maybe he felt some of it, and shared some of her guilt. He would have something to bury, too. That made her feel better, ironically.

*

Next day they went to get the finger whip. It was Saturday, without school, and a carnival had come to the city-dome of Maraud. It was run by traveling Gypsies, and had all manner of marginal entertainments, such as sexy dancing girls, scary rides, and deceptive games of chance. The city authorities did not much approve of the carnivals, but they were so popular that there would have been civil unrest if they were banned. So they were officially ignored, and unofficially patronized by throngs.

There were people of all kinds here, white, black, red, yellow and all shades between, their cultures ranging similarly from

Hispanic through French, American Indian, African, Mongolian, and Saxon. Maraud was a grab-bag of types, because it had originally been part of the Dominant Republic, then taken by pirates who settled it with a number of their captives. It had finally been assigned to Halfcal when the political lines were redrawn to move this entire region into what was politically expedient. Now its city government was Hispanic, with some token Creole to keep the national authorities off its back, and its divergent elements were slowly melding. That was all right with Spirit; she had friends of all persuasions at school, and knew that neither color nor culture defined the whole person. There were great guys and creeps in every section.

She led Hope to the booth where the key prizes were. A laser gun was mounted on the counter, fixed so that it could fire only forward, at a screen across which a number of images danced. Because this was technically classified as a game of chance, it was rated 12+. Only children age twelve or above could play it. Their ages were verified, so there could be no charges of cheating those below the age of partial consent.

This was where Hope came in. "One game," he said, and paid the fare of one dollar. Because the Gypsies traveled widely, they had standardized on Jupiter money rather than divergent local currencies. There were change makers throughout, so that dollars were easy to come by. However, the nation of Halfcal used dollars too, so there was in any event no problem.

"Put up your hand."

Hope held up his right hand, and the booth man aimed an identification reader at it. In a moment its little screen lighted with print. **HOPE HUBRIS, age 14.** He had been minimally verified; that was all that was required.

The booth man touched a switch, and the laser weapon glowed. "Which game?" he asked.

Hope looked at Spirit. "Meteors," she said.

The man looked at Hope. "Meteors," Hope repeated.

Spirit put her hand on the laser. It was obvious that she was the one who was playing, but officially it was Hope. If there were a challenge, Hope would be in as much trouble as the booth man. But there would not be; Hope was playing by proxy. This was the way to get around the age restriction. It was a tacit conspiracy of silence that even the city administration accepted. No children were being corrupted here, legally.

The screen became stellar, with the stars of the galaxy showing above a city dome on a moon. "Captain!" a voice exclaimed in English, which was another standard of these Gypsies. It didn't stop those who knew only Spanish from playing, as they already understood the game. "There's a meteor shower headed for the capital city!"

"We must stop it," the bold voice of the captain replied. "Man the laser cannon. We must not let a single meteor get through, or the city is doomed."

Now the meteors showed as bright streaks. It didn't matter that no such streaks occurred in space, only in atmosphere; this was a game. They were headed right for the dome.

Spirit began firing. A laser beam speared out to strike the screen. Never mind that true lasers were invisible, except for their effects; this was another aspect of the game. The beam just missed the leading meteor. But Spirit's second shot got it, and it exploded beautifully. Already the second meteor was looming, and she got that one too.

After that the meteors came faster, sometimes by twos or threes. Spirit got them all, until one meteor didn't explode, but fissioned into two parts still headed for the dome. Spirit had to reorient the gun to strike first one, then the other, but as she did so, another meteor crashed through, and crashed into the dome. The dome exploded with a display quadruple that of a struck meteor, with fragments of buildings and even people flying outward. The game was lost.

"Damn!" Spirit swore, staring at the wreckage. Then the image faded.

"Too bad," the booth man said to Hope. "You almost got

them all."

"Almost," Hope agreed, and paid over another dollar.

"You're a pretty sharp player."

"Pretty sharp," Hope agreed as the laser gun came back to life and the starry screen returned.

Now there were several spectators, as it was evident that Spirit was indeed a good shot. They were silent, so as not to distract her, but paid close attention. This game was simple in concept, but not easy to win.

This time Spirit got all the meteors, until a group of four cruised by. She got three of them, but could not catch the fourth, and it scored on the dome.

"Four!" a spectator said as the game ended. "Is that legit?"

"Rare but legit," the booth man said. "When one person plays more than once, the subsequent games get harder. So if you want to quit now—"

Spirit looked pleadingly at Hope. "One more game," he said, paying the dollar.

The man took the dollar, but did not turn on the game right away. "Sir, I like your look," he said to Hope. "You're playing well. Let me give you and these following players a hint: you can see the bad ones coming. The clusters are brighter. So its best to clear out all the routine ones and orient on the clusters as early as you can. It's still no easy score, but if you're sharp enough, its possible."

"Thank you," Hope said. He knew the booth man was playing to the crowd, hoping for many more players. In fact it wouldn't bother him if Spirit won, because it would show that it could be done. But she had to earn it.

The third game came on. This time Spirit didn't wait for the meteors to come within easy range; she picked them off at a distance. She missed more, but had unlimited shots, and was able to get them with second shots, still farther away than before. The shower was almost over, and she had the field mostly cleared. Then a bright one showed, the last.

"Oh, damn," the booth man murmured. "That's a boulder."

A boulder was a meteor too big to blast apart. It would have to be chipped down by several shots, and there would not be time to demolish it completely before it caught the dome.

But Spirit knew this game, and knew the strategy for boulders. She caught it with a glancing shot, and a fragment separated from one side. The fragment went wide left, out of play, and the remainder of the boulder nudged slightly right. She caught it with another shot, on the same side, and nudged it right again. She was able to chip it five times before it got by her and flew on toward the dome.

All of them watched as it went. It was only a few seconds, but seemed longer. Then the fragment struck the surface of the planet just beside the dome. A spray of rocks and dust went up, but the dome remained intact. She had won.

A cheer went up from the audience. Spirit leaned back, feeling weak with relief. That had been close!

"Good game, kid!" the booth man said. Then he corrected himself and addressed Hope. "I mean, sir. You nudged it just far enough to miss the dome. You won. What's your prize?"

"The finger whip," Hope said.

"Good choice." The booth man handed over the little package. "May you have much joy of it."

They left the booth. Already others were clamoring to play, so Spirit's effort had indeed been good for business. Hope handed her the package, and she quickly pocketed it. "Thanks," she said, overflowing with gratefulness. This might have been a routine favor for him, but she had truly wanted the whip, and the favor loomed much larger on her screen than on his. "I'll pay you back the money."

Thereafter she practiced diligently with the finger whip. It was tricky at first, and her middle finger got sore, but she was determined and well coordinated, and in due course became so proficient she could snap coins out of the air. When she tackled other finger whippers and won the junior championship of her schoolyard, she knew she was good enough. Never again would anyone sting her with one of these, because she was no longer a patsy. Thereafter she retired, in her fashion, never showing or using the whip unless there was need. But it was always with her.

Similarly she masked her infatuation with her brother, but was unable to abolish it. Others complained endlessly about their siblings, so Spirit did too, but it was all pretense. She wished she could get him alone, maybe asleep, and be able to hug and kiss him without limit. Beyond that her mind balked, but the longing remained. She knew that he would never cooperate in such a thing; Hope was very morally minded. She felt guilty for her forbidden desire, but maybe she would outgrow it when she got her body and became attractive to boys.

CHAPTER 2

BUBBLE

Things were smooth for about a year; then they complicated ferociously. She was walking home with Hope and Faith when Faith was accosted by a wealthy scion. The rich punk floated up on his gravity-shielded saucer and asked her for sex, proffering two dollars. It was insulting and gross, making Faith blush deeply, but he would not give over. Hope was plainly controlling his anger, but Spirit didn't. She impulsively pushed the rim of the saucer with her foot and dumped the scion.

This might have been a mistake, because it led to a fight between Hope and the scion. It seemed unequal, because the scion was older, larger, and better trained, but Hope used his ability to read people, and gave a good account of himself. Until the scion drew a laser pistol. Then Spirit acted, stinging his hand with the finger whip so that he dropped the weapon. That enabled Hope to win the fight, so that they got safely home. They hoped that would be the end of it.

But the scion had his revenge by getting their family evicted. They had to flee Maraud and seek a refugee bubble on the airless surface of Callisto. The scion's closed outside saucer came after them and tried to bomb their vehicle. If any of their suits got holed out here, they would be dead of decompression. Spirit had been nervous; now she was terrified. No finger whip would get them out of this.

The situation was desperate. Hope was trying to use his

captured laser against the saucer, and the saucer was trying to drop a bomb where it counted. So far neither had scored, but that could not last long.

Then Spirit saw something, and had a notion. She jammed her helmet against Hope's. "The ice caves!" she cried, so that the sound would carry into his helmet.

They raced for the ice mine, where ice was quarried to be melted for water. The saucer paced them, still trying to catch them with a bomb. Hope managed to snag the saucer's undercarriage with a rope, tying it to the pedal tractor. But it dropped another bomb, a bright orange cylinder. It was going to blow up their vehicle!

Spirit leaped up and caught the bomb in her hands. It wasn't big, just deadly. She hurled it to the side, where it exploded harmlessly. But her heart was thudding; this was way more danger than she liked.

They hauled the saucer into the mine, but couldn't bring it to ground. So Spirit grabbed an ice stone and threw it at the saucer. But this wasn't enough. So she leaped onto the saucer itself, to smear its window with dirty ice. But when she got on the saucer, its onion-shaped null-gravity section made her light, and she almost floated right back off it. For a moment she floundered; then she caught hold of the ladder dents, and those finger-holds enabled her to anchor herself with one hand while she struggled to use her ice rock with the other. She squirmed across the surface of the saucer, then reached down across the front vision port and rubbed the rock across it. The port itself was invulnerable, but a bit of heat leaked out of the saucer, and than helped melt the ice just enough to make it smear its embedded dust across the port. That would soon foul the saucer's vision, so that the man inside couldn't see to do any more mischief.

The scion inside caught on, and tried to fire his laser through the glass to get her. But Hope fired his own laser from the ground, and must have blinded the scion, because he didn't fire at Spirit. She owed big brother another!

She kept on smearing until Hope jumped on the saucer and pulled her off. She knew why. "We have to get away before he radios for help!" she yelled against his helmet. Because naturally the authorities would choose to believe the scion, not the victims.

They hid in the convolutions of the mine until the saucer and its allies went away, then started bounding on toward Kilroy Crater, where the refugee bubble was supposed to be. They made big long low-gee bounds, but it was too far; they would never get there in time.

But then Spirit spied a utility floater traveling their way, and the family bought passage aboard it to the refugee bubble. So they got there after all, and got three rooms· one for the parents, one for Spirit and Faith, and Hope had to share a room with a strange boy.

They thought they were safe at last, but it turned out to be disaster delayed. The bubble lifted, using its gee shield, then spun to generate trace gravity internally. They were on their slow way to Jupiter—until the crew decamped with the passage money. Then the men of the refugees took over and steered the bubble onward—but discovered there was not enough food. Spirit and Hope and his friend Helse counted the food packs, and found there were only half enough. They had to ration it.

Then there was the first pirate raid, under a brute named Horse. That was a horror, because the pirates tied up Hope and their father, then gang-raped Faith while all of them watched. Spirit was as shocked as the others; she had never seen sex at all, and this was worse than anything she might have imagined.

After that they organized to fight pirate boarders. Spirit participated in a spot course on resisting a rapist, whose operative principles were that girls had knees and rapists had groins; girls had fingers and rapists had eyes; girls had teeth and rapists had noses. Spirit loved the little play, especially where she plucked out a fake eyeball, but she understood the message: pirates would rape women or girls or children, and the females had to be ready to stop them. They had to fight back effectively.

Hope had a surprise for her. He told her that his friend Helse was not a boy but a girl masquerading as a boy. At first Spirit didn't believe it, but Helse showed her breast-filled chest band. Then Hope left, and Helse told Spirit how to play the part of a boy. Helse was sixteen, and actually quite a pretty girl. She told Spirit something of her history, about how she was the plaything of an old man who liked really young girls, and how she had learned all the ways of sex, but finally had grown too old had had to go.

"Too old for sex—at sixteen?" Spirit asked, amazed.

Helse nodded. "That's why I'm going to Jupiter. To find a new career."

Something else occurred to her. "You—my brother—sex?"

"No," Helse said gently. "At least, not yet. He is a very nice boy."

Spirit suppressed a surge of jealousy. "Not *yet?*"

"Sex is an option, to be used when it has to be."

"Like with my sister Faith?"

"No, Spirit, no! Rape is always wrong. But sometimes abstinence can be wrong, too. A girl just has to judge cases, and do what is right in the circumstance."

"I don't understand!"

Helse smiled. "Maybe that's best. Now let's see if we can make you into a boy, so that you never face the question."

But Spirit couldn't let it go. "You mean like when the men are going to do it anyway, so she shouldn't fight, so as not to get beat up as well as raped?"

"That might be a case, yes, but there are others. I don't blame you for being frightened of the prospect."

"I'm *not* frightened!" But she was.

"Well, *I* am. That's why I'm being a boy."

"You?" Spirit asked, astonished. "But you said you had all that sex!"

"Yes. And I think I will never be able to love an older man, because of that. Maybe I can't love *any* man. So I'll be happy not to be touched again. But I've learned not to say 'never.'"

Spirit realized that she had been trying to misjudge Helse, because of the way Hope was taken with her. She was indeed playing the part of a boy, and had fooled all of them. If she was afraid of what might happen, she surely had reason. The specter of Faith's rape gave warning to them all. "Okay," she said. "Make me into a boy."

"First, you have to think of yourself as male. That starts with your name. Mine is ambiguous, so I can get away with it, but yours is too much like a girl. Who do you want to be?"

Spirit considered. Six months ago she had had half a crush on a handsome older boy named Sancho. She had never given any hint, knowing the futility; what would a boy her brother's age want with a girl of eleven, going-on-twelve? Even if there could have been anything between them, her parents would have squelched it immediately. But mostly it was that though the changes were occurring in her body, the pace seemed glacial, and she didn't want to embarrass herself. Her breasts were not a quarter the mass of Faith's breasts, and there was no flesh on her hips. As for her hair—some boys had more on their heads. She wanted to have the body complete before she tried to do anything with it. If only she could have been two years older! But maybe she could have just a little part of that fleeting dream. "Sancho," she said.

"Very well, Sancho. The first thing is how you dress. And how you walk. Men are narrow-hipped; they don't flex much, so think narrow."

"I don't have woman hips yet," Spirit said. That was all too obvious.

"But you're on the way. Your legs are rounding out. You have girl-hips, and they could betray you. Watch the men; see how they walk, and copy that. Get some baggy shorts and bunch them up in front, and wear loose trousers over them. Same thing for your chest, in reverse. A T-shirt would ruin you; get some winding and strap yourself down so nothing can ever jiggle. Try to build up some strength in your arms too; men are more muscular, and it shows. And your hair—let see what we can do about that."

Helse's knowledge was apparent; Spirit's esteem for her was rising. She was privately pleased with the woman's comments about her body; maybe there *was* a little flesh on her hips. She plunged into the lesson with a will, and within two days was becoming a reasonably proficient boy. It was all too easy to reverse her recent efforts to become a girl. She associated with some of the real boys her age, and they accepted her, understanding the threat she faced. The lesson of Faith's public rape had been lost on none of them.

She tried to approach Hope, to show off her expertise, but he repulsed her. Hurt, she tried to conceal her burgeoning tears; boys were not supposed to cry, and she had never been much for that anyway. It was just that she was especially vulnerable to Hope, so much wanting his approval. But she knew he had problems of his own, so she did him the favor of staying out of his way.

It was Helse, oddly, who comforted her. "He's all twisted up inside. He blames himself for being a man."

Oh. Maybe that made some sense. Spirit continued to work on her impersonation, and thought she had it down almost pat. Sancho was now easy to do.

Just in time, for more pirates came. They made ready to rape and loot without even a pretense of decency. "Bind the men. Line up the women—the young ones first." And Spirit was technically a young one.

But this time the men of the bubble were ready. As soon as the pirates showed their foul hand, the men jumped them, two to a pirate, and quickly subdued them.

Then there was a keening sound, and Spirit felt strangely passive. "Oh, no," a man said. "A pacifier."

Spirit had never heard of that, but it wasn't hard to figure it out: it generated a field that robbed the refugees of their volition. The Pirates had nullifiers, so were unaffected. They quickly reversed the case and made the bubble men captive. Spirit saw a box by the air lock, and realized that that was the pacifier. She found she could move a little, and she started inching toward it.

"They will hurt you," Hope said listlessly.

"They won't notice me." But before she got there, there was an interruption: A Jupiter Ringuard patrol boat arrived to investigate. But the pirates took two six year old girls and a younger boy as hostages, threatening to slit their throats if the refugees gave any signal. Then they turned off the pacifier, and the refugees had to pretend that all was well. What else could they do?

And once the Jupiter patrol was gone, the pirates returned the children, naked and staring. The girls had been raped and the boy was dead.

The men leaped for the pirates—and the pacifier came on. Spirit saw the pirate leader raise his sword and strike her father, killing him. It was only the beginning; soon all the refugee men had been slain. The pirates dragged the corpses into a pile, then went after the women. One took hold of Spirit's mother and tore the clothing from her body. She was unable to resist effectively, because of the pacifier.

Spirit focused all her energy on the pacifier box. No one was attending it now:; all the pirates were too busy catching and raping the bubble women. She could move only slowly, but even a tortoise could make good progress when it had to. She reached the box, picked it up, and dropped it. Its internal works had to be delicate; it bounced on the deck, and then she felt the pacification field ending.

With the termination of the pacification came a surge of

such rage as she had never before known, like a rebound effect. To see her father murdered, her mother raped—it was as though Spirit became an attack dog with a single imperative: kill.

Spirit saw Hope running to help their mother. Spirit ran too, but before she got there, her mother kneed the pirate in the groin. He rolled off her, groaning. Hope grabbed at him, catching an arm. Spirit was more direct: she went for his head, jamming a stiffened finger directly into his right eye. She hooked her nail around, trying to pull out the eyeball. The man howled with pain, but Hope's weight was on him, and Spirit had his head. She grabbed both his ears and hauled, pulling up his head, then smashing it down on the deck, again and again.

Somehow the man got away. He was burly, and they could not hold him. His right eye was a mass of blood, and his groin was bleeding where someone had knifed him, but he crawled toward the exit. "Let him go!" their mother gasped. "He's hurt enough."

Then Spirit looked around. Other pirates were retreating, and some were dead. The women of the bubble had piled on, five to a pirate, and rendered the faces and exposed groins of the men into raw sausage. The scene was hellish in its viciousness, but Spirit wasn't sorry. The brutish pirates had deserved it. Most of those who had gotten away would never rape again; indeed, some might never even urinate again without pain.

Hope got up and staggered toward the pile of refugee men. Spirit joined him, horrified anew by the dead face of their father. Others came to stare similarly. An awful silence fell; the killing rage had passed, and what was left was terrible grief.

She turned to Hope, and he turned to her. They clutched each other, sharing their desolation. This horror overwhelmed them both.

But Spirit knew that this would not go away of its own accord. She jammed her dread and fear into some compartment of her mind for forced herself to speak. "We must do something, Hope," she said.

He stood there, trying to recover his common sense. "A leader," he said. "A new leader. But who? All our men are gone."

"Use your talent," she told him.

He nodded, and got moving. "Take care of Mother," he said as he went.

Spirit did. Their mother was in an awful state, with her clothing in shreds, her hair ragged, and blood spattered across her arms and body. She looked as if she were in a trance. Spirit did not know whether she had been raped, or gotten free just before that, and thought it best not to ask. "Come with me, Mother," she said.

She took them to the cell her mother and father had shared. Her mother went without resistance. "Lie down," Spirit said, and her mother lay on the padding that served for a bed. Spirit sat beside her, took a cloth, wet it, and began to clean her face and body, methodically. It was all she could think of to do.

"You darling child," her mother said, submitting.

After a time, Hope returned, with Helse, bringing Faith. "Please join your mother," he told Faith. "You can comfort her better than I can, for you are a woman." And Faith, who had been pretty much out of things since her rape, looked startled, and did as he asked.

But that left Spirit to fend for herself, and she wasn't ready. She had continued to function as long as she had something to do, but now the abyss yawned before her.

"Go with your sister, Hope," Helse said, and departed.

Hope joined her. Spirit let go at last. She flung her arms around him and bawled. It didn't matter that he was crying too; the misery they shared was too great for either to bear in silence. At least they had each other.

CHAPTER 3

Empty Hand

Thereafter things stabilized somewhat. The women assumed the tasks the men had handled, and managed to make the bubble function reasonably well. Having this to do seemed to help them. They also put the men's bodies into bags and stacked them outside the bubble, tied down, where the cold vacuum of space would preserve them exactly as they were. It helped to have the bodies out of sight and the blood cleaned up; then it was easier to pretend that something hadn't really happened.

Hope asked Spirit to help women learn to use the male sanitary facilities, as there was no sense wasting them when there were no men. This entailed pairing off, with one person holding the other in place so she could squat and pee into the urinals set in the walls. In fact Spirit got together with another girl her age, and they demonstrated the technique for others. The women were appreciative, but it was an inconsequential matter; they had more serious concerns. That came clear when they found one woman dead in the head—the bathroom. She had opened an artery and quietly fed her blood into a bidet. The others, when they learned, shrugged; they understood.

But Hope was worse. He was continually morose, rejecting all offers of comfort. Finally Spirit went to Helse. "You've got to do it," she said.

Helse surely did not misunderstand, but was cautious. "What do you mean?"

"You have to get him over this hang-up he has, so he can join the living. Make him not ashamed to be a man."

Helse gazed steadily at her. "You are very close." There was no need to clarify to whom.

"Yeah. I can't stand to have him like this."

"There is only one way I know." She was still looking at Spirit with a disturbing understanding. "Someone might object."

She was being discreet. She knew that it wasn't their mother, but Spirit herself who had the most difficulty with this. "Do it anyway."

Helse nodded, and went to be with Hope. Spirit found an empty cell and clenched her fists, fighting off her unreasoning rage. Helse had asked for her leave, and she had given it, but she hated it.

Hope and Helse were together all night, as time was measured in the bubble. Spirit knew, because she checked several times, hating herself for it, but still doing it. She knew that Helse was showing Hope what it was all about. This was an occasion where sex had to be used, and Helse was using it, to get Hope out of his deep pit. Spirit had asked her to—but still it drove Spirit crazy. Not the least of it was that she could not say *why*, even to herself.

At last they emerged, and Hope was a changed man. His grief remained, but the guilt was gone. The job had been done.

Spirit couldn't stop herself. The first chance she had to catch Hope alone, for all that it was impossible ever to be completely alone in the bubble, she asked him. "How was it, brother?" She tried to make the question neutral, but the tone made it snide.

"I love her." He spoke with such guileless candor that it made Spirit ashamed for her attitude.

"I'm sorry," she said.

He understood, as he always did. "I know I've been a bear. Something had to be done. She did it. But you're still my sister."

"Still, I'm jealous." And there it was. How could she be jealous of *that*?

"When you grow up and love a man, I'll try not to be too jealous," he said.

That was funny, and she had to smile, but there was truth in it. She would like to do just that, and make him jealous back. "Oh, go ahead and *be* jealous!" Then she couldn't stop herself: "Tell me what it's like"

She saw him hesitate, and she knew why: she was only twelve years old, supposed to be too young for sexual knowledge. But after what they had seen and experienced in the bubble, that hardly mattered. "I was inside her," he said. "And heaven was inside me."

"But what about—I mean, the first time—the blood–"

"Only when the woman is a virgin, not the man."

She felt stupid. "Oh. Of course. But still–"

"Give me your hand." He took her hand it his and squeezed it cruelly. "That's rape," he said as she yelped. Then he kissed it. "That's love."

"But it's still sex. Faith–"

"Don't judge all men by the pirates," he said. "That's what Helse taught me. Ask her."

"I will." Because though her jealously still lurked, she really did want to know.

Later, Helse clarified it for her. "He wouldn't come to me, so I came to him. I got him naked, and I spread myself upon him. I put his hard member into me and dared him to say he was raping me. He couldn't."

This was fascinating. "Couldn't what?"

"Couldn't say it. Then I kissed him, and he came."

"Came where?"

"I mean he climaxed inside me. Jetted his semen."

"Oh." She had been stupid again. "That's all it takes?"

"Sometimes. It varies with the situation. Sometimes a man

will spurt even before he gets in; sometimes he has to pump a long time. Usually it doesn't take long. Then he sleeps."

"He just has to get inside her, and then it happens?" Somehow she had thought it would be more complicated.

"It happens, and then his member softens and shrinks, and it's over. He loses interest, for an hour or a night. Sometimes a girl will move things along fast, just so he'll be done and will leave her alone. It's like letting the pressure off a valve."

"Some valve!"

"Sometimes it is necessary."

"I guess," Spirit said doubtfully. This seemed so business-like it was almost disappointing.

"Once a man has done it with a given woman, he wants more of it, on other days. Men think of sex all the time. The nice ones court a woman; the pirates rape. The difference is in their manners, not their lust. I will be doing it again with Hope, perhaps often. I can't tell him no; a smart woman doesn't. You understand."

She was warning Spirit not to be jealous. But she was. "Sure," she said shortly, and left.

But some of the truth of what Helse had said became apparent all too soon. Another band of pirates boarded. It wasn't clear that they were pirates at first; they were polite, and promised to take the refugees to Jupiter. But then it turned out that they had given the children poisoned candy, Spirit included. Spirit fought the drug, but it overwhelmed her and she had to sit down, then lie down. But she could still hear them talking, and learned that the pirates were holding the children hostage for the performance of the women.

And Spirit's mother agreed to buy Spirit's life with sex. Spirit could not protest; she could not move or speak. All she could think of was Helse's remark: "Sometimes it is necessary." Necessary to give a strange man sex, in order to save the life of her child. Because all men wanted it, and the pirates didn't much care how they got it.

Then Faith came forward; Spirit heard her, and knew by the sudden hush that she was dressed to show off her lovely body. She was working at being beautiful. "How many children can I buy?"

And so it was that Faith Hubris saved the lives of all the children who had eaten the tainted candy. She went with the men on their ship, and was gone.

The children recovered. Spirit wasn't sure whether it was because of the antidote, or whether the poison was only a temporary drug, but at least they were all right. She resolved never again to be caught that way.

And only a few hours later, more pirates came. This time the women put all the little children in the cells, while Spirit, Hope, and Helse hid in the netted supplies in the center of the bubble, where gravity was slight. Spirit was still a bit groggy, but saw the sense of it. No children would be drugged this time.

But that left the women. The pirates were armed and ruthless. Their deal was simple: submit or die. If the women died, the children would be left without any remaining protection. Spirit heard Helse explaining it to Hope.

But he would have none of it. "That's my *mother* down there!" he said, and launched himself forward.

Helse caught him, but couldn't entirely stop him. "Spirit!" she cried in a whisper. "Help me hold him!"

Spirit snapped out of her remaining stupor and grabbed Hope's legs. Together they held him back.

"But our mother's getting raped!" he protested.

"I know it," Spirit said, and did not let go. She had come to understand about sex as a tool to do what was necessary. Certainly their mother understood. It was maddening, but it had to be.

Hope continued to struggle, until Helse hugged his face to her half-bared bosom. Spirit felt the fight go out of him then, and marveled at the evident power of a woman's breast.

Still, he protested, wanting to try to save their mother somehow. "Let it be, Hope," Helse told him. "Those women are trying to save our lives."

"At the expense of their honor!" he retorted, and Spirit had to agree with him there.

"Their honor is not of the body, but of the spirit."

That made Spirit jump, though she knew it was a coincidental use of the word. She saw the point, however: the grown women were doing what they had to do to preserve their lives and the lives of their children. How could that be called dishonorable?

So they remained there for a short eternity, letting it happen. Spirit could see very little below, but her imagination filled it in: men thrusting their swollen members into the poor women, getting inside, making it happen. Then, sure enough, they were done, and they went away. It was amazing how quickly men lost interest, once they jetted.

At last they could let Hope go. Helse put her clothing back together, covering her bared breast. "You sure are pretty, when you show," Spirit said enviously.

"You will be too, very soon," Helse said.

They climbed down—and the women acted as if nothing had happened. Hope opened his mouth, but Helse intercepted his words. "Say nothing!" she whispered. That shut Spirit up too.

When they were separate again, Helse explained: "The women don't want us to share their humiliation. We must pretend to be ignorant, and hope that the real children don't catch on. So as not to undermine their sacrifice."

Spirit pondered it, and realized that it made sense. It was a necessary deception, on both sides.

But things did not get better; they just got worse in different ways. There was not enough food; they were running out, even with the men gone. They went down to quarter rations, and Spirit felt hungry all the time. But their natural functions remained, and the toilet facilities were filling and clogging from overuse. "Another head's clogged," Spirit said. That cut them down to three functioning ones, and that was not enough. But she had an answer: "Why not just dump the stuff into space?"

Thus it was that Spirit, Hope, and Helse volunteered to go out on the bubble surface to unclog the heads. They had to use the clumsy space suits anchored by safety ropes. It was awesome, clinging to the little hooks outside the bubble, so as not to be thrown clear by its rotation. The sun was just a star, but Jupiter was huge beyond belief.

Hope made his way to one of the pressure release valves and used a big wrench on it. Spirit was reminded of her dialogue with Helse, about letting off sexual valve pressure, and almost laughed. This wasn't sex, it was shit.

Suddenly the valve let go with a jet of vapor. It carried Hope along with it, which was another scare, but he was secured by the rope, and Helse reeled him in again. Then he and Spirit worked on the tank itself, opening it and getting the refuse out. It slid out in a huge awful mass, and immediately started fragmenting in space, becoming a cloud. She put her helmet next to his, so they could talk, and said "Jupiter rings!" Like the rings of Saturn, only smaller and dirtier. He smiled.

Then they reloaded the empty tank and bolted it back in place. They did the others similarly. The job become tedious, and that gave her time to think, and she remembered how much they had lost: their home back on Callisto, the life of their father, and the honor (or whatever) of their mother. Certainly of their sister. Suddenly it overwhelmed her, and she began to cry. She had been doing more of that recently than she liked, but couldn't help it. Hope understood; he crossed to her and put his suited arm around her for a moment, and it did make her feel better.

They resumed working, getting the job done tank by tank. Until they got close to where the bagged bodies were tied. Then Hope somehow got tangled up with one, and struggled with it briefly. Spirit watched with bemused horror, uncertain what to do. It was almost as if the corpse were alive. Then Hope lay still.

She went over to him—and heard something through the hull. Screaming—someone was screaming. Then she saw into Hope's faceplate. *He* was screaming. Just lying there with his eyes closed and screaming.

She beckoned to Helse. Helse came carefully around, and they managed to disentangle Hope from the bagged corpse and drag him around to the entrance port. The few remaining refuse tanks could wait; they had done most of the job already. What had happened to Hope?

They wrestled him inside the lock, and the women helped them get inside. There they removed their suits, and the women removed Hope's suit. He seemed to be all right, just unconscious. He must have overstrained himself working on the locks; he had after all been doing most of the work, and he had not been eating any better than the rest of them.

He revived. They talked to him. It took some time for them to get his story. It turned out that he had had a vision. He had talked to their father, who had told him there was food available, and extended his hand, saying "Here." But the hand was empty.

The women considered that. They sent Hope to their chamber along with Spirit and Helse, and consulted among themselves. Hope fell asleep, and they watched over him. "What do you think happened?" Spirit asked.

"He had a vision of some sort," Helse said. "It must have gotten really bad. He saw an empty hand, and started screaming."

After a time their mother came to check on them. Hope was still asleep. "Helse, change clothing," the woman said. "There is no need for further concealment."

Helse stared at her. "I don't understand."

"Hope's vision. His father told him that he was to have food for us and for that lovely girl of his. I believe that is you."

"Oh my God," Helse breathed. "The vision told!"

"It's a true vision," Spirit's mother said.

Helse looked helplessly at Spirit. Then she got up and climbed out of the cell. Soon she was back, wearing a dark blouse and skirt that had once been Faith's, and her hair hung loose about her shoulders. Indeed, she looked almost as pretty as Faith.

Spirit stared at her. "You're beautiful!"

"I am what I am. I must admit it's a relief to be unbound." She cupped her breasts through the blouse for a moment, but she meant more than the physical aspect. "Your father called me lovely, so I must be so. For the sake of the vision."

"The vision," Spirit said. "I don't understand where there could be food. All he showed was an empty hand."

Helse gazed at her. "I'm not sure I should say what I think."

"Say it!" Spirit said. "I want to know."

Helse took a breath. "He meant—to eat the hand itself."

"The hand it–" Then Spirit got it. "Oh, no!"

"Now don't start screaming, or you'll get me going too. Try to think of it objectively. We will all die if we don't get more food—and there is—is plenty of—of meat frozen out there. It makes sense to—to use it."

"Cannibalism!"

"You could call it that. But use it or not, your father will not live again. None of the men will. Wouldn't they prefer to see that at least their wives and children live?"

"Yes, they would," Spirit said. "Oh, God, I'm going to throw up!"

"Try to stifle it," Helse said. "You can't afford to lose it."

There could be two meanings there, too. Spirit managed to keep her gorge down. "But if we do that—what does that make us?"

"Survivors," Helse said succinctly.

Spirit looked at Hope. "*That's* why he screamed! He knew—on some level."

"He knew," Helse agreed. "But not consciously. Only the women understood the message, at first. Hope was merely the messenger."

"Not the originator," Spirit agreed.

"I think Hope will not like this, when he wakes."

"Microscopic wonder! I can't stand it."

"I think we will have to help him. I'm less emotionally involved, because I have no relatives on the bubble, but I'm appalled. It is worse for you—and I think will be worse yet for him. He—*feels* so strongly."

Spirit knew what she meant. Everyone had feelings, but Hope was in a class by himself. "Yes." Then she sniffed. "What's that smell?"

"Fresh meat," Helse said. "We shall have to eat it."

"But there's no—"

"The women have been out to fetch it. They are preparing it. They are sparing us that."

This time Spirit's gorge filled her mouth. She clapped both hands over it and forced herself to control her heaves and swallow it back down. This was like rape, only at the other end. Necessary.

Hope woke, perhaps stirred by the sounds of her struggle. Fortunately he was distracted by the sight of Helse in feminine apparel. His gaze fixed on her, while Spirit got herself back in order. "You're beautiful," he murmured.

Helse smiled, being beautiful. "Thank you."

Then he looked at Spirit. "You look serious."

Spirit forced herself to speak. "We have food now. You—you can smell it."

"That's great! But why aren't you eating it instead of sitting here with me?"

How should this be broached? They couldn't express phony delight; he would see through it immediately. But Helse was right: they would have to eat it. So she started cautiously. "We're—we're not sure we should use it."

He frowned. "Where is it from?"

Helse forced a laugh. "From your vision, Hope."

"You think I made that up?"

"No," Spirit said. "I saw our father sit up and talk to you." That was an exaggeration. For one thing, she wasn't even sure it was their father's body he had gotten entangled with.

"I hauled him up. He couldn't have–"

"But I do believe you," Spirit said. Because she knew that Hope would never make something like that up. He was honest to a fault. He had surely had a vision. "Father gave you a message, and Mother understood it."

He didn't want to get it. "He showed me an empty hand."

"He showed you his hand," she agreed. Then, carefully, the two of them herded him into the unkind realization. He had no choice but to accept it.

So it was that they ate the meat. The women cooked it on candle flames and on bits of wood from furniture, and served it in very small portions, so that it was impossible to tell from what part of what animal it might have come. The women ate with the same pretense of unconcern they had affected after submitting to rape, and that told Spirit a lot. She did get sick, and so did Hope, but they both returned gamely to eat again, until they were able to hold it down. After a few days the horror receded somewhat, and became a matter of course.

But for a long time Spirit dreamed of that empty hand Hope had described. It was in its dread fashion her last memory of their father. She knew she wasn't alone; some of the other children evinced odd and ugly symptoms of the underlying guilt for the manner of their survival. But there was no alternative.

Jupiter grew in the vision ports as they slowly approached it. The women were managing to pilot the bubble where it needed to go. The conviction grew that they were going to make it.

But that allowed Spirit to think about other things. Hope and Helse were now an open couple, and they looked wonder-

ful together. That griped Spirit; *she* had been closest to her brother
before. She tried to control herself, knowing that her attitude
was unworthy, but couldn't.

One day she burst in on the two of them in their chamber,
hoping to catch them in the middle of sex. "There you go again!"
she cried. "Father's gone, Faith's gone, Mother's alone—and
you're busy fooling with her!"

Actually she could see that they weren't doing it at the
moment; they were naked, but they had been sleeping. Still,
they were doing it at other times, and certainly Helse was mo-
nopolizing Hope's attention.

"I do not take your brother from you, Spirit," Helse said. "I
can never do that. You are of his blood and I am not. I do not
love him as you do."

Spirit faced her defiantly. "That's space-crock! You love him
more than I do!"

Helse looked as if she had been stabbed. "Oh!" she cried in
pain, and fled the chamber, naked.

Spirit stared after her, astonished. "I vanquished her!"

"But you misspoke yourself," Hope protested. "You said she
loves me more than you do. You know she doesn't love me; she
can't love any man."

"Oh, I shouldn't have said that! I blabbed her secret!"

"What secret?"

"I'd better go try to apologize. I lost my stupid head." She
started to leave.

He held her back. "She doesn't love me, though I love her.
I understand her situation. My talent—"

"Oh, you don't know half what you think you do!" Spirit
snapped. "When your emotion is tied in, your talent cuts out!"

He looked stricken, and she realized that she shouldn't have
said that either, though it too was true. She was thoughtlessly
laying about her with a verbal knife, and cutting up those who
meant most to her. "But she said—" he said haltingly.

Once again she spoke before she thought, and then just

had to continue, because half the truth would be worse for him that all of it. "She *had* to deny it, dummy! She thinks men don't love women who love them back. She's always been used by men who only wanted her body, no matter what they said at the time, and when her body changed they didn't want her anymore. So she knew if she really liked someone, she shouldn't ever, ever let on, because–" She wrenched, trying to break free of his hold on her. "Let me go, Hope! I could kill myself! Helse's an awfully nice girl, and I've got to tell her—I don't know what, but I've got to!"

Now she scrambled out of the chamber, and searched for Helse. She wasn't hard to find; evidently becoming aware of her extreme dishabille, she had ducked into another unoccupied chamber. She was huddled there, alone, sobbing.

Spirit dropped in beside her. "Helse, I'm sorry! I—I—when Hope gets in trouble, he expands his understanding and somehow makes it come out all right. With me, I just start fighting worse. I–" But what could she possibly say to make it right? Suddenly her tears were flowing, making it worse yet. "Oh, damn, damn, damn!"

"I didn't mean to hurt you, Spirit," Helse said. "I thought it was all right with you."

Even through her tears, Spirit managed a form of laugh. "I'm supposed to be apologizing to *you*! You're a really nice person. I just got so crazy jealous—damn! I'm a stupid child. I never should have—what can I do to make it right?"

"You spoke the truth."

"Sure! And we're eating our fathers. Should I speak that truth too?"

"I think I see it now," Helse said. "I've been taking up so much of Hope's attention, you're getting excluded. I shouldn't have been so selfish. I'll try to change–"

"No! That would only hurt him. He loves you."

"And it seems that I love him. That means–"

"No it doesn't!" Then Spirit caught herself. "I've been mess-ing everything up with my big mouth. Maybe it's time I stifled it."

"Your mouth has been speaking truth."

"Truth that shouldn't be spoken! Damn it, Helse, if I could take it all back—"

"No, maybe it is better to be open. What is your point about me?"

"It's about Hope, really. He's not like other boys. Men. Whatever. He truly cares. He doesn't change. He loves you, and it doesn't matter what you do or say, or how you feel, he'll always love you. All this business with other men—it just doesn't matter. He won't change."

"But he accepts me as I am. As I said I am. Without love. He understands."

"He *thinks* he understands. But sometimes his own emotion gets in the way of his talent. You can fool him if you want to, because he really can't read you. And you can love him if you want to, and you might as well, because—" She choked off.

"My love does not conflict with yours, Spirit. I'm not family."

"Yes, damn it."

Helse paused, gazing at her. "I haven't known my siblings since I was six years old. There must be something I don't understand."

"Oh, hell, I'm just a kid. What do I know?"

"You're a woman, Spirit. I think that's the problem."

"I've got a year to go."

"Spirit, I know something about young feeling. It is possible to be a woman long before you stop being a child. You're a woman."

"No, I've never done the woman thing."

"Sex? It's not defined by that either. I had more than enough sex as a child. You have the woman instinct. But what's it like to be a sibling?"

"I wish I could change places with you!"

Helse paused again, piecing it together. "You would prefer to be a girlfriend rather than a sister?"

"No, of course not." She had to deny it, but there was a disconcerting element of truth in it.

Helse nodded. "I think I should go back to Hope. But any time you wish to be with him, just do it, and I will go elsewhere. I never meant to interfere with your relationship."

"You aren't interfering. I *am* his sister."

"But I don't have to take all of his time."

Spirit didn't answer. Helse climbed out of the chamber, and Spirit remained alone. She knew she had said too much, yet again, but she couldn't unsay it. Did Helse really believe that it was just Hope's time she wanted? But it was certainly all she could have.

CHAPTER 4

Children

They came close enough to Jupiter, and were intercepted by the Jupiter Patrol—the real one, this time. Salvation was at hand.

And Jupiter rejected them. The Jupiter crew refused to believe their story, and instead gave them supplies enough to go elsewhere, and towed them back out beyond the orbit of Amalthea, to the outer ring, and let them go with a warning not to return.

"And we thought we had known rape," Spirit's mother said. Hope and Helse just stared out of the port at the receding planet, tears streaming down their faces. Spirit joined them, much the same.

Where could they go? They could not return to Callisto, and Ganymede and Europa were little better. No major moon would accept these wretched refugees.

"Hidalgo!" Spirit exclaimed.

They considered it. Hidalgo was a planetoid no bigger than the moon Amalthea, in a stretched-out orbit between Mars and Saturn. It had been settled by folk from Hawaii back on Earth, and was a major tourist region. Its population was mixed, so the refugees should fit in. But Hidalgo was far distant, and the bubble's gravity shields would take years to get it there, and its little drive jet was insufficient. The food was not enough, either. They would also need an ephemeris, a detailed listing of the locations of bodies in space and time, because otherwise they would never be able to find Hidalgo, let alone rendezvous with it.

So they decided to make a raid on an outpost on Io. Io was a hell moon, the most violently volcanic body in the system. Other worlds, such as their own Callisto, might seem almost dead on the surface; Io was the opposite. It had an erratic eccentric orbit, being hauled about by the next moon out, Europa. Tidal action literally squeezed it, blowing out sulfur. It was mostly uninhabitable, except for small observation stations. They hoped to raid one of these for the supplies they required.

They floated down toward it, looking for a station large enough to have what they needed, and small enough to have a hope of raiding. They were becoming pirates, of necessity.

They found a suitable prospect near a massive rocky escarpment. They settled onto the sulfur. Then Hope and Helse donned their space suits and went with a raiding party of 25 women. Spirit wanted to go too, but her mother told her why not: after losing her husband, she couldn't bear to risk both her children at once. That had to be true.

The party left in the evening. That began the long wait. They knew that it was dangerous outside the bubble. They had to complete their mission before dawn, because Io's day was much worse than its relatively calm night. Day was when the volcanoes blew.

There was nothing to do but sleep, so Spirit settled down in a chamber with her mother. "Will they be all right?" she asked.

"They've got to be," her mother said tightly. That was when Spirit realized that this was no sure thing. The adults had pretended that it wasn't complicated, but her mother's tenseness gave that the lie.

"They'll be all right," Spirit said reassuringly. She wasn't sure she believed it, but what else was there? She slept, but was aware of her mother's restlessness.

When morning came and the party had not returned, the

women held a crisis meeting. "They are in trouble; I know it," Spirit's mother said. "We must go to help them."

They quickly organized a party of twenty five women, led by Spirit's mother. Ten women remained to care for the children. Spirit hugged her mother, and let her go; it was the only way. She watched as the party departed.

They waited tensely all day. The children kept looking out the portholes, but it was useless. Neither party returned. All they could see was swirling sulfur storms.

But then a tiny travel-bubble floated toward them. "It must be from the station!" Spirit cried. "They got through to it!"

Sure enough, it was Hope and Helse. Spirit flew across to hug him. "You made it!" she cried.

But the news was much worse. *Only* Hope and Helse had made it. All the women of their party were dead, taken by the hell that was Io's surface.

And the second party had to be dead too, for they had neither reached the station nor returned to the bubble. The remaining women lifted the bubble and searched the region, looking for telltale tracks of any moving party, but there were none.

Spirit got the story in agonized pieces. They had not known how bad it was. None of them should have left the bubble. Only blind luck had gotten Hope and Helse through; the women had sacrificed themselves to save them, and then they had missed an avalanche only because Helse had spooked and ran, and Hope had followed her. The folk at the station had been kind hearted, but too late.

Hope and Spirit tried to comfort each other, and Helse, true to her word, left them mostly alone, merely bringing them food at intervals. The loss of their father had been awful, but the loss of their mother was worse, because she was all they had had left. Except each other.

"If only we had known," Hope moaned. "All we had to do was float our bubble directly to the station and ask for help.

They would have given it. The scientist—his niece looks like Helse. Or did. She's actually four or five years older."

Spirit grasped at this illusory straw, as if it was better to have been saved in maybe than lost in reality. "What's her name?"

"Megan, he said. Her picture did look like Helse. It was taken when she was that age."

"That makes two girls you could love."

He laughed, and that was a relief, because it was the first break in their terrible gloom. "Maybe so. But Helse's all I need. And you."

Spirit would have been thrilled, if she had not been so steeped in sorrow for their mother. "In different ways," she said.

"In different ways," he agreed, and hugged her again. They cried together some more.

But even the depths of their grief could not suppress them forever. In about three days they came out of it enough to survey the situation. The bubble was on the way to Leda, a much closer destination, as it was the next moon out from Callisto. The scientist had recommended it, and it made sense, because it was a military base with Hispanics in charge; there would surely be refuge there. But the bubble itself was a disaster area. The other children had been mourning similarly for their lost mothers, and a number of them had no siblings. They faced the dread abyss alone—and some of them had found ways to kill themselves. So now the complete bubble complement was ten grown women and seventy two children. The children were moving into the various tasks of operating the bubble; not only was it necessary, it gave them something to do.

But they were passing back through pirate territory. All of them well understood the danger. When a ship overhauled them, Helse and Spirit and several of the older girls became boys, just in case. The ten women garbed themselves to be as attractive as possible, and loosened their hair, knowing that often all pirates wanted was sex, and it was easiest to give it to them and let them go away.

Spirit hid in one chamber, and Hope and Helse hid in another. They listened as the men came aboard. The men were brutes from the start; Spirit heard them hitting the women and swearing. There were screams. The men wanted the women to hurt as they were raped.

It got worse. Soon the screams took on a truly ugly quality, and Spirit realized that the men were killing the women, stabbing them to death. Rape and kill, literally.

Then they started opening the chambers. There were new screams as the children were dragged out. These were the worst pirates yet; they intended to leave no one alive.

Her cell opened. Spirit tried to play dead, but the pirate reached in and grabbed her arm. She screamed.

It didn't stop him. He hauled on her arm, and she was jerked violently forward, for his arm was muscular and gravity was light. Then she got smart and remembered her finger whip. It was on her left hand, which remained free for the moment. She oriented as well as she could, and let fly at his face. She caught him on the cheek, rather than the eye she had aimed for.

He cursed and slapped at his face. Then a form dropped on him. It was Hope, coming to her rescue! The pirate dropped into the cell, and Hope dropped after him. Hope caught the man about the head, trying to draw it back, trying to choke him, but his strength and weight were too slight. The pirate roared and brought a hairy hand back, catching Hope by the hair, yanking him forward.

"Spirit!" he gasped.

That galvanized her. Why was she standing there watching? She pounced on the knife in the pirate's sash and snatched it out. The man wasn't even aware; he was still focused on Hope.

Hope brought up his knees and clamped the pirate about the head. He was doing his part; now she would do hers. She considered, then went for the most likely target. She gripped the knife in both hands and stabbed the pirate in the belly.

Unfortunately, it was only a glancing strike. It drew blood, but was not lethal. The pirate roared and went for her, but Hope grabbed him again. Spirit went for the man's face, but he jerked back and avoided it.

Hope grabbed him once more, giving Spirit a third chance. This time she made sure; she drove the knife into his throat, as fast and hard as she could. And this time she scored. Hot blood spurted, drenching her as the pirate dropped.

Hope took the knife from her hand, and she realized that she had gone into a kind of trance of horror. She had killed!

Her brother did what had to be done. He got them out of the chamber, leaving the dead pirate there, and closed its door, and hauled the dead woman over it so that the other pirates would not find their companion. Then he got her into the next cell, with Helse. "Play dead!"

The three of them played dead. It wasn't hard, for they were covered with gore. Spirit was sobbing, but she struggled to keep it quiet, so that she would not be heard above the tumult elsewhere in the bubble. Hope held one of her hands and Helse held the other, providing silent comfort. It helped.

No one looked in on them. Finally it was silent in the bubble. They heard the lock closing as the pirates departed.

Now they came out to see what remained. It was awful. All ten women and 27 children were dead. Now their total complement was 45 children.

The following days were nightmare, as they cleaned up the disaster. Hope and Helse, being the oldest, hauled the bodies out to join the men. Hope became the den father figure, and Helse the den mother. They organized it to provide comfort to any child who needed it. Spirit helped, and found that comforting others helped her too. The whole group became like a single family.

The children rebounded surprisingly swiftly. It wasn't that they had lost their grief and horror, but that they were, perforce, in survival mode. They spread out to do what had to be done, to clean and operate the bubble, finding solace in the hard work. They cried often, but were starting to smile again too. The family concept lent them all strength. Everyone understood everyone.

And they oriented on defense. They had a big meeting in the bubble commons, and thrashed it out. Every child participated; no child was denied a fair hearing. They knew they were all in this together, and that the price of failure was brutal death.

They settled on a three stage program. Stage One was professional innocence; they would be cute and sweet and beg the intruders not to hurt them, giving the pirates a chance to be decent. Stage Two was to fight; Spirit had a whistle, and when she blew it, every child would bring out a weapon of some sort, be it a sharp knife or only a hard nail, and attack the nearest pirate, going for the eyes and the crotch first. They rehearsed with pirate-sized dummy figures, so that even the smallest child could do some mean damage in that first instant of surprise. With luck they would overwhelm the pirates. They would not stop until all enemies were dead; that was another lesson learned the hard way.

If that did not work, they would go for Stage Three. This was the dreadful one. One of the toilet tank's release bolts had been weakened, set up so that it could be bashed off, letting the fecal matter fly. But its automatic safety lock was jammed open, so that the entire bubble would be blown out in moments, and all unsuited occupants would die. Helse would say "Do it!" and Hope would go out the rear airlock, climb around to the bolt, and do it. All the others would have that little time to get suited and hidden in their cells. With luck the pirates would not catch on in time. They would be vulnerable because they couldn't rape any girls while being in space suits.

They practiced diving into their own suits and sealing them instantly. They held frequent surprise suit-up drills. They knew how much time they would have from the "Do it!" moment, and made sure they could get prepared within it.

Then, ready for anything, they got bored. There needed to

be a distraction, because bored children were mischief, and there was still a distance to go before they found sanctuary. So Hope and Helse decided to get married.

That appealed to the children. It would make it even more like a family. Spirit was put in charge of operations, and she was delighted; she had gotten over her jealousy of Helse, knowing how much Hope needed her. Hope was functioning well as the leader of the bubble in large part because of his love for Helse.

The kids got into it with gusto. They made Helse a wedding gown from swatches of cloth taken from all over. They planned for a wedding cake. They formed a choir and practiced the wedding march. They planned out every detail of the ceremony, lacking only a priest. They even made Hope and Helse rehearse the wedding kiss, which they enthusiastically applauded.

In due course they were ready for a full dress rehearsal. Hope lacked a formal suit, so had to wear his space suit, complete with the helmet, which would be opened for the nuptial kiss. "Take off the suit that night!" one child yelled, and they all burst into wild laughter at the thought of attempting sex in a space suit. All of them understood the mechanics of sex very well, thanks to the pirates. Helse donned her fancy patchwork wedding gown. It even had a name tag: HELSE HUBRIS, just in case she couldn't remember it after the fact.

The lookout sounded the alarm. The children scattered, fetching their weapons. Then they returned to the ceremony, playing the innocents.

Hope went to the rear lock, ready to use it if given the signal. "Get suited!" he called back to Helse. But she was busy organizing the children, and didn't get to it before the pirates entered. Maybe it would be all right, and if not, maybe she could still get suited in time.

Stage One was played out. "Take all the girls for brothel slaves and dump the boys," the pirate leader said. He looked at

Helse, still lovely in her gown. "But this one we'll take for ourselves."

Spirit blew the whistle.

The bubble exploded. The children, well primed for this, drew their weapons and launched themselves at the pirates. The smallest tackled the feet, wrapping their little bodies around the men's legs, anchoring them so that they could not move effectively. The middle sized ones stabbed viciously for the men's crotches, shredding cloth and quickly drawing blood. The largest went for the pirate's heads, slashing at their eyes and noses, jamming stiletto needles forcefully into their ears, and slicing blades across their throats. None flinched or held back; they knew better. Half the pirates were down and screaming within seconds, but their attackers did not quit. They intended to keep cutting until there was nothing left but red meat. Once these children had been innocent; once they had cried at scratches. That had been a long time ago, subjectively. Today they were vicious little killers.

Some men were alert, and defended themselves effectively, surviving the first rush. But there were several children for each man, and they did not hesitate. They stalked their prey like rabid squirrels, closing in from all sides, eyes gleaming, teeth bared. Each child had his or her specialty, and fully intended to score. Even the tough grown men were daunted by this rabid attack. With every second that passed, more children rose from their kills and came to join the ones in pursuit of standing prey. They were taking losses, but none were backing off. The kill fever was on them, and it could have only one end.

Spirit, supervising, kept her eye on the larger scene. She knew that their greatest risk was from the unexpected. She glanced at the front lock, and saw a new man appear, carrying a solid, squat device. It didn't look like a pacifier, but she wanted none of it. "Take him out!" she screamed, and launched herself toward the man.

Five other children turned at her words, saw the man, and

charged him, knives ready. He held his ground, pulling a trigger. The box burped, and something heaved out. It looked like brown taffy as it splattered against the body of the nearest child, with fat strings spreading out. They became tentacles, wrapping the child, pinning his arms and legs, so that he fell helplessly.

Spirit stopped, realizing that they were up against something new and deadly. How could they nullify this taffy gun? The man was squirting shots at all the closest children, tying them up without touching them himself. They weren't hurt, just helpless.

Spirit backed away, and so did others. They knew they were going to have to invoke Stage Three. For a moment there was silence, as the fighting faded.

Then more men appeared at the entrance. "Take your pick," the man with the taffy gun said tersely. "No sense wasting taffy on brats we're going to kill anyway."

Spirit caught Helse's eye. Helse backed away from the pirate she had just stabbed, turned, and spoke to Hope, who was standing in his suit by the rear lock. "Do it, Hope!" she cried, and bolted for her cell to get her own suit.

The pirate fired the gun. A wad of taffy caught her on the back and wrapped around her, bringing her down. She was of course the first one the pirates would rape; even in this scene of mayhem she was stunningly lovely in her gown.

Spirit saw Hope start back from the lock, wanting to help Helse. But she screamed from the floor: "Do it! Don't wait for me! Do it, or we'll all die!"

Reluctantly, he turned back to the lock. Meanwhile Spirit was running to take her place beside their old small drive unit. She had to protect his exit. She closed her helmet, sealing her suit.

He went through the lock, closing it behind him. Spirit stood with her knife held in her suit mitt. But the pirates weren't coming this way. They were already clustering around Helse, pulling the strands of taffy off so as to get at her body. Spirit wished she could help her, but she knew that Helse was done for, one way or the other; there was no longer time for her to get into her suit.

She heard the clank as Hope opened the outer portal of the lock. She hit the switch for the bubble's large drive unit, cutting it off so that Hope could get past without getting fried. It didn't make much difference in the motion of the bubble, because it was now anchored to the pirate ship whose far greater mass stabilized it. In fact the pirates were so preoccupied with Helse's revealed breasts and thighs that they didn't notice.

Spirit counted patiently from one to sixty, giving Hope time; then she hit the switch again, turning the drive back on. Now he was on the hull, and no one could follow him.

Most of the children not caught in taffy or killed by the pirates had disappeared, going for their own suits. Some had been caught by the pirates, who were tearing off their clothes. Spirit had thought that grown girls were what the men really wanted, but realized with an ugly shock that some actually preferred *little* girls. They were grinning as the girls struggled and screamed, relishing it.

The cluster around Helse clarified. They had gotten most of the taffy off, and one man was holding her arms stretched over her head, while another was clasping her bared mid section, getting her into position for the first rape. His erect member looked huge as it shoved toward her. "Hurry, Hope!" Spirit whispered.

Time dragged on. The pirate thrust into Helse, and she screamed, not so much from pain as from despair. Spirit know that she had wanted no other man but Hope to touch her, and that was gone. Helse knew she was about to die, but had wanted to die pristine, in her fashion, for Hope. Spirit shared her horror and anger.

Then, abruptly, it changed. The air sucked out of the bubble, drawing everything toward the hole. Things and bodies swirled madly for a moment, and Spirit herself was drawn toward it. Then it stopped; the air was gone.

The pirates were dead, of course. The ones who had been raping Helse were now so much meat. But so was Helse.

The job wasn't yet done. Spirit went to close off the interior valve, so that the pumps could restore the lost air in the bubble. She dragged Helse's body away from the pirates, so that it would look as if she had died alone. Then she returned to cut off the drive so that Hope could come back inside.

Once he was in, and the air pressure was up, so that they could remove their suits, she saw that he was in a moving trance. He knew what he had done. She realized that he was bereft of his love, and would need support. Spirit was the only one who could give him what he needed. Her own grief would have to wait; it was in any event less than his.

She turned to the six children who were all who survived. They ranged from age six to age ten, four girls, two boys. All were staring, some with tears on their faces, some dry-eyed with shock. "Go to a clean chamber, all together, and cry," she told them. "Comfort each other, and I will comfort my brother. I will come to you when I can. We are family."

"We are family," the eldest girl repeated. She turned to the others. "Come cry with me."

They went with her. Spirit took Hope into their chamber and laid him out on a salvaged mat. She sat by him and stroked his hair, comforting him while her tears flowed silently. Now she had him all to herself, and wished she didn't. If only Helse could have been saved! Then she could be comforting Hope, and Spirit could be with the other children, crying without restraint.

She dreaded the coming encounter, but nerved herself for it. She would have to tell him the truth, but maybe not all the truth. He had to know that Helse was dead, but there was no need for him to know that she had died ravished. She did not think it would be dishonest to keep that secret from him. If he asked her directly she would have to tell him, but if he did not think to ask, then she would not volunteer.

Hope stirred. Spirit dried her face and set her expression. She had to be strong for him.

Then he woke. He clutched at her arm. "Was it all a dream?" he demanded desperately.

She was ready. "I wish I could lie to you, to give you ease, my brother. It was no dream."

"Helse—"

"Dead." There; it was out.

He looked so pained she had to do something. She embraced his head, drawing his face into her scant bosom. It worked to a degree; he relaxed slightly. Maybe if she had had breasts like Helse's it would have been more effective. "Hope, you must seal it off," she murmured. "We need your strength, to survive. There are only eight of us left."

She continued hugging him, and talking to him as if he were a little child. She reminded him that Helse had sacrificed herself so that the rest of them could live. She told him that he could not throw that away.

Finally she got through to him. He sat up, strength returning to his body. "I shall extirpate piracy from humanity," he swore.

She nodded and let him go. Then he turned to her. "And you, my sister—you are sustaining me in my hour of need. But who is sustaining *you?*"

It was like explosive decompression. Suddenly she was bawling, and he was holding her, patting her shoulder in the way he had, comforting her. She had not realized how thin the veneer of her stability was; the merest little question had destroyed it.

After an additional time she settled. "Don't tell," she said with half a smile as he wiped her face.

"Never," he agreed, and kissed her forehead.

They went to the other survivors. Spirit took the two boys, hugging them somewhat as she had Hope, and Hope took the four girls, letting them hug him and cry against him. Hope's magic was returning, and it was especially good with girls; they all loved him in their fashions. Spirit lacked that talent, but she was the closet thing to a woman remaining in the bubble, and that was what the boys most needed. An older, comforting woman.

CHAPTER 5

Woman

After some hours they organized to set the bubble right. First they ate enough to sustain their systems. Then they dragged the bodies to the front lock, and Hope and Spirit hauled them out, one by one, to anchor to the hull. The job seemed interminable, but they kept at it, because the bodies would soon spoil in the warmth and air of the interior. The only exception was Helse; Hope couldn't handle that, and neither, it turned out, could Spirit. But the other children rose to the occasion and did that job, burying her, as they called it, still in her wedding gown. They brought back only the once-humorous little tag, HELSE HUBRIS, and formally gave it to Hope as a memento. They pretended not to notice his tears; how well they understood.

In between they held spot services for the dead. They tried to remember something nice to say about each child they put away, and to wish him or her well in heaven. Some were siblings, some were friends; all had been companions in misery. If the tears came again, as they often did, there was no shame. They were family.

They swept up the refuse, and washed off the decks. Meanwhile there was another, far more positive aspect: they had taken the pirate ship with them. Its lock had been fastened to the bubble's front lock, and all the pirates were dead of decompression. They were treated with less civility: their bodies were dragged into a single chamber, piled up, and sealed off. They were welcome to rot, and their only benediction was an assortment of curses to hurry their way on to hell.

The pirate ship had welcome supplies of food, weapons, and tools. It would be some time, if ever, before anyone had to eat fresh meat again. It also had money and booty from pirate raids, including some mysterious containers marked only with letters of the alphabet. These, Spirit concluded, were illicit drugs, fabulously valuable on the black market.

Hope did a fade-out before they were done exploring the pirate ship, but she managed to steady him. He was like that, often thinking too much; no one knew what so-constantly revved up his brain, and it was best simply to work around it.

Finally they found a fully-stocked lifeboat. That was a find indeed! They strung lines to it so as to haul it behind the bubble. That might come in really useful, if other pirates didn't steal it from them first.

They cut loose from the derelict pirate ship and resumed their journey. One of the things they had picked up was a holo projector and a number of cartridges. Hoping for diversion, the children set it up and put in a cartridge labeled *Animal Fun*. But it turned out to be obnoxious fun: a naked woman indulging sexually with a donkey. There was a cry of dismay, and Hope came from his station to see what was wrong. "Turn it off," he said, disgusted. But then the children got interested, because this was normally forbidden material. So they watched the animals, and also the cartridges showing all manner of human sexuality. Spirit felt guilty, but watched with them, as intrigued as they. This was certainly one way to study the diversity of the act. Despite all its seeming variants, it consisted essentially of getting the male and female parts together, then squirming and grimacing and moaning until a bit of juice jetted from the male. She thought there should be more to it than that, considering all the secrecy about it. Maybe there was, in

non-pirate relationships. Certainly it had had far more significance for Hope when Helse did it with him.

The children were adjusting, one way or another, but Hope
was having more trouble. He slept only fitfully, writhing during
what sleep he got, sometimes crying out inchoately. Spirit stayed
with him, trying to tide him through by holding his hand, stroking his head, or just hugging him. It had been bad when their
father died, and worse when their mother died, but Helse had
taken up much of the slack. Now Helse had died, and it was
the worst, because his loss was greater, and Spirit had less to
offer. It was like trying to sail one of those little boats in a video,
when the water got stormy. She just had to hold on to him,
muttering reassurances, until he settled down again.

But one night it was worse. He thrashed about, and the
name he spoke was Helse. He seemed to be talking to her.
Then Spirit tried to leave, but he wouldn't let her. "Don't go!"
he cried, grabbing onto her. "Love and be loved!"

Spirit tried again to free herself, but realized that she couldn't
do so without waking him from his dream of Helse, and she
didn't want to do that. Helse was his only real comfort, and he
could be with her only in dreams. So she let him draw her in,
and actually she didn't mind being close to him, even if it was
Helse he thought he held. She wished she could truly *be* Helse.

Then he tried to kiss her. She turned her face aside, feeling
guilty. Then she asked herself what harm there could be in kissing her brother, and let him do it. That was perhaps her mistake, because when his passionate lips touched hers she felt a
surge of passion herself. Was this what it had been like for Helse?
Lips were merely lips, but this was feeling fire, spreading through
her body, heating her breasts and her groin. She wanted—what?

Then he paused and began to draw away. "But I killed you!"
he said, perhaps waking just enough to remember reality.

Spirit felt the pain going through his body. She hated that.
She tried to comfort him. "She told you to do it, Hope. To let
the air out. She said 'Do it!'"

He seemed to consider that. Then he said "I love you."

"And I love you," she replied. That had always been true. Did it matter whom he thought he was addressing? *She* was addressing him.

He put his hands on her, ruffling her clothing. She was in a nightie left from one of the women; it was more comfortable for sleep. He was in pajamas, similarly loose. She moved, trying to preserve her modesty, such as it was, but he pressed in more closely. She felt something by her hip, and realized with a shock that it was his member. He had an erection.

He thought she was Helse—and he wanted to have sex with her.

She almost cried out, to wake him, lest they both be severely embarrassed. But something stopped her, and in a moment she realized what it was. She wanted to help him, not hurt him—and waking him from his longing dream to the stark reality of Helse's death would hurt him worse than anything else. He could never again have sex with Helse—unless she came to him in some other body.

Spirit could be that body. She had been jealous of Helse, then sorry when she died. Now she could do something to make it up. She could let Hope love Helse, using her body. Almost she felt the spirit of Helse entering her, seeking Hope.

So she let him draw up her nightie and put his hand on her breast. It seemed to fill out as he touched it, assuming a little of Helse's volume. She breathed, trying to make it fuller yet, suddenly afraid that he would recognize the imposition and wake, angry with her.

But he continued. He kissed her mouth again, and this time she responded better, her feeling fleshing out what her body lacked. Then he moved his face down and kissed her breast, and she let him, her excitement blossoming. He put his mouth on her nipple, licking it, and her body came alive in a new way. She arched, trying to give him more. She had never imagined feeling like this. The pirate holos had shown no such tenderness, no such joy of participation. This was the missing element, this burgeoning feeling.

He got on top of her, and his member was now free of its clothing, pressing hotly against her belly. He wanted to put it into her. How would that happen? In a moment she realized that she had to help him. She spread her legs, lifting her knees on either side of him. His member slid down her belly and dropped into the opening crevice between her legs. She had become hot and slick there. She remembered what he had said about being inside Helse, and heaven being inside him. Had heaven been inside her too?

She wiggled, and the tip of the member found the deepest, hottest recess, and pushed into it. She welcomed that forbidden penetration. There wasn't quite room enough, but he did not stop and she did not try to withdraw. Instead she tried to relax where it counted, letting her knees spread wider. She pictured a cylindrical spaceship docking at a round refugee bubble. The mating of the locks. He was knocking at the lock; she wanted the lock to open. Only in this case the ship was actually sliding *into* the bubble. And it did, slowly, tightly. There was pain all around the rim, as if the surface were corroded, but it was sweet pain, maybe punishment for her doing what she knew she should not, though also joy. Pleasure-pain, like struggling to win a fierce competition. Stage by stage, the valve yielded as the conduit connected, as something somewhat too big nudged into something slightly too small. But the tube was expanding, stretching around the entry vessel. The atmospheric pressure was equalizing. Yet the ship was still driving in, on and on, as if forging through viscous substance, and the bubble was still giving way around it, more readily now. There was a special delight in the tightness; the fit was firm, with no leakage. Overall it was weird and wonderful, a transcendental experience.

At last it stopped; he was all the way inside her, his hull right up against hers, the seal complete. She had not realized how far in it was possible to go; the warm rod of him was throbbing right there in the depths her belly. She surrounded him, she enclosed him, she contained him, she loved him. She reveled in her power to perform, to take the whole of him into her resilient being, and hold him there softly forever.

"Helse!" he whispered, and kissed her again on the mouth. She returned the kiss ferociously. She felt him swelling within; now it didn't hurt, for the tight interior was more flexible than the aperture. She clenched whatever muscles she could find there, squeezing him, caressing him, making him welcome. She felt him responding, becoming increasingly urgent as she stroked him with her substance. Yes! She wanted him to feel her loving power. His body was tensing, his breathing coming hard; something was building to the bursting point. The member jerked quickly in and back and hard in again. And at last there was a rush of fluid heat. It was a signal of his melting joy, erupting from the swollen tip—and after that her own joy came, surprising her, radiating through her body long and slow and strong, wave after wave, making her writhe in the continuing ecstasy. It seemed as if his essence was spreading through all her channels, carrying pleasure everywhere. Who cared about the beastly mechanics of it; *this* was heaven!

They remained a forever moment in that hot wet joy, their bodies perfectly united. *Thy rod and thy staff they comfort me,* she thought, and wondered whether that was the true meaning of those words: the blessed rod of flesh within her. She wanted it never to end. But of course it had to, for men lost capacity after they jetted, as if they had lost the fluid that distended them. What had been huge and hard was softening.

"Oh, Helse," he said as he drew out of her, diminished.

"Oh, Hope, my love!" she said, kissing him again.

He dropped his head beside her and slept completely. That was the way with men; Helse had told her. But as the rapture of the moment faded, Spirit became increasingly uneasy. Hope had perhaps not known what he had done, but *she* had. Maybe Helse was with her, but it was Spirit's body, and who else would ever understand? Also, the fluid heat had come out of him and into her, but it wouldn't stay; it would slide out of her and stain the mat.

Carefully she disengaged from him, and he did not wake. Surely Helse had done the same, many times. It was part of being a woman. She sat up, and felt the wetness below. She got a tissue and put it there, wincing when it touched the rawness. Then she stood, holding the tissue in place, and walked quietly around. The fluid slid down and out cohesively, and she folded the tissue around it.

She climbed out of the chamber and went to the nearest head. She was alone, fortunately. She used the facilities and cleaned up. She was sore, but knew she would recover. She opened the tissue she had brought and looked at it. There was just a whitish blob there, like the translucent white of an egg. So little, signifying so much! She put it down the disposal chute. Then she returned to the chamber and lay down beside Hope. She had to decide what to do, because when he woke he might ask. She didn't want to lie to him, but neither did she want to tell him the truth. Not only had she had full woman-style sex with him, she had reveled in it as the culmination of all her desire. He would never understand.

She worked out the necessary compromise: if he asked her, she would tell. But she would not volunteer it. That way she would not be lying to him. With luck it would remain her secret.

She closed her eyes. "Oh Hope, my brother, my love," she repeated. Maybe it was forbidden, maybe her soul was soiled, but she had at last had what she wanted most of him. She had never really understood what it was she had desired, but now she knew, absolutely. She knew it would never be repeated, but she would cherish the secret memory as long as she lived. It was, in its way, Helse's gift to her. The gift of his ultimate expression of love.

As morning came, she got up and dressed, letting Hope

sleep. He had not slept this well since losing Helse; that much she had done for him. She donned blouse and pants and brushed out her hair, adding a ribbon, making herself respectable. She looked in a mirror. Helse had been right: she was becoming pretty. Her blouse made her breasts show a little, and the pants were tight enough to give her a bottom. She had used that bottom! She also looked innocent, which was much of the point. Her innocence was forever gone, but she would try her best to fake it. Maybe Hope wouldn't ask.

She went out and interacted with the other children, seeing that they got food for breakfast, hugging a girl who had evidently been crying, planning the day. Did any of them suspect what she had done in the night? There was no sign of it. She intended to provide no sign; every hour the secret held made it less likely ever to be exposed. Her mother and the other women had shown her how to fake innocence; it was a lesson she hoped she had learned well.

"You're pretty," a little boy told her.

"Thank you," she said, exactly as she should. The children needed her to be pretty, because pretty Helse had become their mother figure, and now it had to be Spirit. She had taken Hope's early advice to heart, enhancing her body with clothing and hair and expression, though she used no makeup. She needed to be pretty, not adult, right now, for a reason it was best they not understand.

She checked on Hope frequently, and when she saw him stirring, she joined him. "Are you all right, Hope?" she asked, peering down into the cell.

He looked up at her, seeming troubled. Yes, he definitely suspected!

He was going to ask. She could not avoid it, but it was best that this confrontation be private. She dropped down into the chamber beside him.

"Spirit," he said. "Were you with me when I slept?"

There it was. The hour of trial was upon her. But she would

not volunteer it. "Hope, I will always be with you," she replied. "We are family."

"No, I mean—"

She looked at him, bracing for disaster. She had to answer, but she wasn't going to make it easy. "You mean what?"

"I mean *with* me. When—"

"When you screamed for Helse?" That was of course not the same. He knew she had been with him, every night, trying to ease his pain.

"Yes."

"Hope, you had a bad dream. You were thrashing about. I tried to hold you down. Finally I got you quiet." Literally true, but not the whole truth. If he asked her *how* she had gotten him quiet, the game was lost.

He considered. "Did I—hurt you?"

"You can't hurt me, Hope."

"I mean–" But he did not finish. She understood with a flash of revelation that he didn't *want* to know.

She played on that. "Hope, I am your sister. I will do anything I have to, to keep you safe. I would die for you, as Helse did. Does anything else matter?"

Still he struggled, visibly "There are things you must not do for me, Spirit."

She put on her most innocent look. "Like what?"

"Like—" But he choked again.

"Like lying to you?" she asked. "Ask me anything, Hope; I won't lie." *Please God, let him not ask!*

He gave it up. "You are my sister."

"Always," she agreed. Then, trusting her luck no farther, she left him and went on about her business.

Soon he rejoined her. He never brought up the dread subject again. But it lingered long in her dreams.

*

Only a few days later the next pirate ship came. They set up for the three stage defense, this time with only two innocents to greet the visitors, because that was all they could spare. But the men had hardly entered before Spirit blew the whistle.

For an instant Hope and the others were at a loss. "It's the Horse!" Spirit hissed. Then they understood. "*Do it!*" she said, meaning stage three.

But that moment of delay was too long. Even as Hope went out the lock, a pirate leaped forward and caught Spirit. She could not go to turn off the drive, so that Hope could reach the key valve. They were caught.

Horse wasted no time interrogating the captives. "Where are all the others? How did you get this pirate stuff?" he demanded. They refused to answer.

"Then we shall do it the harder way," the Horse said grimly. He pointed to Spirit. "Strip her."

They were going to rape *her*? But of course she had proved she was old enough, and of course no girl was too young for a pirate. She struggled, but soon they had stripped her naked.

The Horse studied her. "Not quite old enough," he said with evident regret. "Another year and she'll be fine, but I don't get my kicks from children. Anyway, that won't make this kid talk; it didn't before. We'll have to go the other way." He drew his knife.

The Horse faced Hope. "This is your little sister, by the look of her." He brandished the knife. "So are you going to talk?"

"He won't!" Spirit exclaimed bravely. But she was terrified. Rape was not necessarily the worst, with pirates.

The Horse sighed. "Okay, we'll start with a finger." He grabbed her left hand and wrestled with it until he had hold of her smallest digit, while the two other pirates held her legs and other arm, preventing her from struggling effectively. So far this wasn't much different from rape. Was he really going to cut her finger?

Then, without further ceremony, he brought the knife up and sliced into the base of her finger, near the knuckle.

The pain was overwhelming. Spirit screamed so piercingly her own ears hurt. She wrenched with all her strength, but the pirate hung on and kept carving. Blood spattered out and the pain continued.

Then it stopped, somewhat. Spirit stared at her hand, which was awash with blood. Her little finger was gone!

"I ask you again," the Horse said, grinning at Hope. "Are you ready to talk?"

What Hope said then surprised Spirit through her pain. It sounded like "Kife."

Spirit was awash in pain and horror, but she was aware that all the pirates took note. She didn't know what the word meant, or how Hope had learned of it, but it had obvious power.

"So you're into that, are you?" the Horse asked, licking his lips. He had for the moment forgotten Spirit. "All right, show me the mark and I'll turn you loose."

"I have no mark," Hope said.

That evidently didn't wash. "There's always a mark," the Horse said.

"Let my sister go, and I'll tell you everything," Hope said, obviously defeated.

The pirates holding Spirit let go of her arms and put ropes on her ankles instead. She tried to put her fist in her mouth, but all she did was smear her own blood on her face. A man gave her a dirty bandanna, and she wadded that against the stump to finally stanch the bleeding. In a moment she found herself sitting on the deck with a blanket over her. She felt cold and faint, and her hand still hurt horribly.

Hope talked, and she listened despite her pain. It seemed that Helse had been a courier for someone named QYV, pronounced Kife. The Horse concluded that she must have been carrying something valuable in her body, and he wanted to know what it was. So while the eight children sat bound on the deck, the pirates suited up and went out on the hull to fetch Helse's body back in. It was frozen grotesquely stiff, so they waited while it slowly thawed, because they did not want to destroy whatever it was inside her.

It was an agonizingly long wait, several days, and all that time the pirates kept the children bound and guarded, released only singly to use the head. They allowed Spirit to rummage ineffectively through her own belongings for better bandaging material for her hand. The tacit deal was that then she would stop moaning so much. There was nothing suitable, so she had to settle for soft undergarments wrapped voluminously around and anchored clumsily with elastic. At least it stifled the bleeding, and she did stop her noise.

Actually she wasn't hurting quite as much as she let on. She had realized almost immediately that the pirates were keeping all of them alive mainly so that they would have plenty of children to torture if they needed to make Hope talk some more. Once they had what they wanted, they would probably either kill the children, or leave them in the bubble without the drive, so that they would inevitably die when their food and air ran out. They were doomed—unless they found some way to overcome the pirates. That was why, in the guise of clumsiness, she fetched her finger whip, and the tiniest of weapons: a knife fashioned from an ancient-style razor blade. It had been one of the weapons they had used in Stage Two. She hid it with in the bandage, next to the gore of the stump. It was unlikely to be discovered there.

But she had no chance to use it, because a pirate was always watching, day and night. One even watched while she pissed in the head, licking his lips; there was no privacy at all. They were children, but she was pretty sure they would get raped before the pirates departed. Not all of the men would be as finicky about age as the Horse. They were just waiting for his word that the mission was done; then they would grab the particular children they had decided on and do it. Spirit had a fair notion which pirate wanted which child for what; they were hardly subtle about their glances. When it was the Horses's turn to return to their ship and sleep, two pirates would stand guard duty in the bubble, and sometimes they talked, not caring who heard. "That one with the finger—she's got half a breast," one said, staring at Spirit. "Got tight little pussy too, I'll bet." They even played a series of games of dice to determine which one of them would get the first dip, as they put it. Spirit pretended she didn't hear or didn't understand, and so did the other children. They had all learned the pretense of innocence, but all knew exactly what the pirates were talking about, having seen it happen before.

Meanwhile in the long hours they sat while Helse's body thawed, and the deathly stench slowly intensified, Spirit reflected on her life and situation, trying to understand why it had come to this pass. She concluded that she had brought it on herself: she had let her brother put his digit into her, so she had had one of her own digits cut off. God's punishment, a tooth for a tooth. If she ever did it again, she would pay again. It was not a lesson she was ever likely to forget. It might be that the whole second appearance of the Horse was to effect that punishment. She had brought it on them all.

But they had not yet been killed. That meant that God was giving her time not only to repent, but perhaps to redeem herself. Maybe she could somehow save them, when her punishment was complete. But she would have to be ready whenever the time came.

At last Helse had melted through, and the Horse was ready. He took out his own blade and sliced carefully into Helse's belly, looking for whatever might be inside. The other pirates crowded around, watching avidly. Spirit knew that Hope was wincing; the woman he had loved was being further violated, even after rape and death.

None were watching the children now. Spirit slowly brought her swaddled left hand to her mouth and worked at the wrapping with her teeth. She found the blade and picked it up with her lips. Then she held it between her teeth and used it to saw at the bonds that held her hands together.

The child next to her turned his head to see what she was doing. She did not try to conceal it from him. Then he looked straight ahead, at the clustered pirates. "Pause," he whispered, and she flipped the blade into her mouth with her tongue and made with the innocence. When no pirate was glancing their way, the boy whispered "Go."

The process seemed agonizingly slow, but the blade was sharp and a single strand was all it had to sever. Her hands were loose, but she kept them together as if tied. When no pirate was looking, she nudged closer to the adjacent boy. He moved his bound hands toward her, and she held the blade in her right hand and sawed more efficiently at his cord. He kept his eyes on the pirates, warning her when there was danger.

When she had his cord severed, she passed the blade to him. It was a good one, holding its edge for a long time; it would cut more bonds before dulling. He knew what to do with it. She rearranged herself and watched the pirates, whispering warning when necessary. At the same time she used her nine fingers to work at the bond at her feet, loosening it without removing it.

What the pirates were doing was awful. Horse had cut Helse open from breast to crotch, and across the belly, and now they were drawing out her intestines and inspecting them length by length. They did not want to miss whatever it was inside her.

Finally Horse found it, and drew it out of her: a tiny capsule. But Spirit could not look at that; she was trying to catch Hope's eye. The child next to him nudged him, and he looked at her. She made a gesture with her hand as of cutting, indicating that she had a knife. Then the blade itself reached him. Not all the children between them had had time to sever their bonds, but they knew that Hope should be first, being more effective when free. So the child beside Hope was sawing at Hope's bond.

Meanwhile the pirates were trying to figure out the capsule. They were hesitant to break it open, lest it contain a deadly poison, or some precious oil that would be lost.

Hope gave Spirit a signal with a finger: when they acted, she should go first for the weapons. She nodded; that had been her idea, and she was glad to have it confirmed. She was closest to the cache.

"To hell with that," the Horse exclaimed, settling the pirates' dispute. He twisted the capsule apart.

An object fell out. Another pirate caught it. They looked at it. "A key!" the Horse said, disappointed. "A stupid little plastic key!"

But they didn't know what lock it might be for. It was useless to them.

The man threw it to the deck. "Three damn days gone—for this! For nothing!"

The children could wait no longer; it was time. Spirit got up quietly and walked toward the weapons. She tried to project an aura of innocence, as if she had been released to go to the head.

She almost made it. But then the Horse spied her. "The little bitch is loose! Who forgot to tie her ass?"

She saw Hope launch himself toward the Horse. He crashed into the man, distracting him for a moment. The other children were attacking the other pirates. Spirit broke into a run. A pirate intercepted her, but she flicked him in the face with her finger whip. He clapped his hands to the wound. But another pirate was between her and the weapons cache. She hesitated, looking wildly around.

Hope had been thrown aside, and the Horse, all too quick to catch on, had drawn his laser pistol and was bringing it to bear on Spirit. She couldn't outrun that!

But Hope acted with hellish inspiration. He was going for

the corpse. He was going to hurl that at the pirates! But it would be too late for Spirit; the Horse was about to fire.

She changed direction, leaping up into the upper baggage section, curving as she did because of the spin of the bubble. The laser shot missed her, burning a food package. Then she was scrambling through the packages, effectively losing herself among them. Unfortunately there were no weapons there, so her objective had been blunted.

But she had thought of an alternate way. It was deadly dangerous, but this was a desperate situation. She passed right on through the baggage compartment and dropped out of it on the far side of the bubble, out of sight of the pirates for the moment. There was the little drive unit.

She picked it up and wrestled it around so that it pointed down the center of the baggage section, the way she had come. "Down!" She cried. "Flat!" She braced herself as well as she could and turned it on.

"Someone shoot that brat," she heard the Horse saying. Then the rocket came on.

A blast of propulsive flame shot out of its aperture, shoving her violently back against the rear lock. She spread her legs, fighting to maintain her balance, hanging on to the monster. The fire spread in a narrow cone, singeing the netting and packages of the center of the bubble and bouncing off the rim of the front air lock. Then her grip slipped, and the drive cut out.

"Get their weapons!" she screamed as she struggled to reorient the drive. She hoped the blast had fried the standing pirates, and missed the fallen children, but she couldn't see its effect through the expanding smoke.

She heard Hope's voice. "Spirit!" Then there was a thump.

She pushed the switch on again. The frame erupted, and now the metal of the drive was hot, burning her hands, but she hung on regardless, as long as she could before her damaged flesh could no longer do the job and the drive went off again. The bast of hot air around it stung her eyes so that she could no longer see, but she bluffed: "I'll burn you all if you don't get those pirates!"

There was a scramble at the other side of the bubble. Then Hope called again. "Spirit!"

Blindly, she lifted the hot tube and aimed it by hope and guesswork. She found the switch, and felt it blast again. But she couldn't hold it, and in a moment it bucked from her grip and stopped. She lay on the deck, unable to do any more.

She heard people coming. Who was it? She had done all she could.

"Spirit!" Hope cried. Then she knew it was all right. She let go of her dwindling consciousness.

When she woke, she was in agony. She felt the burst on her hands, arms, and face. But she was able to move, and to see; she had been singed, not destroyed. Hope had the pirates captive, and was trying to decide what to do with the Horse.

She had hoped that brute was dead. But maybe it was better this way. She knew what to do with him. She held out her left hand, which was slightly better off despite its missing finger because the bandaging had protected it to a degree. That bandaging was gone, but her stump wasn't bleeding, maybe because of the ferocious heat.

Hope put a laser pistol into it. The contact stung her hand, but she gritted her teeth, aimed it at the Horse's crotch, and pulled the trigger. He screamed as smoke puffed out. She held the beam there until she was sure his groin was bare of all external flesh, then dropped the pistol. She had castrated him, avenging the rape of her sister Faith. The destruction of Helse's body. The man might live or die, but he would never do that to another maiden.

Spirit and the other burned children rested, trying to heal, while Hope and the well ones cleaned up. Hope saved the plastic key, putting it with Helse's wedding tag, HELSE HUBRIS. They had survived, losing no more children, but they had suffered, and it was not a happy occasion.

CHAPTER 6

Hidden Flower

Things steadied for the next two weeks. No more pirates came, and the burned skin scabbed over and healed. Naturally they got bored. So they found a diversion: making Hope into a girl. He was starting to grow fur on his face; they made him shave, and get into a dress, and put a red ribbon in his lengthening hair. They made him don pantyhose, and feminine slippers, and wear a padded halter. The idea was to enable him to pass for a girl, in case pirates came to kill any men they found. The risk had to be taken seriously.

Spirit donned male clothing and postured as a boy, gleefully ordering him about. "I am here to stop you from getting raped, unless you really want to be. Say 'sir' to me, sister!" The other kids laughed as if that were the humor of the century, though Hope didn't seem to find it quite as funny.

Then another ship was sighted. They ran for their space suits, not having time to change. Spirit and Hope were the fastest, because they had drilled specifically for the decompression stage; the others were younger and had less practice, having inherited their positions by random survival.

"You sure look cute, sister," Spirit teased Hope. "In your ribbon." She saw him try to remove the ribbon from his hair, but his suit gauntlets were too clumsy.

There was a crash, and then another. "They're shooting at us!" Spirit cried, and jammed her helmet closed.

Hope did the same. They were just in time; a third shot holed the bubble, and the air sucked out. They were drawn along with it, but managed to grab on to things and delay their flight until the air was gone.

No others were in motion. The children had not been in time for this devastatingly unexpected attack. They were dead.

The pirate ship docked, and used the airlock. Suited figures appeared in the bubble and began checking around.

This must be a pirate salvage operation, looking only for supplies and parts, not rape or slaves. Spirit and Hope grabbed armfuls of food packages, pretending to be looters. With luck the real pirates would not know the difference, since all of them were similarly suited.

They carried their burdens to and through the lock, and made their way into the alien ship. It had docked side-fashion, rather than nose-on, and they found themselves in a vertical central tube. This was a Navy ship, with a cannon at the nose instead of a civilian lock. Yet it was obviously a pirate.

Unused to this layout, they had to grab on to handholds, letting their packages fall outward. This gave them away, and the pirates quickly made them prisoner. But they took Hope for a girl, and he had to play the part, while Spirit maintained her role as a boy. It was a weird reversal, but maybe for the best.

They faced the pirate captain, who wore a Naval uniform. This was a renegade Navy vessel, a deserter from its assignment.

"You are young," the pirate officer said to Hope. "But that perhaps makes you cleaner. You will serve one man per night, commencing this night. You will cooperate gladly—"

"No!" Hope cried, horrified with better reason than the pirate officer could know.

"Otherwise your little brother will be flogged—by the man you do not please—and you will go without food or water till the next. I believe in time you will cooperate willingly enough."

Spirit quailed. This was not remotely funny any more. These

brigands obviously knew had to make a girl perform.

The pirate medic sprayed Spirit's stump with a plastic bandage, and took away her finger whip. Fortunately he never thought to check her gender.

They were put in a bedroom suite. For a moment they were alone, while the pirates drew their straws for the first liaison. "We're in trouble," Hope said in a gross understatement.

"*You're* in trouble, paleface!" she quipped. But she turned serious immediately. She knew what she had to do. "I can take your place. We can change clothes—"

"No good," he said. "They won't fit." But she thought his objection was more than that.

"We could make it dark—"

"I won't stand by and watch you be raped!" he said.

She sighed, relieved on one level. "That too, of course."

They tried to make some wild plan for escape, but it seemed hopeless. Then a bearded pirate entered the chamber. He grabbed Hope and fell on the bed with him. Spirit had to admit that Hope looked just like a girl, with his skirt flaring up as he fell, showing legs that looked nice in their panty hose. But the masquerade was about to be brutally unmasked.

"Kife," Hope said.

That stopped the pirate instantly. Spirit had inquired, and learned from Hope what that was about; Kife was some sort of super-pirate who used ordinary folk as couriers, and took dreadful revenge against anyone who interfered with a courier. Helse had been a courier.

Hope quickly followed up with a scary story of what Kife had done to the last pirate who interfered, freaking out the would-be lover. Soon they were back before Captain Brinker. Hope continued to play his scene; he was really good at that. He parlayed this into a private interview with the captain— then asked Spirit "Do you remember Helse's secret?"

She was puzzled. Was he referring to the way Helse had

masqueraded as a boy, hiding her gender identity? "I remember."

"Another shares it."

In a moment she caught on. The dapper captain was a woman!

Hope played it out, revealing that all three of them were in reverse gender. He had to show his masculine parts to convince her, then bargained for freedom for the two of them: set them loose in a stocked lifeboat, and they would not reveal the captain's secret to her crew.

It worked—to a degree. The captain agreed to let Hope go, but kept Spirit as a hostage.

Hope didn't like that. "Make another offer," he said curtly.

"No other offer," the captain said, now assured that Spirit was important to him. "I may neither kill you nor let you go entirely free without imperiling myself. It must be all or nothing—or this. Take the compromise—or the consequence."

"Hope, she means it," Spirit said. "Do it. She will not harm me, for I have the same secret. I can be the cabin boy, and I will not be molested. You must go free, to complete your mission." That was nominally his job as courier for Kife, but actually his best chance to survive.

Still he balked. "My father, my mother, my fiancée—all sacrificed themselves for me!" he exclaimed in anguish. "You are all I have left, Spirit! I can't let you go!"

That tore at her heart. He had always been the biggest thing in her life, her idol, her love. It was gratifying to verify that he cared so much for her. But she was perhaps more practical than he. This compromise had to be. "Hope, I said I would die for you. This is not nearly as bad. We may someday meet again." She felt the tears on her face, for once not ashamed of them.

"Agreed," he said at last to the captain, almost choking over the word.

The captain nodded. It occurred to Spirit that the captain might actually like the idea of having female company; it couldn't be easy being the one member of her gender on a pirate ship. Certainly this seemed safer for Spirit than exposure or destruction.

They fashioned a device whereby Spirit would make a break for it, take the ship's self-destruct mechanism hostage, and win freedom for her "sister." It seemed viable, if the three of them played their parts correctly. But she felt constrained to give warning. "One thing," she said to the captain. "If my brother doesn't make it safely away—"

"You will do what I would do in the circumstance," Captain Brinker finished.

"Yes."

"Spirit isn't bluffing," Hope said.

The captain smiled grimly. "I think we shall get along."

Probably so. Spirit had learned to be tough minded, especially when dealing with pirates. If Hope was betrayed, she would not hesitate to destroy the pirate ship if she could. She would have nothing to lose, her life being worthless without Hope. The captain was in a roughly similar position. They had to trust each other, not because of any conceivable friendship, but because of their mutual dependency.

"Beloved sister," Spirit said to Hope. "I love you." Then she kissed him with a passion that perhaps disconcerted him. She knew she might never see him again.

He turned to the captain. "You will see that my brother is well treated," he said, his voice cold.

"You can be sure of it." Captain Brinker was no gentle creature, but she understood. There was no bluffing in any of this; they were all killers. The penalty for betrayal was death.

They played out their charade most convincingly. The two of them exchanged one final look, and Spirit wondered almost irrelevantly whether Hope had really believed it was Helse he had last clasped in his sleep. How could he not have known? Was it possible that he desired Spirit in the same way she de-

sired him, but had to play a charade to indulge that passion?
Was it after all a mutual secret?

Then Hope turned and moved toward the lifeboat. Spirit
remained with her hand on the destruct lever until the lifeboat
detached and jetted away from the mother ship. When it was
out of range of the ship's guns, she finally relinquished the lever.
It was theoretically possible to pursue the lifeboat and blast it
out of space, but that would not get the girl inside for pirate
use, and would represent an open violation of the captain's
publicly given word. It wouldn't happen.

Thus it was that Spirit became a member of the crew of *The
Hidden Flower*. She found the name of the ship intriguing, for it
described the Captain. Was that coincidence? Who had named
it?

Brinker took the lever and secured it as if this were routine.
"Now we shall go to my cabin," she said tightly. "Your life is
spared, boy, and neither I nor any member of my crew will
harm you. But you are now a member of this crew, my cabin
boy, and if you fail to perform efficiently and loyally, you will
be subject to standard discipline. Do you understand?"

That meant anything from verbal rebuke to execution, but
normally was a beating on the back with a given number of
whip lashes. Spirit would never be required to bare her back,
because her front would show. "Yes, sir," she said.

"You will never again touch the destruct lever."

To ensure that the captive boy did not try to renegotiate
the compromise now that his sister was safe. "Yes sir."

They went to Captain Brinker's cabin. "I believe you will
serve as agreed, and I will treat you well as long as you give me
no reason for discipline. But we must establish ground rules.
You are inexperienced in pirate operations; you will make mistakes. You will accept prescribed penalties boldly or with tears,
but never will you remove your clothing or indicate in any way
that you are not male."

"Never," Spirit agreed.

"Because if your secret is discovered, so may mine. My crew will know that you could not have concealed your gender without my knowledge, and that I am therefore suspect. That will be death for both of us."

"Yes sir." This made sense. The captain was taking a risk. The cabin boy would be sharing the captain's private accommodations, such as the head, and of course in sleep something was bound to show. "Except–"

Brinker's tone was deadly. "Except?"

"If some freak accident betrayed me, I could say that you knew all along, and kept me for yourself. So you had no need to take regular women."

The captain considered. "That I have not taken women because I have found none to my taste. I want a guaranteed clean one. So I have said before."

"Such as a young one, shared with no one."

Brinker nodded. "Exception accepted. But it would be much harder to protect your person if your gender were known; there would be restlessness in the crew. The men do like their indulgences. I will take death before betrayal, and would give you to the men for continuous use."

"Yes, sir. I will not betray you." She hesitated. "My elder sister was well endowed. I may become so. So someone may suspect, in time."

The captain considered again. "We shall strip."

They stripped. Naked, Brinker was a fully formed woman, using a chest band similar to the one Helse had used to mask her upper development. Her posterior was shapely but small, so did not give her away.

"You sister was more endowed than this?" Brinker asked.

"Yes, top and bottom."

"Then we have perhaps a year before you become difficult to conceal. In that time I will arrange to obtain a ship's whore. That will alleviate possible interest in you."

"I hope so, sir. I am not trying to threaten you, only to

acquaint you with my liability."

"Understood. If you are discovered, you will have to indulge the men. I can limit it, but not eliminate it. So you must be prepared for that."

"Yes, sir. If I am discovered, I will serve as I have to, without revealing any other secrets."

The captain nodded curtly. "Now you will learn to urinate like a man. Observe and do likewise." Brinker brought out a small section of tubing. Spirit realized with a small shock that it was an emulation of a penis, complete with attached scrotum. "This is an adapted dildo, normally used by women who crave penetration without a man." She put it to her cleft, so that the curved back of it made a tight fit. Then she walked to the suite's head section and stood at a urinal. She urinated, and the urine emerged from the forward tip without spillage. "When you are away from this cabin, you will on occasion urinate in the ship's regular head, in this manner. Any man there will know you have a penis."

"Yes sir," Spirit said, impressed.

"Now you do it. Here is your penis." Brinker gave her a different one.

Spirit tried, but didn't hold it quite right, and urine leaked out around the edges.

"You will use this every time," Brinker said. "Only when you never leak will you use it elsewhere."

"Yes sir."

"You will wear these." The captain brought out a kind of uniform. It included underpants with a stuffed crotch, and a chest band.

Spirit donned it, and looked in the mirror. She looked even more masculine than before, especially with her slightly bulging crotch. It would do.

"Your facial scars help. Do not cover them. But your hair must change."

Spirit submitted to a crude haircut. Brinker was good at

making her into a boy; no one would know, if she did not give herself away.

"What is your prime desire in life?" Brinker asked.

"To reunite with my brother," Spirit said immediately.

"Give me your complete loyalty, and I will allow that, at such time as it is feasible."

Spirit didn't trust this. "You already have power over me. What else do you want?"

"You have rare nerve for one your age. I want to be able to trust you, so that I need never kill you."

"I gave my word!" Spirit said angrily.

"Your brother is a man of honor. Are you the same?"

Spirit had to think for a moment. "I guess not. I'm still learning from him."

"So your honor needs buttressing by motive. I will help you search for your brother, and let you go to him when you find him. No one else will do that. Your best interest is to see that I am not betrayed before you find him."

Spirit nodded. "It's a deal."

"There is a second destruct switch. This one you may access." She opened a cabinet to show a small unmarked lever. "If I face mutiny, you will bargain on my behalf as you did on your brother's behalf."

"But that was a setup! We had already made the deal."

"But you could have destroyed the ship."

It had been a deal, but no bluff. Brinker was giving her similar power. "If you face mutiny, I will bargain. If you lose, I will destroy the ship."

"That suffices. What shall we call you."

Spirit didn't hesitate. "Sancho."

*

Thereafter Spirit quickly fell into the routine as cabin boy. She carried messages for the captain, and did chores. When the pirates went after booty, she was locked in a supply chamber, because the men did not trust her out of the ship. They teased her, sometimes cruelly, but only verbally or by arranging for her to foul up; there was a do-not-touch order on her, and they knew better than to violate that. So they confined themselves to words, and to musings about the taste of some men for boys rather than girls, and what would the precious lad do when he grew hair on his balls and was no longer appealing? She tolerated it, satisfied that they were off the mark.

Once a man asked her directly what use the captain had for her. She had rehearsed an answer, and gave it with just the right amount of awkwardness: "I knew when he spared my life it wasn't just because he wanted a cabin boy. So whatever he does once or twice a week, I keep my mouth shut."

"Or open?" he asked with a leer.

The implication was oral sex. She did not refute it. "Whatever he wants."

Naturally the word circulated. It didn't bother either Spirit or the captain. But the fact was that Captain Brinker had no apparent interest in sex of any kind. Spirit, in contrast, did. She thought a lot about what she had done with Hope, that single night, and wondered whether it would be like that with any man, or only with Hope. As her breasts and hips expanded, making concealment more difficult, she regretted that she could not *be* a woman. She wanted to complete her education in that respect, and find out what it was all about. But that would have to wait.

The captain did not abuse her. Everything was by the book, in the tradition of the navy the captain had abandoned when she and her crew turned pirate. That did not mean Spirit liked her; the memory of the fate of the last six children remained with her. But Spirit knew that her situation was quite good, considering the alternatives. She was alive, and treated well, and she had a hope of getting back together with her brother someday. That was what sustained her.

After several months, the captain issued her a laser pistol. She practiced diligently with it, and it was soon apparent that she had excellent control and aim. Now the teasing by the men abated, as her technique was reminiscent of that of the captain.

The Hidden Flower was fortunate to obtain a replacement lifeboat from one of its salvage ships. Captain Brinker had been uneasy without one, but a pirate vessel could not simply requisition such equipment.

The *Flower* had a specialty business: handling sexual feelie chips. Feelies were shows recorded in three dimensions, to be played on special helmets that enabled the wearer to be in the scene. The helmets interacted with the trace electric fields of the brain, evoking the senses of sight, sound, smell, and touch. It was very effective; a walk in a flower garden seemed completely real. Naturally what the pirate ship handled was of another nature. Deviant sex was a popular subject, and the market for this was brisk, so this trade was the main source of income for the ship. Most of the feelies were made in private studios on the major planets, but *The Hidden Flower* had some editing capability, and put its own brand names on particular lines.

True to her word, Spirit presented a notion to the captain. "I don't know where my brother is, but I want to let him know I'm all right. Maybe I can do it through the feelies. Is this okay, as long as it doesn't get the ship in trouble?"

"What do you propose to do?"

"To set up a brand called THE EMPTY HAND, with a picture of an empty hand to illustrate it. To put titles on individual chips that he will recognize, such as the name of our father, mother, sister, and his girlfriend."

"You think you can edit feelies?"

"I think I can learn."

"The mechanics are easy. It's the content that can make a female blush."

"So I'm female, and only twelve. I've seen plenty already."

"Show me your power."

"Sir?"

Brinker smiled thinly. "It's a Navy term. It means to demonstrate what you can do. Show your competence. Impress me, if you can."

Spirit got into it with a will. She viewed hundreds of feelies, and zeroed in on those calculated to appeal most strongly to sex-hungry men. Because she was not a man, she was relatively objective. At first she found some of them shocking, especially the sado/maso or weird animal liaisons, but soon enough they became dull in their repetition of what was, after all, a straightforward act: copulation. Men did seem to have rather repetitive tastes. Spirit focused on the peripherals. She considered originality, artistry, humor, clarity, coherence, and theme, seeking some story value along with beauty of the women and virility of the men. She also had a special criterion: reverse roles, where men played the parts of women, and women of men. In the feelies that was sexual, so that male users could experience the sensations of women as they participated sexually. That made this line distinct from most others, so that it would not get lost in the welter of similar offerings. Her choices became the EMPTY HAND line.

It sold well. She did seem to have the touch, mainly because she was considering the larger picture. She continued with the line, giving the feelie participants names: Major, Charity, Faith, Hope, Helse. But not Spirit. That would give her away, and part of the point was that at such time as Hope discovered this series, the omission would tell him who was behind it. Meanwhile her position was secure; she was contributing to the welfare and comfort of the ship.

After a year she was allowed to go on salvage missions. One man was assigned to be her buddy; they would look out for each other while off-ship. She thought it was just a formality, but didn't object. His name was Bruiser, and he was a powerful man, but he had never razzed her. In fact he had quietly helped her on occasion, and seemed to be decent as pirates went.

"Why not?" she asked him as they suited up.

He knew what she meant. "I was second in line for your big sister," he said. "I figure if we ever see her again, maybe you'll put in a good word for me."

He didn't know that Hope was male; none of them did. They all watched the feelies, but had never made the connection to the one they knew as the boy Sancho. But she was touched, because it was evident that Bruiser didn't like beating on children, and was using this as a pretext. "I will," she said.

They locked on to the derelict. All ships and bubbles this crew boarded were derelicts, even if they had not been prior to contact. This one contained a number of grotesque bodies. The pirates ignored them, being used to this, but Spirit thought again of the bodies of the children, and Helse before them.

This ship contained stores of spices, valuable on the black market. They carried the boxes into *The Hidden Flower*, where they would be sorted and indexed for marketing. There was a considerable trade among pirates, with different ships specializing in particular things. This one marketed whatever it found, and made a marginal living as such things went. The idea that all pirates had hoards of gold and rare liquor was false; most had mean existences, always with the threat of being blown apart by a Navy vessel that wasn't on the take.

When Spirit picked up the last box, something felt strange. Bruiser was on it immediately. He put his helmet to hers. "You got a pinhole leak! A splinter on that box."

So she did; she could see the tiny vapor jet. He whipped out a patch and slapped it on her glove, but the seal was not complete; she was still losing air faster than her tank could replace it. She tried to hurry back to the ship, but the thinning air got to her, and she passed out. The last thing she was aware of was being picked up by her buddy. He flung her over his shoulder and charged back.

When she recovered, she was in the spare bedchamber, her suit was off and she was breathing from an oxygen mask. Bruiser was staring down at her. "Kid, I didn't know," he was saying. "The captain was busy, so I just got to work to get you breathing again. If I'd a known, I'd've covered for you, buddy style."

That was when she realized that in his haste to get her out of the suit for resuscitation, he had dislodged her shirt and chest binding. Her breasts were showing, and they were no longer token.

Captain Brinker appeared. She appraised the situation in an instant. "Damn! Now I'll have to share her."

Spirit was still woozy, with a headache. But she knew what was required. "I guess you will, sir. Make—make Bruiser the first. I owe him." Then she passed out again.

The captain compromised by setting up a weekly raffle. Sancho would remain officially male, but the winner of the raffle would have him as a woman for one hour alone. The rest of the time Sancho still belonged to the captain. Anyone caught referring to Sancho as female would be eliminated from the raffle. The first winner was declared to be Bruiser. No one argued with that; he had earned it by saving her, and by revealing her, however inadvertently. For regular sex there was the whore they had installed; this was special sex, higher class. Not only did they know and respect Spirit as a good worker with uncanny aim with a laser, she was considerably cleaner and prettier than the whore, apart from her scars.

Privately the captain was grim. "Damned bad break! A splinter!"

"I'm not sure I could have hidden much longer," Spirit said. She was now thirteen, and her breasts were almost full.

"Maybe not," Brinker agreed. "Can you handle it?"

"I think so. If there's no violence."

"We'll post rules of the game: no violence, no perversions, just the straight goods. For perversions, they can continue to use the feelies." Then she paused, thinking of a better variant.

"Make it your choice. He gets the hour, you choose the type and position. I don't want you spoiled for my own pleasure."

"Yes," Spirit agreed.

"But you will have to perform. Some of those brutes are so horny they'll do it six times in that hour. You can't tell them no."

"I'll find six positions," Spirit agreed with a wan smile. "I'd better practice them now."

Brinker described a considerable assortment of what should be acceptable positions. She knew about sex, and must have had experience; she just didn't care for it. They were all variants of what were called the front and back positions, augmented by oral sex, which was also of two kinds: male mouth or female mouth. "You've got to do it, because they think you've been doing it all along."

Spirit agreed. She had of course seen much more in the feelie chip sequences, but this time it was personal. She rehearsed exactly how it and other sexual exploits were done. It didn't look great to her, but surely wasn't as bad as eating human flesh had been. She was ready; she would surely improve with practice.

The hour came. She entered the bedroom chamber that she and Hope had first used. This time she really was taking his place—but now she was far better prepared for it, in flesh and mind. She didn't expect it to be bad, because she had control, and she knew all the men of the ship, whose attitudes had changed significantly since they learned her gender. There would be no rape and no sex with strangers; in fact there would be nothing she did not choose, so long as she did choose often enough.

Bruiser was there. He was standing, and clothed. "Kid," he said awkwardly. "If you don't want to do this—"

"You saved my life. You earned it."

"I woulda done that anyway, buddy style. I never knew—I mean, I thought your sister—"

She realized that this hulk of a man was being diffident. He had been decent throughout the past year, which was why he had been assigned to be her buddy on the mission. Brinker had known that he would do his honest best to safeguard her welfare. He wasn't shy about sex; he was lusty enough with the whore. It wasn't her age, because the whore was hardly older; the men didn't care about age as long as the grown body was there. But Bruiser knew Sancho as a person, and this complete shift was evidently awkward for him.

"You figure you didn't agree to be my buddy to get sex from me," she said.

He looked at the floor. "Yeah. Even if I'da known. I mean—"

"We both know I'll be doing it with the whole crew before I'm through," she said. "One hour a week. Some of the men I don't like, but when they win, I'll give them their hours. But you I asked for, to be first, because you are my buddy, and I know you wouldn't hurt me."

"Yeah. Still—"

She was actually going to have to seduce him! Because she did want him to be first, so that she could do a favor for a decent guy before she had to do favors for the bad ones. "Come on, Bruiser. I know I won't be very good at this, but I've got to learn, and I'd rather learn from you."

He looked more positive. "Well, if you're sure—"

For answer, she began to disrobe. Her hair had grown back some in the past year; now she let it flop loose. She was wearing a light robe; she opened it to show her breasts and belly. She was considerably better fleshed than she had been at age twelve, but not yet of the stature of Faith. "If you like, I can do you instead of you doing me," she said, going to him and addressing his clothing. The feelies had many active women; some men preferred their women passive, but others liked them lively.

"Naw. I just—hell, let's get it on." He loosened his belt and was quickly out of his clothing. He had a full erection.

She got on the bed and spread her knees. But then he hesitated again. "I don't know; maybe I shouldn't."

"You don't like me?"

"I do like you, kid. That's the problem. You're no whore."

"Shouldn't that make it better with me?"

"Yeah, it should. Except–"

Now she was genuinely perplexed. "Except what?"

"Except I know you. I know you don't really want to. I don't want to do that to you, even if you say it's okay."

It was like a light flashing. "You know me. You like me. You want to treat me right—not like a whore."

"Yeah," he said gratefully.

"Would it help if you know I want it?"

"Yeah. But–"

"Here's the truth, Bruiser. Sex I think I can take or leave. But since my secret's out, and I have to do it anyway, I want to start with someone I like. I like you."

He seemed surprised. "You do?"

"You saved my life, Bruiser. I'm not going to be your girl-friend—I belong to the captain—but you're a decent man and I owe you. So this hour I'll repay you. You're the only man on this ship I'd really like to do it with."

"Gee." He was like a ten year old boy, despite his powerful man's body.

He joined her on the bed, but still he hesitated. "There is something else?" she asked.

"The—how we do it—it's supposed to be your choice."

"That's to protect me from weird perversions. I'll go with what you prefer."

"Naw, you got to choose. It's the rule."

She considered. She had lain on her back for Hope. She would prefer not to have another man use that position just yet. So she rolled over on her side and drew up her legs. "This way." In terms of feelie sex, this was boringly tame, but for her first open sex, it was challenging enough.

He was glad to oblige. In a moment he clasped her from

behind and was thrusting into her. She remained tight, and it was a stretch, but not uncomfortable. His climax was instant. She wasn't looking for any herself.

He was done, but most of the hour remained. "Now let's talk," she said as he disengaged. "I'd like to know what really pleases a man." She donned her gown so that she could conceal her midsection while she unobtrusively cleaned up.

"You just did it," he said with a rueful smile.

"I just let you get your edge off. What would make you happiest right now?"

He seemed bemused. "You really want to know?"

"Yes. When I'm a boy, I try to be the best boy I can be. When I'm a girl, I want to be the best girl. I'm not into role-reversal for this."

"Honey, you're doing it now."

"I am? But I'm just talking to you, trying to get information."

"You're treating me like a person. The whore kicks me out the moment I'm done. I'm just a chore, and she wants me out of the way. It's nothing *but* sex, and she sure lets me know it."

This was another revelation. "You want something else?"

"Like you said, you're not my girlfriend. But I'd like it if we could be friends. Sure, I'd always like sex with you, but it's much better if you like me too."

"You want respect."

"That too."

"A relationship."

"Yeah. I know it's not possible, but you asked me what I'd like, so I told you."

Her understanding was expanding. "You know you can't touch me, outside of this hour."

"Yeah."

"But we can get along."

"Yeah."

"And in this hour you *can* touch me. And you're telling me

that the way I feel about you is more important than the sex, or at least greatly enhances it."

"Yeah, I guess."

"Tell me how I can fake it."

He shook his head. "That's no good, kid."

He had misunderstood. "There will be other men after you, every week. For them I'll have to fake it."

"Oh. You mean—?"

"For you I'll mean it." That wasn't entirely true, but also not untrue. He was far from her notion of the ideal lover, but she did want to make him feel good, in thanks for the way he had helped her.

He wasn't entirely fooled. "I think you know it already. But men want to be fooled. If you smile, and maybe sit in my lap, and–"

"Like this?" She smiled and sat on his lap. Then she turned enough to embrace him and kiss him.

"Yeah."

They continued with increasing passion, and before the hour was out had had sex again, this time more rewarding for them both. As she left, Spirit kissed him once more. "Thank you, Bruiser, for everything." Then she left for the captain's quarters.

"How was it?" Brinker asked as Spirit cleaned up more thoroughly.

"He's a good guy. He didn't want to hurt me. We did it twice, and I learned a lot. He doesn't want feelie sex or whore sex, he wants caring sex."

"True, for Bruiser. But some of them aren't good guys."

"I think I can handle them, as long as they follow the rules."

"They will follow them, or be removed from the eligible list. If anyone forces you, report him. Your word will not be questioned."

But Spirit knew they could push the limits, putting her in an awkward position, not wanting to draw too narrow a line.

There turned out to be no problem about that. When

Bruiser was questioned about his session, all he said was "I'm in love." That meant that he would take it personally if another man abused her. When Spirit, as cabin boy, went on routine chores, and some men started obliquely razzing her, Bruiser appeared, closing his big fists. The razzing stopped.

As it happened, the winner of the next raffle was one of the razzers. Spirit played up to him shamelessly, pretending to like him. He wasn't fooled, but he liked the notion, and thereafter he treated her with greater courtesy. It was true: men wanted to be fooled, to think that they were doing their women a favor.

In the course of the next year, she won over the whole crew, and it was clear that it wasn't just the sex. It was that, for an hour, each had had the taste of what she might be like as a girlfriend, and that appealed. She was only fourteen, but by now fully formed along the lines of her sister Faith, and she had perfected her courtship strategy. She was satisfied that she now knew how to impress and win any man she chose to, despite her scarred face and hands and her missing finger. Actually, for the hour sessions, she donned gloves with one stuffed finger, and applied foundation makeup to mask her facial scars. She became beautiful; she knew the men were not lying when they told her so.

"You're doing what you have to do," Brinker told her. "But you do have a talent for it."

Meanwhile she pursued the search for her brother. The pirate network was imperfect, but Brinker was able to access certain records, which showed that Hope had made it safely to the receiving station at Leda, then disappeared. But after a year he had reappeared as a Navy recruit. The feelies were big on the military gray market, so she was sure Hope had access to them. He would know that she survived, and remained on the pirate ship, and was doing all right for herself. When she turned sixteen she would be eligible to join the Navy; the minimum age was a year lower for women than for men, perhaps because they matured earlier, or maybe because men preferred younger women.

She was in no hurry. She wanted to be reunited with her brother, but her situation here was good, and she did need to be somewhere until she was old enough. Brinker had promised to let her go when the time came, because Spirit had more than paid her way. She watched Hope Hubris from a distance as he made E3 rank and took a buxom Hispanic woman his own age as a roommate. As he made E4 and trained in ship-raiding. As he made E5 and disappeared on a mission.

Meanwhile Spirit was now sixteen. It was time.

"You don't have to go," Brinker said. "You have captivated all the men, and done good work on the feelie trade. You can make it as a pirate." She did not pretend friendship; they had mutual respect and convenience, but were personally wary of each other, as many pirates were.

"I know. But I've got to be with my brother."

"We can't go to Leda," Brinker said, unsurprised. "But we can trade you to another ship, and you can transfer from there to a gray market ship that transports feelies to Leda."

"That's good enough," Spirit said. But she was cautious. "You know I have not betrayed you, and will not. You have no call to betray me."

"I will not send you to your death," Brinker agreed. "I have treated you more generously than I needed to. Have you wondered why?"

"Yes. That's why I suspect there is unfinished business between us."

"It is this: the tenure of no pirate is secure. The time will inevitably come when I lose my position. If I survive, I will need an ally in the Navy. You are my reserve knife."

Spirit nodded. "Come to me then, and I will do what I can. That will acquit the debt. We are not friends."

"That will do."

But as it happened, things changed before Spirit could go.

They came across a Naval vessel, the *Hammerhead*, that had lost its drive and become a derelict. The personnel must have been evacuated, because the Jupiter Navy did not desert its own. Probably there was a caretaker crew to maintain the vessel while a new drive unit was requisitioned and transported to the site. Meanwhile it was vulnerable. This was a rare opportunity to sack a destroyer-class vessel.

"I don't trust this," Spirit told Brinker privately. "A derelict Navy vessel right in our path? It's bound to be a trap."

"It is," the captain agreed. "But we have a countermeasure."

"It's still too dangerous. Better to leave it be and get the hell out of here."

"I appreciate your opinion. Now report to your battle station."

Spirit knew better than to argue. The captain had made up her mind. She remained where she was: her battle station was the captain's cabin, guarding the captain. She quickly removed all her clothing, retaining only a knife. That was so she could move silently. Now that her gender was known, this had become standard practice; she was naked for every salvage mission, and no man touched her. She was also the courier for the captain's orders, so that no electronics had to be used. It was said with a smirk that nude news had to be believed.

"This will be a swift mission," the captain told the crew. "It surely will not be long before the Navy comes on the scene. We must clean it out and get away before that happens." Then she shut down the intercom; the rest would be done silently.

They oriented on the Navy ship and fired. The third strike holed it; they saw the air puff out. They moved in to mate locks, and the suited three man boarding party moved through efficiently. They would make sure the ship was secure: that all aboard it were dead.

Then the *Hidden Flower*'s power died.

"What happened?" Spirit asked, alarmed. "Our power

shouldn't fail like that."

"They have a suppresser."

"A suppresser!" Spirit said. "They were ready for us! We've been betrayed!"

"Carry the word: all personnel back off. Do not engage the enemy until I give the word."

Spirit moved into the passage. She knew exactly where everything was, so needed no light, and the men knew her voice. They would obey without question.

The locks remained mated, and the Navy personnel were boarding. They must have ambushed the *Hidden Flower* boarding party, and taken out the backup party. Six men gone—and Brinker wasn't concerned? But Spirit went rapidly to the other stations, gave the word, and retreated to the captain's cabin before the Navy men got there.

"They had suited men waiting for their ship to be holed?" Spirit asked the captain.

"They have a double hull."

"A double hull! You knew—and mated anyway?"

"Yes."

Then, suddenly, the Navy boarding party withdrew. "Damn," Brinker muttered. "Have they caught on, or are they merely suspicious?"

"Caught on to what?" Spirit asked.

"We have an agent aboard their ship. He will turn off the suppresser."

"An agent?" Now it was coming clear. The Navy had set a trap for whatever pirate ship it could catch, but the pirates had infiltrated a man to turn the tables on them. Play and counterplay.

Then the Navy boarders returned. "Did they catch on—or didn't they?" Brinker asked rhetorically.

"We should close the lock and disengage immediately," Spirit said. "Don't gamble on it." She didn't like the chance of the

Hidden Flower losing its air pressure; she would be the first to
die.

"They would shoot us out of space. We are in this until it
finishes, win or lose."

"That sounds like a 50-50 chance," Spirit said glumly.

The ship's power came back on. "Engage!" Brinker said,
satisfied.

Spirit moved out to the stations, carrying the word. In her
wake the pirates moved out, ready to kill the boarders. They
had lasers and knives, so that there would be operative weapons with or without the suppresser.

There was a period of silence after Spirit returned to the
cabin. The pirates should be reporting back, but they were not.
Then the suppresser came back on.

"Damn!" Brinker whispered. "Betrayal."

Spirit nodded in the darkness. She had not trusted this from
the outset.

"They will come for me," the captain said. "You will engage
them first."

"Yes, sir." It was now a matter of life and death, and Spirit
was pledged to defend Brinker. She gripped a knife in each
hand; she had trained with these too.

There was a noise in the passage. A hand drew the cabin's
entrance panel aside. Without power, it was not locked in place.
Beyond it Spirit was aware of a suited figure, pinpointing it
more by smell than sight. She hurled the right knife into the
figure. It would not kill the intruder, but would hole his suit,
and his reaction should distract him a moment. A holed suit
was always a matter of immediate concern, even in a pressured
environment.

The suit fell over. By the sound if it, it was empty. She had
fallen for the old hat-on-a-stick trick, but she was already moving through the aperture in her follow-up attack before she realized.

Of course the man was lurking. He dived for her in a tackle.

She knew why; in darkness one needed to be sure of the enemy's location before making a lethal strike. Or maybe he simply wanted to capture the captain alive. It had to be something like that, because this counter-trap had been too well planned to be for a simple elimination of a pirate ship. They surely wanted to interrogate Brinker and get information on other pirate ships.

These thoughts were parallel to the action. Spirit was already turning, twisting to avoid the tackle. If the man did get hold of her, he would have a surprise: a naked woman in his arms. That should make him pause that instant necessary to allow her to make a deadly stroke with her second knife.

He sideswiped her, but was already countering her move. He caught her right arm, yanked her off-balance, and used a foot to sweep her ankles out from under her. She realized she was up against a trained hand-to-hand fighter. This was mischief indeed.

She had not even hit the deck before she swung hard with her left hand, trying to knife him before he knew. It was her only chance.

But he caught that hand, somehow knowing, and clasped it with his strong fingers, seeking leverage on the knife. They landed on the deck, torso to torso. She inhaled, trying to make sure he picked up on her gender now, while their hands wrestled. If she could free that hand even a moment—

His finger fell across the stump of her little finger. "Spirit!" he whispered.

She froze. Then she placed the voice. "Hope!"

"I got your message. EMPTY HAND. Where's Brinker?"

Then it was his turn to freeze, for the captain had come upon him silently during the struggle. Spirit knew Brinker's knife was touching his flesh—and he could not get away, being entangled with Spirit. "What is your offer, Captain?"

"Life for life," Brinker said. "Yours for mine."

"Agreed." Thus simply the two had bargained and made the deal. Hope kissed Spirit, giving her a two-second taste of heaven, then disengaged and got to his feet, addressing the captain in the darkness. "You can take your lifeboat out, as I did before."

"Yes. I know you are a man of honor, Hubris."

"Spirit," he said. "Go get dressed, then stay clear while we deal."

They had already dealt! But Spirit didn't argue. She returned to the cabin and donned her clothing, becoming Sancho. It was only a moment.

They were still talking in whispers as she returned. "Company," she murmured. She meant that another person was approaching from the far side.

"We're done here," he said. He raised his voice. "Navy in charge here. Is the ship secure?"

"Secure, Sergeant," one of his men agreed from the control room.

"Losses?"

"One, inside. No report from outside."

They had taken the ship with only one loss! This had indeed been a polished mission.

They went to the lifeboat in single file, Hope, Brinker, and Spirit. "You knew!" Spirit said.

"Kife informed me," the captain agreed. "I planned to capture the ship and ransom him back to the Navy, letting you go with him. But he outmaneuvered me."

So Brinker hadn't tried to have Hope and Spirit kill each other, though it would not have bothered her unduly if that had happened. Spirit suppressed a surge of anger. The captain had remained within the letter of their understanding, but hardly the spirit.

Brinker entered the lifeboat. "Perhaps we shall deal again, Hubris," she said.

"Perhaps," Hope agreed noncommittally. He was no better pleased with the captain's ploy than Spirit was; she felt the controlled anger in him.

The hatch closed. Hope found Spirit again, this time embracing and kissing her like a long-lost lover. Indeed, she was all of that, in her heart. They had so much to catch up on!

"You are going to join the Navy," he told her.

"Of course," she agreed, as if there had never been any question. Because he was already there.

The power returned. They separated in body, but not in soul.

CHAPTER 7

Gerald

The next two years were quite busy, but in terms of Spirit's life represented a necessary interstice. She entered the Jupiter Navy's basic training; Jupiter citizenship was not necessary for this, and indeed it was a route many immigrants took to facilitate citizenship. Hope entered officer school at the same time, and about the time he made O1, she entered officer school herself. Training was tough on both levels, but she had little trouble with either, because her soul had been hardened as a refugee and her mind and body had been trained aboard the pirate ship. The requirement to patronize the Tail did not bother her either; she was long accustomed to weekly sex with indifferent men.

Actually she had come to know the men of *The Hidden Flower* quite well, and had prevailed on Hope to arrange for lenient treatment for the survivors: one year's imprisonment followed by service in the Jupiter Foreign Legion, where they could earn immunity from further punishment if they merited it. Bruiser, by special dispensation, was allowed to enlist in the Navy, provided he kept his nose clean. She made it a point to meet him once in the Tail, just for old times sake.

"God, kid," he said when he recognized her. "I love you."

She knew it. "You saved my life; I gave you back yours. We won't meet this way again; I'm going to officer's school. But I do care for you in my fashion."

"I love you," he repeated as he climaxed in her. She knew she had given him a gift that he would cherish indefinitely. Not the sex, for that was always available in the Navy, but the contact. He did love her, knowing they would never have a social relationship.

They did not see each other again until a year later, when she, as an officer, brought him into her brother's forming unit. They did not speak of their former association, but she knew his loyalty was guaranteed. He became her informal bodyguard, when she needed one.

Hope, as an 02 lieutenant, made contact with one Lieutenant Repro, a drug addict with no future in the Navy, who nevertheless had a dream of the perfect unit. He had a list of the best possible officers for it who were not otherwise committed, and urged Hope to assemble that unit. The first target was Lieutenant Commander Phist, a whistle-blower who had blown the whistle on a billion dollar cost overrun, whose Navy career had of course been destroyed by his honesty. He was thirty five years old and on the verge of retiring from the Navy.

Hope discussed it with Spirit, as he did anything of consequence. She was the lowest of officers, an O1, but that had nothing to do with their relationship. "I need to get Commander Phist's commitment to my unit," he said. "He is the best logistics officer in the Navy. Repro points out that though he ranks me by two grades now, mine will rise while his will not. But until I rank him, I can't bring him in, even if he should want to come, and I'm not at all sure he would be interested in someone's dream of a perfect unit. So this seems impossible to put together. What can I do?"

Spirit had an answer. "I will fetch him for you."

He shook his head doubtfully "How?"

She smiled. "Just give me a little time, Hope."

Thereafter she oriented on Commander Phist, learning everything about him. He was a good man, an outstanding officer, well worth recruiting. He had absolutely no future in the

Navy—unless Hope was able to reverse the blacklist. When she was ready, she sent him a message:

> May I meet with you on private business?
> Ensign Spirit Hubris

Evidently bemused by this contact from space, as the phrase went, Phist agreed. Spirit took a taxi rocket to the spinning administration bubble that was his station, and made her way to the complex where he was posted. She reported to his office in uniform, but took along a civilian outfit. She intended to make an impression on him, and she had a fair notion how to do it.

Commander Phist turned out to be a tall, handsome, well formed man, the soul of courtesy. He was efficient without being pushy, and did not waste time on small talk. "Lieutenant, I admit I am perplexed by your wish to meet me. Is there some small problem I can help alleviate?"

She smiled. She had not tried to mask the scars on her face, or her truncated finger; she intended to be honest with him throughout. "My business is of a somewhat personal nature, and may require considerable reflection on your part. I can express it in one minute, but would prefer to express it in an hour or a day, in a less formal setting. I would greatly appreciate it if you would humor me on the presentation, though not on your decision."

He reflected only a moment. "What do you know of me?"

"Everything that is on the record."

"Does this affect my career?"

"Yes, in part."

"I know nothing of you. Show me your power."

She held up her hands, demurring. "Please sir, not here."

"Will you trust yourself in my private apartment?"

"Yes."

"Then I believe I can free the afternoon for your presentation. Will that suffice?"

"It may, sir."

He smiled. "You intrigue me. But I trust you already know that I have very little influence on Navy policy."

Just in case she were some kind of agent seeking military favors. "Yes, sir."

They walked to the street level where his personal floater was parked. Gravity shielding did not work on spin-gee, so the vehicle did not literally float; it had wheels. But truly floating vehicles were so common on planets that the designation had spread more generally. They rode to his apartment complex, which was not fancy. Gerald Phist was evidently not much for personal display, conforming her research on him.

But his apartment was reasonably spacious and quite well kept. He was meticulous in personal habits. She appraised it at a glance, liking what she saw.

"May I change to civvies, sir?"

"As you wish."

She stepped into his toilet cubicle and put on a blue dress. She let her hair down and tied it back with a matching blue ribbon. She applied foundation makeup to her face, hiding the scars. Finally she donned white gloves, the left one with a stuffed finger. The whole procedure took very little time; she was well familiar with this particular transformation.

She stepped out and walked to the center of the room. She twirled, letting her skirt flair decorously. She was slender, but her legs had ripened nicely. "This is the artificial me," she said. "I will change back if you prefer."

He studied her with obvious appreciation. "Why should I prefer?"

She sat in the chair opposite him and crossed her legs so that some thigh showed. "Because my appearance and manner may distort your judgment."

"At this stage I am not clear whether your business is professional or social in nature."

"Both, sir."

"I am now more than intrigued."

"I will show you my power now, sir, if you wish."

"I believe you already have. You have transformed from a battle scarred ensign to a lovely woman."

He had obliquely agreed receive her presentation. She gave him the blunt summary: "My brother, Hope Hubris, wishes to assemble an ideal military unit. You are the best logistics officer extant, and he would like to have your association, when this becomes appropriate. Because you outrank him at present, this is not yet feasible. I am here to obtain your commitment. This is a business matter, in support of my brother, who is my galaxy. I am prepared to marry you and make you as satisfied in that respect as a man can be."

His mouth had not dropped open, but his features had gone still. She had impressed him, all right, but not necessarily positively. "This is more business than I anticipated," he said.

"I want there to be no deception as to my nature or my mission," she said. "I can not promise you love, but I can promise you the semblance of it for the duration of our association, which will be as long as you choose it to be. But I would like to say also that I believe you will find my brother worthwhile, perhaps more so than me, and that he may in due course be able to improve your career. We need you, Commander, and we are prepared to pay our way."

He frowned. "I think I am not for sale in quite that manner. But I confess that your personal appearance is appealing to me, I assume by no coincidence."

"No coincidence," she agreed.

"However there is more to a woman than appearance. I would like to know more about you personally."

"The one minute summary is that I was a refugee from Halfcal, witnessed the destruction of my family and companions, was captured by pirates, and after four years was able to rejoin my brother and enter the Navy. It is the kind of background that leads to survivalist traits. I am a hard woman, but a loyal one."

"You would do anything for your brother."

"Yes. I am here for him."

"Tell me about Halfcal."

"Sir, do you mean historically, culturally, or my participation in it?"

"All of them. Call me Gerald."

She flashed him a smile. "Thank you, Gerald. Stop me when you tire of detail; I don't wish to bore you."

"I think you know how not to bore me."

She smiled again. Indeed, she did know. He had lost the early love of his life when his career foundered, and had not taken a regular woman since. Spirit had disposed herself to resemble that woman in subtle manner. Her dress, her style of hair, her smile—all were roughly reminiscent, considering that the woman had been Saxon rather than Hispanic. "Halfcal echoes Haiti on original Earth, whose people were descendants of free slaves that revolted against the French in the 18th century, during the rein of Napoleon. French buccaneers took over the west side of the island of Hispaniola and harassed the French until they gave up in disgust and let the revolutionists have it."

"What of the original inhabitants?"

"Those were the Taino, American Indians, who welcomed the explorer Columbus but died out because of European illnesses like smallpox and the brutal treatment by the invaders. The French then brought many thousands of black slaves from Africa. There were fifty or more slaves for every Frenchman. Eventually these slaves revolted and threw the French out, naming their land Haiti. But that was not a happy conclusion, even for the slaves; there were racial tensions between mulattos—that is those of mixed white and black ancestry—and the blacks. Halfcal was colonized by those descendants, and by some from neighboring regions, a renewed melting pot. Our situation mirrored our origin; there were border tensions between Halfcal and the Hispanic Dominant Republic. Thus my family lived in a border city, and is Hispanic rather than mulatto."

He seemed interested, but she decided not to leave it to chance. She got up and went to sit beside him. When he looked at her, she learned forward earnestly, showing more breast than before. She was seventeen, and now fully formed. She had no picture of her sister Faith at that age, but Hope said she was similar. She would rivet the gaze of a man, when she tried, and she was trying now. "So racially and culturally I am Hispanic. But we ran afoul of an aristocrat, and had to flee the planet. That was our mistake; the pirates—"

"I know about pirates," he said, gazing into her bosom. He really had no choice. "Their tentacles extend well into Naval supply procurement."

"Yes, they prey on refugees." She frowned, remembering the horrors of the refugee bubble. "But I think you would not care to hear those details."

"Yes, I would."

So she told him, but the telling crept up on her, especially when it came to the loss of her father and then her mother. She had blocked those memories off for years, but the bitter edge was still fresh when she reviewed it. "I apologize," she said. "I am unprepared for this particular narration."

Then she was in his arms, not by her decision, and crying against his shoulder. "Damn!" she said. "I don't like to cry, especially not in public. Especially not now."

"I apologize."

She was startled. "Sir?"

"Gerald."

"Gerald. Do I misunderstand? I have bored you with my pain, and wet down your shoulder. You should be angry."

"Spirit, I wanted to see the genuine you, under the pretense. I did not mean to hurt you. I apologize for leading you on."

"This is not what I had in mind. I have ruined the effect."

"I appreciate the effect. You are a most attractive woman. But I prefer to keep company with a genuine person."

"I am not sure of that. I have maimed men. I have killed. I have been the woman to an entire ship of pirates. My core is grief and bitterness. I am ugly inside. There was no need to burden you with that."

"Then let's leave that behind. Tell me of your brother."

She cheered almost immediately. "He is smart, and honest, and courageous. When there is a difficult scene, he has such nerve he can face down a pirate or an officer. He can read people, understanding their natures. And his effect on women—"

"You pause?"

She smiled ruefully. "Women love him. They all want to do his bidding, to be near him, to have sex with him. It's like an aura he carries with him, even when he was young. And I—am jealous."

"Jealous of his magnetism?"

"Of his women."

There was a silence. Then she got up and went to clean her face. When she returned, Gerald had changed to civilian clothing, and looked like any man on the street.

"I believe I am twice your age," he said.

"Does it matter?"

"I think not. If you still wish to associate with me, I am amenable."

"You have just seen me at my worst. Are you sure?"

"My career is going nowhere. I am neither young nor virile, neither bold nor wealthy. You obviously have the ability to fascinate any man you wish to. Are *you* sure?"

"Yes!"

"Then so am I."

She nodded. She lifted the hem of her skirt. "Do you wish to—?"

"It is tempting. But perhaps not appropriate at this time."

"As you prefer." She kept a straight face, but she was hurt.

"Am I missing something?"

"No, you are a sensible man. I am the one who has foundered."

"I assume that having won your case, you are ready to return to your unit."

"Yes, of course." But her hurt remained.

"I fear I have offended you."

"No, not at all."

"Or failed you in some other manner. I ask you to tell me how, for you have made a considerable impression on me."

"No failure. I am the one out of line."

"Please tell me, Spirit."

She took a breath. "I came to persuade you to join our unit, in spirit now, in reality later. I came prepared to win you by my body if not my logic. I find that you are a nice man. I am not used to nice men."

"You have had brutal experience," he agreed. "This is one reason I do not wish to require you to do what does not derive from your own preference."

"I—I did not mean to expose my own emotions. You have been courteous and kind. You have seen my depths and not been repelled. I wish we could–"

He shook his head. "I do not have your brother's ability to read people. I think you will have to tell me exactly what you mean."

"I want you to desire me beyond the point of politeness."

"Spirit, I do! But–" Then he reconsidered. "The men you have known—they leave you alone only if they lack interest."

"Or if they are forbidden to touch me. I have had sex with many men; it was not really a matter of choice. The desire was theirs rather than mine. Now—now the desire is mine."

"Spirit, if I relax my discipline, I will become like the men you have known. I thought to spare you that."

"Don't spare me that."

He paused only a moment. "I will desist when you tell me

to." He came to her and embraced her.

"I won't tell you to." She kissed him. The passion rose up, and the kiss deepened. She knew it was in significant part a product of her savage emotions evoked by her memories, positive and negative. But she wanted him to possess her with abandon.

They moved to the bedroom alcove. "Undress me!" she panted, and put her hands on his clothing. He obliged, and soon they fell on the bed. She was on top, pinning him down. She wrapped herself around him, seeking his member, setting herself on him and around him. "Take me!" she gasped as she took him, feeling her climax starting before his.

The sexual aspect was soon done, but the emotion lingered. "Do you mind if I continue to kiss you?" she asked.

"I do not mind, but I am bemused. Normally the girls of the Tail are not interested in any continuation."

"Nor have I been, elsewhere.," she confessed.

"I am pretty sure it is not my average body or my indifferent personal magnetism."

"You do want candor?"

"Always."

As she had known. "I come to you on behalf of my brother. I studied you, doing my homework: your history, your likes and dislikes, your philosophies. In the course of that research I discovered a man I liked very much. You are not like those I have known, in so many ways. I became taken with the idea of you before I ever met you, and I know that I want you in my life. My mission is to recruit you by offering you a package you will not care to refuse: my body, my loyalty, and the career my brother may be able to offer you. But it has become personal; I also want you for yourself. I think if you decline to join my brother I shall have to leave you, to seek some other man, but I think I could love you, and I do not readily love anyone. I know I am not in your class, and that is not a matter of age; your entire existence is apart from what I have known. You know this, even

if you can not read people, even if you did no research on me.
I know that you could obtain a woman of your class. So I have
perhaps just this day, this hour to possess you, and I can't help
myself; I must have all I can of you, for fear there will be no
tomorrow."

"I am cautious about love."

"And if you loved me, and our circumstances changed so
that our relationship was no longer feasible, I would leave, as
she did. I wish I could deny that." She did not need to clarify
who the "she" was; it was his former love.

"It is that simple?"

"No! It is that complicated. My brother roomed with a
woman as an enlisted soldier, and when he became an officer
and she did not, he had to leave her. They had agreed that love
was not part of their relationship, but they both hurt, and I
know that if they were not in love, they approached it. I think
I can not afford to love you, or you me, but I think it will
happen anyway, at least for me, if we associate. Such is my
desire for your company that I am prepared to find myself in
love with you, without expecting reciprocity, for such a period
as we associate. This is not a wise course for me, but neither is it
wise to deceive myself. Viewed objectively, it is a paltry offering I make to you. I would have made the association even if I
disliked you, and perhaps that would have been better. As it is,
it is a treacherous course for us both."

"A treacherous course," he agreed. "Yet why do you believe I would not love you in return?"

"Your love is already taken, and when it passes, you will be
reluctant to give it elsewhere. You will not give it for a body, or
for return love. Only for a woman who is worthy and willing to
commit completely. I am neither."

"The limit on commitment I understand; it is the Navy
way. But the unworthiness I do not understand."

"I am in essence a pirate lass, and before that a non-Saxon
refugee. These are not your worlds."

"Yet you may be more woman than any I have met before."

"No. I do what I do for reason, and that includes the sexual aspect. I am not a feminine creature, though I will emulate one if you wish."

"That is not what I said. The girls of the Tail are highly sexual, and can be feminine. They lack intelligence, discipline, and integrity."

"Those are masculine traits."

He laughed. "Perhaps with your background you would think so."

"Yes."

"I will make you this compromise: in public, with or without me, be the smart, hard woman you are. In private, be the soft, loving woman you also are."

"The emulation," she agreed.

"If you think it is that."

"I do think it is that." But he had shaken her. She kissed him again, and realized that her face was wet. "I suppose I could be mistaken."

"I will keep company with you," he said. "This will require us to register as a sexual couple, to abate the need for the Tail. We shall have to arrange to meet for that at least once a week. No larger commitment is implied."

"No larger commitment," she agreed.

"But neither is it denied."

"Thank you." She was not being ironic; he was opening the portal to the deeper relationship she desired.

"We shall give it time to jell," he said. "This is the sensible course."

"Yes."

"But I must say that I find myself as intrigued with the idea of you as you are with the idea of me. I never anticipated such an approach by such a person, but it occurs to me now that I may have been too restricted in my notions of women. There can be diamonds amidst the refuse."

It was a nice analogy, for her background could fairly be considered refuse. Spirit doubted that she was in any sense a diamond, but she liked the notion of being separate from her situation. Gerald was accepting her as she was. "Thank you," she said again.

"Now perhaps we should register, and be seen together."

"Gladly."

"However, there may be a complication."

"They are harassing you in little ways," she said.

"Yes. They are trying to encourage me to leave the service. It is never too obvious, but they may discover a pretext to interfere."

"I will handle it."

He shrugged. "As you wish."

They cleaned up, dressed in their uniforms, and went to the nearest personnel office. "Lieutenant Commander Phist registering as a sexual correspondent to this woman, Ensign Spirit Hubris," he said.

The clerk took their names and verified their prints. Then he looked directly at Spirit, who had arranged to look severe in the military fashion, and had not covered up her facial scars. He kept his eyes on her but spoke to Gerald. "This is irregular, sir," he said.

Gerald frowned. "How so?"

"This woman is obviously not a sexual creature. That suggests a commitment in name only."

"I can not choose which woman I want?"

"Sir, it is known that you want only one woman. The navy does not support tokenism."

"Tokenism!" Gerald was evidently too surprised to see what Spirit saw: this was an aspect of his harassment, part of a continuing campaign to drive him out of the Navy. Spirit's research had established its existence, and she recognized the pattern. They wanted to force him to do what he disliked, using the common Tail.

She stepped into the fray. "Summon your superior," she said to the clerk.

"That is not required." Then, after a significant pause, he added "Sir."

Spirit's knife was in her hand, its point touching the man's nose. "Are you refusing to obey an order by an officer?"

The clerk was not so dull as not to realize he was in over his head. "Nosir!" No break between words this time. He touched a button on his desk.

Spirit put away her blade, removed her military shirt, and let down her hair. She faced the officer's aperture as she efficiently applied spot makeup by touch. Gerald faced away, tacitly disengaging from the proceedings. Possibly he had a notion what was in the offing.

The aperture opened and a lieutenant senior grade appeared. He had not yet gotten his mouth open for an imperious query before he spied Spirit, standing straight and proud in her well-filled military bra, her gaze smoky from beneath aggressively tangled locks of hair, her facial scars gone, her mouth accented by bright lipstick.

She gave him no time to catch his mental balance. "Sir, this rectal martinet claims my liaison with this fine officer is tokenism, a commitment in name only, because I am obviously not a sexual creature. I challenge this assessment."

The lieutenant of course knew that his clerk was honoring the Navy's private policy of harassment against a whistle-blowing officer, but at this moment this was clearly unfeasible. It wasn't just that Spirit was outstandingly female, but that she was so clearly eager to fight. No small office wanted the kind of public scene this threatened to be. That was one reason Spirit had come prepared. Had she dressed civilian she might have been challenged as an opportunist or prostitute.

"I think he meant that an officer of your qualities does not normally associate with one of the Commander's qualities," the lieutenant said somewhat lamely. Beautiful women generally avoided career-dead men.

"I am a red-blooded woman who can have any man she chooses," Spirit said, shaking her hair artfully across her face. "I choose the most decent, honest, and courageous officer in the Jupiter Navy. Do you have a problem with that, Sir? Show me your power."

And what a scene that would make, if the news-media got hold of it, for Commander Phist was a hero among civilians. The lieutenant backed off, literally. "Approved," he muttered to the clerk. He retreated through his aperture, and it closed behind him.

Spirit quickly put her shirt back on and jammed her hair in a wad under her cap. Gerald turned to face her, keeping his face straight.

The clerk made on entry, then touched a button. Spirit recognized it as the mute, cutting off the recording of this interview. "Sir, may I speak off the record?" he asked.

"Speak," Spirit snapped.

"Damn good show. Well played. Congratulations."

"So it's not your personal blackball?"

"No sir. The commander's reputation is excellent among enlistees."

She smiled graciously. "Thank you."

"Maybe he is finally getting some of what he deserves. You popped my eyeballs, sir." His hand hovered near the mute button; obviously it could not remain tuned out long, lest the gap in the record arouse suspicion.

"Thank you," she repeated.

He touched the button. They were back on the record. "Your liaison with the commander has been approved, sir," he said formally. "There may be another time." The implication was that the office would make further difficulties if it could.

"If so, you may regret it," Spirit said coldly. Her threat

was obviously directed at the clerk, so that no one would suspect the nature of their private dialogue.

Then she took Gerald's arm, and they departed.

Back at the apartment, Gerald finally allowed his military bearing to relax. "May I kiss you, Spirit?"

"Any time!"

He did so. Then he held her slightly away from him and looked at her as if reappraising her qualities. "May I fondle you?"

"How far do you intend to go?" she asked, smiling.

"As far as you allow."

"I thought we had already done that. There is no requirement for twice in a week, let alone in a day." She was teasing him as she undressed.

"This time it is of my volition rather than yours."

"Gerald, if you want it ten times an hour, you are welcome. But I am curious: is it merely physical?" She sat on his lap.

"No." He accepted her proffered bare breast.

"A reaction of the moment stemming from a small victory in the field?"

"In part."

"A suggestion that there is a greater potential in our relationship?" She repressed her desire to take over the sexual process; this time it had to be his initiative, not hers.

"Yes." He kissed her breast.

"Do I need to say how happy that makes me?"

"No."

She followed his lead, and soon they were on the bed again, and in the throes of a more extended and lingering act of lovemaking. She tried to school herself not to expect too much, for potential was not actuality, but the prospect of winning his love thrilled her. She had taken a calculated risk at the personnel office, knowing that she could surely win her point, but might alienate Gerald in the process. Now he had a better notion of what she was capable of, and it seemed he had reacted positively. That was a great relief.

When the sex was accomplished, he surprised her again. "May I continue to kiss you?" he asked.

That was what she had asked *him* before. "You may, but I am bemused. Normally men go to sleep."

"So I have done, elsewhere."

"Your kisses imply developing commitment."

"You desire candor?"

And they had completed the inversion. "Always," she agreed.

He kissed her, and indeed it was not a sexual gesture despite their situation. Then he got serious. "I have some questions you may find awkward."

"I fear the answers may be awkward, but you shall have them."

"Is your brother like you?"

"No, not really. We are both Hispanic refugee orphans who have seen truly ugly things, and we love and understand each other, but our strengths and weaknesses differ. We complement each other."

"How so?"

"Hope is idealistic, and he thinks a lot, trying to understand everything philosophically, and often succeeding. I try merely to understand the situation of the moment, so that I can control it. He writes down his experiences periodically; I do not. He is like a fine actor who can play a scene brilliantly, improvising when he has to, but normally others will write the script."

"You did not say that he is ambitious."

"That is because he isn't."

"Then why does he want an ideal unit?"

"That is the dream of Lieutenant Repro. The man is an addict, and his career is stultified, but he has conceived the perfect unit, and believes my brother can implement it. You are the first step in that implementation."

"Yet no ambition there?"

"His ambition is to extirpate piracy from the Jupiter Ecliptic, perhaps from the entire Solar System. This unit offers an avenue."

"There must be something you have not yet told me about him. Please amplify. Why do you support him so completely that you will put your entire life and future on the line for his whim?"

Spirit considered, not certain how much of an answer was feasible. "I would prefer to avoid that discussion."

"If I am to associate, I need to know why. I have had bad experience in the past."

Indeed he had! "Then I must answer. My brother has two, maybe three special qualities. One is his ability to read people, as I mentioned. He knows whether they tell the truth and what their nature is, so he can't be deceived except by one he loves; then his talent is nulled by his own emotion."

"Can you deceive him?"

She hated this. "Yes."

"No shame there."

"His second quality is perhaps a result of the first: his effect on others, as I also mentioned. He compels deep respect in men, and love in women. Any woman who associates with him more than in passing would gladly do whatever he wishes of her."

"Including sex?"

"Especially sex," she said shortly.

"Would you?"

So that was what he was after. She refused to lie about it. "I did, one time."

"I do not wish to misunderstand. What did you do?""

"I committed incest with him, when there was no other woman."

He paused a moment. "When?"

"When I was twelve, and he fifteen."

"I think then that your guilt is limited. You were too young to understand."

"No. I understood. I desired it."

"The fact that a thing is consensual does not necessary mean it is understood. The ramifications—"

"I understood," she repeated.

"But you did not do it again."

"There was no opportunity."

"I think I am coming to understand the depth of your commitment. Is there anything else?"

"You wish to know the worst?"

"Yes."

"My brother has sieges of madness. He can see visions, he can do things he does not know about."

"Such as having sex with his sister."

"Yes. But normally he is completely rational. I—I try to protect him from stress that can madden him."

"And helping him to fulfill his dream protects him."

"Yes."

"I think your brother is dangerous."

"Oh, no, he would never do deliberate evil! His intentions are the best."

"That is the most dangerous kind."

"I don't understand."

"I pray you never do. Spirit, you do share his traits to a degree. You are intelligent and motivated, capable of what some would call madness, and you can influence people when you try, even against their will. I saw that today at the personnel office, and here in my apartment."

"I am rational, with the discipline to do what has to be done. That is not the same."

"Yet it is similar. I feel it myself, and I am not readily influenced."

"I offer you sex and passion and the hope of an improved career. Your rational decision is to take what is offered."

"Had I been rational in that manner, I would never have blown my whistle."

That set her back. He was right. "I concede the point."

"But you do have some power, for I have been moved to cater to you since you first approached me. I have tried to resist it, but I must now concede that I see in you the capacity to replace my lost love. This is why I have questioned you in uncomfortable detail; I do not wish to be hurt again."

"I can not promise not to hurt you."

"But you can promise never to do it by your choice."

"I do so promise."

"And your brother is more than you, in this respect."

"Yes."

"I will associate with your brother's unit, to the extent feasible. But I gather it is really you who will make unit policy. Suppose I differ with you?"

"Then we shall thrash it out in a private top level meeting, and a majority vote will decide the issue. Or my brother will. But we must not allow any single issue to become a wedge between us."

"I agree, with the exception of a matter of conscience."

"Agreed. Your conscience may become our guide."

He kissed her again, as he had been doing throughout their dialogue. "I think a third sexual completion is more than I can manage at this time, but will you remain the night with me without that pretext?"

"You can fail to have sex with me ten times an hour, and I will remain with you as long as you wish."

He laughed, and she laughed with him, though it was not exactly humor. She had no desire to leave him.

She remained the night, and thereafter was with him whenever it was feasible. Fourteen months later she married him in a military term ceremony, to endure as long as both wished it, or as long as both remained in the Navy. She was then eighteen, and he thirty six, twice her age. It didn't matter. He had not yet met Hope Hubris, who had been away on a special mission. It took them some time, even after marriage, to speak of love, but as their relationship solidified, they did so.

CHAPTER 8

Betrayal

Two days after the marriage ceremony, they had a house-warming, and Gerald finally got to meet Hope. The two had a private dialogue, for Spirit wanted them to come to their own understanding without her interference, but they seemed to get along well.

"You are right," Gerald said that evening. "I like your brother, and can feel his personal magnetism. I also like his dream, and not merely because it promises something for my own career."

"I knew you would," Spirit said. They made love, as they had been doing more often than once a week, and it was indeed love rather than sex.

Hope's special mission had been to the troubled planetoid Chiron, and he had played his scene well and emerged not only with a medal for heroism and a promotion to 03, but a number of field promotions he had made there in an emergency situation had been confirmed. There were some quite grateful soldiers, and thereafter they began transferring into Hope's unit as they could manage. Spirit was active doing the detail work for consolidating the unit, forging it into an efficient and responsive organization. That kept her apart from Gerald for much of the time, but they managed to have their weekly dates throughout, as required by Navy policy.

Lieutenant Repro gave Hope the next name on his list: the most brilliant unrecognized military strategist of the century, doomed to nonentity because of lack of political connections, wrong color, and wrong gender: Lt. j.g. Emerald Sheller, of mixed ancestry and 22 years old. He went on a date with her, they talked, had what was rumored to be ferocious sex, and married the same evening. Next day she joined the unit, and Spirit met her.

Emerald was a small lanky plain brown skinned woman with a sharp attitude that often rubbed Spirit the wrong way. But there was no question of her genius in her specialty. She took over management of Hope's career, and within three years got him promotion to 04 and herself to 03. Spirit made 02 and then 03 on her own, so the two were often rivals in rank and activity. Despite Spirit's chronic annoyance with the woman, she could not question Emerald's devotion to Hope and his career, or her effectiveness as a strategist on both the military and personal levels. So she tolerated the annoyance, schooling herself not to repeat her unfortunate jealousy of Helse; she had nothing to gain by the loss of Hope's woman.

Also, Hope had brought in as his secretary the lovely enlisted woman Juana Moreno, with whom he had roomed for two years before he became an officer. Emerald was hardly keen on that, as it was clear that the two still had feelings for each other, but had to let it be. Juana was a good secretary, and absolutely loyal and discreet. So Spirit knew that Emerald had a jealousy of her own to contend with.

Lt. Repro came up with another name for the unit: Lt. Mondy, a top intelligence specialist whose career was stifled because of post-traumatic stress syndrome deriving from prior bad experience. He was middle aged and pot bellied, and he needed the constant psychological support of a woman. He seemed like no bargain, but Repro said he was what the unit needed, and that he would surely pay his way, whatever it cost to get him. One of the unit's top women would have to marry him to bring him in.

"What's his type?" Spirit asked nervously.

"Lieutenant Sheller answers the description."

Spirit was both relieved and concerned. Relieved because it wasn't her; concerned because neither Hope nor Emerald would go for a dissolution of their marriage. The two never spoke of love, but it was clear that their mutual attachment was of a similar nature. "I will have to find a suitable occasion to bring this up," she said. "It will require some finesse."

That occasion came when the news of an agricultural riot broke. The Navy would have to handle it, because Jupiter could not tolerate any extended interruption of farm produce; if its people went hungry, there would be riots of a far more serious nature. The unit that took this on and settled it would win significant acclaim. But the potential for disaster was huge. They could have this mission for the taking, but they needed competent Intelligence in a hurry.

"Now is the time," Spirit said, and had Juana send out word for an immediate staff meeting. It was early morning, but this couldn't wait.

She marched into Hope's room with Juana trailing, for the secretary had not had the nerve to disturb Hope when he was in bed with his wife. "Rise and shine, Hope! Our mission is on the horizon," she said.

Hope came logyly awake. "What?"

Spirit couldn't wait. "Get up, Brother!" she said, whipping the top sheet off the bed to expose the two of them naked.

Emerald woke and sat up, not at all pleased. Spirit traded barbs with her as the other staffers arrived, among them Gerald. "Have I missed anything?" he asked, perplexed.

Emerald, thoroughly annoyed, reacted with a flair Spirit had to admire. She threw back her shoulders to emphasize her breasts, which while not large were well formed, and spread her legs wide in his direction. "You tell me, sir. See anything here your busy wife hasn't shown you recently?"

Gerald, astonished and abashed, turned away. As it happened, Spirit *had* shown him just as much quite recently, but he had been caught completely off guard.

Meanwhile the staff was complete. "Sit down, all," Spirit said, and most of them sat down around the edge of the bed, thus trapping the two naked ones in the center. Then she hit them with the challenge of the mission, and the need for the intelligence man, and how to get him.

Indeed, Emerald did not take the news well. "I'm not going out whoring for personnel!" She looked directly at Spirit and Gerald as she spoke.

Spirit felt Gerald flinch, and for an instant she felt blind rage. But she was experienced in masking her reactions. The meeting continued, and the staff consensus was soon apparent: they did need that mission, and also the new officer. Even Emerald conceded that. She agreed to dissolve her marriage to Hope, but tackled him for one last phenomenal act of sex, starting even before the others had left the room.

Thus it was that Emerald brought in Lt. Mondy in much the manner Spirit had brought in Gerald. And Mondy showed the unit his power. Using his information and the expertise of the others, not only did they succeed in settling the migrant labor strike, they obtained a blanket promotion: one grade increase for every single member of the unit, from Hope at the top to the lowliest private. Hope made Commander 05, and both Spirit and Emerald made Lt. Commander 04. Only Gerald missed out, ironically, because he was not at this time directly associated with the unit. But now, with Hope ranking him, he joined, and that simplified Spirit's married life considerably. She owed it in large part to the sacrifice Emerald had made, and with the issue of Hope no longer between them she found herself warming to the woman.

The unit soon expanded to become a battalion. Spirit was extraordinarily busy organizing the new lines of command and communication as its personnel roster grew. In the middle of it, Hope experienced a siege of madness, and wound up at the

enlisted women's barracks looking for sex. Spirit quickly col-
lared Juana. "Take care of him!" The woman was glad to oblige;
it was the only way she could have Hope in bed again. Spirit
acted to cover up the affair, and Juana never told.

But there was one addition that was special. A woman came
to see Spirit. Her eyes were deep gray and penetrating, and she
moved with an odd melding of diffidence and assurance. She
seemed to be about fifty years old, and she was oddly familiar,
yet strange. Then it registered. "Brinker!" she exclaimed. "Captain of the *Hidden Flower!*"

"Please, just Isobel," the woman said nervously. "My past is
not healthy for my present."

"Whatever brings you here?"

"I need work, and I need discretion. Will you help me?"

Spirit considered. "We did make a deal, as I recall. I won't
say I like you, but I will honor it if my brother does."

"I will serve in any capacity, with perfect loyalty. I am competent in administration and in combat."

"I know. You taught me to use a real laser pistol accurately.
Come on; I will speak for you, but Hope will make the decision."

Hope took only a moment to catch on. "Captain Brinker
of the *Hidden Flower*—in drag!"

The woman grimaced. "It is the only way to conceal my
identity. A necessary evil." She glanced with distaste at a lock
of her hair, and at her nails. Her tresses were shoulder-length
brown-red, and her painted fingernails were color-matched. She
was actually an attractive woman for her age. But as Spirit understood, she was accustomed to masquerading as a man, and
felt uncomfortable in a dress.

Hope returned to Spirit. "You know this woman a good
deal better than I do. Do you speak for her?"

"I don't like her," Spirit said, determined to be objective.
"But she treated me fairly and kept my secret, and she is the
most competent fighting woman I know. If she will serve you,

you can't afford to turn her down. I gave her my word not to betray her to the authorities."

"That word shall be honored, of course," he agreed. "But she is a pirate."

"Was," Spirit said.

He turned back to Brinker. "My friends died because of you." Hope was not much for forgiveness of such murders.

"I lost my ship because of you," she said evenly. "It happens, in war." Spirit saw that Brinker had set him back, for the rules of war were not those of peace.

Their dialogue continued, and it became apparent that sex was at the root of Brinker's difficulty. She was not lesbian, but neither did she like sex with men. Hope could of course enable her to bypass the Navy Tail requirement, which was probably the deciding factor. Also, this was the third time she had interacted with Hope, and Spirit knew that his magic was having its effect; the woman probably wouldn't mind being close to him. But she also saw that Hope remained in doubt. "Bring Repro," he said.

That meant he was on the verge of rejecting Brinker's application, and wanted an acceptable reason. Spirit went looking for Lt. Repro, who was nearby; he was the unit's psychologist, and she had anticipated his involvement. She quickly explained the situation, and he nodded. He would do his job. Then they went to join Hope.

"What is your advice?" Hope asked him.

Repro considered. "She was not on my list, because I did not know of her. She belongs on it. Hire her."

Spirit managed to keep her jaw from dropping.

"But she is a pirate!" Hope protested again, clearly dismayed by Repro's ready acceptance of her.

"Sir, you swore to eliminate piracy. You can do that by conversion as readily as killing. You must be ready to accept those who genuinely reform. This women will be a significant asset to the unit. She has abilities it is likely to need."

Hope almost sighed. "It seems I have been overruled by my staff." He turned to Spirit. "Hire her."

As it turned out, Repro was right. Brinker had to remain in female guise, because that made her past anonymous, but she was absolutely loyal to Hope, Spirit, and the unit, and sometimes had excellent practical advice, especially relating to pirates. Later she was to serve on occasion as Hope's bodyguard, when he did not want such guarding to be obvious, and later yet she even commanded a ship for him and fought against pirates. She obeyed directives without question, accepting Spirit as her superior, and was quite satisfied to fade into the woodwork when not on duty. She became a de facto member of the unit's inner circle. Spirit had known her for years as a pirate, but now came to know her from another vantage, and her dislike of the woman faded. She was indeed an asset to the unit.

Hope had adopted an informal policy unique to the Navy, deriving from his experience as a migrant laborer: every member of the unit had to have a song and nickname bestowed by his or her associates. This had seemed foolish at first, but it had a marvelous bonding effect, and had become quite popular with enlisted and officers alike. When the songs were sung, there was no rank; every person had equal status. The songs could be quite perceptive in obscure ways. Hope's own song was "Worried Man Blues," and he was called Worry. Now in the throes of leadership he hardly seemed worried, but those close to him knew how much he cared about them and his mission, and though "concern" might be a more appropriate term, "worry" would do. Spirit's song was "I Know Where I'm Going," and those who did not know her thought it reflected her sureness of direction as Hope's closest associate. But its real message was more subtle: "I know where I'm going, and I know who's going with me; I know who I love, but the dear knows who I'll marry." That dated from before her marriage to Gerald, but its message remained: there was one she loved more, but could never marry. Her nickname was The Dear. Gerald Phist, as the master of equipment, was Old King Cole, from the song of that name, where the merry king called for his pipe, bowl, fiddlers three, and other equipment. True to the song, Gerald did requisition the finest brand of beer for the "fighting infantry," and the enlisted personnel loved him for it. And Isobel Brinker became Little Foot, from the song "Who's Going To Shoe Your Pretty Little Foot?"; the point being that she needed no man for that or anything else. She was able to escape both a personal relationship and the Tail because she was a civilian. There was a certain delicious irony in the fact that she did have small feet.

Meanwhile, Hope, having forged The Beautiful Dreamer's ideal unit, got his chance to go after the pirates of the Jupiter ecliptic. The pirates had been getting bolder, perhaps running out of Hispanic refugees to harass, and had taken to raiding Saxon pleasure craft. That finally struck a Jupiter nerve, for the government was Saxon. Hope's battalion got the mission, and made its preparations.

This was where Gerald Phist entered the picture. Logistics lacked sex appeal as a profession, but it was the lifeblood of any organization. All the equipment, from spaceships to paper clips, were in his domain. As the unit's S-4 Logistics officer, he now had the authority to requisition the best, thanks to this pressing mission, and he knew exactly what that was. Spirit loved watching him forge an apparatus that was considerably better than it should have been, given the tight budget. Old reconditioned ships were quietly becoming superior fighting pieces. It was like providing an indifferent street fighter with a set of brass knuckles.

"If I am not careful, I could get to like you," she murmured as they lay embraced. They had been married for three and a half years, and their delight in each other was still growing. They were now of the same rank, though he had seniority.

"Of course I tolerate you for the sake of your brother, Dear," he said, reversing their original relationship and facetiously invoking her nickname. But the fact was that Hope had put Gerald back to work in his specialty, and Gerald delighted in that; he did indeed support Hope independently of Spirit's encouragement.

"What, nothing else, Old King Cole?" she asked teasingly.

"Well, you are more convenient than the Tail."

"I had better be!" She wrapped herself around him, making him react. She had been able to take or leave sex before, but with him she enjoyed it, and knew that he did too.

Lt. Mondy, nicknamed the Peat Bog Soldier because his mind was a concentration camp, had done his intelligence homework, and had the current information on the location of every private vessel known to the Jupiter Navy. Thus Spirit did know exactly where she and the unit were going, and what they would find there.

Thus, in due course, they zeroed in on the pirate ship *The Caprine Isle*, notorious for gun-running to guerrilla groups on the Hispanic moons. It was the prime suspect in the abduction of the Saxon heiress that had triggered this mission. Now they would see just how well Spirit's organization and Gerald's equipment worked in real combat.

The pirate ship's captain was, of course, Billy the Kid, as bearded and shaggy as any randy buck. When Hope got him on the video, he rejected the demand to surrender in explicitly vulgar language. That was rebroadcast to the Jupiter news media, surely making a fine impression on the civilians. However, he was given an hour in which to surrender, so that it was clear that the Navy was not being unduly hasty. At the end of that hour, Billy the Kid did surrender, but it was a ruse. He tried to destroy the Navy cruiser by treachery, but got his own ship blown up instead. Lt. Mondy had anticipated the ploy exactly, and arranged to counter it before the engagement was made. Thus seventy two bad men were suddenly dead, in much the way the refugees of the bubble had died.

So the Navy had won, and the pirates had been literally destroyed. Hope played the scene through perfectly, and it made headlines on Jupiter; he was entering the beginning of his planetary fame. But Spirit knew her brother, and intercepted him as he retired to his cabin. He was alone because Emerald, the Rising Moon, had left him to marry Mondy, but he needed someone. He was not at heart a creature of cold killing, and he would suffer a severe reaction.

She found him in his hammock, sobbing. She touched him on the shoulder, and he reached up and caught her four-fingered hand in his, finding ironic solace in her familiar deformity. He brought it to his face and kissed it. She came down to the hammock and embraced him, hugging his head to her bosom in the manner of a mother, and he cried into her comfort. She understood what he felt, for she shared his heredity, his culture, and his experience. She, too, had seen their parents die; she, too, had lost her friends to pirates. And she loved him. Now he needed that love.

After a time they talked. "I never killed before like that," he said.

"It was their bomb, their deceit."

"But I knew of it!"

"You *suspected*. And you warned the pirates."

He nodded. The justification of his act became more convincing to him. The pirates had set up their own demise in the manner of a person who strikes at another and scores on himself instead.

"Are you better now?" Spirit asked gently.

"Vital signs stable," he agreed.

She smiled wanly. "Now *you* hold *me*."

He laughed with bitter understanding. He sat up straight and held her head to his chest and enclosed her in his arms while she cried. She felt the same pain, but had had to tend to him before letting go herself. It had always been that way between them.

Then they went out and saw to the other officers of the unit, who were suffering similarly in their own ways. They had been blooded. They had trained diligently for it, but it just wasn't the same. Mondy was particularly hard hit; he had suffered a nervous breakdown from guilt over the killing he had done in a prior military action, and Emerald, one tough woman in her own right, was discovering the softer side of herself that her husband had to have. Fortunately they had several days to recuperate, as the ship oriented on the next target.

Gerald suffered too, but handled it better. He had been blooded not by killing, but by being betrayed, and learned how to endure in adversity. Spirit had maintained emotional neutrality in public, but had some crying left to do, and he was there for her for that. "Do you know," he murmured, "I have heard you called the Iron Maiden, because you are always so tough in handling personnel matters and in implementing your brother's directives. They say you don't yield, you chip around the edges."

She lifted her four fingered hand. "Yes, part of me has broken off," she agreed. She touched the scars on her wet face. "And I must have gotten scraped by a passing meteor."

"But they don't know you as I do." He kissed her. "Soft inside."

"Molten."

"When you are passionate." He paused, looking intently at her. "Spirit, I was lost, until you came into my life."

"Now you have your career back."

"That, too." He kissed her again.

*

The second pirate ship bolted the moment they hailed her. They fired one torpedo and rendered her into another derelict. Again they suffered reaction, for again they had killed, and this time they had done it directly. But their pain was not as bad as before; already they were getting hardened.

By the time they tackled the third ship, the news had evidently gotten around, and it surrendered. Its officers were put on trial and later executed, but its personnel were treated more leniently, and some were retrained for useful work.

The full mission took almost a year, and took out some fifty pirate ships. It did indeed make Hope and the unit famous, as well as extirpating piracy form the Juclip. Hope's original mission had been fulfilled, his vengeance against the pirates complete.

But there was a complication: on one of the last pirate ships was a QYV courier. Helse had been a courier, and it had indirectly brought her love and death. This was a fifteen year old boy named Donald Beams who was somewhat cocky, thinking himself protected, until Hope had a private interview with him. When they rejoined the other staff members, it was evident that the boy's assurance had been severely shaken.

"Treat Donald as a hostage," Hope told Spirit. She took charge of him, knowing Hope had made progress. QYV would want whatever the courier carried, and would have to deal with Hope to get it. For the first time he had the sinister power at a disadvantage.

"Ready an escort ship," Hope told Sergeant Smith. "Program it for Europa." He intended to go there to brace Kife directly. Fortunately Mondy persuaded him to send an emissary instead, with a hint that Hope might be in QYV's power.

In due course the man returned, bringing QYV's envoy: a middle aged woman, heavyset with iron gray hair and weird trifocal contact lenses. Her name was Reba Ward, and she was nominally a Jupiter government research assistant for a minor USJ congressional committee.

Hope met privately with her. They talked for some time. When they emerged, it was Hope who was shaken, to Spirit's astonishment. What could that dull woman have told him?

Hope gave Reba Ward the hostage boy, and she returned to Europa. As far as most observers could see, nothing of significance had occurred. The two must have talked and come to no agreement. But Spirit knew better. The woman had had a profound effect on Hope, and it had nothing to do with sex or fear.

When they were alone, Hope hold her: "Kife is a Jupiter organization with no reasonable limits other than convenience. She asked me what I wanted, and I told her promotion to Captain, and a fleet to go after the nest of pirates in the Belt. And she agreed."

"Kife has that power?" Spirit asked, amazed.

"So it seems. They are restrained only by expediency and their desire to stay out of the news."

"But you did not give her Helse's key?"

"Not yet."

"What in the universe could she offer you to match your memory of Helse?"

"Megan."

"Who?"

"Megan is the one other woman I could love. But we have not yet made that deal."

Spirit feared that her brother was suffering an incipient siege of madness. But she decided to wait and see whether any part of what he claimed the QYV woman had promised came to pass.

In two more weeks they wrapped up the last of the Juclip pirates. And Hope received a promotion to O6 and command of a mission to go after the pirates of the asteroid Belt. The agent of QYV had shown her power.

*

The task force was impressive: one battleship, one carrier, two cruisers, six destroyers, fifteen escort ships, and a number of service boats and patrol craft. Hope would have eight months to shape it up for the mission, which was his most challenging one yet.

Gerald was thrown into his most busy time, checking and upgrading the fleet. He had hardly gotten started before he received his own promotion to full Commander, O5. The block against his promotion had been lifted! Spirit suspected it was because this mission was highly newsworthy, and reporters might inquire why its logistics officer was below standard rank for such a fleet position. Still, it was a gratifying breakthrough, and she could see how pleased he was. He maintained his composure in public, but that night he could not get enough of her. "This is your doing, in some devious way," he said.

"My brother's doing, maybe."

"Same thing. You have transformed my life."

"We merely enabled you to get what you deserved."

"I love you, Spirit."

"I love you, Gerald."

It was an exhilarating truth. But it made her uneasy. "What if my brother makes the deal with Kife?" She had shared as much of the information Hope had given her as was allowed, including this part. "Suppose they give him Jupiter citizenship and the chance to go after Megan, the woman he could love? If he goes to Jupiter, I shall go with him."

"And our relationship will end," he agreed.

"Our marriage. Our association. But not our love."

"Not our love." He shrugged. "We knew it when we signed. Navy marriages exist no longer than Navy service. If it happens, I know you have the courage to do what you have to do, and so do I."

Spirit found herself crying—from the mere possibility of their breakup. "My brother believes he can love only two women he might marry. Is it possible that I am the same? I can't conceive of loving any other man as I love you."

"If you do, I am sure he will be worthy."

"Not more worthy than you."

He shrugged again. "All is relative. Can we get off this subject?"

"How the hell did we ever get *on* it? Is it your turn to make love to me, or mine to make love to you?"

"I have lost track."

"Then we had both better do it."

They almost attacked each other, and it was very good. But the premonition of destruction was on them, a cloud looming on a distant horizon.

When the fleet was ready, it sailed to the Belt and tackled the several major pirate bands there. Emerald was eager to test her mettle in open battle between fleets, something they had not had occasion to do before. She was a scholar of ancient warfare, and fancied that the early principles of deployment and surprise would still obtain.

"The operative concept is Kadesh," she said. "The Egyptians met and defeated the Hittites in the vicinity of the town of Kadesh in 1299 B.C."

"Now wait, Rising Moon!" Gerald protested, using her song-nickname. The applicable words were "For the pikes must be together with the rising of the moon." The pikes of the infantry as it massed for the coordinated attack. Emerald's moon was certainly rising. "Those were marching land armies; this is space! There's hardly a parallel!"

"You worried about your hardware, King Cole?" she inquired with a glance at his trousers. "I'm trying to protect it for you."

As it turned out, Emerald had a good battle plan, but unanticipated events interfered, such as enemy reinforcements. They wound up in a messy pitched ship-to-ship battle, and Emerald transferred to a smaller ship to participate more directly. Hope, the idiot, went with her, while Spirit remained on the lead battleship. "Stay out of mischief!" Spirit called after them, knowing they wouldn't. They had the delusion that direct combat was honorable.

The battle was joined—and in the course of it Spirit had to watch helplessly as the ship the others were on, the *Discovered Check*, got incapacitated by a lucky enemy shot, and grappled, and boarded. But she knew the officers there were competent; they would reverse the case with the pirates. Soon enough they did; they used a light grenade to blind the pirates and mopped them up.

Meanwhile the larger battle was falling into place, and in due course won. Emerald's strategy had been sound; her only real mistakes were in putting herself and other officers at unnecessary risk, and in not allowing for the random breaks of combat.

But there was an unpleasant aftermath: notifying the families of the personnel lost in battle. Hope, as Commander, did it competently enough, sending careful messages, but it hurt him. Spirit joined him again as he slept, and held his hand when he woke screaming, and kissed him and mothered him until he stabilized.

"You are my strength," he told her gratefully. She merely nodded; she was as strong as she had to be for him, but it was mostly a façade he would have seen through instantly, had he not been her brother. She took no joy in battle; she merely did what she had to do, and hurt in private, thankful for Gerald's understanding embrace.

But the next engagement was hard upon them. Hope took Isobel Brinker to a neutral zone Belt tavern station to reconnoiter, and there encountered a highly significant figure: Straight, the pirate leader of the Solomons, engaged in organized gambling. And the pirate's wife Flush, and startlingly beautiful eighteen year old daughter Roulette. Hope danced with her, and was instantly smitten. The others learned about this at the staff meeting he called immediately after.

"Brinker will command the captured pirate destroyer on a de facto basis," he told Sergeant Smith. "Cobble together a competent crew in a hurry."

"Yes, sir." He got on it, taking Brinker with him. She maintained a straight face, but radiance was leaking from the edges. She lived to command a ship, and had been long denied. Her loyalty, even against pirates, was certain; she was now in Hope's orbit. She had no use for sex, but would have leaped into bed with Hope if he asked it.

Spirit exchanged a glance with the others. Repro had put the idea of putting Isobel to work this way into Hope's head, and evidently it had taken. They needed this kind of competence for the coming battles, especially considering Isobel's experience with pirate ways.

"We're going to meet the Solomons in battle in deep space in forty-eight hours," Hope said to the others. "Make the preparations."

"But our supply ship arrives in thirty-six hours," Spirit protested. "That won't give us enough time to organize."

"We'll locate a vacant planetoid and use it as a temporary supply base," Emerald said, taking this surprise in stride. They had all learned to roll with the punches of Hope's sometimes sudden decisions. "Our lesser ships will be able to protect that with the pincushion defense." She turned to Hope. "You agree, sir?"

He looked blank. "I suppose so."

She was on it in a strategic flash. "You have something more important on your mind, sir?"

"No," he said, obviously embarrassed.

It was a pleasure watching her zero in. "A woman?"

"Ridiculous!"

"Tell us about her," Emerald urged mischievously. "You haven't had a really good woman since you had me."

Juana smiled obliquely at that, but held her peace. She had taken Hope on during a siege of hallucinogenic madness, but officers were not supposed to mix sexually with enlisted, so it was a tacit secret.

He sighed. "It seems a pirate chief is trying to fix me up with his daughter, for political reasons. Covering his bets."

"A pirate wench?" Spirit asked, intrigued. "Is she clean?"

"This one would be," he said. Then he reacted against the

mere supposition. "It's ludicrous! She has killed two men who wanted her."

"That fatal appeal," Emerald said. "I must remember it."

"Not this marriage!" Mondy objected, and they laughed. The two were getting along well, and their humor showed it.

They returned to the details of strategy, but Hope seemed to be mostly out of it. Obviously the pirate wench had made more than a casual impression.

Sergeant Smith returned with Brinker. "I have set it up, sir. If you will just sign this waiver—"

"Waiver?"

"She's a civilian employee, sir. For her to command a Navy ship—it's irregular."

"She will not command a Navy ship," Hope pointed out. "It is a captured pirate vessel; and anyway, this is to be mostly off the record." Nevertheless, he signed the waiver.

Brinker started to go, but Hope stopped her. "Sit in on the strategy session, Captain. You may have input."

"Yes, sir," she said gratefully. Oh, yes; she would have danced naked on the desk, at his whim.

Emerald leaned toward her, her quest not yet done. She retained a serious interest in Hope's social status, as was the case with all his women throughout his life. They never fell out of love with him. "What does she look like?"

Brinker was startled, glancing at Hope. She had been rather suddenly admitted to the inner circle, and was understandably cautious. "My staff has will and mischief of its own, Little Foot," he said with resignation. Actually he hardly minded; he never fell out of love with any of his women either. "Satisfy their curiosity, so we can get on with business."

Brinker glanced briefly around the circle. No one indicated objection. She nodded. Then she made a gesture with her two hands, the classic hourglass shape. "Eighteen. Fire-hair. Face would launch a thousand ships. Imperious. Deadly."

There was appreciative laughter. "No wonder he wants her!"

Mondy exclaimed. "There's nothing like that in this task force!"

Emerald slammed a backhand into his chest because of the presumed slight. It was her way of displaying affection. She was not ashamed to show it, now.

It was a scramble to get ready for the battle with the Solomons. Hope had arranged with Straight to meet at a designated site in space, so that no inhabited asteroids would be menaced. There was a certain chivalric honor to it, but the battle itself would be serious. Emerald planned on her pincushion, but first invoked a remarkable open-space device that completely fooled the pirates and took out over half their deadly drones in a single sweep. Her genius was scoring.

However, the Solomons were no pushover; they had cut off the Navy supply ship, and that was a serious reversal. Without those supplies, the fleet would soon be hurting.

Then the situation changed: another pirate band, the Fijis, was approaching rapidly. They were not allied to the Solomons; they were coming in to clean up after the two combatants had decimated each other. This was bad news for both sides, for the Fijis were scum, even as pirates went.

The staff held an emergency meeting without Hope. Repro, the Beautiful Dreamer, had a provocative notion: "We need to ally with Straight," he said. "He is honest as pirates go, and stands to lose as much as we do."

"But we're at war with him!" Emerald protested.

"Not entirely. He is playing for an alliance, in case he loses the battle. That's why he proffers his daughter to Worry." He meant Hope. "He is into gambling, technically illegal, but only technically; throughout human history men have always gambled. We have no inherent quarrel with him."

"But he won't just surrender," Emerald said. "Why should he trust us?"

"Because we must surrender to *him*," Repro said.

They stared at him. But after a moment Mondy nodded. "I

believe it would work. He will trust us if we trust him first. And if his daughter marries Worry, the alliance will be secure."

"*What?*" Spirit and Emerald said almost together. Juana, too, looked shaken.

"A woman can be a powerful incentive to join a cause," Gerald said, and Mondy nodded. "In this case she will bring her band in with her."

"We don't need any more whoring for personnel!" Emerald snapped.

"Especially not when my brother is the whore," Spirit agreed.

But as the men argued the case, it came to make more sense, and in the end the women had to agree. It was a weird and risky ploy, but it stood the best chance of success in this adversity.

They put it to Hope, without mentioning the prospect of marriage. "Sir, we have thrashed this out," Spirit said, speaking with atypical formality. "We have concluded that our best course is to proffer our surrender to the Solomons' fleet."

He found his gee-couch and sank into it. "Please say again?"

"Straight is a halfway decent man," Spirit continued, arguing the case Repro had made. "He generally keeps his word, and he's not bloodthirsty. Go to him under flag of truce and present our situation."

He resisted the notion, understandably. But when he saw his staff unified behind it, he reluctantly yielded. "You won't explain?" he asked almost plaintively.

"After this crisis passes, sir, we will explain," Spirit said.

He sighed. "I hope you have not lost your collective wits! All of us will be court-martialed for pusillanimity when we are ransomed back to Jupiter. All of our careers will be finished."

"But we will suffer no further losses," Emerald said. "We are thinking not of pride but of the greatest good."

Once resigned, Hope played the scene with his usual flair. He got Straight on the video and asked to parley under flag of truce. He went alone to negotiate the terms of surrender—and returned in due course with the pirate's surrender to *him*, and Straight's daughter Roulette with him in the shuttle ship as hostage.

The ploy had worked. Straight had decided to trust Hope and his cadre of officers, after seeing their trust of him. His daughter was his earnest of integrity. And she was indeed mind-bendingly beautiful, exactly as Isobel had said.

"This is Roulette—our hostage for the Solomons' surrender," Hope said somewhat lamely.

Spirit didn't bother to seem surprised. "I recognized the figure. I'll see her to a cabin."

"You knew," he said.

"We thought it likely," she agreed. "We showed Straight our power, and he responded."

"The game is not over yet," Roulette said darkly. This was evidently no choice of hers.

"Arrange for rendezvous with our supply ship and for transfer of food to the Solomons fleet," Hope said. "Establish liaison for working out the fine print of the surrender. And quickly; the Fijis—"

"I can help," Roulette said. "I know the personnel to contact in our fleet, and what they need."

There was one reason Straight had sent her. Her cooperation would greatly facilitate the process.

Spirit glanced at her appraisingly. "You have practical training?"

"I'm my father's S-3." S-3 was the Operations section, which was vital.

"At your age?"

Rue smiled. "Pirates aren't subject to Naval regulations. I've been an officer since birth. It's a family corporation."

"We shall test you." Spirit conducted the wench to an officer's cabin. "You will be given the freedom of the ship," she said. "You're not really a hostage."

"So you say," the girl said. But then she mellowed slightly.

"Did you really castrate the man who raped your sister?"

"He told you of that?"

"Did you do it?"

"Yes. And I would do it again."

"Then you understand pirate ways."

"Oh, yes. I was a captive of pirates for four years. Now the captain of that pirate ship works for us."

"I would like to meet him."

"Her. Isobel Brinker."

She pondered, but evidently drew a blank. "What was her ship?"

"The Hidden Flower."

"Oh, of the Juclip! I thought a man commanded that one."

Spirit was surprised. "You know every ship by name?"

"The significant ones. That one was a feelie porn conduit."

"The Empty Hand."

"That was one of the better lines."

"That was mine."

Roulette looked at her, surprised. "I think you and I will get along."

Spirit found herself liking this young woman. "But you know, we just took out the Carolines."

"Too bad, if you like porn."

"Its pirates we don't like. No offense."

"We don't like the Jupiter Navy either. No offense."

Spirit changed the subject. "I will ask Captain Brinker to meet with you at her convenience."

Then Roulette did a doubletake. "Brinker—age about fifty, red-brown hair, gray eyes, lightning draw?"

"You have met?"

"She bodyguarded Captain Hubris at the tavern. I didn't make the connection when I heard the name. She looked so feminine."

"So she did. It is how she masks her past. I didn't realize you two had interacted."

"She's a captain again?"

"She commands a ship for us."

"We will get along," Roulette repeated.

They got her set up in her cabin, then returned together to the communications center. "You're S-3?" Spirit asked, giving her a chance to back down.

"Try me."

Spirit did. She put her on the video contact. "Integrate our fleets."

When the first Solomons ship came on, the young woman evinced no uncertainty. "This is Roulette, hostage aboard the Navy flagship," she said to the screen. "The Navy has food for us, and time is short. Get me Cap'n Snake-eyes on the double." It went from there. There was no question of her competence.

Spirit turned her head to look at Hope behind Roulette's head, nodding affirmatively. But then Roulette herself turned to send him a glare of hate. She really did not like him, no matter how well she might get along with others. Rather, Spirit realized, she did not like the idea of having to marry him. But she would inevitably be captured by his subtle charm, as all women were. She fought, but would lose.

And Hope, astonishingly, averted his gaze. She had stared him down. Oh, yes, he was already smitten.

Meanwhile the Fiji fleet, seeing that they had broken off the battle with the Solomons, pounced instead on the planetoid where they had set up their pincushion defense, before abruptly evacuating. They had had to leave supplies behind, annoyingly. The pirates were scavenging, and the Navy couldn't stop it.

Spirit was unconcerned, knowing what Emerald had cooked up. "Call them, sir," she told him. "Give the Fijis an ultimatum of immediate surrender—or destruction."

"But that would be foolish! We have no—"

"Or delegate someone to do it."

"But—"

"Roulette, maybe. She'll enjoy this."

He spread his hands. "*You* delegate it."

She smiled knowingly. "Rue, would you like to deliver the Navy's ultimatum to the Fijis?"

Roulette came over to the screen. "I hate the Fijis almost as bad as I hate the Navy. But a bluff's no good. They're smugglers, and lying is their pride. Bloodstone would laugh in my face."

"Is there any redeeming quality about the Fiji?" Spirit inquired.

"No. They captured one of our parties once, and sent us back their hands, one finger at a time, each one flayed. Our biolab said the skin had been pulled off while the fingers were still attached and alive."

Spirit stiffened, then slowly raised her left hand, showing her missing finger. "We have met that kind," she said. "The Horse didn't flay my flesh, though."

"I noticed. But you settled the score." Roulette settled herself before the screen. "Is this a bluff?"

"No."

"Then I'll do it." She went to work, and in a moment she was in touch with the Fiji operator. "Get me Bloodstone," she snapped imperiously.

"Who the hell wants Bloodstone?" the man demanded.

"Roulette."

Another face came on: grizzled, grim, with earrings in the classic pirate style. "What you want, you luscious tart?"

"Surrender this instant, or be destroyed."

Bloodstone bellowed out his laughter. "Listen, you juvenile slut, when I clean up Straight's mess I'll screw you to the damn bulkhead. You never had a real man before."

"I never had a man at all," she responded. "Only with my knife. You have one minute to surrender to the Jupiter Navy."

Bloodstone just laughed coarsely, making obscene gestures with his hands.

The minute finished. Spirit signaled a technician.

The planetoid exploded. "We mined it," Spirit explained.

Roulette watched the expanding ring of debris in the screen. "Beautiful," she murmured, licking her red lips. "You really don't bluff, do you!"

"No," Spirit agreed.

Soon came the next stage of the liaison with the Solomons: Hope's marriage to Roulette. This was a horrendous event, because he had to rape her, which he didn't want to do, and survive her knife attack. But Isobel Brinker was firm: this was the only way to fashion an enduring alliance with a pirate band.

They rehearsed the abduction, with Juana playing the part of the bride. She was in a low-bodiced pink nightie that revealed somewhat too much of her lush torso, and when the light was behind her much of the material become translucent. Spirit and Emerald had presented Hope with a model who was guaranteed to turn him on, while being forbidden. She had a rubber knife to defend herself, but she was laughing so much she couldn't even threaten him with it.

Then came the rehearsal of the rape itself. Emerald played the part of the to-be-ravished bride. Spirit slipped the rubber knife to her. "You poor, innocent damsel," she said in honey-drip tone. "I cannot stop my evil brother from this cruel assault, for I am only a woman, but at least I can give you some chance to defend your treasure."

"Bless you, sister," Emerald said, smiling maliciously. "I'll disembowel him!"

"Hey!" he protested.

But it was time for the humor to end. The threat was real, and Hope was all too apt not to take it seriously until too late, because of his crush on the wench.

"Roulette will use her knife," Spirit reminded him. "Don't trust her for a moment, Hope; that's how she got her other two suitors. She's your enemy—until you conquer her."

Despite their best intentions, it was hilarious. He managed

to disarm Emerald, but she managed to seduce him, in a fashion. The staff, watching, critiqued the performance, to make sure he would be able to handle the real rape properly.

And of course the real rape, in the manner of a battle, turned out to be quite different from the rehearsal.

Spirit, in her ritual guise as secret friend, slipped Roulette a knife, a real one, in accordance with pirate protocol. The girl accepted it, handling it quite competently. But she looked doubtful. "I'm not sure this is smart."

"Not smart?" Spirit hesitated to guess what she meant.

"Spirit, I like you. You've had solid pirate experience. I don't want to kill your brother."

"He's a martial expert," Spirit said. "He'll disarm you."

"Maybe he could. But *will* he?"

"We have rehearsed him. He knows what to do."

"He thinks it's a game."

Spirit sat down beside her. "I know he does. He's not a rapist. Should we stop this?"

"Yes."

"Then how will we make the alliance both our sides need?"

"Maybe we could get some other pirate girl. One who wouldn't really fight."

"He's already smitten with you."

"Damn it!" Roulette flared. "I'm trying to spare us disaster! That weakling's going to die."

"If he does, we'll return you safely to your father."

"You'll do that?"

"It's the protocol."

"And you're tough enough to follow it to the letter."

"Yes." And she would, though her heart broke.

"I wish I could marry *you*."

Spirit knew what Rue meant: that she had the iron gumption her brother lacked in this instance. "I wish I could rape you."

Roulette turned, leaned into her, and kissed her on the

mouth. Spirit accepted it—and caught the girl's knife hand as it moved. It was a feint, without real power, but move and countermove had been quick. They understood each other. Were Spirit a man, she could indeed perform the rape.

"Look—you'll be witnessing it."

"Yes, with video cameras. To prove you did not submit willingly."

"Be there physically too. Then you can overpower me before he's dead. I'll make the first strike non-lethal."

"No. It has to be played out straight, or it doesn't count. You know that."

"It must be," Roulette said sadly. "Once we engage, there'll be no stopping it."

"Yes," Spirit agreed. Then she stood and departed before her emotion overcame her. The girl had figured Hope correctly, and her chances of killing him were all too good, because he would hold back. It would indeed be better if Spirit could substitute for him, but she couldn't.

Then she went for the final session with Hope, to try to stiffen his spine. That was little comfort; he had somehow overlooked or blocked out the fact of the witnessing.

"*What?*"

"It's the pirate way, Hope. The groom's clan has to witness the victory, so that no one can claim he didn't perform. And if anything happens to the bride, I will be obliged to seek revenge—"

"*You?*"

"I gave her the knife, Hope. It's real; no rubber one this time. I'm responsible for her until you win her. So whatever you do, don't kill her, because if she dies and I don't kill you, her clan will be honor-bound to do it, and—"

He stared at her, suddenly knowing that she would do it. That might be a positive sign.

Spirit sent Isobel to talk to him, to impress on him the reality of the need. Then he called Straight, who advised him to strike fast and hard, and to give up the marriage if he didn't succeed in the first minute. He even put his wife Flush on, who clarified that she would never have respected Straight if he hadn't conquered her first. But Hope still seemed uncertain. Spirit dreaded the coming encounter.

The time came. They took their places in chairs set around the sides of the bride's chamber: Repro, Phist, Mondy, Emerald, and Spirit herself. Brinker operated the video camera, and Juana was in a corner making shorthand notes. The Groom's official witness team.

Roulette was beautiful as she sat on the bed; she wore a pale blue negligee that offset her red hair dramatically. Her tresses were artfully wild, making her resemble a waiting predator. Her figure was so full and lithe it would make any man pause, even the three male witnesses. In fact when Rue caught them looking, she opened her décolletage, giving them a better view of her fine breasts, and let her full thighs part. Repro and Mondy smiled briefly; Gerald blushed. Spirit appreciated the tease; the girl had some humor. Even Juana, a well formed woman, looked envious. Only Isobel was unmoved.

Spirit checked her watch. "Time." The room darkened, though not completely; they had to be able to see the event.

Roulette got silently off the bed and went to stand beside the door panel, her knife ready. She intended to ambush him as he entered, and the witnesses could not interfere in any way.

The panel slid quietly open. There was a pause, then something entered rapidly. Roulette was on it, stabbing downward. Then a second form leaped through the door, caught her from behind, and rendered her unconscious with a neck strangle. She had fallen for the oldest trick in the book: a decoy shirt thrown in first. It was a good start.

Hope used the shirt to bind her wrists, then used the bed sheet to tie her ankles and tore off a section to gag her. She recovered consciousness quickly, but was helpless. She didn't even struggle; at this point it was useless. He had won the first round by abducting her.

They moved to the groom's quarters and took new chairs. Spirit untied the bride and restored her knife to her while Hope stripped. This was according to protocol; the bride had to be able to defend herself from the rape.

He approached her; she struck with the knife, and he disarmed her again. He let her go, and she went after him with nails and teeth. He nullified her again, and whispered something in her ear, then let her go. She attacked again, but he caught up her negligee and entangled her in it, whispering to her again. He let her go once more.

The utter fool! He was playing with her.

And it cost him. She got her hand on the dropped knife, and this time she managed to graze his leg. Yet still he played, snatching parts of her negligee away as she slashed at him.

Then he turned strange. Oh, no! He was going into a madness vision. He stared at Roulette, muttering something. Then he approached her, neither feinting nor dodging, as if she were welcoming his embrace.

She stabbed him in the left shoulder. He merely shrugged as the blood flowed. She stabbed again, and this time the blood jetted; she had severed an artery. But he ignored it and closed for a kiss. She bit his lip, hard, but he remained as if it were a true kiss.

He had to finish it quickly, before he bled to death. Yet the blood no longer jetted.

After a moment he drew back, and the cloud left his face. "You stabbed me!" he exclaimed, perceiving the blood. "And you bit me!"

"Well, you hugged and kissed me!"

"And you're not Megan." Then Spirit understood at least part of it: Megan was the other woman he thought he could love. He must have seen her in the vision.

"Who the hell is Megan?"

He struck her, a slashing openhanded blow across the side of the head. Her head rocked back, her mouth open, but he caught her again on the other side with a backhand. She fell on the bed, blinking. "Who the hell are *you?*" he demanded.

And the blood stopped flowing from his wounds. They simply closed up, leaving only red scars. Roulette saw it, and her mouth hung open. It was as if she faced a bloodless ghost or zombie.

This was a side of Hope Spirit had never seen before. He had not returned to his normal self. The madness had taken over. It gave him weird control of his entire body.

"I never saw you like this!" Roulette gasped.

"You never saw me at all, you arrogant bitch!" he snapped. "You like me better now?" He jerked his right hand and forced her right hand to strike her face.

"You brute!" But it was neither fear nor horror that governed her now. Her tone was one of discovery and admiration. "Kiss me again; I won't bite!"

Was it another trick? She might be feigning surrender, hoping to recover the knife.

Instead Hope spat blood and saliva in her face. "I'd as soon kiss a snake!"

She shuddered, not with anger but with rapture. She spread her arms and her legs. "Do it now!" she breathed. "I can't fight you when you're like this. You're a real man after all!"

It seemed real. Now was the time for him to do it.

He drew away from her and stood by the bunk. "Look at me," he said. "I don't want you. You're not Helse, you're not Megan. What good are you?"

"Revile me!" she whispered. "Hit me! Make me scream!"

"You aren't paying attention, you pirate slut," he said. "Look at my member. You don't turn me on at all."

And indeed he showed no sexual desire. "You have failed as a woman," he told her.

Enraged as a woman scorned, she snatched the knife from

the bed beside her. She pointed it at his groin. "I'll cut it off!"

"Go ahead." He raised his arms and set his hands behind his head, not retreating from her. The total fool!

And she couldn't do it. Spirit saw her shudder. Hope had entirely vanquished her.

But she had another ploy. Slowly she brought the blade to her own throat. "If you won't have me, no one will."

"Spirit," he said.

Oh, damn! But she had to play along. Spirit rose from her chair. "Yes, Hope."

"If she dies, you are bound by honor to kill me."

Spirit hesitated. She wanted to call a halt to this awful alternative, but she could not oppose her brother. Especially when he was like this; she was in awe of him now. "Yes," she whispered.

"Set the laser."

Slowly she brought out her laser pistol, adjusted it, and aimed it at his face.

His eyes had never left Rue's. "You see we honor the pirate convention. Do you believe Spirit will kill me?"

Roulette turned her head a moment to gaze at Spirit's face. "Yes," she breathed. "She doesn't bluff."

"So you may safely kill yourself," he continued. "You know you will be immediately avenged, and there will be no onus for your father to bear, no embarrassment to your clan."

Roulette flung the knife away. "You bastard, you have mastered me! Finish it!"

And finally, as it were reluctantly, he did. Roulette made no resistance; rather, she cooperated vigorously. He had not raped her body so much as her soul.

And when it was done, she demanded that the videos never be played, and the witnesses be silent. She and Hope had visible injuries; those would suffice to tell the story. This had been a rape like none other.

*

Thus was the alliance made. Roulette was assigned a song, "Rue" whose words suggested the wasting of women by men, and her nickname became The Ravished. She liked that. She was, as it turned out, a masochist; she could not truly turn on unless brutalized. Thus their marriage was an ongoing contest, as he tried to make her respond to gentleness, and she tried to make him treat her cruelly. Each seemed to be making progress with the other.

The fleets merged, and with Emerald's genius guiding them, they defeated the other pirates, band by band. Then, when they were on the verge of completing the cleanup of the Belt, there came the betrayal.

Gerald was the first to learn of it, and it appalled him. "What is it?" Spirit asked.

"I am ordered by the Jupiter authority to assume command of the Task Force and place your brother under arrest for insubordination and other charges."

Spirit stared. "But he's guilty of none of that!"

He shook his head. "He is guilty of being too effective in fighting crime. Pirates have nerves extending to high places. I am in a position to know."

For he had lost his own career that way. "Oh, no," she breathed.

"And I must arrest you too," he continued miserably. "And ground the fleet."

It was as though the Solar system had foundered, but for the moment it was the personal aspect that stung her. "Is this the end for us?"

"I very much fear it is."

She kissed him. "Then do your duty, Gerald."

"Consider yourself relieved of your position," he said. Then he braced himself and went off to find Hope.

Gerald Phist did his duty like the good soldier he was. All

of the top officers were interned and held incommunicado as the fleet headed back for Jupiter.

Then several significant things happened: The Beautiful Dreamer, deprived of his drugs, died. The marriages of Hope and Roulette, and of Gerald and Spirit, were dissolved, and on Mondy's insightful suggestion Gerald married Roulette, to preserve the necessary connections. It was an irony, as Gerald and Roulette loved not each other but Spirit and Hope, but each understood the other's position perfectly. They were to be a successful long-term couple publicly, and possibly privately, perhaps because of that common passion.

Hope wrote the narrative of his migrant and military memoirs, settling his soul in a way that Spirit could not. She suffered her loss of Gerald alone. She was, after all, the Iron Maiden.

The woman of QYV met with Hope, and they made a deal: Helse's key for Jupiter citizenship and information on Megan. Hope and Spirit, at the ages of thirty and twenty seven respectively, were honorably discharged from the Navy—in fact Hope was hailed as the Hero of the Belt—and they came at last to the planet of Jupiter. It was not by their choice, at this stage, but was the best compromise settlement they could manage. As it turned out, Hope's core unit was not destroyed; it merely became invisible, and his officers went on to consolidate power in the Navy, supported by a solid cadre of enlisted personnel. Some liaisons did not follow official chains of command, but were as potent. That was to have significant later effect on Jupiter politics.

CHAPTER 9

Second Love

It was as though they were starting their lives over, leaving all they had known to join a new world. Both Hope and Spirit knew that they would never recover their Navy relationships; they might as well be dead, just as their family and refugee friends had been dead when they first came to the navy. Hope was in depression, and Spirit sustained him as well as she could, whether by diverting him with inconsequential talk, or holding him. He was not ashamed to show his weakness when they were alone together; she could not afford to show hers, needing to be strong for him. It would take time for their pain to fade. Meanwhile they faced the future with nominally positive attitudes.

Jupiter up close was ferociously beautiful, with its mighty bands and spots. It was also somewhat daunting, because the atmospheric pressure at the residential level was five bars: five times that of Earth's surface. Spirit tried to bury the feeling of being crushed. She was used to vacuum, emotionally, dreadful as it was.

They came to the city of Nyork, a giant bubble about one and a half miles in diameter. Once they were inside, Spirit's tension eased; it was like being in any other bubble, except that this was larger. It hardly mattered whether the surrounding substance was atmosphere or vacuum; both were similarly lethal to unprotected human beings.

They were treated to a parade in their honor. They rode in a wheeled vehicle with the mayor of the city, and throngs of people cheered. This was weird; could it really be for them? It seemed it was. Theoretically Jupiter's press was open, but it was clear that the real situation had not been publicized. So they were retired champions rather than cashiered outcasts.

When they entered the Hispanic section, the chant became monstrous. "*Hubris! Hubris!*" The car was pelted by flowers. This conspicuous waste embarrassed them, for ornamental plants were precious in space. Spirit made the most of it: she picked up several that fell inside the car and made a bouquet that she set in her hair, and there was a deafening roar of approval. She made another, her nine fingers nimble enough, and put it in her brother's hair, and the noise swelled yet farther.

A girl launched herself into the car, and flung her arms about Hope. "Hubris, I love you," she cried in Spanish.

A Saxon policeman pursued her, but Spirit interceded. "Let her stay, officer," she urged. "She will be no trouble, I'm sure." She put her arms protectively around the girl.

But the girl had another notion. She snuggled closer to Hope. "Hero Hubris, why don't you stay here in Nyork and become mayor, and I will be your mistress!"

He was so surprised that he choked. Spirit knew why: the girl was obviously under the age of consent by a year or two, though her anatomy was fully formed. Hope had sex with women of all ages, but in recent years had settled on nominally legitimate ones. He had never anticipated such a bald proposition by a stranger.

Spirit decided to rescue him. "My brother has already arranged to settle in Ybor, in Sunshine. He will get married."

"Married!" the girl cried, clutching him.

"He is not for you," Spirit said. "You would be too much woman for him. He is thirty years old."

"Thirty," the girl repeated, evidently shocked that anyone could be such an age. Then she reconsidered. "Still, a married man needs a mistress, too, and May-December liaisons can work out. Sometimes an older man can be very considerate and not too demanding—"

"And he has been long in space," Spirit continued, keeping her face straight. "The radiation—"

"The radiation!" The girl glanced down at Hope's crotch as if expecting to see crawling gangrene. Of course space radiation did no apparent physical damage; it merely sterilized men who remained off-planet too long without taking special precautions. That was why the navy needed no contraceptives. Most men had stored semen samples in shielded reserve if they later decided to become fathers. Regardless, the notion had done the trick; the girl was no longer much interested in seducing him.

But soon the crowd became a riot, and they were in danger as the car was stalled by aggressive Saxons who thought Hispanics were taking their jobs. Spirit exchanged a glance with Hope: they knew what to do.

"Crowd control procedure," he said. "Cover me, Spirit."

She reached into her blouse and brought out a pencil-laser pistol. "Covered."

"Hey, you aren't supposed to be armed," the mayor protested. "Weapons are banned in—"

Spirit pointed the laser at his nose and he stopped talking. Hope jumped out of the car and ran ahead. For a moment no one realized what he was doing; then a worker pointed at him and shouted.

But by that time Hope had reached the leader. He caught the man by the right arm, spun him around, and applied a submission lock.

"You can't do that!" another man cried, reaching for Hope. Spirit was ready; a beam from her laser burned a hole in his shirt and stung his chest. It was only a momentary flash, just enough to make him jump. Jump he did, falling back, staring at the car.

"That was just a warning," Hope told him. "Stand clear."

The others stood clear, realizing that the Navy personnel did indeed know how to conduct themselves in a fighting situation, and that the presence of the weapon made them far from helpless. Lasers did not have to be set at trace level.

A kind of hush descended on the crowd as Hope marched the labor leader to the car. Spirit's gaze remained on the crowd, not on Hope, and she fired again, stinging the hand of a man who was getting ready to throw another brick. She had always had acute reflexes and perfect marksmanship with whatever weapon she chose. Hope got the leader into the car.

"Sit there. Put your arm around the young lady."

"That spic?" he demanded angrily. "I wouldn't touch her with—"

Spirit's laser tube swung around to bear on his nose.

"Uh, yeah, sure," he said, disgruntled. He took the seat and moved his left arm.

"Keep your filthy Saxon hands to yourself!" the girl snapped in Spanish.

"Suffer yourself to be touched by this man," Hope told her in the same language. "We want to show the crowd how tolerant their leader is."

Her eyes widened as she caught on. She smiled sweetly. "Come here, you Saxon tub of sewage," she said in dulcet Spanish tones. "Put your big fat stinking white paw on me, snotface."

It went on from there, with the publicity cameras watching. Hope exerted his genius and in due course got the labor leader and the Hispanic girl to agree on a city program for the mayor to implement, that would bring more jobs for both factions. And the two natural enemies actually began to warm to each other.

"Know something, Captain?" the mayor said to Hope. "You're a born politician."

And that profession was exactly what Hope had in mind. It wasn't that he craved notoriety or power, but that he had a woman to win and a score to settle. Spirit would support him in both quests.

They took a shuttle flight to the state of Sunshine and the city of Ybor, and to the suburb of Pineleaf, which was a small spinning bubble reminding her of their early life in Halfcal and the disaster of the refugee bubble.

"Do you still have your finger-whip?" Hope asked her as they explored it.

"I can get one," she replied, laughing. It was good to laugh; she was beginning to reorient on the new reality, putting the pain of the Navy betrayal half a step behind her.

Within a day they discovered racism: an anonymous neighbor did not like the fact that they were Hispanic. But a non-anonymous neighbor went out of her way to counter it, and they were made welcome. As Hope put it: "Prejudice, racism, and unprovoked hate do exist in our society, though normally they are masked; they do their mischief in darkness. But they are more than compensated by the elements of openness, tolerance, and fairness that manifest in light." When it came to conceptual expression, Hope was the one.

They had funds from their Navy retirement to sustain them for some time, so did not have to obtain paying work immediately. Instead they oriented on Hope's next objective: Megan, the woman he believed he could love. He was a dreamer in his fashion, but that was all right; Spirit had enough practical sense to keep him functioning. She envied him his fancy; he had lost his first love, but at least had hope of a second one. Spirit had no such hope. She was not about to delude herself that any other man could ever take the place of Gerald in her life and heart.

Gerald. She hoped he was satisfied with Roulette. It had been a marriage of convenience to salvage what the Beautiful Dreamer had dreamed and Hope had made, but the girl was smart, nervy, beautiful, and passionate, and had essential connections. They would be having sex, of course, with or without love, because it was the Navy way, but Gerald was so gentle and Rue so masochistic that it was probably perfunctory. Spirit hoped they found some viable compromise. She discovered that she was motivated not by jealousy, but by the wish for Gerald to be happy. Maybe Rue could fake it, letting her unparalleled body carry the onus. Maybe Gerald could fake brutality with a feather whip, making The Ravished come truly to life.

But for now Spirit could sublimate her core of grief by focusing on her brother's prospective romance. "Call Kife," she told him once they were settled in.

He needed no second urging. He put in a call to a code he had memorized. The letter Q appeared on the screen. "This is Hope Hubris."

In a moment the screen lighted with a silent schematic of the Pineleaf apartment complex, with one apartment briefly highlighted. Then it faded, and the connection broke.

He looked at Spirit. "Here?"

"Are you surprised?"

"Yes. I thought they'd just arrange to print out the data—"

"She's a woman, Hope."

He laughed. "She's interested in my career, not my body!"

"So am I."

He glanced at her, for a moment fathoming the farther reaches of that statement. Spirit *was* interested in his career, as hers was bound to his, but that was hardly the limit of their association. The JYV woman, Reba, had recommended that Hope get into politics, and hinted that she, and therefore QYV, would lend its potent subtle support; he would be expected to reciprocate as convenient and/or necessary. But no woman was immune to Hope's magnetism, and so it figured that however coldly ambitious Reba was, she also had at least a small worm of desire for his favor gnawing in her core.

"But it is to locate Megan that I need Kife," he said.

"You haven't located her yet."

He got the point: therefore he was not yet committed. So he could exercise his charm on this smart, tough, ambitious older woman, and perhaps gain by it.

He went alone, taking along his manuscript of Navy experience to give her for safekeeping. Reba had obtained the Refugee manuscript, and there was no reason to doubt her sincerity in protecting it.

He returned some time later, visibly awed. "She's young— my age," he said. "And she does have an interest."

"Of course."

"She says I am potentially Jupiter's next president."

Even Spirit was floored by that. "President! I thought some state office, maybe mayor of a city."

"She is ambitious, and means to use me to further it. I am daunted by the power of her mind and her grasp of reality. If we associated, I might orbit her."

Instead of the woman orbiting him in the usual manner. Any woman could impress Hope with her body, but few impressed him with their minds. If he was shaken, Spirit needed to take warning: Reba was dangerous.

"I kissed her," he added.

"Then you set her back."

He nodded. "I had to. She is too strong not to counter in some way."

Spirit nodded. That worm of desire would now be a snake. Reba might have power to affect Hope's career, but she would have a continuing hunger for his embrace. That would mitigate her sternness in dealing with him.

"She gave me something."

It was a case similar to the one he had had containing his Navy manuscript. That hinted at the woman's research; she had been prepared even in that detail. It was filled with material relating to Megan. They studied it together.

Megan had a considerable history. In her youth she had been an excellent singer; then she had entered politics and run for Congress. She had served as congresswoman, then run for senator—and been sabotaged by a completely unscrupulous opportunist. Megan was a liberal, concerned with human values and the alleviation of poverty and oppression on the planet, and her political record reflected this. Her opponent, an aggressive man named Tocsin, was a creature of the affluent special interests. He promptly denounced her as "soft on Saturnism," that being the dirtiest political accusation it was possible to make. Theoretically the government of Saturn represented the comrades of the working class; actually it was a leftist dictatorship that suppressed the working class as ruthlessly as did any other system. Megan certainly had not supported that; she believed in human rights. It was a scurrilous tactic, an open smear campaign—but it worked. Tocsin won the election. Megan had supposed that competence, experience, and goodwill should carry the day; she had been brutally disabused.

"That woman was raped," Spirit murmured.

Megan was five years Hope's senior, a pedigreed Saxon, but that would not matter when he got close to her. She was beautiful, and as Reba had said, she dwarfed Helse in intelligence and competence, though Spirit did not bring that up. She did indeed seem like an excellent match for him, and not merely because of his fixation stemming from her slight physical resemblance to Helse. Hope needed a woman to take care of him, and Megan could certainly do that. With Megan in his life, Spirit would have greater freedom to focus on other matters, as had been the case when Emerald handled his career.

Megan had probably never heard of Hope Hubris, but he intended to marry her. And Spirit would do her best to make it happen.

Megan lived well around the planet from Sunshine, in the state of Golden. So they traveled there, and went to her residence without an appointment. They asked for her by intercom. And Megan declined to see him.

"She was a singer," Spirit murmured.

He grasped at that straw. "Tell her Captain Hubris will sing her his song!" he exclaimed. "She need only listen, then I will go. Surely she will grant this much to one who has crossed the planet to meet her."

The gatekeeper, plainly impatient with this nonsense, nevertheless buzzed her again. "Ma'am, he is insistent. He promises to depart if you will listen to his song." There was a pause, then he repeated, "Captain Hubris. He says he has crossed the planet to meet you. There is a woman with him." He paused again. Then he glanced at Hope. "Sing your song, sir."

Hope sang his song: *Worried Man Blues.* "It takes a worried man to sing a worried song . . . I'm worried now, but I won't be worried long."

Now Megan spoke directly to Hope. "Who is the woman with you, Captain?"

"My sister, Spirit Hubris."

"Does she also sing?"

Startled by this unexpected reaction, Spirit sang her song: "I know where I'm going, and I know who's going with me; I know who I love, but the dear knows who I'll marry."

When she stopped, they heard Megan's voice clearly. "Miss Hubris, you love your brother, don't you?"

"I do," Spirit agreed, bemused by this interest in her.

Megan agreed to see them.

Megan's beauty of youth had not paled; it had matured. The more recent pictures in the material QYV had given Hope had suggested it; life confirmed it. "It is not often I am visited by military personnel," she remarked.

"Retired," Hope said. "We are civilians now."

"So you knew Uncle Mason," she said.

"Only briefly," Hope said, surprised. Evidently they were not complete strangers to her. Perhaps the scientist had mentioned the episode before he died. "I was with—Helse. She—looked like you."

"Of course," Megan said, as if it could have been no other

way. She had that certain presence that facilitated this. "But that was some time ago."

"It's still true," he said, gazing at her. The sight of Megan was casting a spell over him; Spirit could see it happening.

"You still identify with the working class?"

"I do."

She nodded. As a politician she had sponsored social legislation; she was a friend of the working class, though she had never been part of it herself. "Yet you achieved a certain notoriety in that connection as an officer in the Navy, I believe."

"I helped make peace between the migrants and the farmers," Hope said defensively.

"Indeed you did," she agreed. "At one stroke you forged a settlement and set a precedent none of the rest of us had been able to arrange in years."

He was surprised again, and so was Spirit. "You—were watching that?"

She laughed. "My dear Captain, it was the headline of the day! I knew that you would be going far."

"You were aware of me before then?" Hope asked.

"Uncle Mason had mentioned you. He said it was like seeing me again, as I had been in my youth . . . that girl with you. I was then in my early twenties"

Spirit made a half-humorous sigh of nostalgia: the notion that a woman in her twenties was beyond her prime. Megan responded with a smile. Spirit found herself liking the woman.

"Then when you showed up at Chiron," Megan continued, "which I know was a very ticklish situation, I recognized you. Naturally I was curious. But I hardly thought you were aware of *me*. You caught me quite by surprise, coming here like this. Perhaps I should have realized that a military man normally takes direct action."

"But if you recognized my name why did you refuse my letter?"

"Did you write? I'm so sorry. I refuse all posts from strangers because of the hate mail."

"Hate mail?" Spirit asked, surprised. It turned out that Megan still received nasty letters from conservatives.

"Yet you refused to see me," Hope said.

"Captain Hubris, I have put that life behind me," she said firmly. "I knew the moment I heard your name that you were here on a political errand. I shall not suffer myself to be dragged into that mire again." She grimaced in a fetching manner. "Then you sang, and it was a song of the working class . . ."

"But you were wronged!" Hope protested. "You should not let one bad experience deprive you of your career!"

"Didn't *you*, Captain?" she asked, scoring.

Soon Hope got down to his real business: he wanted her to guide him in his forthcoming political career.

"My dear man, whatever makes you suppose I would do such a thing?"

"I'm sure you are loyal to your principles and your family. Therefore—"

"But we are not related!"

"Not yet," Spirit murmured.

"What are you trying to say, Captain?"

"I want to marry you, Megan."

Her mouth actually dropped open. "Have you any idea what you're saying?"

"You are the only living woman I can love," he said.

She was stunned but rallied quickly. "Because I once resembled your childhood sweetheart? Surely you know better than that!"

Hope tried to explain, but for once failed to get through. Megan looked at Spirit. "You are his sister, and you love him more than any other. What do you make of this?"

Spirit shook her head. "I'm not sure you would understand."

"I suspect I had *better* understand! Describe to me his nature as you appreciate it."

Spirit dropped her gaze, frowning, but made the effort. "Hope

Hubris is a specially talented person. He reads people. He is like a polygraph, a device to record and interpret the physical reactions of people he talks with. He knows when they are tense, when they are easy, when they hurt or are happy, when they are truthful and when lying. He uses his insight to handle them, to cause them to go his way without their realizing this. He—"

"You are describing the consummate politician," Megan exclaimed.

"So we understand," Spirit agreed. "But that's not what I'm addressing at the moment. Hope—is loved by others because he understands them so well, in his fashion. The men who work with him are fanatically loyal, and the women love him, though they know he can not truly return their love. But he—his talent perhaps makes him inherently cynical, emotionally, on the deep level. On the surface he is ready to love, but below he knows better, so he can not. Except for his first love, Helse. She initiated him into manhood, and there was no cynicism there. But having given his love to her, he could not then truly give it elsewhere—with one exception. The woman who looked like Helse."

Megan dabbed at her forehead with a dainty handkerchief, as if becoming faint from overexertion. "But he doesn't even know me."

"He doesn't need to," Spirit said. "This has nothing to do with knowledge. It has to do with faith."

"It is also true that I need your expertise in politics," Hope said. "So there is a practical foundation. Marry me and it will make sense."

Megan, naturally enough, resisted the notion. She did not want to return to politics, and was not about to marry a stranger.

"Convince her," Hope said to his sister.

Spirit made the effort. "Megan—may I call you that?—I must argue that your life has indeed developed toward this union. You are a fine person, an outstanding political figure, and a lovely woman, though my brother still would have come for you had you been otherwise. You deserve better than what the maelstrom of Jupiter politics has given you. You deserve to wield power, for you do know how to use it, and you have a social conscience unrivaled in the contemporary scene. You did not lose your last campaign because you were inadequate but because you were superior. You refused to stoop to the tactics your opponent used. As with money, the bad drove out the good, and you lost your place in the public eye, while your opponent flourishes like a weed. But whatever the politics, the bad remains bad and the good remains good, and this my brother understands."

Thus Hope's courtship of Megan, the woman of his dreams. She did not acquiesce immediately, but with further acquaintance his power and qualities slowly eroded her resistance, and four months after their first meeting, she did marry him. At first it was a marriage in name only, but in time that too changed. It was not accurate to say she came into his orbit; rather they orbited each other. Hope had won his second love, and it was a fully worthy relationship with no stain on it.

Except, perhaps, for one aspect, which was not the fault of either. It was Spirit's fault.

*

They delved into political issues, under Megan's competent tutelage, trying to learn everything. This was their homework for the coming political effort.

Meanwhile, their limited activity had not gone unnoticed. The political columnist for a local newspaper was a man who signed himself simply "Thorley." Between elections he was evidently short of material, so minor things warranted comment.

"Guess who's coming to town," Thorley wrote conversationally, showing by this signal that this was not a subject to be taken too seriously. "Remember the darling of the bleeding-heart set in Golden, Megan? It seems she married the gallant of the Jupiter Navy, Captain Hubris, a man some years her junior. Rumor has it that one of them has political pretensions."

"That's insulting," Hope said angrily. "What right does he have to—"

"We are, or were, public figures," Megan said. "Our names are in the common domain, his to play with at will. He tosses them about as a canine tosses a rag doll, entertaining himself. You will have to get used to this sort of thing if you wish to survive in politics. Words become as heated and effective as lasers. Perhaps you can better appreciate, now, why I was not eager to return to the arena myself."

Indeed, Spirit was coming to appreciate that. "He's our demon."

"Just keep in mind that though Thorley is at the opposite end of the political spectrum, a thorough conservative, he is a competent journalist and an honest man."

"You would find good in the devil himself," Hope charged her, smiling.

"That might be a slight exaggeration. But Thorley is no devil. His beliefs may be wrong-headed by my definitions, but he is no demagogue. He will not compromise his principles, and that is to be respected."

Much of the evil of the political system seemed to center on money. Politicians needed a lot of money to campaign effectively, and it soon corrupted them. There needed to be reform of campaign financing. They oriented on this, and Hope began speaking of it in citizen meetings.

Columnist Thorley had another comment in print: "Captain Hubris, he who tightened the Belt, has been delving into the arcane lore of Campaign Finance (his caps, not mine). Could he be interested in something of the sort himself? Stranger things have been known to occur in the murky by-paths of the liberal establishment."

They let that pass, with an effort. They continued their research and participation in citizen initiatives. Three years passed.

In that time Hope's marriage to Megan became real, so it was not a dull time for him. But Spirit was restless, though she did not express it. She missed having a man in her private life. She even missed the Navy Tail. She had thought she could take or leave sex, but after Gerald she appreciated it more.

They hired an executive secretary. Megan selected her, somewhat in the manner the Beautiful Dreamer had selected ideal officers: she located the best who were otherwise barred. Thus Shelia—and that was the spelling—joined their small group. She was a lovely girl, seventeen years old, highly qualified, and confined for life to a wheelchair. But she was a very quick study and a dedicated worker. Soon she had a clearer notion of the campaign strategy than Hope did. Of course she loved Hope, and served him in the best way she could: with absolute loyalty.

Hope ran for state secretary. He told the truth, eschewed special interest money, and refused to dig for any dirt. Consequently he looked like a likely loser, and the polls confirmed it.

Thorley summarized the situation succinctly: "Hope Hubris constituency: Belt 20. Hispanic 20. Total 35." Allowing for overlap. Of a likely voting population of millions.

Hope's ire focused on Thorley. "I'm about ready to do something about that guy," he muttered. "I'd like to debate *him* before an audience."

"Great idea!" Shelia agreed enthusiastically. She was then barely eighteen, and subject to enthusiasm.

It had been a joke. But Spirit considered it. "You know, I wonder—?"

Megan nodded. "That would be truly novel. We really have nothing to lose at this point."

So the joke became real. Hope made the ludicrous gesture of challenging the columnist Thorley to a public debate, since he couldn't get the incumbent to share the stage with him. They expected either to be ignored or to become the target of a scathingly clever column.

But Thorley accepted.

Bemused, they worked it out. "He must find this campaign as dull as I do," Hope said. "This will at least put us both on the map of oddities."

"True," Megan agreed. "But do not take it lightly. Now we shall find out what you are made of. Debates are treacherous."

"Like single combat," Spirit said. Hope had always been good at that.

They prepared as carefully as if it were a major public event. They had acquired a certain cynicism about politics and the electorate as they experienced the insularity of supposedly public spirited organizations, but Megan had been completely unsurprised. She had been through it before. "Even the most bleeding of hearts becomes a trifle cynical," she observed. Now she believed that this debate would be a formidable test, and Spirit had learned to heed Megan's judgments on such things. She drilled Hope on every conceivable aspect of the subject. He was letter perfect. But was it enough?

Thorley showed up on schedule. He was a handsome man of about Hope's own age, a fair Saxon, slightly heavyset, with a magnificently modulated voice. He shook Hope's hand in a cordial manner, then greeted Megan similarly. "It is an honor to meet so respected a figure," he told her, his evident sincerity setting her back. "You are indeed beautiful." He turned to Spirit. "And so are you, Miss Hubris. Had I a sister like you, I should have run for office myself." Spirit was so surprised by the muted compliment she had no answer. He turned to Shelia. "And I would have needed a secretary like you to keep me organized." Instead of shaking her hand, he lifted it to his face and kissed it. She, too, was momentarily stunned.

Thorley settled into the comfortable chair assigned to him as if he had been there all his life. In the space of hardly more than a minute he had fairly set back all three women support-ing his debate opponent. His manner and presence disarmed them; he was completely charming.

Hope chatted with Thorley in the few minutes before the

formal program, and it was clear that Hope also liked him. They had expected a sneering, supercilious snob, despite Megan's assessment; they had been disabused. In person he was not at all like that.

"I feared I would be late," he remarked with a momentary slant of one eyebrow to signal that this was a minor personal crisis. "Thomas was not quite ready to come in."

"Thomas?" Spirit asked. "I thought you were childless."

Thorley grinned infectiously. "Naturally your camp has done its homework on the opposition, but perhaps imperfectly. Thomas is our resident of the feline persuasion."

Spirit had to smile in return, touching her forehead with her four-fingered hand as if jogging loose a short circuit. "Oh, a male cat. We did not have pets in the Navy."

"The Navy remains unforgivably backward in certain social respects," he said. "Cats are admirably independent, but in this instance, with my wife visiting Hidalgo to cover for a discomfited relative, the burden of supervision falls on me. Regulations"—here he made a fleeting grimace to show his disapproval of regulations as a class of human endeavor—"require the confinement of nonhuman associates when the persons concerned are absent from the immediate vicinity." His nuances of facial and vocal expression made even so small a matter as a stray tomcat seem like a significant experience. The man had phenomenal personal magnetism, and Spirit had to fight to maintain her objectivity. She realized that Hope might be in for more of a debate than they had anticipated, for Thorley could surely move an audience.

"Well, in a couple of hours you'll be back to let him out again," Hope said.

"I surely had better be," he agreed. "Thomas is inclined to express his ire against the furniture when neglected, as any reasonable person would." That fierce individualism manifested in almost every sentence he uttered, yet now it became appealing.

Then the hour of the debate was on them. There was no holo-news coverage, but there were a couple of cub reporters and a still-picture photographer, and of course each side had its own machine recorder. The audience was reasonable for the occasion, hardly filling the hall, about two hundred dutiful citizens.

There was no moderator, no formal rules; it was discussion format. Spirit knew that could be awkward, but Megan had assured them that it could also be the most natural and effective. They had agreed to alternate in asking each other questions, with verbal interplay increasing after the initial answers. They flipped a coin, and Thorley won the right to pose the first question.

Megan and Spirit moved to either side of the small stage, while Shelia merged her chair with the front row of the audience and took notes, which were bound to be the most relevant.

"I understand that you, Captain Hubris, in accordance with many of the liberal folly, are opposed to capital punishment," Thorley said, his attitude and his language hardening dramatically as he got down to business.

"I am," Hope agreed.

"Yet you are, or were, a prominent military man," Thorley continued. "You could have been responsible for the deaths of hundreds of living people—"

"Thousands," Hope agreed.

"How do you reconcile this with your present stand opposing the execution of criminals?"

It seemed like a trap, but Megan had anticipated it and prepared Hope for it. "The two situations are not comparable," he said carefully. "As a military man, I was under orders; when killing was required, I performed my duty. I never enjoyed that aspect of it, but the Navy did not express interest in my personal opinions." He smiled, Thorley smiled with him, and there was a ripple of humor through the audience. This was merely a warm-up interchange, and they all knew that it was the audience reaction that counted. "There is also a distinction between the violence of combat and the measured, deliberate destruction of human life that legal execution is. If a man fires his weapon at me and I fire back and kill him, that is one thing; but if that man is strapped to a chair, helpless, that is another. To my mind, the first case is defense; the second is murder."

"Well and fairly spoken," Thorley said smoothly. "But can we be sure there is a true distinction between the cases?" Thorley then proceeded to make Hope's position seem paradoxical, and it was apparent that he was scoring better with the audience than Hope was. Spirit realized that the man was not only privately charming, he was quite intelligent and thoroughly prepared. He was at least a match for Hope, and Hope was no slouch at playing scenes or moving audiences.

It was now Hope's turn to pose a question. He asked about the conservative's opposition to big government: did he prefer anarchy? Thorley fielded it with grace and felicity of expression, employing incidental metaphors that carried his meaning without being unkindly blunt. Spirit saw the audience nodding agreement, and when he likened too much government to a bloated stomach, they laughed. What an image! There were things to be learned from this man, and Spirit would make sure that Hope did learn them.

With the next question, Thorley got serious. "It has been said that a free press is the best guarantee of honest government. Where do you stand on that?"

This was a difficult one. Hope had practiced censorship of the news during the campaign in the Belt, to keep the pirates from anticipating the Navy moves. Thorley would surely make much of that.

There was a commotion in the audience. A burly Saxon man was striding forward, brandishing a portable industrial laser unit. "You spics are stealing our jobs! We don't need none of you in office!" He brought his laser to bear on Hope and fired.

But both Hope and Spirit were already flying out of their chairs. Megan, no creature of physical violence, was standing stock-still, gazing at the worker with horror.

The first bolt seared into the floor where Hope's chair had been. Hope and Spirit were closing in on the man from the sides. But it would take them seconds to reach him; they had not come armed.

The Saxon worker's face fastened on Megan. "And we don't need no spic-lovers, neither!" he cried, and swung the laser to bear on her. Still she stood frozen.

Thorley launched himself from his chair just as the man pulled the trigger. The deadly beam sizzled and was muffled by Thorley's body. Steam spread out, and in a moment there was the horrible odor of fried flesh.

Then Hope reached the worker. Knowing that her brother would make short work of him, Spirit veered aside and went to Megan instead, leading her away from the violence.

In another moment Hope kneeled beside Thorley. The man was curled up in agony, trying to grip his left leg. The laser beam had seared into his thigh, not a lethal wound but certainly a hellishly painful one. It could cost him his leg if a key nerve had been burned out.

There were other urgent things to do at this moment, as the hall erupted into pandemonium. Thorley needed immediate medical attention, the police needed to take charge of the murderous worker, and Hope had to get Megan away from this place before she went into shock. But for the moment Hope remained with the wounded man. "Thorley," he said. "Why did you intercede?"

"I don't believe in assassination," Thorley gasped. "Not even of liberals."

"How can I repay you?"

"Just—keep the press—free," Thorley whispered, and passed out.

"Always!" Hope swore to the man's unconscious body. It was a vow he would keep.

CHAPTER 10

Secret

Spirit was bringing heavy bandages from the hall's emergency supply, knowing that prompt attention to the wound was essential. All officers in the Navy had paramedic training; she knew what to do.

"Spirit," Hope said. "Take care of this man."

She nodded, knowing that he meant more than bandages. She worked efficiently, cutting away his burned trouser leg, applying the bandages to the seared flesh. No cauterization was required; laser wounds were already cauterized. It was necessary only to protect the surrounding flesh.

When the medics came for him with the stretcher, Spirit picked up Thorley's holo recorder and went with them. "His cat!" Hope called after her, and she nodded again. Thorley would be in competent hands.

No one questioned her presence; she was taken as a family member or employee or friend. She was that last, as of the moment Thorley had sacrificed himself to save Megan.

They took the ambulance to the hospital, where there was a flurry of competent activity. Thorley came partly conscious, in pain, and Spirit took his hand. "It is all right," she murmured to his ear. "You are severely injured, but it is not lethal, and the doctors are tending it now."

He nodded. "Thomas—"

"I will take care of him, if I may take your key."

"Wallet–" Then he passed out again.

She felt in his jacket and found his wallet. It would contain his key card. But first she had to see to his registration. She went to the check-in window and used the information in the wallet to get him properly checked in and verified for insurance.

"It will be eighteen hours," the clerk woman said, not needing any other medical input; she was going by the insurance limit. "Pick him up then at the outlet bay."

That was it. Thorley would be booted from the hospital then, and someone had better be there to convey him elsewhere. She checked his wallet to see whom to contact, but found no one. Apparently there was only his wife, who was on another planet at the moment, and Spirit did not have her address.

Why would Thorley have expressed concern about his cat, unless he were living alone at present? Spirit had promised to take care of the animal; she would do so. With luck she would find information on some neighbor or relative or friend who could be trusted to see to the man's welfare during his recovery. Certainly she could not leave this responsibility until she was sure it was safe to do so.

She took a taxi to the address listed on his identity card. It was an unpretentious suite in a mid-level residential complex, not poor but far from rich. She had had the careless notion that all conservatives were rich, but obviously that was no more true than the notion that all liberals were poor. She used the identity card to key open the door.

A stately white Persian cat was walking across the room toward her, but halted to deliver a hostile stare, his tail switching. That would be Thomas, dismayed to discover a stranger instead of his master.

Spirit had had no direct experience with cats since leaving Callisto at age twelve. Now she was thirty one. She remem-

bered practically nothing. She would have to do some homework before doing anything.

She explored the apartment, discovering the family room,
bathroom, kitchen, bedroom, and an alcove chamber lined by
physical books that had to be Thorley's office. Everything was
in order except the bedroom, where the bed was unmade, and
the kitchen, where old fashioned dishes were stacked in the
archaic style sink. She smiled; for all his verbal and literary
eloquence, Thorley was a typical man, unable to keep up with
mundane housework on his own.

She pitched in, made the bed, washed the dishes, and then
focused on the cat. There was a pan of sand in the bathroom
that looked competent for a feline potty, but what about food?
What about company? She gathered that the animal did not
like to be alone too long, but Thorley would not return for a
day and a half, so it seemed that Spirit was it.

She found cat food. She did not know the feeding schedule, so guessed that it would be the same time as the humans
ate. That would not be for a couple of hours yet. And what
would she eat, if she did not leave the apartment? She checked
the kitchen supplies and found them depleted; Thorley's wife
had surely left plenty, but she must have been away for some
time. More would have to be ordered.

She was about to use the vidphone, but paused. She was
here to help, not to bring a whiff of scandal to Thorley's household. A strange woman calling from his apartment during his
wife's absence might look amiss, never mind the circumstances.
In fact, anything done on his behalf in her name could compli-
cate his life unkindly.

She considered, then made a decision. She went to the bathroom and drew back her hair, which had become more femi-
ninely long since she left the Navy. Then she rummaged in his
clothes closet and borrowed one of his work shirts and a set of
trousers. She had to do some spot stitching to make them fit
her, but their bagginess was to a degree an asset. She changed

clothing, washed her face clear of all makeup, and donned the gloves she kept in her purse. She looked in the mirror. Still not right. She doffed the shirt, removed her bra, and found a suitable section of white cloth in the wife's closet. She bound this tightly around her chest, flattening her breasts, then put the shirt back on and tucked it in. Now she looked the part: the teenaged boy Sancho had reappeared after a lapse of fifteen years.

She took inventory of both the food remaining in the apartment, and the empty but not yet disposed of cans and packages in the garbage. This gave her a fair notion of the original store of supplies, including catfood. Then she took Thorley's identity card from his wallet. "I shall return," she told the tail-switching cat as she left.

She walked to the nearest food store and selected her purchases. "I shop for Mister Thorley," she told the checkout clerk as she presented Thorley's card.

She carried the bag back to the apartment, and put the supplies where they belonged on the kitchen shelves. So far so good. Then she tackled the cat again. She went to Thorley's cubbyhole and was relieved to spy what she sought: a book on cats. This one was on the Angora Cat, and its pictures made her realize that she had misjudged the breed; Thomas was not Person but Angora, surely pedigreed. "Sorry, Thomas," she said apologetically. "I misidentified you. Now can we be friends?" She squatted and held out her hand.

The cat kept his distance. "Oh—I'm wearing the gloves," she said. "That's the artificial me." She removed the gloves and extended her four fingered left hand.

To her surprise, it worked. The cat approached and sniffed her fingers, then suffered himself to be stroked. She sat on the floor, crossing her legs, and in a moment he climbed into her lap. He had accepted her.

"But you want to know what happened to your master," she said. "Or more properly, your associate. Well, he suffered an injury in a noble cause, and will not be here tonight. But to-morrow night I will bring him home, and then all will be well."

The rest was routine. She made a simple supper for herself and for Thomas, watched the evening holovision, and slept in Thorley's bed, with Thomas curled up beside her. In the morning she showered and did some hand laundry, so that she would not use up more of Thorley's clothing than necessary. In the afternoon she phoned for a taxi to pick Sancho up and take him to the hospital. She was falling surprisingly readily into the male routine as the old habits and cautions came back; originally it had been a matter of life and death, and that had been excellent incentive.

The taxi waited while she entered the hospital to check Thorley out. The clerk never bothered to question why a Hispanic boy should be doing it; just so long as the patient did not run up any bill beyond the insurance limit. She found him at the outlet bay, parked in a wheelchair. She thought of Shelia with a certain obscure fondness; Sheila was a good girl.

"Thorley," she murmured.

He glanced at her. "Evidently you know me, young man, but I doubt I have had the pleasure of knowing you."

"I hope you will trust me, nevertheless," she said, slipping off her left glove to give him a flash of her hand.

He took the hand, noting the missing finger. "I do. Your hand, my leg: we are compatriots of the left." His smile was pained, yet still warming.

The taxi came up, and she had to help him to stand and to get into the vehicle. He was well bandaged, but it evidently hurt when he moved his left leg. She had to take hold of his knee and lift it slowly for him. He winced, but did not complain.

As they sat beside each other in the relative privacy of the cab, he turned to her. "There is a reason?"

"I did not know who else to ask to take care of Thomas."

"There *is* no one else. I fear I was not thinking coherently the other day. I apologize for inconveniencing you."

"You saved my brother's wife."

He shrugged. "It was necessary. Are you aware of her history?"

"Yes."

"I would not say this in public, but I respect her more than I do Toxin." It seemed that even an arch troglodyte preferred an honest liberal to a shifty pseudo-conservative.

The taxi reached the complex. "Can you make it?" she asked.

"I shall have to."

She used Thorley's card to pay the driver, then helped Thorley out of the taxi. They walked somewhat jerkily into the structure and to the internal lift.

Two husky young men in maintenance livery came to help. Spirit was glad to relinquish the support to them. "Mr. Thorley!" one said. "You are a hero!"

"I am?"

"It's in all the holos! You made a gallant sacrifice to save a woman."

"One does what one has to do."

They helped him all the way to his apartment, and set him in his chair. Thomas immediately jumped into his lap. "Do you need anything else, sir?"

"Thank you, no. My borrowed houseboy suffices."

They nodded, then departed, leaving him alone with Spirit. "Thanks for not telling," she said.

"You disguised yourself to spare me embarrassment."

He had been quick to catch on. "I thought a woman in your apartment would be misunderstood, in the absence of your wife." She fetched his wallet and returned his card to it. "I used your credit, because–"

"Yours would have been similarly misunderstood."

"Yes. I will repay you–"

"You have already more than repaid me. You must return to your brother; I'm sure he needs you."

"Yes." But she hesitated. "You have friends to help?"

"I will manage."

"I'm not sure you will. You have no insurance to cover home nursing."

"It is expensive."

"Who will help you?"

He frowned, dismissing the matter. "I will manage because it is necessary for me to manage."

"Thorley, I don't want to interfere in your life. But I promised my brother I would take care of you, and I don't think my job is done."

"You owe me nothing, Spirit. You have been more than kind enough already."

"I owe my brother. I owe Megan. The job is not yet done."

He looked up at her. "I seem to be unable to dissuade you from this sacrifice."

"It is not of the level of the sacrifice you made."

"I fear I am constrained to accept, though I am not easy about this."

Spirit smiled. "I promise to do you no liberal mischief."

He sighed. "That too, of course."

She let down her hair and called Hope. "Whom did you appoint to care for him?" he asked Spirit when he saw her face on the screen.

"Sancho," she said.

He was taken aback. He remembered Sancho from their time as refugees in the bubble. "Are you sure that's wise?"

She grimaced. "It's necessary. We can afford him."

It was true that their finances were as limited as those of Thorley, and Sancho was as cheap as it was possible to get. Hope shrugged, refusing to interfere. "He can certainly do the job—if no one suspects."

"No one will."

"*Thorley* will! That man is no fool!"

"Thorley knows," she said, meeting his gaze.

He made a motion as of washing his hands. "It is your affair, Spirit."

She shut off the connection. "Affair?" Thorley inquired.

"Figure of speech. I have already promised not to molest you. How soon will your wife return?"

"That is problematical. Her sister has a terminal malady, and needs special care. I hesitate to summon her away from that."

"Then it seems I am with you until you mend."

"It grieves me to restrict your life in this manner. Perhaps you can return to your brother by day—or better, by night."

"No. It is best that I travel as little as possible, in any guise. I dislike crowding you, but–"

"That is not the problem. I fear that I am not completely competent to rebandage my injury, or even to get around without assistance. This could embarrass both of us."

She shook her head. "I bandaged it the first time. I am a Navy woman; I can handle blood."

"The location–"

"I am long familiar with male anatomy. Think of me as a nurse."

"I shall make the attempt, Miss Hubris."

"Spirit."

"It is an appealing name."

She helped him lie on the bed, then fetched blankets for herself on the floor. "Please," he said. "There is no need to visit this additional indignity on you."

"No problem."

"Please, I am embarrassed to allow a woman to be treated so. There is room for you on the bed."

"As you wish." She lay on his wife's side of the bed, and slept.

She settled in. She made his meals and took care of his household chores. She changed his bandages, cleaned him up, and helped him to use the bathroom and the shower. When she needed to clean up herself, he faced politely away.

She laughed. "Don't bother. I have seen all of your parts; you can see mine. It's only fair."

"There is where there is a difference. You are a lovely woman."

"I am Sancho, your Hispanic houseboy."

"You are my liberal angel of mercy."

"I am no angel!" Yet she was flattered.

The days passed, and gradually he recovered. She helped him get settled in his desk chair to write his columns, and between times they debated politics and policies, but never with force.

"You are a remarkably savvy woman, Spirit."

"My intellect is not in a class with yours."

He shook his head. "You believe that?"

"I admire intellect."

They exchanged life histories to alleviate the developing dullness of the wait. Thorley loved his wife, and would never leave her; his present separation from her was uncomfortable. Spirit still felt the pain of the loss of Gerald. But a pleasant tension was building up between them.

"I fear I am coming to appreciate you too much, Spirit," Thorley said. "You are a woman like none other I have known."

"I am an orphan Hispanic refugee, pirate wench, Navy officer, and unashamed liberal. Not much to like there."

"I feel constrained to be honest. You are forbidden fruit, with its illicit yet powerful appeal."

"Forbidden fruit is intriguing," she agreed.

"More than intriguing. Spirit, I believe it is best that we end this arrangement, lest I embarrass you."

She laughed. "You think you can embarrass a woman with my history?"

"I fear I can. But there is no need. You have tided me safely through the worst of my recovery, and I believe I can manage on my own hereafter. I am sure your brother needs your services."

"My brother has an excellent wife, thanks in significant part to you, and an excellent secretary. He can manage for a time."

"Surely so. But that does not justify my taking more of your time, however sincerely I appreciate it."

"How long before your wife returns?"

"That is indefinite. Her sibling's demise is a drawn-out process."

"Thorley, you are not used to being on your own. You are the original absent minded professor type: intellectually brilliant, but a duffer in minor practical matters. Things were piling up and running out before I came, and it's bound to be worse during your recovery. You do need someone, and I think that means your wife, or me."

"This is an aspect of the problem."

"I mean someone to cover your incidentals: spot shopping, laundry, dishes. You can't afford to hire a real houseboy, so I think I have to remain it."

He smiled ruefully. "At this point you understand my finances better than I do. You are surely correct. But I doubt I can afford you, either."

"I feel that my brother's obligation is not fulfilled until you are well and able to proceed with your normal life. I think you don't understand how seriously we appreciate what you did. Megan is Hope's life, and Hope is my life. Money is no part of this."

He looked at the floor. "I know it, Spirit. I see I must after all embarrass you. The reason I can't afford your services is that your nature and proximity are causing me to become enamored of you. There can be no future—"

He broke off, for she had had to sit down suddenly. Why hadn't she seen this coming? They had been getting along *too* well. They were complete opposites politically and socially, but their practical closeness was another matter.

"I apologize for inflicting this embarrassment on you," he said. "But I trust you will agree that a continuation of the present situation is unfeasible."

She scrambled to recover her poise. "No. The apology is mine. I have been vamping you, forgetting that we are strangers. The Navy—when I was with Gerald—never mind. Somehow I lapsed into an unconscionable informality. My reflexes are not appropriate to this situation."

"Unconscionable? Dear woman, now you are sounding like me! You do have a beautiful body, but that is not my concern. It is your competence and caring that stir me. I am no longer able to tolerate your presence in any attire without suffering foolish notions."

"Thorley, you know what I am! It's not just a matter of being liberal. I have consorted with pirates; in the Navy they called me the Iron Maiden for my brutal efficiency."

"They also called you The Dear."

"I never should have told you about my song."

"I do know what you are, Spirit, and it is totally at odds with my prior experience, and an education in itself. You have become The Dear to me."

"I know who I love, but the dear knows who I'll marry," she said, echoing her song. "Actually, if I could marry Gerald again, I'd do it. But I must stay away from him, for the sake of his restored military career and my brother's political career."

"And I could not marry you either, for similar reasons. But if you do not depart, I shall wish I could."

"What of your wife?"

"I do love her, and shall never leave her. That is why I must no longer be near you."

She considered for a minute, then spoke sadly. "I think it is too late."

"Perhaps it is. Perhaps I was already too far gone before I realized it. But at least now you understand why you must return to your brother. I would not compromise you any farther, or embarrass you by–"

"Thorley, I meant too late for *me*. I thought I was staying with you because of loyalty to my brother, and being informal with you for convenience. Now I realize that I was already on that slippery slope. I admire your intellect and your integrity of philosophy. I *was* vamping you, unconsciously."

"No, you were merely being natural. I am the one who–"

"Come off it, Thorley! Against all superficial logic, we're attracted to each other."

He frowned gracefully. "Spirit, you are not making this easy. We must separate."

"Not until you can make it on your own."

"I shall *have* to make it on my own. You know why."

"I think I must remain with you until your wife returns. Then I shall depart without fuss or recrimination, and we will not see each other again. The job will have been done, and our private feelings need never be known elsewhere."

"You offer an infernally tempting compromise. But is it right?"

"It is not right. It is necessary. And maybe it is not wrong, if we don't act on our foolish feelings."

"This will be difficult."

"We can do it."

"We *must* do it."

But it turned out to be harder than they expected. Spirit's emotion, once realized, did not retreat, it expanded. She had a hunger to love and be loved romantically. She had catered to that hunger without realizing it, and now was trying to brake a ship that was falling into the sun.

Thorley's wound was healing, but it remained awkward for him to change the bandages; he was not competent in incidental medicine either. So she did it. The wound was high in the inner thigh, and she had to work around his genitalia. This did not bother her, but she knew it bothered him. Now she noticed something. "My touch does not arouse you."

"At least I am spared that additional humiliation."

"I think you are avoiding the issue. *Can* you be aroused?"

"I fear not," he said heavily. "The burn seems to have rendered me impotent."

"Then my job has not yet been done, regardless."

"You are not responsible for my sexuality!"

"My responsibility is to leave you in the condition I found you, before the debate. I know something about sexuality. I should be able to help."

"But we agreed not to act on our feelings."

"Let's reason this out," she said. "If we did what we would like to do, we would exchange expressions of love and desire, then embrace and kiss and have sexual intercourse."

"Unfortunately true."

"But we are not doing that. We are addressing a particular problem. I have a responsibility to you that must be completed. I have had experience in stimulating men to sexual performance. I will draw on that experience to stimulate yours. I will not do any of the forbidden things."

"Your logic seems impeccable, but I do not understand."

"I think the heat of the laser did some partial damage to certain key nerves. It may be that the main ones have been destroyed, but that peripheral ones can take their place and in time restore your capacity. We need to encourage that reprogramming."

"I still do not understand what it is you propose to do."

"Bear with me, then." She completed the bandaging, then took hold of his penis and massaged it. It responded by expanding and hardening. "The mechanism is there, just not the line to the brain. Try to locate that line."

"Obviously you have expertise, as you indicated. But I confess I have no idea how."

She backed off and stood before him. "Think what you would like to do, if you could. Try to react." She removed her shirt, and then her bra.

"This falls into the arena of forbidden expression."

"This is not romance. It is therapy. What would you do with my body, if you had no constraints?"

"I would kiss those marvelous breasts."

"Think lower." She drew off her skirt and panties, then turned in place, doing a small hula dance.

"Spirit, you torture me!"

"Precisely. React."

But he could not. She got down and addressed his member again. "Maybe if we take you through the process, it will encourage the nerves."

"Process?"

She took his member in her mouth and worked on it until it swelled to full proportion. But it would not respond beyond that. "Let's give it a rest," she said after a while. "I'll try again this afternoon."

"You are amazing, but this is useless. The connection is not there."

"We shall remake it." She got up and dressed.

"Every time I think I have the measure of you, you take the measure of me," he said. "I have never encountered a woman your equal, all aspects considered."

"You haven't met some of the women I have known. But you do know Megan."

"She is unparalleled in her area of expertise, which is broad. But she could not do what you just did."

That was true. "She was never a pirate wench." But Spirit was flattered. She had made it a point, among the pirates, to learn exactly how to please men, and that knowledge had served her well among the pirates, and in the Navy, and with Gerald. Now, with luck, it would enable her to restore to Thorley what the laser attack had taken. But she wasn't sure; she had never before tackled physically derived impotence. Could she get the key nerves to reconnect? Suppose she failed?

She went about her business, keeping house for Thorley,

feeding him lunch, then reading and critiquing a draft of his latest column. He did several drafts of each, struggling for up to an hour on a single not-quite-perfect turn of phrase. Eloquence came naturally to him, but he lifted it to the status of art by working hard at it. She admired that too.

The cat approached her. She picked him up and stroked him. "Thomas likes you," Thorley said. "This, too, is important."

"Thomas brought us together." For it was Thorley's concern for his cat that had made her first call necessary.

Then it was mid afternoon. "I will address you now," she said as he sat in his chair.

"Must you? I find this procedure discomfiting."

"I must. I am trying to stimulate regrowth or repositioning of nerve functions. There may be no seeming progress at first, but in time you may get a twinge of response, and then we shall know it is feasible." She opened his trousers and reached inside.

"Your words make sense, but it distresses me to allow you to degrade yourself in such manner."

"One day we shall debate what is degrading about acquiescent sexual performance," she said, and put her mouth to his member. She sucked on it as it swelled, but could not rouse it to further accomplishment. Still, she must be stimulating the essential nerve paths.

Three days later he reacted. "I felt a twinge!"

"Wonderful!" She kissed the tip of his member. "Can it stand alone?"

It seemed not. But the next day the twinge was stronger. In several more days she was able to make it swell without touching it. They were definitely making progress.

Then it leveled off. The arousal would go to a point, but not progress beyond. She seemed to come close to swallowing his member, but it would not perform.

"Enough of this child's play!" she said. "I'm bringing in the first team." She stood, tore off her skirt and panties, turned around, and carefully sat on the member, guiding it in. "Go go go!" she cried, clenching her vaginal muscles as her bare bottom made full contact with his lap.

And it erupted. She felt the pulses, and rejoiced; she had at last brought him to climax.

When the throes of it eased, she lifted herself, then fetched a cloth and cleaned up the two of them. "You did it," Thorley said, amazed. "You completed the process."

"There is farther to go," she said, pleased. "You must be able to do it all yourself."

"But you overstepped the boundary."

Then she remembered. "There was not to be intercourse. Oh, Thorley, I'm sorry. I didn't think—I just got so frustrated with incipience–"

"Perhaps there was no other way. To me, oral activity is not—not completely natural. I had an emotional reservation that stifled the culmination. When you—Spirit, I'm glad you forgot. At least you were innocent of evil intent."

She had to laugh. "And you were not?"

"I was not innocent. I should have warned you before you did it. But temptation overwhelmed me."

"Then we are both at fault. I think we had better reconsider our program. Shall we eliminate the restrictions and have a full affair?"

"Again, you tempt me wickedly. But where is the justification?"

"To restore your full sexual capacity. Then there will be no remaining debt."

"But my wife–"

"Would she be satisfied if you lost your potency during her absence?"

"She would prefer there to be no change."

"When she returns, I will go, and it will be over. You will have your full potency for her benefit. She will have lost nothing."

"That is perhaps how it must be."

"We are agreed." She glanced sidelong at him. "May I do the honors?"

"What can you do, that you have not already completed?"

"I can speak the unspoken, and do the undone."

"Do the honors," he agreed wryly.

She leaned down and kissed him on the mouth. "I love you, Thorley."

"And I love you, Spirit, idiot that I am."

"We are both idiots. Idiots in love."

"May I make a confession?"

"It seems to be confession time."

"You have brought delight back into my realm. I am not speaking sexually. Had I at this moment the ability to go back in time and eliminate the injury that brought you into my life, I would not do it."

"Nor would I, though I would spare you the pain of it if I could."

"Yet we know that this must soon end, and never be acknowledged elsewhere."

"I know who I love, but the dear knows who I'll marry," she murmured.

"You are my dear."

Thereafter their affair was full-blown. They made love in the chair, on the bed, in the shower, and on the floor, to Thomas's disapproval. They did it in the daytime, evening, and in the middle of the night when they happened to wake. Thorley's responses were slow at first, but steadily quickened, until he seemed to be fully normal. Between times they spoke of love, and kissed, and embraced, and teased and tickled each other like children.

But always they knew and accepted that it was temporary, and would end when Thorley's wife returned home. That was in fact one reason for its abandon: they had to do in a limited period what should have taken a lifetime.

Thorley's repute as a conservative columnist increased greatly, because of his recent notoriety. More media outlets signed up for his byline, and there was more income from the existing ones. His act had been good for his career, and Spirit was glad for him, though she agreed with few of his positions. Sometimes she teased him about that: "You would be a better lover if you endorsed weapons control."

"How so?" he asked as he penetrated her body.

"You would have more control for your gun."

"All I need is a bit more target practice."

"That must be true, because you haven't worn out this target yet." She clenched on him, bringing the culmination.

"It is a quality target."

Meanwhile Hope Hubris won the election, profiting from his share of the notoriety. He became a state senator, and thus a further target for Thorley's poisonous pen. But the private relationship between the two men had changed.

Thorley's wife's sister finally died, and his wife returned to Jupiter. Spirit collected her things and made ready to move out. "It is over," she said as she transformed to Sancho, as she always did before leaving the apartment.

"It is over," Thorley agreed.

"I love you."

"I love you."

Then they couldn't help themselves; they made love standing by the door. "You had better not let anyone catch you having sex with a boy," she said mischievously as he climaxed.

"Only with a glorious woman," he agreed.

They cleaned up, kissed, and she left. Only when she was well clear did she find a private spot and let the tears flow.

She returned to join Hope, who had hired a Gofer named Ebony, a black woman without pretensions. It was clear that Ebony was already in Hope's orbit, utterly loyal.

Megan welcomed her back. "We missed you."

"It took his wife longer to return than expected."

Shelia, savvy for her age, took one look at Spirit and caught on. "But he had a Navy wife in the interim."

"It's over."

But it wasn't over. Hope made it a point to inform Thorley of any political news that might interest him, regardless of its sensitivity. Sancho became a courier for it. She left a message with his service: Sancho. They had arranged a rendezvous site, where she handed over a briefcase.

But when they were alone, everything changed. Wordlessly they kissed and embraced, and found a position for clothed sex. They didn't dare speak, for it was not possible to know who might overhear, or what recorders might be in the vicinity. They could not afford to dally long, for similar reason. So in a few minutes they were done and parted, their efficient act substituting for the words they could not speak.

This continued for months. They simply could not terminate their love. But they were able to keep their secret.

As Spirit was to determine later, on the day Hope hired a female bodyguard named Coral, Spirit conceived a baby. She had never thought to take any contraceptive precaution, for all the men of space were sterile, and Thorley was childless. She had just assumed that he was sterile too. Now she knew better.

She told him. They found a sound-secure spot and discussed it. "I can abort it," she said.

"I cannot countenance that!" he protested. She had known it; he was conservative on this score too, of course.

"But neither can I keep it."

He was in agony. "This is true. Your brother's career and mine would both be ruined by the scandal. Yet it is not possible to give up such a blessing."

"Blessing!"

"A child of yours. How can it be other than blessed?"

"And of yours. Oh, Thorley, I want it! There has to be a way."

He considered, then nodded. "There may be. Confide in

Megan."

"But I wouldn't inflict her with such a burden!"

"One day we must debate whether a child of love can ever be a burden."

So Spirit, having no choice, broached Megan. "I will adopt it, of course," Megan said without hesitation.

"But a bastard baby–"

"There are no bastard babies, only bastard adults—and I think this is not the present case. This is as close as I can ever get to having a child by Hope."

Suddenly Spirit saw it. "Hope's bloodline!"

"Hope will want it too. We must arrange anonymous confinement for you until the time."

Thus it was that Thorley and Megan found rare agreement, and when the time came, Hope and Megan adopted Spirit's baby. They named her Hopie Megan Hubris.

CHAPTER 11

Hopie

"It wasn't just that the bloodline is mine," Hope remarked to Spirit privately. "It is also Thorley's. He took the shot meant for Megan. She remembers." In the complications of the situation, Spirit had lost track of that aspect. Of course Megan would value that child. It was her way of repaying Thorley for his formidable service to her.

But it was quickly apparent that Hopie was also wanted for herself. Megan had evidently missed having a family, and plunged into the sudden new business of motherhood with rapture. Hopie had the very best of attention and care from the outset. Spirit was now peripheral, but she could see it happening. There simply could not have been a better placement for this baby. Spirit herself was welcomed as "Aunt Spirit," and given free access, but she kept it minimal for fear of betraying the secret.

Hope himself was a marvel. He delighted in his daughter, and was pleased when others suggested that she resembled him. Of course political enemies suggested that Hopie was his bastard child by some unknown Saxon woman, and he accepted that too. "Show me that woman." They were of course unable, though there were several claimants. Hope knew that as long as others were looking for a Saxon woman, they would never find the true mother. In this way he protected Spirit's secret, and she truly appreciated it. The really amazing thing was that no one thought to remember that Hope, as of former man of space, was sterile.

The child was a delight. She did favor Hope, perhaps because he gave her so much time that she picked up his little mannerisms. She seemed to have an eerie rapport with him, knowing where he was without being told, and crying when he suffered any pain, though they were in different cities at the time. But that took time to manifest, and was always subtle; perhaps even as an infant she learned discretion.

She was also a favorite of the office. Shelia watched her when necessary, and it seemed that she, too, liked the notion of a baby. Shelia herself could never have one of her own. Ebony, as gofer, toted the baby from place to place, seeming quite satisfied. Even Coral, the martial artist from Saturn, liked to be involved. Every woman, it seems, liked a baby, but it was more than that; Hopie seemed to share some of Hope's magic of personal magnetism.

When Hopie was one year old, there was a storm. "Storm watch," Megan announced, viewing the news while she fed Hopie her bottle.

"Watch?" Neither Hope nor Spirit were familiar with this, as airless Callisto had never had storms.

"It could strike this area within thirty-six hours."

"It can't hurt this bubble, can it? A little rain?"

She didn't comment. She just tracked the weather reports.

Next day it was a storm warning. "It could strike within a day," Megan said worriedly. "I think we had better take refuge in Ybor." She sounded genuinely concerned, so they packed the auto-bubble for overnight, checked out of Pineleaf, and blew out to the highway leading to Ybor. Spirit was on other business, but learned about their scary trip later. Hope drove while Megan held little Hopie in her arms. The baby evidently picked up the tension, for she began to cry and would not be pacified. But they were stuck for the drive, however long it took. The traffic was slow, and they watched nervously as other bubbles crowded closer to theirs. The velocity of the highway current changed, causing the bubbles to jam in closer yet. There were accidents, which were serious matters in the swirling eddies of Jupiter atmosphere, because to get lost there could be lethal.

They thought they were safe from the storm once they were ensconced in a hotel in Ybor, but they were wrong. They watched on holovision as the storm's approach was recorded. Small bubbles were rocking like chips on a wave of liquid, and large ones were being shoved from their normal positions. The city-bubble of neighboring Pete was struck first. They watched with awe as the cloud layer broke up, dropped down, and enveloped that bubble, lightning radiating.

The holo switched to another locale. "One of the suburbs is moving out of control!" the announcer exclaimed. "It's starting to drop. Power seems to be out—" Then, with open horror: "The gee-shield's failed!"

They watched, appalled, as that small bubble, about the size of Pineleaf, started its fall. Nothing anybody could do could save it now as it spiraled down into the immense and deadly gravity well of the planet. All its occupants were doomed to implosion and pressure extinction.

There was a shudder through the city. The walls creaked. They were encountering the high winds. Suddenly it was much easier to believe that the hull of the city-bubble could crack and leak, or that the gee-shield could fail.

The power flickered, causing them both to start. "Oh, Hope, I'm afraid!" Megan cried.

"Let me take Hopie," he said gruffly. Wordlessly Megan gave up the baby and huddled alone on the bed. He paced around the room, holding the screaming baby, no better at comforting her than he had been with Megan.

Then the door alarm sounded. "Not more bad news," he breathed, and went to answer it.

It was Spirit. "I would have come sooner, but the traffic—"

Then she saw their situation. She reached out her arms, and he handed Hopie to her. "You take care of your wife," she said, holding Hopie close.

He went to Megan and took her shivering body in his arms. "Spirit is here," he said, as if that made everything all right.

Megan sat up, listening. "Hopie—"

Hopie had stopped screaming. "She's with Spirit," he explained. "Now relax."

"Yes . . ." she agreed, relaxing.

Spirit supported Hopie close to her bosom and sang her a lullaby. "Sleep, my child, and peace attend thee, all through the night."

Megan heard. Suddenly she animated. She sat up and joined in, her fine voice filling the room. "Guardian angels God will send thee, all through the night!"

Hope joined in, too. Soon they were singing others, including their Navy identity songs. Spirit sang "I know who I love," while the baby slept blissfully. She had indeed found love, again—and could not marry. But what sheer bliss it was to hold her baby for these hours. And Hopie had stopped crying when Spirit took her, as if she knew something.

In the morning Spirit was tired but relieved. She gave the baby back to Megan and went her way. She had not had much sleep, but she could handle that, considering the secret joy of the experience. They were all nervously eager to get back to Pineleaf, which had survived merely shaken.

In 2640, when Hopie was four, Hope ran for governor of Sunshine. Spirit returned to be Hope's campaign manager for this effort. Megan remained as his strategist, preferring to take no overt part, but she consulted frequently with Spirit. Shelia knew exactly how much money they had to work with and where their contacts were. Hope's bodyguard and gofer were drafted to handle the details of campaigning; this was the way it had to be, for a lean campaign. Together, these five women decided where the candidate should go and how he should spend his time. Hope said it reminded him of his time as captain in the Navy, when women had mostly run his show, and done an excellent job of it.

What they could afford, it turned out, was a rental train, which was a chain of transport bubbles linked by means of special flexible airlocks and towed by a tug. There was an old dining car converted to residence after being retired from active duty and now used mainly for novelty occasions. It was shaped like a cylinder rounded off at the ends, so as to be aerodynamic; that was important for any vehicle traveling rapidly in atmosphere. They used it to go from city to city, campaigning at each.

Then Hope encountered a new phenomenon that mystified him. Men kept shouting from the audience, interrupting his campaign speeches.

"It's heckling," Megan explained. "Every politician suffers it eventually. It's a sign of success."

"Success! They were interfering with my speech!"

Spirit was more practical. "I gather this is a tactic of the opposition?"

"Of course," Megan said. "Such men are for hire, relatively cheap. But a candidate who is sure of success does not bother with such a minor tactic."

"I still don't like it," Hope said. "How can I stop it?"

"Let me consider," Spirit said.

Megan glanced at her. "I don't think I want to know what you are going to come up with," she murmured.

They moved through a long highway that was a scenic wonder. It followed the five-bar contour, but the dynamics of the planet and the fringe of the band caused the cloud cover to dip, so that first it loomed low, then intersected the route, so that special fog-cutting buoys were necessary. It was like an eerie tunnel through foam that seemed always about to stifle out. Spirit and Hope gawked, while little Hopie, sat in Hope's lap and shared his enthusiasm; she liked traveling. She was a charming child, and increasingly people were remarking how much she resembled Hope.

As they rose somewhat above the cloud surface the light touching it sharpened the fringe so that it resembled an enormous mountain slope. Rifts in it seemed like reaches of dark water, as Hope explained to Hopie while Megan smiled tolerantly. Thus they were, in their innocent and childlike fancy, driving along a narrow length of land, or a series of islands, bright fragments surrounded by the enormous silent sea. It was like the kingdom by the sea, and Hopie loved it.

Meanwhile, Spirit took note of the hecklers, identifying each. She arranged to touch them with a Navy formula called Mustard Six. This burned like fire when activated by a particular electronic signal but was otherwise quiescent. Hope proceeded with his address, and when the heckling commenced, he said, "I would like to take an impromptu survey. Will all those who harbor un-Jupiterian sentiments please rise and make yourselves known?" Then he switched on the mustard-six activator.

Six hecklers leaped out of their chairs, exclaiming loudly.

After a while the heckling resumed. Hope paused. "Is there by chance any person here whose mother was a baboon?" he inquired, and hit the switch.

Again the six hecklers jumped up, cursing. Hopie clapped both little hands over her mouth, trying to stifle her giggling. This was great sport!

Hope had no more trouble with heckling. But he was as yet too new to the larger political scene, and he lost the nomination of his party. Spirit knew that he could have won had he accepted special interest money. He had paid the usual price for integrity.

But he had attracted national notice, and received an appointment as ambassador to Ganymede. It came about because President Kenson wanted a token Hispanic in his administration, and because no one else wanted this particular assign-

ment. None of them were deluded about the underlying reali-
ties of the situation, and it was a good position for a Spanish-
speaking politician who might otherwise quickly disappear from
the national scene.

Hope received a call from New Wash, inviting him and his
family to visit the White Bubble for a private conference. Megan
know this was important, and of course they went: Hope, Megan,
Spirit and Hopie. The child was almost five, and ran joyfully
around the halls, enchanted by the complex that was the White
Bubble. "They're darling when they're little," the president remarked, smiling. Then he glanced at Megan. "And beautiful
when grown." That was when Spirit realized that Megan had
pulled a string to get Hope an appointment. Hope wasn't pleased
when he caught on, but she turned on him that certain wide-
eyed stare of challenging innocence, and he was helpless. She
could wrap him around her little finger any time she chose, and
this was one of the few times she chose.

Ganymede was the historic Cuba, under Communist government, long estranged from Jupiter. But now cautious signals
of rapprochement were occurring, and this new embassy was
the main one. The announcement generated a predictable furor among opposition party members in Congress, who seemed
to hate the very notion of peace instead of war, but they could
not stop it.

Thorley's comment didn't help: "The liberal set may be
about to experience the end product of its naïveté." Naturally
he considered liberalism to be three-quarters of the way toward
Communism and liked to imply that the true liberal would be a
Communist if he only had the courage of his convictions. Spirit
chided him for that, when they next rendezvoused. "Liberal-
lover," she whispered as he climaxed within her. He professed
to be mortified by the charge.

Hope went to Ganymede with Megan and Hopie, and his
three-woman staff, while Spirit remained on Jupiter to caretake
his affairs there. There turned out to be disturbing truth in

Thorley's prediction, for it seemed that the Premier of Ganymede did not like the embassy, but had been forced to allow it by pressure from Saturn. They were treated like outcasts, in the manner of the Navy campaign against Gerald: nothing overt, but continuously unpleasant. For example, there was a bogus flood of refugees demanding sanctuary, threatening to overwhelm the facilities and generate an embarrassing scene for Jupiter, whose government discouraged such defections. But Hope rose to the occasion by calling their bluff. He put in a call to Emerald, now a Navy Captain, and they played out a scene:

"What can I do for you, Ambassador, that wouldn't gripe your spouse and mine?" For Emerald remained one of Hope's women. Her husband was managing her career with genius, and she was rising to significant power in the Navy, but she would have leaped into bed with Hope if she had the chance.

"You can contact Roulette for me and ask her to approve immigration of approximately one hundred defectors seeking political asylum from Ganymede," he said. "If the Belt will take them, then I'd like a transport ship dispatched here to pick them up."

Emerald considered, after the transmission pause. "I'm sure the Belt will take them," she said. "The Belt is always short of men. I will start the scutwork and have a ship dispatched in forty-eight hours. But, you know, Ambassador, it's not exactly cushy living in the Belt, especially for untrained recruits. How many speak English or French?"

"None," he responded. "They'll just have to learn. Thank you, Emerald; give my respects to Rue."

"I won't give her those," she replied with mock severity. "She's still hot for you, Captain, and she's only thirty, you know. Lot of juice left in her." That, too, was more literal than it sounded; Roulette, too, would gladly leap into his bed.

It was all a bluff, but it worked beautifully. Within a day all the pseudo defectors were gone. What would a paid agent of Ganymede do in a non-Hispanic section of the Asteroid Belt?

But that was only one episode. When Hopie screamed in the night, frightened by a live rat, Hope got serious. Rats did not occur naturally on the planets; it had to be a plant. He braced the Gany Premier directly and with finesse, having Megan sing to the man's autistic son, causing the boy to respond. This utterly destroyed the man's enmity, for it gave the shame of his family hope of improvement. Thereafter the treatment of the embassy improved dramatically, and Hope and the Premier, became in their limited fashions, friends. In fact, Hope set about a devious process that was to lead to the return of the Jupiter Naval base Tanamo to Ganymede authority. In return, Ganymede released a number of prominent political prisoners. Real progress toward peace was being made, and Hope's reputation was growing.

Hope also met Mikhail Khukov, a captain in the Saturn Navy, a figure he described as a meteor: one destined to rise fast and far in his government. Khukov had a talent similar to Hope's own, that of reading people and influencing them. The two men, from opposite poles of power, understood and trusted each other. That was to prove crucial in later dealings. Like Lieutenant Repro, who had started Hope on his own meteor career, Khukov had a dream, and Hope found it worth supporting. So Hope's time as Ambassador, nominally successful, was far more significant than others knew at the time.

The two also exchanged personal favors that Spirit herself did not know about for some time: they taught each other languages. Hope learned Russian, and Khukov learned Spanish. This was to give each a significant advantage when dealing with others who thought their private dialogues secure.

After a year and a half Megan returned to Jupiter with Hopie, because of the political indoctrination on Ganymede. Hopie was a bright child and a pleasant one. She got along well in school, as she mastered Spanish, made friends, and learned the lessons well. When she began debating the liabilities of capitalism at home, Megan grew uneasy. When Hopie challenged some of the Jupiter versions of history, such as the manner the so-called Mid-Jupe Canal was arranged, Megan became angry. And when the child began praising the dedication of Saturn to System peace, Megan had had enough. "I shall not suffer my child to become a Saturnist!" she exclaimed.

So they left, and Hope was in pain that Shelia, Ebony and Coral could not assuage. They had respected Megan and liked Hopie. But it was good news for Spirit, who now took over much of the care of Hopie, theoretically to relieve Megan of the burden. Megan had always given her every chance to be with her unacknowledged daughter, and such time was precious to Spirit. She knew that Megan was suffering as Hope was, but she did what she had to do for the sake of the child. At least Spirit was able to provide some genuine affection for Hopie that the girl had lost when she left Hope and his staff.

The Premier did Hope one favor that was not to be forgotten: he located Hope's elder sister Faith and returned her to her family. She became Hopie's Aunt Faith, and Faith herself did not know that this was literally true.

In the course of the Tanamo negotiations, Hope met Gerald Phist, by then an Admiral. Phist caught on to Hope's political ambition to become president. He shook his head. "You know I'll serve you loyally if you succeed, and I'm not the only one. The careers of the officers in your unit did not end when you resigned from the Navy." Phist typically understated things. Hope's friends in the Navy now had a good deal more power than showed.

"Give my regards to your wife."

"Rue is a good woman," Phist said seriously. "It is unfortunate that she and I both love others."

"Still?" Hope asked, though he had heard as much from Emerald. He had not realized that Phist still longed for Spirit.

"Still. But we do have a good marriage. We understand each other's positions exactly."

After two years as Ambassador, Hope returned to Jupiter,

having made a considerable name for himself by his actions on Ganymede. He resumed political activity, with Spirit and his staff falling naturally into their prior roles, and this time was successful. He became Governor of Sunshine. He immediately set about implementing populist reforms. Partly as an example of his opposition to ageism he hired an old woman, Mrs. Burton, as stage technician, and not only was she competent, Hopie adopted her as a grandmother figure. He also put his sister Faith on the state payroll in open nepotism, for she worked with the state's sizable contingent of Hispanic refugees, and her relation to the governor made them realize that their plight was now being taken seriously. Spirit had had a hand in that assignment, and it proved to be an excellent one.

Thorley, of course, had the earliest news of what was in the offing, and used it to craft a clever excoriation. No one knew how he got his information; it was as though he had a bug in the governor's office. He did, and her name was Spirit. Hope guaranteed that the press was never muzzled, by keeping Thorley fully informed, and the news was always delivered with love. He concluded: "If this man Hubris had ambition, he would be dangerous." And of course Thorley knew exactly what Hope's ambition was, but some secrets he kept.

But Faith's participation was to lead to a serious crisis in Hope's administration. There had been a riot in the Black community before Hope's administration, and four men were on death row for crimes supposedly committed therein. Faith believed they were innocent, and that there would be much worse riots if they were executed. Hope investigated and concurred. So he pardoned them. And there was outrage. His popularity as governor dropped thirty points in the polls. He was excoriated by conservatives and much of the general press, with one seemingly odd exception: Thorley. The columnist was not free to support the pardon, but his commentary suggested that the authorities had brought it on themselves by making an inept case that allowed a liberal governor the technical grounds to overturn it. That was correct, and Thorley had the grace not to say more. The public outrage softened, for Thorley was now a potent conservative voice. Spirit rewarded him with special passion the next time Sancho met him.

Two years later something happened that led to Hope's finest political hour as governor, and a very special union for Spirit, Hopie, and Thorley. An interplanetary passenger ship that had been headed for Titan had somehow drifted off course and passed through restricted Saturn-space. The Saturnines had tracked it, fired on it, and holed it. All its crew and passengers were dead. Including fifty Jupiter citizens, eight of which were residents of Sunshine, and one of whom was a representative from a Sunshine district. Two were Hispanics, and Faith wanted to know when their bodies would be recovered for proper burial. As governor Hope had a responsibility to all residents of Sunshine, but this was not state or national business, it was interplanetary.

"You know, Hope—" Spirit murmured thoughtfully.

"But it's crazy!" he protested, though she had not actually voiced the thought.

"Yet, correctly played . . ."

He knew what she meant. There was a daring opportunity here. "Still, it could mean my life."

She put her hand on his. "*Our* lives."

He sighed. It was time to be a hero again.

Sancho notified Thorley that day. "But please do not break the news until after we are on the way, because—"

"Credit this old conservative with some modicum of discretion," he said as they made love.

"I will give you a full private report when we return," she promised, kissing him.

"You are going too?"

"He's my brother."

He pondered only a moment. "Then I will go as well."

"You? Thorley, you can't possibly—"

"News somehow leaked out, I saw my chance for a scoop, I demanded to come, in the name of the free press. Can your brother stop me?"

"I think not. But Thorley—you and I together on such a trip—suppose someone catches on?" For she was thrilled with the notion, and knew they would have a torrid sequence of love during such a trip.

"It will be a hostile association, and I will report it as such. I doubt your brother will refute it."

"He won't," she agreed.

They chartered a yacht, a sleek and swift civilian ship with a competent crew. Hope made sure that her captain knew the nature of the project, off the record, so he could turn it down if he chose. He paled but accepted. "It's time someone did something like this, sir," he said.

Hope told Megan and Hopie, of course, expecting them to condemn this as idiocy. Indeed, Megan did: "You're going to Saturn? Hope, this is preposterous!"

"I want to go, too!" Hopie exclaimed, clapping her hands. She was eleven now, and Hope claimed she reminded him hauntingly of Aunt Spirit at that age.

"You will do nothing of the kind!" Megan exclaimed, horrified. "This thing is suicide!"

Hopie frowned. "You mean Daddy's supposed to go die alone?"

Her words were a question, not an accusation, but Megan was wounded. "We'll both go," she said shortly.

Hopie jumped up and down, oblivious to the subtle pain. "Oh, goody! I'll do a school paper on it!"

They wasted no time. They issued no public statement, but Thorley phoned Hope. "Governor, is this an official excursion?" he demanded. "Then you cannot bar the press. I will be there in two hours."

Hope glanced at Spirit as the screen faded. "You put him up to this?"

She spread her hands. "Please, Hope."

"What of Hopie?"

"We didn't realize she would be coming. But she does not have to know everything."

Hope nodded, and went to inform Megan of this new detail.

They set out for Saturn. When they were safely in space, Shelia in Hassee issued the press release that announced the governor's intention. He was going to Saturn to recover the bodies of Sunshine citizens, demand an apology, and obtain reparations.

There had been a national election, and Megan's enemy Tocsin was now president. They received his signal, coded for privacy. "What the hell do you think you're doing, Hubris?" he demanded.

"Mr. President, I am doing my duty by my constituents," Hope said evenly, and Spirit knew he was pleased to see the man so angry.

"You have no business dabbling in interplanetary matters!"

"When those whose business it is renege on their responsibilities, it becomes necessary for others to take up the slack," Hope said. Spirit, standing beyond the camera range, bit her tongue to stop from laughing. Hope could be so fiendishly annoying when he tried.

"You shithead spic! Turn back or I'll blast your wise ass out of space!"

He was bluffing. He could indeed order the ship to be downed, but such an act would carry a horrendous political penalty, for the early news holos showed that the people of Jupiter were overwhelmingly with Hope on this matter. "You do your duty as you see fit, Mr. President," Hope said calmly. "I will do mine." He was doing what he did best, playing a scene.

"I'm going to see you hung by the balls for treason, Hubris," Tocsin snarled, his face mottling red as he cut off.

"At least I've got them, Mr. President," Hope muttered under his breath to the blank screen, smiling. Now Spirit let her stifled laugh burst out. What a naughty pleasure this was! Hope had hated Tocsin since he learned of what he had done to Megan, and Spirit shared his sentiment.

Megan stepped into the communications chamber, followed by Thorley and Hopie. "I wish you hadn't done that, Hope."

He gazed at her levelly. "That man destroyed you politically. I will destroy *him*."

"And become just like him?"

That set him back. He promised not to bait the president any more.

"What does shithead spic mean?" Hopie inquired.

Megan, who evidently had been unaware that the girl was close enough to overhear the dialogue, seemed about to faint. "Please, allow me to explain privately," Thorley said. He took Hopie by the hand and let her out of the chamber. Spirit knew the man would find a way to defuse the language. Perhaps Hopie had been too protected.

In due course, Thorley sent his dispatch from the yacht. It was remarkably gentle to Hope, almost suggesting that the notorious Hubris might for once have done something of which a conservative could approve. "Why all the fuss? One would almost suspect that the errant governor of the Great State of Sunshine had pardoned someone. Doesn't it make perfect sense to challenge the Saturnines on their home turf when they have done something slightly more than routinely reprehensible? Somebody has to, as it were, pick up the pieces."

"You don't like Tocsin either!" Spirit exclaimed when they were alone. They had adjoining staterooms, with locking doors and a private portal between them, so that nobody's daughter could accidentally discover the governor's sister making love with the governor's most persistent critic.

"Sometimes it is expedient for a good conservative to stand aside and allow events to take their natural course."

"Such as when a good liberal does what no conservative

dare do, and stands up to the Saturn bear?"

"Liberals may have their uses, on rare occasion."

"And liberal wenches have only one use?"

"Bait me at your own risk, wench, lest I make that use of you."

"Show me your power!"

They made love, delighting in doing it in a bed after twelve years. "Oh, Spirit," he said. "I wish I could marry you!"

"Perhaps if you converted to Mormonism, so that you could have plural wives?"

"It is a thought." But of course they knew that marriage between them had never been in the picture.

The journey took several days, and boredom soon threatened. But Thorley was in person a most engaging companion; he kept his politics out of polite conversation. He joined the liberals for meals and made a fourth for games of old-fashioned cards, teaming with Spirit against Megan and Hope, and his smooth wit made him a delight. He also taught Hopie to play chess, which he claimed was a game of royalty. Spirit was privately thrilled to see them getting along so well, for a reason no one would speak aloud.

Then it threatened to fracture. "You seem like such a nice man," Hopie told him. "Why are you always so mean to my father?"

Thorley laughed, as if this were rare wit. "It is my profession, child. I do to public figures metaphorically what your father does to them politically."

Megan and Spirit and Hope, theoretically engaged in their separate pursuits at that moment, paused to listen without interfering. "Is it true you saved his life?" Hopie asked with her typical directness.

Thorley smiled. "That might be an exaggeration. It is true there was an incident some time ago."

"And you got lasered instead of him?"

He shrugged. "It could be put that way. Actually I believe

it was your mother the man was aiming at, as a target of opportunity."

"Back before I was born?"

"Prehistoric," he agreed wryly. "So the matter need not concern you, Hopie, if I may address you so familiarly."

"So if it wasn't for you, I wouldn't exist."

Thorley knew what she had for the moment forgotten: that Hopie was an adopted child, not Megan's own. But he did not remind her of that. "It is certainly possible."

"So I suppose I can't hate you, even if you deserve it."

"I would be distressed to have you hate me, Hopie, however deserving of the sentiment I may be."

"Then will you stop writing those mean things?"

Thorley spread his hands. "I can no more change my nature than your father can change his."

Surprisingly she smiled. "Well, at least you are honest."

He smiled back. "I fear I may not merit such an accolade. Let's just say I am consistent."

"Okay." She returned her attention to the chess game. She was doing well, there, for Thorley had spotted her the queen, both rooks, a bishop, and a knight. There was a savage battle among pawns in progress.

Spirit and Megan exchanged a glance. It seemed that a necessary hurdle had been navigated. And indeed, the two continued to get along well. Thorley was a marvelous font of arcane and sometimes odd humor, and he made Hopie laugh often. He taught her other games, and did not try to feed her any conservative lore. Soon she was calling him Uncle Thorley.

And in private at ship's night, and often also in the day, Spirit and Thorley found time to make more love. They were both in their 40's, but pent-up longing made them lusty. They spoke often of love and desire, and not of marriage.

"But you know," Spirit reminded him "this mission is dangerous. Saturn could blast us out of space."

"It could indeed. Why do you think I wanted to come along?"

"But you're not suicidal!"

"I wanted this last chance with you. If you are to die on a foolish extravaganza, let me die with you. Then I will not have to endure the loss of you."

"But you have a wife to console you."

"And an excellent wife she is, and I do love her. But you are my forbidden passion. If I live for her; I may die for you."

"Forbidden fruit," she agreed.

"Fruits," he said, kissing her breasts.

"Always the tastiest, I'm sure." She delighted in this by-play, so long denied.

In due course they approached Saturn, with its phenomenal rings, the splendor of the System. They were hailed by a Saturn cruiser. "Jupiter ship, you are intruding on private space. Turn back immediately."

Hope took the screen. "I am Governor Hubris of the state of Sunshine of the United States of Jupiter Planet," he replied in English. "I am coming to claim what belongs to my state and my planet."

That did not seem to faze the officer. "If you do not turn we shall fire on you."

"I am sure that will make excellent news," Hope said, playing out his scene. "I am Governor Hope Hubris, and the members of my party are my wife Megan, my sister Spirit, my daughter Hopie, and the correspondent Thorley."

"We are firing one warning shot," the officer said.

Indeed, the in-ship report came immediately: "Laser beam at twelve o'clock."

"Saturn does seem to be competent at holing unarmed ships," Hope reminded the officer.

The screen went blank. "Bluff successful," Thorley remarked laconically.

"Even the Saturnines do not knowingly shoot down a governor," Hope said. But Spirit knew that Megan was as relieved as she was; it had been a formidable risk.

Two hours later they were signaled again. "Governor Hubris," a new officer said. "Please adjust course for orbit at Ring Station; a shuttle will convey your party to Scow."

"Understood." This was victory indeed, for Scow was the capital bubble of North Saturn, the seat of government for the Union of Saturnine Republics. They were now accepting the visit.

"If you will pardon the curiosity of a political innocent," Thorley said with his special brand of irony, "what guarantees do you have against arrest and execution as a spy?"

"The Governor of Sunshine, former ambassador to the Independent Satellite of Ganymede? Our esteemed president would be forced to make an issue."

"And you have placed Tocsin in the same bind you have placed Saturn," he said. "However much he detests your intestines in private, Tocsin can not undermine you in public. This could precipitate Solar War Three."

"Oh, I doubt it will come to that."

Thorley laughed. "One must admire your finesse, Governor, if not your politics. To make the Eagle and the Bear waltz to your tune involuntarily."

"Finesse does have its compensations."

"Still, I want to advise you in advance that I will be most perturbed if this leads to my obliteration in SW III."

"I will take your perturbation under advisement at that time."

"You characters would make light of Sol going nova tomorrow," Spirit muttered.

Thorley raised an eyebrow. "Indeed, there would be much light then."

Hopie tittered, and even Megan smiled. Spirit aimed a mock laser pistol at his head and pulled the trigger. They were releasing tension, knowing that they had not yet won the day. Not nearly.

They were conducted by grim non-English-speaking troopers that made Hopie quite nervous; she stayed very close to Megan, hanging on to her hand. In due course they were in the giant bubble of Scow.

The adults were guarded about reactions, but now Hopie was thrilled. She had never before been to a city-bubble of this size. They were ushered into a private chamber where three Saturnines sat behind a long table. One of them was Khukov, the officer Hope had met on Ganymede. He stood up and leaned over the table to shake Hope's hand. "Welcome to Saturn, Governor Hubris," he said in English. "Please be seated, you and your party. We have much to discuss."

"Indeed we do, Admiral. Are you empowered to arrange for reparations?"

The other Saturn officers spoke to each other in Russian. By their tones, Spirit gathered that they were not pleased about this forced meeting. But Khukov smiled at Hope graciously. "The Commissar wishes to reassure himself that your party is quite comfortable. He is eager to change your status if you are not."

Spirit was sure that was not the nature of the Russian dialogue. But Hope returned the smile. Then, in Spanish, he said to Spirit, "These characters haven't decided how to handle us."

"Now I am sure you are reasonable people," Khukov said in English. "You know we cannot make reparations!"

"Reparations and an apology—and the bodies," Hope said firmly.

"My companions are not sanguine about that," Khukov said. "You know it was a spy ship."

"You know your gunners got trigger-happy and shot down a civilian ship by accident!" Playing the scene.

"And now the fools are locked into their error," Spirit said in Spanish.

Khukov glanced at her, nodding.

"He understands Spanish!" she hissed, alarmed.

"Now how could that be?" Hope asked her blandly.

She shook her head. "I don't know! But—"

"He speaks Spanish no more than I speak Russian," he told her, and turned to face Khukov.

Spirit eyed Hope. She was catching on now—to both parts of the deal. They had exchanged languages!

"For abating the menace of the spy ship we should apologize?" Khukov asked Hope in English.

"Tell the communist clown to go spy his own posterior," Spirit told Hope in Spanish, picking up the nature of this dialogue. Hopie stifled a giggle, and Megan frowned; she had learned enough of the language to grasp the insult.

"For mistaking a strayed civilian ship," Hope said in English, without hint of humor.

Thus they continued their devious bargaining, finding devices to allow the return of the bodies with token reparations.

Khukov smiled grimly. "Your president will be pleased, no?" Spirit, Megan, and even Hopie smiled, and Thorley coughed. The Commissar chuckled. All knew that Tocsin would be privately furious at Hope's success but would not dare to disparage it openly. That was perhaps the deciding factor for the Russians: the prospect of obliquely taunting Tocsin, who had made a career of bashing communism.

Khukov and Hope shook hands formally, sealing the understanding. "And while we wait for the arrangements to be complete, we shall give your party a welcome that will please your president even more," the Russian said.

Hope then stood and shook hands with the other officers, one of whom said something in Russian, smiling broadly.

"And you irritate my penis, you ignorant double-dealing pederastic Bolshevik," Hope returned in Spanish with just as broad a smile.

Khukov almost visibly bit his tongue. "It is nice to overhear the exchange of such sincere remarks between supposed adversaries," he said in English. "I'm sure you hold each other in similar esteem."

"Why do I get the feeling I'm missing something?" Thorley murmured.

"You're not missing anything," Spirit returned darkly.

Then came what had all the aspects of a head-of-planet formal visit. There was a banquet with distinctly unproletarian trimmings. Megan and Hope were feted at the head table with the high-ranking dignitaries of the supposedly classless Saturn society, while Spirit, Thorley, and Hopie had a table with the ranking wives. There were translators to render the remarks of the hosts into English. After that there was even a parade in their honor. They rode under a massive red hammer-and-sickle banner while the enormous crowd cheered.

"Tocsin will be apoplectic," Spirit remarked, enjoying it. Hopie giggled; she had long since picked up on her family's antipathy to Tocsin, and had caught on to Saturn's similar sentiment. She knew that this celebration was not for the visitors so much as for interplanetary show. She loved it.

"I fear I will never live this down," Thorley muttered, but he didn't seem to be as unhappy as he might have been. He would have an excellent story to write. His hand, where it didn't show, was holding Spirit's hand.

Hopie happily waved to the crowd. "What's a pederastic Bolshevic?" she asked without turning her head.

"Later," Spirit and Thorley said together, laughing.

In due course they returned to their yacht with a cargo of four frozen Sunshine bodies that included the two Hispanics and the representative. The rest would follow in a Saturn freighter. They weighed anchor and put out to space with an escort of Saturnine Naval vessels.

The usual dullness set in during the long trip home, but Spirit and Thorley made the most of it. If Hopie caught on that something was going on, she had the wit to pretend ignorance. It really wasn't her concern if two unmarried people were finding a way to alleviate boredom.

By the time they docked at Sunshine, Hope was notorious

across the System, as the governor who had braved the Bear's jaws and won. He really was a hero, in a culture that loved heroes. For some reason there was little other than silence from the White Bubble.

Thorley write a fine series of articles on the excursion, and Hopie did a nice paper for her school class. She showed a definite flair for written expression. "Uncle Thorley told me how," she explained. That seemed to cover it.

CHAPTER 12

Campaign

But the following six months were not kind to the Hope Hubris political fortune. Hope and Spirit were dedicated to the elimination of the illicit drug trade, and Sunshine was a major conduit. Prior governors had paid lip service to the effort, but now it got serious, for this governor had special connections. He contacted Roulette Phist of the Belt, his lovely onetime wife who remained hot for him, and she used her connections to locate a crew of about fifty drug experts to loan. These were folk who could, in some cases, literally smell the drugs and who knew the sinister by-paths of illegal distribution. Hope interviewed them to verify that they intended to serve the cause faithfully. In general, Rue's selection was excellent; they quickly formed the most savvy drug-control team extant.

First they merely identified the routes, taking no action. The agents were instructed to accept any bribes offered and to report them privately, spending the money for themselves in ways that no ordinary enforcement agents would, so as to allay any suspicion. They enjoyed that part of it. For six months they infiltrated the delivery network of Sunshine, satisfying the professionals that business remained as usual; the new governor would not be any more effective at cutting the pipeline than any other had been.

Then the force struck. They went after the personnel, not the drugs, and got them. The line had been cut, and ninety percent of the drug flow ceased overnight. They used the confiscated wares for a comprehensive detoxification program, providing drugs free to acknowledged addicts as long as necessary. This reduced the incentive to commit crimes to support habits, but it meant that the State of Sunshine was now in the drug business. Thorley got supposedly private information and condemned the program, but the fact was that crime was declining. Outrage faded; other states were considering similar programs. In three years both illegal drug traffic and crime were at their lowest ebb in a century.

Then the crime cartel struck back. One of the tame addicts blew the whistle—he claimed—on the biggest secret of Hope's administration: a massive payoff by the drug moguls. "I was a courier for the money," he said. "I took it from the laundry in Ami and brought it to Hassee every week."

His figures were staggering: twenty five million dollars delivered to the Governor's secret account every week. That was the price to keep the governor's minions off the *real* drug traffic.

"And to whom do you deliver them?" the interviewer inquired.

"A guy called Sancho."

"Sancho!" Hope exclaimed. He and his staff members were of course watching the broadcast. "That can't be!" Indeed it could not, for he knew that Spirit herself was Sancho. She had tried to keep out of sight, but must have been observed from time to time.

"Who is Sancho?" the interviewer asked.

"Some spic who works for the governor's sister. That's all I know. Always wears gloves, has a scarred face. I think he's an illegal. Small guy, talks in a whisper."

"Sancho works for Spirit Hubris?"

"Yeah. Or maybe for the governor direct. I don't know. He's the one who takes the money, anyway. I don't give it to nobody but him."

The courier went on to describe the warehouse where he

delivered the money to Sancho. The station went to look, with its cameras. It was a warehouse for campaign literature—and under it was half a billion dollars in used bills, exactly as the courier had indicated. It was of course a frame. They had planted the money there, then planted the "courier," and suddenly Hope was in trouble. It *was* his warehouse, and the money *was* there.

That was enough for the hostile State Legislature. A bill of impeachment was introduced and debated, and somehow it sailed through with phenomenal velocity. Objections were brushed aside or voted down by bloc—and therein was another pattern. A narrow majority was held by the members of a coalition formed of the more conservative members of Hope's own party and those of President Tocsin's party. It was evident that Tocsin, perceiving an opportunity, had issued a private directive, and they were obeying with partisan discipline. This was his chance to, as he had put it during the trip to Saturn, see Hope hung by the balls. It hardly mattered what the facts were; the opposition was determined to see to his undoing. He, it seemed, had been fool enough to provide them an opening.

There seemed to be no easy way out of this. Spirit could reveal her identity, but that would merely seem to confirm her brother's complicity. They had been caught flat-footed, and were unable to marshal refuting evidence fast enough to prevail. The Senate quickly voted, and just like that, Hope was impeached, found guilty, and removed from office.

But neither Hope nor Spirit were easy targets. Hope called QYV. That nefarious organization had caused him trouble in space, but was now more or less on his side.

Reba answered. She was older than she had been, and had been rising through her echelons just as Khukov had been doing through his and Hope through his, until recently.

"It's about time you called," she said severely. "You made the perhaps fatal error of losing your paranoia and allowing the conspirators to catch you. Tocsin made a deal with the drug moguls to eliminate a mutual enemy. But you can still prevail if you get the truth before the public. You merely need to use the appropriate avenue. Send Sancho to Thorley." She clicked off.

Spirit nodded. "Why didn't *we* think of that?"

She went to Thorley, this time making quite sure she was unobserved. "I don't like to ask this, but–"

"I am aware of the news, and of Sancho's innocence," he said with a grim smile. Of course he was; they had been making love some of the times Sancho was supposed to have been accepting graft from the courier.

"But our secret—we can't reveal–the scandal—" She was near tears. Never before had she been put in the position of having to betray either her brother or her lover.

"I believe this is an occasion for partial truth."

"I don't see how–"

"Leave it to me. Now may we proceed to more urgent business?"

She flung her arms about him, gladly setting aside the crisis in favor of love. Their normal separation made them always eager for closeness.

In due course Thorley wrote an essay titled "Let Justice Be Done." In it he blew the whistle on Sancho:

Sancho is in fact a disguise used for convenience by Spirit Hubris herself. It is not necessarily appropriate, even in these enlightened times, for an attractive woman of any age to travel widely alone, particularly when she is closely related to a prominent politician whose life has been threatened more than once. Therefore Spirit Hubris has assumed masculine guise, donning gloves with a stuffed left finger to conceal her deformity and removing the makeup she normally employs to mask the abrasions on her face. In this guise, as "Sancho," she has had no difficulty and has required no cumbersome protection; her complete anonymity has been her safeguard. Naturally she preferred not to have this revealed, because a cover blown is a cover useless. This clarifies why Sancho was mysterious and had no formal identity. He was not an illicit immigrant, merely a fictive connivance.

In this guise Spirit has on occasion provided me directly with pertinent information about her brother's activities. It was she who informed me of the governor's planned venture to Saturn—an expedition that for obvious reasons could not be publicly advertised in advance. When such conflicts between principle and expediency arise, Hope Hubris has compromised by informing me in this direct and private manner, trusting my discretion not to nullify a particular thrust by premature exposure. At times the line between legitimate news and counterproductive exposure becomes extremely fine. In this instance I took advantage of the knowledge to force my attendance on the Saturn sally, in this manner amplifying my eventual report.

It happens that my records indicate that on two of the occasions in which Sancho is supposed to have accepted money at the warehouse, he—that is, she—was present at my office, delivering information to me. I can therefore vouch from direct personal experience that the charge against Sancho—and therefore against Governor Hubris—was on these occasions unfounded. I have also verified that on several other occasions Spirit, herself, was attending public or business functions in other cities, so could not have been at the Hassee warehouse when the courier claims.

Now simple logic suggests that if part of a statement is demonstrably false, all of it becomes suspect. Certainly the courier's rationale is questionable; it is nonsensical to suppose that he could "go public" about the covert activities of the drug moguls without being promptly and nastily dispatched, unless he was, in fact, acting on their orders. I submit for public consideration the supposition that the entire charge against Governor Hubris is false, and I invite challenge by independent parties. But for the moment let us assume that my case has been validated and that an innocent man has been impeached. Let us now consider motives.

Thorley then proceeded to destroy the opposition case against Hope Hubris, showing with devastating logic the corrupt and political nature of the charges and the impeachment process itself. He clarified that the governor, however obscenely liberal in other matters, had suffered grievously from criminal pirates and was dedicated to extirpating the drug trade. Suddenly the campaign of the Hero of the Belt was remembered.

I suggest that, unable to take Hubris out physically—the governor's female security force is remarkably loyal and efficient—the pirates at last devised a scheme to do it politically. The money was not to *bribe* him but to *frame* him. This was effective; he was promptly ushered out of office. It is evident that the drug business quickly reverted to normal, increasing in Sunshine to its former level. Recidivism is rampant among treated addicts, and crime in the streets is rebounding at a rate that has swamped the minions of the law. In a few brief weeks the halcyon days of Hubris's term have been eclipsed. Certainly this was a victory for the drug moguls, who thrive on political corruption, and for crime in general. At the present rate of activity, their parcel of half a billion dollars, surreptitiously planted in the governor's warehouse, should be redeemed within months. It was, it seems, a very sound investment. In addition I understand that much of that warehouse money has mysteriously disappeared from storage and that the proprietors are extremely reluctant to permit a recount by qualified parties. Perhaps the money was not an investment but a loan.

He concluded: "We have witnessed a rare perversion of due process. Now let justice be done."

If there had been furor before, there was absolute chaos now. By the time it was over, approximately fifty percent of the state senators of Sunshine had resigned in disgrace, the White Bubble itself had a political black eye because of its covert involvement, Hope was retroactively exonerated, his drug program was reinstated, a grand jury set out in pursuit of the mysteriously missing warehouse money, and Hope was launched into his candidacy for the office of the president of the United States of Jupiter.

In the early days Thorley had interposed his body to protect one Hope loved from assassination by laser. Spirit had repaid him in her fashion. This time he had interposed his literary talent—and lo! his pen was mightier than the sword. He had at one stroke laid waste the entire array against Hope. Historically it was to be known as "The Sunshine Massacre," but that hardly told the real story.

"If I had not loved you before, I would do so now," Spirit whispered as they made love thereafter.

"I would have done it for you," he replied. "Fortunately I didn't have to. Your brother, by sheerest liberal coincidence I'm sure, happened to be on the right side of the issue this time."

"Oh shut up, troglodyte!" she protested, stifling him with kisses.

*

It was two years before the next presidential election for the United States of Jupiter, but that was barely time to do the job. Spirit was Hope's campaign manager, of course; Megan was his strategist, and Shelia his coordinator. They worked together, organizing a complex political entity of publicity and fund-raising, hiring specialists for particular aspects, and dictating the very footsteps of his climb. Hope himself had very little to do with this; he was not apt at the details of organization. He merely did as directed, much in the manner of Ebony, their gofer. In fact, sometimes when Ebony was overloaded, he helped her out; she promised not to tell on him, as if it were any secret. Hopie, when not in school, happily joined them. The operation was somewhat like a military campaign, with every effort made to apply maximum force to the key vulnerabilities of the enemy. The enemy in this case was the apathy of the public and the reputation of opposing politicians. Specifically Tocsin; somehow they had always known that Hope would one day try his strength against him, to the political death.

"But we're going to have to travel, to campaign effectively," Spirit said. "Across the nation, efficiently and cheaply." For of course their funds remained lean, the chronic condition of honest politicians.

"Take the train," Ebony said. "Just like before."

They laughed, but in a moment the notion jelled. Hopie loved the idea. They wound up with a fine cheap old luxury train, the *Spirit of Empire*, with seven ornate coaches. Spirit liked the name, foolishly

Each coach was about eighty-five feet long and ten feet wide, and looked very much like its ancient terrestrial ancestor. The engine puffed clouds of dissipating smoke. Hopie was thrilled; she was thirteen years old now, not yet too old to glean joy from new things. Spirit remembered her own life at that age, packaging porno feelies and having weekly sex with pirates; how young Hopie seemed in comparison!

They boarded, officially, as a group: Megan, Spirit, Shelia in her wheelchair, Ebony, Coral, the grandmotherly handyman Mrs. Burton, Hopie, and Hope. There was a small crowd of supporters to cheer them on, and, the train had its own staff of two engineers, cook, maid, and porter. So they were to be a group of a baker's dozen, touring much of the planet. It promised to be interesting, even if the quest for high office proved unsuccessful. Spirit, for the moment attuned to her unacknowledged daughter, experienced it with the heightened excitement of youth. Oh, to be a child again, and not among pirates!

The railroad station was in the basement of Ybor, below the residential section, where gee was slightly high. It seemed cavernous, because it was mostly empty and poorly lighted. Gee and illumination combined to provide an illusion of great depth at the outer rim of the bubble. The cars stood beside the long loading platform, the tops of their wheels barely visible in the crevice at its edge. The glassy windows reflected the things of the station, making the whole scene seem stranger yet.

"Ooo, I like it!" Hopie exclaimed, clinging tightly to Hope's hand. She was now almost as tall as Spirit herself, and had young breasts and dawning appeal of feature, but she wavered back and forth between child and adolescent. "A real old choo-choo train!"

Hope let the girls board first, with Hopie and Ebony helping Shelia get her wheels across the gap between platform and train floor. He turned at the entrance platform, before the lock closed, and smiled and waved to the crowd, and they cheered. Then he and Spirit entered the coach.

It was like an elegant dayroom, with swiveling couch-chairs and ornate pseudowood tables and fluffy curtains on the windows. Light descended from hanging chandeliers. The floor was lushly carpeted, with protective plastic over the spots where wear was likely to be greatest.

"Please take your seat, sir," the porter said. "If you dim the lights you can see out the windows better."

Hopie plumped into a seat next to Hope and clasped her hands. "I want to see us pull out!"

There was a jolt; then they began to move, ever so slowly, seeing the platform with its burden of people pass behind. Gradually they accelerated, so that the platform moved back at a walking, then at a running, pace. The vertical support pillars started to blur. Their weight increased because they were moving in the direction of the bubble's rotation, adding to the effective centrifugal force.

"I like this part," Hopie said, her hands holding tight to the arms of her couch-chair.

There was a warning whistle, a double note. Then the coach flung out of the station, going into free-fall. In a moment they were out of Ybor's gravity shield. Now they felt Jupiter's real gravity, diffused more than halfway by the train's own gee-shield, to reduce it to Earth-normal.

They got up and toured the train. The dining car was domed, with a restaurant that seated as many as eighteen people; they could peer out to either side and above, seeing the sights while they ate. There was also the sleeping car, with neat cubicles containing wall-to-wall beds; Hopie could hardly wait for evening to come so she could try it out. There was a conference car, with an office-like section and equipment; Shelia's files were already ensconced. There was a playroom car, set up for games and entertainments ranging from pool to commercial holovision; Hopie's mouth fairly watered at that. There was a baggage car, used also for supplies. And there was the caboose. This was where the train's own staff resided; they ate and slept there when not on duty, staying out of the way of the paying clientele. Naturally Hopie found it the most fascinating one of all, perhaps because it was tacitly forbidden; they were not supposed to intrude on the crew's privacy.

The seeming wheels of the train opened out into propellers that drove it forward through the atmosphere. They could also see the railroad tracks ahead. These were actually two beams of light, used to guide the train on its course; as long as the engineer kept it between those tracks, all was well.

Satisfied with the tour, they returned to the dining car, where the cook was serving lunch. For this first meal aboard the train, all eight of them gathered in the dome restaurant where they could further admire the distant smoke through the curving ceiling. Theoretically Hope was the leader and Megan his consort, while Ebony, Shelia, Coral, and Mrs. Burton were mere employees, but they had long since abandoned pretense in private; they were more like a family. Hopie excitedly told the others about the wonders of the engine, and they listened with suitable expressions of interest. At first the cook and waitress (in other cars she became the maid) evinced muted disapproval of this un-hierarchical camaraderie, but slowly they relaxed, perceiving that it was genuine. A long train journey, like a space voyage, was a great leveler; social pretensions faded.

But the joyride rapidly became something else. Hope returned from the male restroom with Casey, the engineer. They had narrowly missed being electrocuted by a wired urinal. The train was booby-trapped, and that was unlikely to be the only one.

Mrs. Burton dismantled the urinal trap and discussed its details with Coral. They would have to check the entire train before any of the party could relax. "Meanwhile," Coral told Hope firmly, "you stay with me, close, Governor. I will taste your food first; I will use your facilities."

"But the sanitary—"

"You want privacy at risk of life?"

He looked helplessly at Megan, but she merely nodded agreement. "Coral is only doing her job," she said. She was pale, not from the notion of another woman staying so close to her husband, but because of the immediate threat of death.

"Good luck using the urinal," he murmured to Coral. Hopie tittered, but she too was shaken.

It went well beyond that. When they were ready to sleep, Coral took Hope's whole bed apart, remade it, then stripped and climbed in herself. "Now, wait—" he protested.

Coral smiled. "No seduction, sir," she reassured him. "Maybe chemical on sheets, or radiation; I know if I feel."

She climbed out and stood for a moment, nude, considering. She was well formed; her Saturnine skin was silken, her torso slender and extremely well toned, her breasts not large but perfectly shaped, her waist so small that her hips and posterior became pronounced. Coral was every bit as pretty in her fashion as her reptilian namesake, and as lithe, and her face was of matching quality. She certainly had not had to go into this sort of work; any man of any planet would have been glad to marry and support her. But she was her own woman, and matchless at her profession.

Hopie had of course seen the inspection; Hopie saw every-thing. "I wish I had a figure like yours," she said wistfully.

Coral laughed. "Yours will be more like Spirit's."

Hopie considered that, and smiled. "That's good enough."

Spirit felt foolishly flattered.

Next day the quest for traps resumed. Coral stayed so close to Hope that she often touched him, suspicious of everything. But it was not only that. "I am jealous of Megan," she confided when he looked askance.

Spirit nodded to herself. The woman had no animosity to Megan, nor would she ever betray Megan's interests. She was merely in love with Hope, as all his women were. As Spirit herself was, in her twisted way.

Still no traps turned up, and that was bad because they were sure they existed. All of them felt the tension, especially Hopie. "I don't want anything to happen to you, Daddy!" she cried, hugging him tightly.

"Or to you," he said, kissing her on the forehead. Indeed.

"Her, too," Coral muttered. That was a corollary aspect: If Megan had his love as wife, Hopie had it as daughter, and the others were excluded. They suffered an amicable jealousy of any such attachment.

Hope went to the men's room to wash his hands, and Coral went with him. He picked up a bar of soap and began to un-wrap it.

"Me first," Coral said, taking it from his hand.

"Harpy," he muttered. She ignored him, wetting her hands and squeezing the bar through them, pausing to smell it.

"No poison," she concluded, satisfied.

"Unless it's just male poison," Hopie put in, laughing. She had followed them in; there was no longer any such thing as privacy for Hope.

It was a joke, but Coral stiffened. "Sex-differentiated en-zymes—it just could be!" She took the bar and hurried away. Soon she was back with grim news. "It was, sir. I ran it through my chem-kit. Affects only Y chromosome, so no effect on fe-male. But you—if not death in hours, brain damage in days."

Hopie seemed about to faint. Spirit put her arms about the girl, comforting her, though Spirit was privately appalled by the narrowness of the escape. "I thought it was humor," Hopie whispered.

"That enemy not laughing," Coral said grimly.

The train approached the site of the first campaign speech. As they passed through the maneuvers for entry to the station, Hopie was at Hope's elbow, trying to tell him something. He was distracted and not paying attention; this really was not the occasion for the indulgence of childish prattle. "You'll have to let me go now, honey," he told her gently. "I have a campaign address to give."

"Daddy, you aren't *listening!*" she exclaimed, and it became apparent that she was crying.

"I'm sorry," he said sincerely. "I'm listening now."

"Daddy, I had a dream, sort of," she said, her tears abating. Sunshine followed rain very quickly, with teenagers.

"A dream," he agreed.

"Sort of. I don't think I was exactly asleep, so—"

"A vision," he said. "I have them sometimes. Maybe it runs in the family."

She smiled gratefully. "Maybe." It was a running joke: How could an adoptive child inherit a genetic trait? But behind it was reality: as Spirit knew so well, Hopie *was* blood kin, and might indeed share traits. "But this was a bad one."

"Sometimes they are. But often there is truth in them."

"Daddy, I saw you start to talk to the crowd, and then—then it all blew up. Daddy, I'm terrified!"

They discussed it, and Hope agreed to be alert for anything explosive. But there was nothing. He took the mike, to address the small crowd—then backed off, signaling Mrs. Burton to turn off the mike.

Coral started forward, concerned. "Sir, is something—"

Mrs. Burton switched off the mike. "What's on your mind, Governor? Surely not stage fright!"

"Let's try a test record," he whispered. "One with my voice."

"Sure." They had made several recordings of single-issue spot discussions for backup use in case his voice got strained; that was another standard precaution. She put one on and turned on the mike, while the crowd outside looked on curiously. They retreated to another chamber.

"Hello, friends," his voice said on the loudspeaker. "My name is—"

The mike console exploded. Metal shrapnel blasted into the wall and cracked the shatterproof pseudoglass window. Hopie screamed.

In a moment there was silence. The broadcast chamber was a shambles; anybody in it would have been damaged beyond repair.

Coral nodded ruefully. "Voice-activated bomb, coded to your voice only," she said. "Sir, I failed you. I did not anticipate that."

"Fortunately Hopie did," he said, putting his arm around her heaving shoulders. "I think you saved my life, cutesy."

"Oh, Daddy," she said, sobbing into his shoulder.

In due course Mrs. Burton rigged another mike, one not booby-trapped, and he gave his address from the shambled chamber. He kept Hopie with him, holding her left hand with his right. "Someone tried to assassinate me," he told his audience firmly. "Don't worry; it wasn't anyone from here. My daughter anticipated it and saved my life; but for her I would have had trouble addressing you now. I think she deserves to participate." And he lifted her hand in a kind of victory gesture.

The crowd cheered so hard that the train vibrated, and Hopie blushed. No one had ever cheered her before. But Spirit was concerned. The girl's vision had saved Hope; was it sheer chance, or did she have some power of vision? Was it a real ability, or an early signal of the kind of internal delusion Hope was capable of?

Hope's first presidential campaign address was a great success. But all of them were sobered: a deadly anonymous enemy was out to kill the candidate, and only a girl's nervous anticipation had prevented it. This time.

During the long hours of intercity travel they had to have a distraction, as much for Megan's and Hopie's benefit as Hope's, so they played cards. There were all manner of computerized games available, of course, but none of them had any present taste for these. They had been checked safe, but it was too easy to imagine a unit blowing up when a certain configuration was achieved, such as the code word *Hubris*. And, despite all the advances in game-craft, the old-fashioned physical cards still represented an excellent all-around repertoire of diversion. They taught Hopie how to play partnership canasta, and she and Hope tromped Megan and Spirit. Then Hope and Hopie played two-person games, like Old Maid, War, and Concentration, but even these palled in time, perhaps because Hopie, with the wit and luck of the young, kept winning. In the afternoon they were at the point of staring out into the Jupiter atmosphere, watching the cloud formations just above the train, as they were augmented by the drifting column of train smoke. They fancied they saw shapes and pictures there—goblin heads, potatoes, dragons' tails, and such. Imagination was wonderful stuff, and Hopie's was akin to Hope's.

Then Casey passed by, and they roped him into a game of imaginary sightseeing. He turned out to be good at the game. "You can still see the old molybdenum mine, there by the cattle herd; it's reclaimed land now, converted to pasture."

"Brown cows," Hopie said. "With white faces."

"You got it," Casey agreed.

Spirit nudged Megan. The three spectators were evidently starting to see those sights. That was the sort of thing Hope could do, in the lighter stages of his madness. *Did* Hopie share the ability?

"Oh, see the flowers!" Hopie exclaimed. "Pretty yellow ones!"

"Yeah, they got golden pea here, Indian paintbrush—wild flowers galore, in summer. We'll be passing nigh Enver real soon; see, we're crossing the South Platte River; got to follow the river channels to find the best passes."

Hopie peered ahead. "Those mountains look awful tall," she said. "Can we really get over them?"

"Don't have to," Casey said grandly. "Got us a bridge—and a tunnel."

"A bridge *and* tunnel?" she asked, awed.

"There's a chasm just before the face of the last peak," he explained. "Train has to go level, or at least stay within a three percent grade. Can't yo-yo up and down the jagged edges. So the track bridges across the valley and bores right through the peak. You'll see."

Spirit and Megan watched the three, seeing them seeing the marvelous scenery. "I think that's half of what I love about him—and her," Megan murmured. Spirit understood. There was certainly something special there.

Then Shelia rolled up. "Train approaching, boss," she said. "Overtaking us from behind."

"Hey, there's no train scheduled now," Casey said.

"We know," she said. "That's why we're suspicious."

Hope held a quick council of war with Spirit and Coral. Spirit and Hope had both had battle training and experience in the Navy, and Coral was generally knowledgeable about in-close violence. Together they decided on their strategy for defense.

Hopie and Casey and Hope peered back, and now as the track curved they saw the pursuing train, steaming up the grade, definitely closing on them. "We'll pick up speed as we start down the other side of the Divide," Casey said. "But so will she.

The grade don't make no difference for this. She'll catch us, sure."

"Grade?" Shelia asked.

Hopie glanced at Hope and winked. "Come here, Shel," she said. "Look out the window. See the mountains out there? The snow? We're crossing the Great Divide, and it's been an awful climb, but now we're almost at the top, about to start down the other side. We old railroad hands call the slope the grade."

"Oh," Shelia said, nonplused. She was a fine woman, but it was evident that she did not see the mountains or the snow outside.

Casey smiled. "Most folks are mundane," he murmured. "That's their curse. They don't even know what they're missing. You and your little girl're the first real folk I've met in a long time, Gov'nor."

"We're very rare species," Hope agreed, and Hopie nodded emphatically.

"She sure favors you. I'd a known she was your kid right away, even if you hid her in a crowd. Bloodlines run true."

Spirit averted her face. The man was right in essence.

"Hang on," Casey said. "Reality's 'bout to take a beating."

Hopie and Hope smiled and took firm hold on the anchored furniture, as did the others in the chamber. This was going to be weird. But would it be strange enough to balk the enemy train?

First the train slowed on the track, and the enemy train overhauled it rapidly. Then, just as the other was drawing up parallel, the home train left the track and floated into the sky. Hopie gave a little sigh of amazement, locked into the vision, and Spirit was startled she had known what to expect.

They left the other train below. They maneuvered on the small wheel fans of the cars, angling them down to provide propulsion. The enemy train blundered on ahead, caught by surprise by the maneuver. Then the cloud enveloped the train, and darkness reigned outside. They had disappeared into their own great cloud of smoke.

"We got away from them!" Hopie exclaimed happily.

But the other train would soon enough zero in again, and then it would lock on and invade, in the manner of a pirate ship with a refugee bubble. Spirit did not like the odds.

Hopie glanced at Hope cannily. "But you're cooking something, aren't you?"

"I think you'd rather not know, honey."

"I think I'd rather *not* not know, Daddy," she countered. "I'm scared."

She spoke for those other than herself. It seemed better to reassure them all, especially Megan, who was sitting pale and tight-lipped. They were not combat personnel. Only Spirit and Hope had been toughened to this sort of thing, and Coral could handle it. The others were in trouble. "Mrs. Burton is arranging to shunt some steam inside," Hope said.

"Steam?" She didn't grasp the relevance.

"It will make them uncomfortable," he explained.

"Oh." She still didn't get it but did not pursue the matter further, and the others who did comprehend did not comment.

Megan, Hopie, and the other noncombatants retreated to the restaurant chamber, while the others took laser pistols and went out to defend the train from either end. Spirit guarded the entrance to the sleeping car. But she was merely part of the delaying action; what counted was what Mrs. Burton was preparing.

The pirates (for so Spirit thought of them) boarded. They did not come cautiously; they came with the abandon of grossly superior numbers, seeking to overwhelm the few defenders in an instant. Every lock opened simultaneously, and men came through each, holding their lasers ready. Spirit could track the action in different sections by Sheila's announcements on the intercom. Shelia was a noncombatant, but her calm coordination was vital.

The pirates were met by the careful fire of the defensive lasers. One beam from Spirit, one from Coral, and two men fell, each holed efficiently in the throat.

"Shoot for the face," Hope told Casey. "One beam per man, no more; they outnumber us." Of course, the enemy could also hear the com speaking, but that couldn't be helped.

"Progress, Mrs. Burton?" Hope asked, his voice sounding calm. He was playing his scene, but time was running short—very short.

"Close enough," she said. "I'm rigging a line; I can pull the cork from the diner; I think it'll work."

"Then unroll your line, Mrs. Burton. Get back here quickly—you and the engineers."

She strung her line, and the three of them retreated from the engine, entering the passenger car. But, as they reached the center, more men burst in at the now-unguarded engine lock, threw themselves into the crannies of the cab, and began firing into the passenger car.

"Cover your heads," Coral called. Then she hurled something. It skidded along the floor, rolled, fetched up at the far end, and exploded. A small grenade. "Now get into the diner—fast!" she ordered.

Mrs. Burton lifted her spool of line. "It's been severed!" she exclaimed, horrified. "I've got to reconnect it!" But that turned out to be unfeasible. "I'll set it off," she said. "You scoot back to the diner. I'll give you thirty seconds."

"But—"

"Better do it, boss," Shelia said on the com. "They're moving against Spirit; she'll have to retreat in a moment." True words; Spirit was already retreating.

"You want it this way, Mrs. Burton?" Hope asked.

"I'm old, boss," she said. "You gave me a good retirement. Now move!"

Spirit heard a loud hissing from the cab as she entered the chamber with the noncombatants. She knew what it meant.

"Farewell, Mrs. Burton!" Hope gasped as he launched himself at the door to the final chamber. It opened as he reached it; he stumbled in, and it closed behind him. Hopie was operating it; she had been alert and timed it perfectly.

Now they watched what happened beyond their sanctuary. The screen showed it clearly. A great rush of steam was pouring from the cab, billowing out, funneling through the locks from car to car in both trains, spreading throughout the length of both. They heard the screams of the men being burned. They could not escape; the steam quickly permeated every crevice of both trains, and it was super-hot. It was the steam that normally drove the propulsion propellers; Mrs. Burton had tapped into one of its lines, routing it into the passenger section. It reminded Spirit of the time she had fired the propulsion jet in the refugee bubble, scorching the pirates. It was having similar effect.

They checked Coral. She had been burned through the abdomen. She was alive but unconscious. They gave her a sedative to keep her that way; she would live but would only be in pain while conscious, until they got her to a competent medical facility.

"She did her job," Spirit murmured.

Indeed, she had. Coral had taken the shot that might otherwise have caught Hope. She was the loyal bodyguard to the last.

The battle was over. They let the steam dissipate, then went out to explore. Hopie wanted to come too, but all the adults forbade it.

There were dead men everywhere; the steam had suffocated them all. Spirit exchanged a glance with Hope. Yes, he too remembered the bubble in space!

Mrs. Burton was dead, too, of course—and that also echoed the past. "Helse," Hope murmured. Spirit winced. There was no similarity between the young, beautiful girl of the past and the old woman of the present, except this: each had knowingly sacrificed her life in horrible fashion to save theirs.

Hope leaned against Spirit and cried. She held him an comforted him as well as she could, stifling her own pain of the occasion. It had ever been thus. Hope was the feeling man, she the iron maiden.

*

The campaign continued, as Coral recuperated physically and the others did so emotionally. It was especially hard on Megan and Hopie, who had never been exposed to such malicious physical violence before. Hopie mourned "Grandma Burton," feeling guilty for surviving. But Shelia and Ebony, who had some prior experience, rallied to help them through, and so did Coral, despite her injury.

Hope entered the first state primary at Granite. He did not win, but came in second, significantly stronger than predicted. That, in the legerdemain of politics, translated into an apparent win. Suddenly he was a much stronger candidate than he had seemed before, and the media commentators were paying much more attention to him. In their eyes he had become viable. They had much fun with the Hispanic candidate, but his issues were sound, the unrest of the populace continued to grow, and the aspirations of those who were sick of the existing situation focused increasingly on him. He showed up more strongly in the next primary, becoming a rallying point for the disaffected, and the third one he won. Then he was really on his way.

Spirit was breathlessly busy organizing the details of the campaign, but it was successful. They played off the several factions of the party, and in the end Hope became the first Hispanic nominee. He chose Spirit as his running mate. The victory was sweet, but there was no pause in the campaign, for the incumbent Tocsin remained ahead in poll percentage points.

Slowly Hope gained, until he drew almost even, and the election was rated a dead heat. Then Tocsin pulled out all the stops. Among them was the old scandal of Hopie's origin: the charge that she was Hope's bastard baby. The fanatic press tried to get at Megan, but she was ready for this. What really finished it was Thorley's interview with her, in which the conservative gadfly asked her point-blank why she had agreed to adopt this child, who could not have been her own.

"I love her; she is mine now," she said, echoing Hope's response.

"But surely you have wondered about her origin—"

"I know her origin. That's why I adopted her."

Thorley shook his head eloquently. "Mrs. Hubris, you are a great human being." Very few understood how sincerely he meant that. His career, as well as Hope's, had been safeguarded by Megan's constancy. The issue faded; Thorley had defused it. That fact that this also saved Spirit's hide was politically incidental.

Another threat involved the Jupiter Navy. The first signal of trouble was when a formidable task force approached the planet for extensive maneuvers, with battleships and carriers hanging over individual cities as if targeting them. The public was assured that it was only a routine exercise, but it was a massive and persistent one.

Hope talked to his old Navy wife Emerald, who was in easy communication range because she commanded one of the wings. She was an admiral now, her brilliance as a strategist, proven in Hope's day, having enabled her to rise impressively.

"What's going on up there, Rising Moon?" he asked forthrightly. "As a candidate for the office of commander-in-chief, I believe I should be advised if the Navy has any problems."

Her dusky face cracked into a smile. She still loved him, and would help him any way she could. "Hope, you know there's been increasing civil unrest recently. There is concern that the election itself could be disrupted. So the Navy is on standby alert, ready to keep the planetary peace if that should prove necessary."

A form answer—with teeth in it. The Navy was under the ultimate command of the civilian president, Tocsin. Was he preparing for a military coup in the event he lost the election?

"It is good to have that reassurance," Hope said. "We know how important it is to preserve order." Which was another formal statement. "Give my regards to your husband." And there was the hidden one: her husband, Admiral Mondy, was the arch-conspirator of Hope's once tightly knit group within the Navy. He prized out all secrets and fathomed all strategies; he liked to know where every body was hidden. Hope was telling her that something was up and to alert Mondy if he was not already aware. He might be retired, but they knew he kept his hand in. That sort of thing was in his blood.

"Have no fear, sir," she responded, and faded out. That concluding "sir" was significant, too; she was tacitly recognizing Hope's authority. There would be a quiet unofficial alert among Hubris supporters in the Navy—and Spirit knew how strong that support was, and not just because Hope was a former Navy man. There had been considerable anger about the way he had been cashiered.

But these were incidental concerns compared to what came up next. Spirit received a special visitor on the campaign train: Reba of QYV. She didn't even inquire about Reba's business. "I'll fetch Hope." The woman nodded grimly.

"Hubris, this is off the record," Reba said immediately when Hope arrived. "It could mean my position—and your life. The press must not know."

"Let me bring one member of the press here, now, while I hear what you have to say. If he agrees to keep it secret—"

Reba sighed. "Thorley."

He nodded. "He happens to be aboard now." Indeed, Thorley was on temporary assignment to cover a leg of the campaign, and was a great comfort during Spirit's off moments.

She went to fetch Thorley, explaining the situation on the way. He nodded, evidently recognizing Reba's identity. He did have sources of his own. He joined them, sat down and waited.

"I am—an anonymous source," Reba told him.

"Understood."

"This woman knows me as well as any," Hope said. Thorley raised an eyebrow and glanced at Spirit. She nodded. He might be surprised that any woman should know Hope as well as his wife or sister did, but did not question it.

"I am in a position to know that a plan is afoot to kidnap Hope Hubris," Reba said carefully. "To destroy his credibility as a candidate for the presidency."

News indeed! Trust QYV to be the first to fathom Tocsin's mischief.

"This is not a plot to keep secret," Thorley remarked. "I differ with Candidate Hubris on numerous and sundry issues, but I do not endorse foul play."

"Some secrets must be kept until they can be proven," Reba said. "If this is published now the plot will fold without trace, and an alternate one invoked—one I may not be in a position to fathom in advance."

"Ah, now I see," Thorley said. "This fish you have hooked but not necessarily others. From this one the candidate may be protected, if the perpetrator does not realize that the subject knows."

"Exactly," she agreed. "The perpetrator is playing for high stakes and will not stop at murder as a last resort."

"Yet surely the Secret Service protection—"

"Could not stop a city-destroying bolt from space."

Thorley glanced at her shrewdly. "Certain mischief has been done, and hidden, the details accessible only to the president. Revelation of that mischief could put a number of rather high officials in prison and utterly destroy certain careers."

"You seem to grasp the situation," Reba agreed.

"And it seems that the details of that hidden mischief could no longer be concealed, if a new and opposing person assumed the presidential office at this time."

Reba nodded. "That office will not be yielded gracefully, regardless of the outcome of an election."

Thorley smiled. "Perhaps you assume that one conservative must necessarily support another. This is not the case. Some support issues, not men, and their private feelings may reflect some seeming inversions. I might even venture to imply that there could be some liberals I would prefer on a personal basis to some conservatives. Strictly off the record, of course." He smiled again, and so did Spirit. Thorley was an honest man, with a sense of humor and a rigorous conscience.

"Then you will withhold your pen?" Reba asked. She of course knew about his affair with Spirit.

"In the interest of fairness—and a better eventual story—I am prepared to do more than that. I prefer to see to the excision of iniquity, branch and root, wherever it occurs."

"Then perhaps you will be interested in one particular detail of the plot," she said grimly. "Candidate Hubris is to receive a message, purportedly from you, advising him that you have urgent news that you must impart to him secretly, in person, without the presence of any other party. When he slips his SS security net and goes to meet you, he will be captured by the agents of the plotters, taken off-planet, mem-washed, addicted to a potent drug, sexually compromised, reeducated, and returned to his campaign on the eve of the election armed with a speech of such nonsense as to discredit him as a potential president. He will be finished politically."

Thorley blew out his cheeks as if airing a mouthful of hot pepper. "This abruptly becomes more personal. As it happens, I have no need to summon the candidate to any private encounter; I have another contact."

"So you have said," Reba agreed, glancing at Spirit, who smiled. "I know that Hope Hubris would not fall for such a scheme. But it occurred to me that, considering the alternative—"

Now Hope caught her drift. "That I might choose to!"

"Choose to!" Thorley exclaimed, horrified.

"Hope Hubris is immune to drug addiction," Reba said. "His system apparently forms antibodies against any mind-affecting agent. His memory will return far more rapidly than is normal, and he soon will throw off the addiction to the drug. Which means—"

"That the attempt is apt to backfire," Thorley finished.

"Particularly if the candidate is forewarned and properly prepared," she agreed.

"And we would finally establish our direct link to the guilty party," Hope said. "Which would at last put him out of commission. No fifty-fifty gambling on the election; no waiting for a bolt from space. At one stroke, victory!"

It was hardly that simple, of course, and by no means safe, but they made the plan. In due course Hope Hubris, falling for an urgent counterfeit message, disappeared.

CHAPTER 13

Tyrant

The following two months were especially difficult, because not only did Spirit have to coordinate the campaign, she had to cover for Hope's absence. Because of course they were not about to admit that the campaign had lost its candidate. That would simply wash Hope out of the running and probably get him killed. They had received a terse note from an anonymous source saying that Hope Hubris was safe and well cared for, and would be returned to them in due course, provided they did not go public. He was being held hostage for their good behavior. So like any baffled organization, they covered up, hoping for the best.

They put out word that Hope was working very hard on a special project and was unable to campaign at the moment. Spirit took his place for existing engagements, and while she did not have Hope's flair for audience rapport, she did increasingly well. The staff did its part. Shelia maintained an effective wall, saying that she could not interrupt the candidate for anything. Coral, largely recovered from her injury, reported regularly to Hope's private office on the campaign train and guarded it physically from intrusion. Ebony ran constant errands to and from that office, never letting slip exactly what business she was on.

Even Thorley participated in his fashion, marveling in print what business could keep a candidate too preoccupied to campaign. "One must conjecture that it is of transcendent importance. Could he even be reconsidering the validity of liberalism itself? That were an end devoutly to be wished."

Hope was not returned until the eve of the election. He looked well, but somewhat vague; obviously he had been drugged for transport and was still coming out of it. A man stood close at his elbow, obviously an enemy guard to make sure he did not bolt or deviate from his script. Hope winced as if suffering a moment of pain, and that gave a hint: There was a valise there that surely contained a pain box. Spirit remained well clear, waiting for her people to scout the hall and identify every enemy agent. They needed to know all the enemy's tricks before nullifying them.

How much did Hope remember? He had been prepared for the mem-wash, and had marvelous powers of recuperation, but had they been enough? Hope looked around—and Spirit saw a small flash of recognition in his face. He had spied Thorley, who was in the press section. That meant he knew that Spirit's people were present. But they would have to nullify that pain box and that guard before they could do much else.

But they were not given time to neutralize anything. The broadcast light came on, and Hope had to start his speech, reading from the script before him. He spoke, describing a series of reform initiatives that aligned with what he had always supported. So far so good, but that could hardly be the whole story; there had to be a kicker coming later in the speech. Still, that gave Spirit's crew the time it needed to do its job. They had been prepared, and operated efficiently to neutralize the enemy agents. All except the one on stage with Hope. She signaled Thorley, who in turn gave Hope a cautious thumbs-up sign. Would Hope understand its full import?

"Now, I have been making promises," Hope said. "I realize that some of you are doubtful. You don't believe I can or will fulfill these promises as president. I would like to reassure you specifically." He glanced about again. "I see that some of my most effective critics are in attendance. You, sir—" He pointed at Thorley. "Do you doubt?"

Thorley smiled with that relaxed-tiger way he had. "I confess I do, Candidate."

"Well, I shall refute your doubt!" Hope declaimed. "Come up here if you have the nerve! Debate me face-to-face, and I shall destroy your silly points!"

Yes! He had caught on that he needed to get Thorley close enough to nullify the pain box.

The others in the small audience smiled now; this was more like his old form. "You are a glutton for punishment, my liberal Candidate," Thorley responded, rising huffily. "I came here ostensibly to report the event; however—"

"Report the event!" Hope exclaimed indignantly. "When did you ever do that, you sly provocateur? You have been sniping at me from the safety of your wretched column for years." He was playing his scene.

Thorley puffed visibly with indignity and marched up to the podium, carrying his briefcase. "Since you have seen fit to fling the gauntlet at my veracity, sir, I must advise you that in this valise I carry complete refutation to all your foolishly liberal postures."

And more than that. "Well, Sir Conservative, let's see you refute this: my position on tax reform. Do you oppose elimination of the nefarious loopholes that favor the rich?"

"Allow me to bring forth my armament," Thorley said, lifting his briefcase and twiddling with the latch. "A moment, if you please; it seems to have jammed."

"The way all your positions jam when challenged!" Hope retorted, and a ripple of mirth traveled through the audience. It was not that they were taking sides; they were merely enjoying the repartee, as they might the sight of two pugilists scoring on each other.

Thorley grimaced. "If you believe yourself to be so clever,

perhaps you can operate the latch more effectively than I can," he muttered.

"Certainly I can, you conservative incompetent," Hope agreed, taking the briefcase from him. In that manner he took possession of the pain-box tuner inside the briefcase. Now he could use it to nullify the box that controlled him. Now he was truly free of coercion.

But Thorley had done more. He had given Hope a small paper, on the advice of Emerald's husband Admiral Mondy, who had zeroed in on the psychology of the Tocsin campaign. It was a notice of significant news that Hope's captors had surely concealed from him: "One week past, Tocsin broke relations with Ganymede on suspicious pretext. Candidate cannot afford to ignore issue."

Hope smiled. Now armed, he was about to play another scene, something he could do better than almost anyone else. "I know you are waiting for me to address the issue of the hour. As you know, I was at one time Jupiter's ambassador to Ganymede. Naturally I regret what has happened. But before I commit myself, I would like to be sure I have the facts." He glanced at the camera. "Please establish a connection directly to Ganymede and ask the Premier to do me the kindness of speaking with me now."

There was another ripple of surprise. Few people were aware how close Hope had been to the premier of Ganymede, despite their differing politics. It was not to the Premier's interest to torpedo Hope; it was Tocsin he would be after.

They put through the call, of course. Formal relations might have been severed, but a public call from a candidate for president of Jupiter was too dramatic a move to deny. In a moment the Premier responded. His familiar face came on the hall monitor screens. "Where have you been, Ambassador?" he asked.

"That is a special story, Premier," Hope said. "I would appreciate it if you would tell me—and our Jupiter audience—as concisely as you can what happened to alienate our two planets."

The premier was amazed. It took seven seconds for his answer to return, because of the delay in transmission. "This is being broadcast? Alive?"

"Yes. You can verify it on your monitors." They waited another seven-plus seconds.

He had evidently done so. "*Señor*, all we know is that our ship left our port carrying a cargo of sugar bound for south Jupiter. Then these pirates board it and claim it carried Saturnine arms, and diplomatic relations are broken."

"*Did* it carry Saturnine arms?" Hope asked, nailing this down.

"Not when it left Ganymede, *señor*."

"But then how did the arms get aboard?"

"They were put there."

"By whom?" This might have been tedious, with the delay between each response, but Spirit saw that the audience was rapt.

"By your Navy, *señor*. Who else had access to our ship?"

"But why should the Jupiter Navy do that?"

"That I would like to know, *señor*. We have been selling sugar to your ships, and we have gotten along until this."

Before long, they had established that it was a frame done as a foul political ploy. The potential torpedo had been defused.

Then Hope got serious. He put through a public call to Emerald, and told her of the sub aboard which he had been imprisoned. The Navy bracketed it and demanded its surrender. Unfortunately the sub itself had been mined, and it blew up before it could surrender. Still, it was mute evidence of the complicity of the opposition party.

Hope played it through to a resounding endorsement. Then he fainted. But the crisis was over, and while he recovered from the abuse he had suffered in captivity, he won the election.

Later, Spirit talked with him, explaining how she had carried on the campaign in his stead. "If Tocsin had been smarter," he told her, "he would have kidnapped you instead of me!"

Then he had a longer session with Megan, and with Hopie. For he had indeed been sexually compromised while captive, placed in a cell with a lovely Hispanic woman who was supposedly another prisoner. He had promised her to save her baby, who had been used as a lever to make her cooperate. That baby was Robertico, and now that his mother was dead, he became Hope's responsibility. This took some explaining, but Megan and Hopie understood.

Meanwhile Spirit continued busy. She was in constant indirect touch with Emerald and Roulette, tracking the threatening Navy maneuvers, tracking the opposition effort to subvert the electors of the electoral college, watching the Jupiter congress where sneaky legislation was in the making, the state legislatures where the electoral results were being challenged, and had a special project going in a number of key Jupiter states. Hope had won the election, but as Reba of QYV had warned, that did not mean that Tocsin would give up power. They had to be prepared to foil the remaining dirty tricks that were in the pipeline. Shelia was coordinating the assorted watches, with Ebony on the computer constantly gleaning spot information. It was like hanging onto a barrel of slippery snakes; if any one got loose, there would be an election to pay.

The containment effort was generally successful, but one snake did get loose: a bill appeared in Congress, concerning something routine, bearing an obscure amendment relating to the political process. The bill passed shortly before the turn of the year, and the nature of the amendment became belatedly clear. It was a "clarification" of the requirement for holding major office in Jupiter. Above a certain level it was now illegal for any foreign-born citizen to hold office.

Spirit and Hope were foreign-born, technically, as they had come from the independent satellite of Callisto and had been naturalized as full Jupiter citizens when they left the Navy. Suddenly they were barred from taking the offices to which they had just been elected.

Naturally they challenged this bit of skullduggery on several grounds. They pressed for a rehearing and revote in Congress but were stonewalled; by the time that course was run, the day of taking office would be past. So they sued and got an expedited hearing before the Supreme Court itself, a week before the deadline of January 20, 2651. This was highly unusual, but the entire situation was extraordinary. Only direct access to the highest court could settle this in time.

The technical question was whether Congress had the right to pass ex post facto legislation affecting a candidate already elected. They argued that this was inequitable at best, and a mockery of the entire election process at worst. The opposition argued that this was not properly considered as new legislation but was merely a clarification of existing policy and therefore was valid. They succeeded in obfuscating the real issue—that of who was to be president—to the point that it became a question of Hope's fitness for the office. They were actually required to summon character references.

So while the twelve Supreme Court Justices listened in seeming passivity, Hope and Spirit suffered through the ordeal of being publicly judged as persons. All manner of innuendo was brought out in an evident effort to make them lose their tempers. They survived that, but we were almost torpedoed by their friends.

Hope's first Navy roommate, Juana, now a master sergeant, testified to his excellent character and confessed that they had first met in the Tail—i.e., Navy institution of sex. It was the Navy way, neither right nor wrong, but it was a way that was not generally understood in civilian life. It made both Hope and Spirit look like sexual perverts. Emerald gave similar evidence, except that she had actually married Hope, until it became expedient for her to go to another officer in order to obtain his expertise for the benefit of their unit. Again it was the Navy way; again it was damaging in the present context, as was the fact that Emerald had obvious Black ancestry. The Navy strove to extirpate racism from its midst, and mixed marriages were accepted without question, as were interracial liaisons in the Tail. But the civilian sector had not applied similar discipline to itself; interracial marriages, though legal, were socially problematical. Another black mark against Hope.

But the worst was Rue. Admiral Phist (Retired) and his wife Roulette, Ambassador from the Belt, were brought to Jupiter, to the court in the bubble of New Wash. They were cross-examined like criminals by the lawyer from the other side. "And isn't it true that you are a pirate wench?" the lawyer demanded of Roulette.

Roulette was now a striking woman of thirty-nine, retaining fiery hair and a figure that caused even the venerable heads of the Supreme Court Justices to turn. She had been in her youth the most physically beautiful of Hope's women, the veritable incarnation of man's desire, and her hourglass figure remained intact.

"Objection!" Hope's attorney protested, but Roulette waved him away.

"I can answer for myself," she said. She turned disdainfully to the interrogator and fixed him with a gaze that actually made him step back. "Yes, I was a pirate wench—until Captain Hubris made a woman of me."

"And how did he do that?"

"He beat me and raped me," she said with pride.

The attorney straightened up with over-dramatic shock. Obviously he had been fishing for exactly this response. "And did you press charges?"

"For what?" she inquired archly.

"For abuse! For rape."

She laughed. "That gentle man? He never abused me!"

"You love him yet!" the lawyer accused her.

"I have always loved him, ever since he mastered me. I

always will."

The lawyer pounced. "And what does your husband make of this?"

Admiral Phist smiled. "I understand completely."

"Your wife loves Hope Hubris, and you *understand*?"

"Of course. I love his sister." He made a nod in Spirit's direction, and Spirit smiled. She loved another man now, but considerable feeling for Gerald remained.

The Justices sat stonily. How was this affecting them? The lawyer's gaze cast about the chamber as if he were looking for something to hang on to. They fixed on Hopie. Suddenly they widened in wild surmise. "A Saxon woman," he said. "Still in love with her former husband, free to travel where she wishes, without objection by her present husband—" He whirled on Roulette. "*Where were you*, Roulette Phist, fifteen years ago?"

Roulette straightened, quickly assessing the situation. She glanced at Hopie. "Why, I don't remember. But—"

"Will you submit to a maternity blood-typing test?"

"You'll have none of my blood, mate!"

"Do you deny that you are the mother of that child?" And he pointed dramatically at Hopie, who seemed equally startled.

Roulette considered, playing her scene. "Where *was* I, that year, dear?" she asked her husband, her lovely brow furrowing in seeming concentration.

Admiral Phist grinned. "You have certainly traveled widely, Rue."

"This is no laughing matter!" the attorney snapped. "As you, Admiral, should be the first to recognize!"

Roulette studied Hopie openly. "She certainly is a pretty one," she said, turning once more to her husband. "She does favor Hope. Do you think I could have. . . ?"

Gerald had been looking at Spirit, and it was evident that he was catching on. Slowly he nodded, as if coming to a conclusion. "It does seem possible," he agreed.

"But if I claim her she would have to leave Jupiter."

"True," he agreed soberly. "It had better remain secret."

The lawyer was flushing, aware that he was being mocked. One of the Justices was quirking half a smile. "Madam, your blood type is surely on record. We can verify—"

"Lots of luck, shithead," she said sweetly. "I'm not a Jupe citizen. I came here only for the chance to see the man I love."

There was a muffled chortle from another Justice; evidently he understood about lovely women coming to see powerful men. But Spirit knew that none of this was doing Hope's case or her own much good. The executive and legislative branches of the government were already against him; where would the judicial be when its limited mirth abated?

There was a brief recess following this interview. Admiral Phist and Roulette approached the section where Hope sat with Megan, Spirit, Hopie, and Shelia. "Maybe we?" Roulette asked Megan.

Megan smiled with a certain gentle resignation, then swung her chair around so as to face away. Spirit and Hope stood up, and Gerald took Spirit into his arms and kissed her, and Roulette did the same to Hope. Hopie's eyes widened, as did those of a number of the other folk present.

Then they separated. "You have secrets yet," Gerald murmured to Spirit.

"You remarried another pirate wench almost before I was gone," she said with mock reproof. "What did you expect?"

He smiled wistfully. "But the dear knows who you'll marry."

"Iron maidens don't marry often."

They departed. Megan turned around again, ending her symbolic ignorance. "She's beautiful," she said to Hope. "She does still love you."

"I gave her up for you," he reminded her.

"I can't think why." In her view she was his fifth wife, following Helse, Juana, Emerald, and Rue, and she was jealous of none of the others.

But the scene was painful for Spirit. She had married only

The Iron Maiden

once, but loved twice, and lived a lie.

Next day the news arrived: the decision of the Supreme Court, by a vote of six to five, with one abstention, was in favor of the legislation. The interpretation stood, and Hope and Spirit were barred from assuming the offices to which they had been elected. All three branches of the government were against them, and they had lost, thanks to dirty politics.

But Spirit had prepared for this. "The game has not yet been played out," she said. "Tocsin has been concentrating on controlling the branches of the government; we have been concentrating on the will of the people. Ultimately that will must prevail."

Hope did not know what she had in mind, but trusted her to get it done. There was certainly a reaction from the people. Demonstrations erupted in all the major cities, from Nyork to Langels, so fervent that they overwhelmed the police, who, it seemed, were not unduly committed to their suppression. All across the planet the chant sounded: "Hubris! Hubris!" Hope and Spirit had been elected, and the popular mandate was being thwarted by a technicality, and even some pretty solid conservatives, such as Thorley, questioned that. The common man was angry. The migrant workers of the agricultural orbit rioted, doing no damage to the crops but hardly bothering to conceal the threat—in the event Hope did not take office. They regarded him as one of their own, with some justice. Likewise, women of every walk of life made a more subtle demonstration, as even some opposing legislators confessed ruefully; and those men who sought relief at establishments of ill repute discovered that the girls there were boycotting any man who did not support Hope's candidacy. Something very like a revolution was building.

The great ships of the Navy moved closer yet, and Spirit realized that Tocsin had anticipated trouble like this. If he declared a national emergency he would assume extraordinary powers—and would not use them to benefit democracy.

4206-ANTH

Hope had to pacify the animals. He addressed his supporters, in their separate categories, pleading with the Hispanics to
keep the peace so as not to reflect unfavorably on their kind,
which included himself and his sisters and daughter; he assured
the Blacks that he was doing everything in his power to see that
justice would be done; he begged the women to wait a few days
more, for something good might come of our various appeals
on technical grounds, or from the upcoming special election.

It worked. The tide of violence receded, and life returned
to an approximation of normal. But everyone knew that phenomenal activity could break out almost instantly if triggered.
The Navy ships orbited very close, ready and ominous.

Naturally Thorley commented. He pointed out something
few people had noticed: There was one of the perennial move-
ments afoot for a constitutional convention to balance the budget. Now the constitutional convention, he explained, was a
truly venerable device; it rose directly from the people, by way
of the several state legislatures, and once it passed certain hurdles,
it could not be denied. This one was now only two states shy of
the necessary two-thirds majority of state approvals to become
viable, and once it became established, it could not be dissolved by any power other than itself. The present system of
government, he reminded Jupiter, had been instituted by the
first constitutional convention, close to nine hundred years ago,
and could conceivably be overturned by another. Such a convention might be brought into being for a specific purpose, but
it was under no binding directive to stick to that purpose. "You
may suppose this is a simple matter of balancing the chroni-
cally unbalanced planetary budget," he concluded, "but it could
conceivably be the route to tyranny. A fire, once started, may
spread beyond the original site."

Exactly. That was Spirit's secret weapon, carefully honed.
The measure was currently up for consideration in five states,
and two of them were Golden and Sunshine. Spirit had been

shuttling her attention back and forth between them, working to get them to vote to establish the constitutional convention. In one of the brief interstices, as Spirit waited for a ship to transport her to Golden, Shelia approached her. "This is going to go that route," she said.

"Yes. Thanks to our planning and organization. You have performed splendidly, Shelia."

"I—we need to know," Shelia said hesitantly.

This was different. "Know what? You already know more about this campaign than anyone else. You're our communications hub."

"When it happens, Megan won't go along."

Spirit hadn't thought of that aspect. "I suppose she won't. Hope will have to go without her. He won't like that."

"He will be in pain. I—we can't stand to see that. If we can help."

"He has lost wives before. He'll survive."

"Yes. He will do what he has to do. We all will. But if we can—"

Something was skew. "Shelia, spit it out. What's on your mind?"

"When the time comes—will there be staff privileges?"

"Staff privileges? I don't follow."

"We love him. Coral, Ebony, and I. If he separates from Megan, are we entitled?"

Then Spirit caught on. The loyal staff members were also Hope's women. Like all of his women, they wanted him physically as well as emotionally. They had served loyally for fifteen years, risking their lives in the course of the campaign. They were indeed entitled.

"You—confined to the wheelchair—can you–?"

"If he helps. I—I have never been with a man, but I know I could, if he wishes."

And of course Coral and Ebony were able and more than willing. It might even help alleviate Hope's coming distress, and enable him to function better as leader. So it made sense on more than one plane. "Yes. If he wishes."

"Thank you."

Then it was time for Spirit's ship, and they separated. She leaned down to hug Shelia. "In fact, I hope he wishes," she said. "You—all three of you—are more than deserving." The woman smiled, seeming to glow.

And the political ploy happened. They had strong support in both states, for one was where Megan had been a representative, and the other was their own political base. On January 18 Sunshine ratified the bill, and on the nineteenth Golden followed suit. They could have done it earlier, but Spirit had arranged for the delay in order to keep this from being a public issue before it had to be. Timing was vital—and now was the time.

On the twentieth, the day the presidency was supposed to change, the constitutional convention convened. A clear majority of the delegates were Hope's supporters. The whole time Hope had been captive, Spirit had been touring the planet in his stead, giving public speeches and privately seeing to the selection of the delegates for this convention, so that there would be no confusion or delay at the critical moment. The skids had been greased, and the whole thing came into being with amazing ease, fully formed. Tocsin's forces, supposing they had victory in hand as long as they held Hope captive, had not been aware of this. They had been blinded by their own connivance, not recognizing Spirit for what she was: the mistress of their undoing. They really *should* have abducted the Iron Maiden instead.

So Spirit was in the state of Golden, where she had gone to oversee the final ratification. She caught a few hours of sleep she desperately needed, before tuning in on the national proceedings again. The skids were greased, but might still need attention.

Now the constitutional convention, governed by that majority, acted with extraordinary dispatch. First it declared that the budget should be balanced. Then it declared that, inasmuch as neither executive, legislative, nor judicial branches of the government had proved able or willing to do this in the past century, all were to be disbanded forthwith. Then its spokesman addressed Hope publicly:

"Hope Hubris, as the evident choice of the people of the United States of Jupiter, do you pledge to balance the budget without delay or compromise, if granted the power to do so?"

"I do," Hope replied. It really was not a difficult answer.

"Then this convention hereby declares Hope Hubris to be the new government of this nation, effective immediately."

And there it was. Spirit's counter-ploy had just trumped Tocsin's machinations.

There was political and social chaos. Ex-President Tocsin acted instantly. He renounced the validity of the constitutional convention, declared planetary martial law, and postponed the date of the changeover of the office of the presidency, to preserve, as he put it, "the present constitutional system of Jupiter." In the name of this preservation he directed the Jupiter Navy to enforce his edicts. He was, in fact, assuming dictatorial powers himself, as Thorley recognized.

But the states knew that the Constitutional Convention was valid, and there was open rebellion against Tocsin's machinations. Violence was incipient. What was the answer?

"We are hoist between Scylla and Charybdis," Thorley said when the news service was scrambling for precedents and comment. "Faced with a choice between a tyrant of the left or of the right."

"But which side is correct?" the interviewer persisted.

Thorley grimaced. "Appalling as I find the situation, I have to say that technically the constitutional convention is correct. This is a horrendous abuse of its office, but it does have the power to void our entire system of government."

"But the Navy—"

"Ah, yes, the Navy," he agreed. "If the Navy answers to President Tocsin, then perhaps might will make right. We are in an unprecedented pass."

The interview was interrupted for more pressing action. Tocsin was on again. "I declare Hope Hubris to be a traitor to Jupiter, and I order his immediate arrest. I am directing the Navy to dispatch a ship for this purpose."

The picture shifted to the representative of the Navy. Emerald's dusky face came on. Spirit smiled; they had labored to see that this admiral held this position at this time. There was no way Emerald would arrest Hope. "The Jupiter Navy recognizes the authority of the legally constituted government of the United States of Jupiter," she said. "This authority, as we understand it, now lies with the constitutional convention. The convention has appointed Hope Hubris as the government. Accordingly, the Navy answers to Hope Hubris." She paused, her gaze seeking Hope, and quickly the news cameras shifted to him. "What is your will, sir?" There was a certain relish in the way she accented that last word. The military was answering to the civilian, and a woman was answering to the man she loved.

But this was something Megan could not accept. She knew that Tocsin had to be stopped, but she could not support this mechanism. "Do what you must, Hope; I shall not deny you your destiny."

Hope reached for her and brought her to him while the planet beyond the camera watched. "Megan, I must have you with me!"

Her eyes were bright with tears. "No, Hope. I cannot go there. You must go alone."

"Megan, I'll turn it down."

Spirit suffered a siege of anxiety. This was a slip she hadn't anticipated. Megan could derail this train.

"You cannot, Hope. You must do what you must do, or all the planet will suffer worse. You—must be—the Tyrant." She was borrowing from Thorley's characterization: a tyrant of the left. That, as it turned out, was to name Hope's government.

"Not without you!"

"No!" she flared, jerking away from him. "Do it, Hope! Do it!"

Do it! Spirit saw Hope wince, and she knew why: Helse, his first love, lying in her wedding dress, entangled on the deck of the space-bubble, cried out those words to him, knowing they would destroy her. The first love of his life, sacrificing herself for the good of their group. Megan, in his heart, was the reincarnation of that girl, and in this respect she was the same. *Do it!*

Spirit could not help him; she was far away, watching the new video as his crisis unfolded. Hopie was there, sobbing; she knew this was family disaster. Shelia, Ebony, and Coral watched from the sideline, unable to intercede. The news holo cameras showed them all. This was in effect the victory of Hope's military wives over his present wife.

He had to do this himself, just as he had in the refugee bubble. With tears standing on his cheeks, he turned to the camera to give his first order to the Jupiter Navy. He had indeed assumed the mantle of a tyrant, by taking power outside the framework of the prior government, but he was clearly miserable. He had lost Megan.

But there could be no further hesitation. "Get me the most knowledgeable expert on the budget," he said to Emerald, the camera still on him, sending this historic scene to the entire System. "I promised to balance the budget and I shall do it."

"That would be in the civilian sector, sir," she said.

"I *am* the civilian sector," he said, taking hold. "Get me the personnel I need to do my job."

"We'll get on it, sir," she agreed with a certain muted satisfaction. "Meanwhile we'd better get you aboard ship."

"Aboard ship?" he asked querulously. "Why?"

"To guarantee your safety, sir."

Hope looked across at the Secret Service men who had been guarding him through his political campaign just past. "My safety is already guaranteed."

"Sir," Emerald said seriously. "There is a sub homing in on your bubble."

A sub! They all knew what damage a sub could do and who had control of one or more. Hope had defeated President Tocsin and now had taken power from him, but Tocsin was not a man to allow legality to stand in his way.

"We have detached a destroyer to pick up you and your personnel," Emerald continued. "But if that sub opens fire before we nullify it—"

"There are other people here!" he exclaimed. "Innocent residents! I can't go and leave them to be—"

"When you go, the bubble will no longer be a target, sir," Emerald said. "Wait there and be ready for pickup in fifteen minutes."

A Secret Service man nodded affirmatively. He knew this was best. Hope shrugged. "Shelia," he said. "Coral. Ebony."

They stepped forward. "Sir, better get suited," Emerald said.

"Suited?"

"That sub is firing. That will help us pinpoint it. But until we take it out—"

"But the other residents—"

"Had all better get suited," she said grimly.

Hastily they broke out the emergency suits, still on comera. The law required all bubbles to have suits for every resident, in case of accidental pressurization, as might happen if there was a leak. There were regular drills, but seldom was there really a need. The suit-alarm sounded, alerting everyone in the bubble.

However, Spirit knew that suiting was a complicated process for Shelia, because of the wheelchair and her inoperative legs. It was possible to get her into a suit, but it would interfere with her ability to function in her chair.

"They are finding the range," Emerald said, evidently reading her battle indicators. "Proceed to confinement alert."

That meant that each resident had to get into his or her chamber and seal it shut. This was to maintain normal pressure in individual apartments even when the bubble itself was holed.

"But I can't—" Hope protested, evidently thinking of Megan. He knew she didn't want him with her in their apartment now.

"Mine," Shelia said, propelling her chair rapidly down the hall. The Secret Service man followed, glancing around warily.

Her apartment was next to Hope's. She shared it with Ebony, so that the two were always handy for notes or errands. Coral's was on the other side, and she shared with Spirit, when Spirit was home. Coral went to join Megan and Hopie, to be sure they were all right.

They entered Shelia's apartment, and the Secret Serviceman took up his position in his suit, in the hall.

Spirit looked away from the scene on the screen. There was no pickup within the private apartment, of course, and it was pointless to watch the hall. Except for the evidence that the residential bubble still existed. If that sub scored before the Navy took it out—

Yet at this time of crisis, she found herself diverted by another matter. Megan had left Hope, though she loved him. He was now alone with his loyal secretary who also loved him. No one knew whether they would survive the next minute, let alone the next year. What would he do with Shelia?

Actually Shelia had a video transceiver built into her wheelchair, so they remained in close touch with Emerald. But that was closed circuit; the news service could not tap into it unless invited. Still, there was evidence of Hope's directives, because suddenly the bubble's gee-shield cut off, causing it to drop as the gravity of Jupiter took hold. Pineleaf, like all the towns and cities of Jupiter, was a good deal more solid than the atmosphere and would plummet to the hellish depths if not shielded from the main effect of the planet's gravity. The pressure at this level was about five bars—five times the pressure of Earth's atmosphere at sea-level—which the bubbles and suits were constructed to withstand. The pressure below was much greater. Too great a drop would cause a bubble to implode—a far more certain demise than depressurization. But it was the only motion it could quickly make. This was an extremely nervy ploy.

The exterior pickup came onscreen, and Spirit found herself watching, unable to keep her gaze away. The bubble was now spinning loose, precessing like a failing top, as it dropped. It had been struck a glancing blow by the sub's shell. Had it remained in proper orbit, that shell would have holed it.

The invisible sub exploded. The Navy had zeroed in on it, tracking its fire, and destroyed it. There was an intolerable flash. That threat was gone.

But the bubble was still falling. They were surely struggling to reactivate its gee shield, but meanwhile its survival was horribly uncertain. There was no signal from within.

Spirit closed her eyes and focused on the only thing that might divert her from the incipient threat to her brother. He was perhaps about to die, with a worthy woman who loved him. Of course he would love her. That was his nature. He loved every woman, and every woman loved him. Normally it was muted, but at times it got naked, and this would be such a time. Staff privilege . . .

Spirit pictured him lifting Shelia out of her wheelchair—easy to do in the lack of strong gravity—and laying her out on the floor. He stripped away her clothing, and his own. He stroked her breasts. Shelia might be paralyzed from the waist down, but she had fine breasts. He kissed her and she clung to him, her face wet with her tears or his, and her tongue met his as her legs lifted to wrap around his. He was on her in an instant, pumping his essence into her, and she sighed and convulsed against him and relaxed at last. They lay embracing, the sweat of their exertion between them, delighting in their union though their sexual passion had passed. And of course he had a vision of Helse. Helse was always his cover when he loved illicitly.

Shelia's legs lifted? They *couldn't* lift. He would have had to lift them for her. Yet for a moment Spirit had seen it happen in her mind. As if she herself were the woman, doing what she could do. Perhaps *would* do, in such a situation. If no one else could know. She loved her brother in all the ways a woman could. "But the dear knows who I'll marry," she thought in song.

Then the news came: Hope Hubris and his staff had been rescued. They were on the Navy flagship. Spirit had been day-dreaming while others acted. She was ashamed.

Meanwhile, hell was breaking loose on Jupiter. Emerald and the Jupiter Navy were handling it, but Spirit knew she needed to get back to her brother's side in a hurry. He was not a detail man, not an organizer, and not invariably tough minded; that was her job. He was not the iron man; she was the iron maiden.

Spirit took a flight directly to New Wash, and the White Bubble. Former President Tocsin, whose name was justly pronounced "toxin," had bartered for a pardon and safe passage off the planet. That galled her, but they had had to settle the old order quickly, to be able to focus on the new. She slept on the flight, knowing it might be long before she had the chance to rest thereafter.

She arrived just before the Navy delivered Hope, so waited for him in the air lock of the White Bubble.

They met and embraced, and for a moment it was as if she were twelve again, and he fifteen. He needed her, and she had always known that, but she needed him too. Together they could face almost anything.

But there was no time to be maudlin. Spirit got right to work. "You have done a good job of consolidating power, Hope. Now you need to establish a government, at least a temporary one."

"I will declare the present mechanisms of government to

continue until further notice," he said. "Then I will revise them as convenient, piecemeal."

She nodded appreciatively. "You are better organized than I thought you might be."

"It's not my notion," he confessed.

"Oh?"

"Beautiful Dreamer."

"Oh." She understood the reference, of course, but took a moment to digest the implication. Hope had been consorting with the dead, again. "Then let's make notes on your speech." She turned to Sheila. "Set up a planetary address at the earliest auspicious moment."

"Twenty-one minutes hence," Shelia said evenly.

That was a shock, but it was Shelia's business to know. "We'll make it," Spirit said. What choice did they have?

They huddled over it, working out suitable phrasing. Hope was to declare himself to be the new government of North Jupiter, by the authority of the Constitutional Convention to Balance the Budget. He would declare all the current institutions to remain in force until further notice, on an advisory basis. The leaders of Congress and the governors of all the States of the Union would have twelve hours to publicly acknowledge their acceptance of this state. The members of the Supreme Court would acknowledge similarly. Hope would not actually say "Or else," but he would pause meaningfully, letting the implication sink in.

They made the deadline. Fortunately Hope had always been apt at public speaking. He made it sound like a well considered and orderly program. That was an aspect of his genius. It seemed to go over well enough; the people did support him, and the politicians were not slow to catch on to political reality.

Immediately after the speech, they turned to the matter of appointments. There were many good men and women; the trick was to spot them rapidly and obtain their cooperation. Hope would have to do a lot of personal interviewing, because that was another aspect of his genius: to know people. But he seemed doubtful. She would have to snap him out of that.

She laughed. "Sometimes I think of you as the fifteen-year-old boy I knew when our situation changed." Then she leaned across and kissed him on the mouth, as he sat startled. It had the desired effect: he forgot about uncertainty. It was a real pleasure for her, but also pain. If only—

She refocused on present business. Soon they had a number of key appointments, based on military associates they knew they could trust. Loyalty was not supposed to be more important than competence, but in this wild new situation it was vital.

And in the middle of it, a baby arrived. It was the child of Dorian Gray, the woman Hope had seduced while captive on the sub. He had promised to rescue her son, Robertico. The woman herself had perished with the sub, but here was the baby. And so while they discussed the nationalization of Congress, to deal with recalcitrant opposition members, and tried to handle international negotiations, Hope came to be holding a wet baby boy.

Fortunately Shelia took him over, for a while. Then Hope tried to change the damp diaper, but lacked recent experience. Spirit did not offer to help; she had even less experience. It would have been a minor crisis in the best of times; as it was, it was downright embarrassing. What a beginning for the Tyrancy!

It was Senator Stonebrigdge who made the obvious suggestion: fetch Hopie. Spirit called her, and Hopie, delighted, agreed to come to handle this emergency. She arrived in due course and set up shop in a corner of the room. That was the beginning of a long association; Hopie became Robertico's big sister, and all was well with him thereafter.

It was time to rest; they had been working hard for ten hours without respite, and they had to stop. Coral took Hope away; Spirit realized that it was her turn for staff privilege. She was the most athletic of the women, and surely as knowledgeable in sexual matters as she was in martial arts. She would give him a good night.

And what would Spirit do? Thorley was far away.

Stage by stage, somewhat hit or miss, they assembled the new government. But in two more days Hope received a gift from Saturn that was to change his life. It was actually to facilitate the operation of the Tyrancy, by distracting Hope so that the others could handle most business their way, but at first it was just a mystery. Its name was Amber.

CHAPTER 14

Tyrancy

Hopie, enlisted to take care of baby Robertico, soon had larger missions. She was a fine spirited girl at age fifteen, and Spirit found it difficult to mask her pride in her unacknowledged daughter. When Hope told her she would need to be tutored to complete her education, she alertly set him back with examples of the uselessness of contemporary studies. She made her point, but he had the last laugh: he appointed her head of the Department of Education. When she protested that she lacked the knowledge to institute an effective reform of education, he sent her to see his leading critic: Thorley. Her unacknowledged father. Sometimes Hope lucked into decisions of genius.

Meanwhile Saturn, ever ready to seize an advantage, was working over the new ruler of Jupiter. It sent troops to take over the government of its nominal minion Ganymede, deposing the Premier, who was Hope's unacknowledged friend. So much of reality was unacknowledged! But appearance was at times more important than reality.

Shelia sent word out, and soon there was a literal council of war with Emerald, Mondy, Spirit and Hope. Mondy was fading physically, but his mind remained sharp; he understood the issues perfectly, and had excellent advice. He also sought and got input from Reba Ward of QYV. All this was necessary because of the dire nature of the threat. If Saturn took over

Ganymede, the balance of interplanetary power would shift significantly in its favor. But if Jupiter invaded Ganymede, it would be clearly in violation of interplanetary protocol, and the Tyrancy would lose what little credibility it had.

They were between Scylla and Charybdis again—or in the contemporary parlance, CT and BH. To be caught between contra-terrene matter, whose very touch would render a person into something like a miniature nova, and a black hole, that would suck them in and crush them to the size of the nucleus of an atom. Politically, they were between capitulation and potential holocaust.

QYV recommended the use of one of Jupiter's anonymous subs to take out the Saturn ship approaching Ganymede. It would seem that it had struck a mine by accident, and therefore would not be an open act of war. But this remained an exceedingly chancy ploy.

Meanwhile, Hope held a press conference, necessary to reassure the public that things were under control and that the press really was not being censored. Spirit decided to make the point in a mischievous way: she planted a question without telling Hope.

It was from a respected member of the Holo Guild: "Tyrant, suppose I were to call you a gnat-brained, pigheaded, philandering son of a spic?"

It took Hope only a moment to recover. He hauled his open mouth closed. "I really don't think of myself as gnat-brained," he responded.

There was laughter, timorous at first, but soon swelling into heroic proportion. If the Tyrant could be openly insulted with impunity, there was no suppression.

Then the Ganymede crisis intensified: Saturn had anticipated Jupiter's ploy, and sent one of its own subs along with his ship. That sub took out the Jupiter sub. The Saturn ship was not stopped.

Spirit sighed. "Brother, we are in trouble."

"Double trouble," he agreed morosely.

"Maybe we can still pull it out," she said. "We can take the offense. We can accuse Ganymede of blowing up one of our strayed vessels and demand reparation. We can get so outraged by the unprovoked attack that we invoke the Navy. We could pick that ship out of space long-distance if we used a saturation launch of homing missiles."

"But that would be an overt act of war!"

"If that ship docks, we'll soon be at war regardless," she pointed out.

He pondered, ill at ease. "It would also be a lie," he said. "Covert activity is one thing; a lie is another."

"The truth is that the Premier of Ganymede tipped us off," Spirit reminded him.

"No. To preserve a confidence is not to lie. We must find a way to act without violating either the confidence or the truth."

She shook her head as if in frustration. Then she took hold of him and kissed him. Sometimes she just couldn't help herself. "My brother, you are my conscience. Without you I would be lost."

Coral exchanged a glance with Shelia and nodded.

Spirit regrouped. "Well, Saturn now knows that we had a sub in there. Would it be fair to say that we had a suspicion about their ship, that we now feel is confirmed?"

"Yes," he agreed. "But we can't say what our suspicion is."

"Suppose we accuse them of renewed arms smuggling? That's not exactly what they're doing, but it is something Jupiter has always been sensitive about. After that business with the impounded ship . . ."

So it went out to the media: the accusation that Ganymede was violating the covenant and shipping arms again. An alert went out to the Jupiter Navy, and the ships changed course and made for Ganymede. Of course, it would be days before the majority of them were in position, but the order was dramatic enough.

Saturn bluffed it out. Spirit exchanged a glance with Hope. "He thinks I am made of putty," he said.

"Saturn does not respect putty."

"What can we do to dispel the putty image?"

She was ready for that. "We can put the Navy on Full Alert." That would signal the seriousness with which Jupiter viewed the present situation.

"Do it," he said.

Shelia made the call. Within a minute Emerald's dark face was on the main screen. "You sure, Tyrant?" she demanded.

"Full Alert," he repeated. It was an indirect signal, but a potent one.

Saturn did not heed the signal. It refused to stop the ship. So Jupiter sent a stronger signal: it fired on the ship. That was an act of war, but could still be stopped short of war.

There followed an informally but carefully scripted shouting match with the Premier of Ganymede, its real purpose being to show that the Premiere had no complicity in what Jupiter was about to do, which was to invade Ganymede. At this point, Hope Hubris was a far better friend to the Premier than was Saturn, but neither party could say that.

They tracked Saturn's ships in the Jupiter sphere. They were now on alert. Jupiter's moved into position to oppose them, even as Saturn ships defending Saturn moved to counter Jupiter formations there. The invasion of Ganymede might be a rather serious joke, but the siege of Saturn was not. If any missile was fired at a Jupiter city—

Spirit's stomach was knotted. They really were at the brink of System War Three. Any tiny miscalculation by either major party could set it off. She looked at Shelia, and saw her face composed, evincing no concern about anything other than her immediate business. What a woman she was, crippled in body but absolutely reliable in performance. Of whatever type. Hope trusted her absolutely, and so did Spirit. Spirit hoped her own mask was as good.

Now the White Bubble was deluged with calls from its own population. They had not censored the news; the people were catching on that real trouble was brewing.

"Sir, you may want to watch this," Shelia said, glancing up, and put on a local interview.

It was Thorley, speaking editorially. The startling thing was who was in the background: Hopie. Evidently she had been consulting him about the prospects for education when caught by the Saturn crisis, and the news pickup caught them both.

"*That* will make tongues wag!" Spirit murmured appreciatively.

"... seems to be madness," Thorley was saying. "There is no reputable evidence I know of that the Saturn ship carries contraband, and to launch an attack on the mere suspicion—"

"My father's not mad!" Hopie exclaimed. "He always has good reason for what he does!"

Spirit winced inwardly. The girl was loyal, but should have known when to keep her mouth shut.

Thorley gave a wry smile. "Such as appointing a child to be in charge of education?"

"He told me I could do the job if I got the best advice!" It was clear to Spirit that despite the extreme seriousness of the occasion, they both were enjoying this. Hopie because she loved argument, and Thorley because he loved to see her doing it. There was a certain similarity between them, by no coincidence. It seemed obvious to Spirit, but she was hardly objective; she loved them both.

Thorley shook his head. "Mayhap he is but mad north-north-west; when the wind is southerly, he knows a hawk from a handsaw." He returned to the camera, smiling in the eloquently rueful way he had. "It seems the Tyrant sent his daughter to me for advice."

Spirit heard someone laugh; it was Shelia, losing her composure for the moment. She knew their relationship, of course;

she knew everything. There was no way Thorley would ever give Hopie bad advice, but the public would suspect it.

" . . . yet it remains difficult to see the logic in such brinksmanship," Thorley was continuing. "In a matter of hours the Tyrant has brought us closer to the brink of holocaust than has been the case in twenty years. I am, candidly, appalled."

He was hardly the only one. The rest of the System did not know that the invasion of Ganymede was a sham. Ganymede even carried it live, so that everyone could see. That was dangerous, because troops were not necessarily good actors.

There was a blazing battle at the perimeter as the Gany forces charged. They had to expose themselves in the straight access tunnels, and the Jupiter troops mowed them down.

It was beautiful. The Gany troops clutched themselves and collapsed. Had Spirit not known they were not hurt, she would have winced. They had been well coached. Spirit knew it would not deceive Admiral Khukov for an instant, but she also was pretty sure that he would not expose the ruse.

He would read it correctly, censor the Saturn records of anything that would undermine the effect, and send the tapes on to his superiors: the clear violation of Gany territory the Tyrant had initiated. Then he would wait for his orders.

The Saturn Premier Karzhinov temporized: he issued an ultimatum. "Withdraw your troops from Ganymede by 1200 hours, January 28, 2651, or the Union of Saturnian Republics will be forced to consider your action an act of war."

"You're sure Karzhinov can be bluffed?" Spirit inquired.

Hope laughed. "Who's bluffing?"

Spirit smiled, but she was worried. She understood her brother well, but she got nervous when he got like this. His nervy diplomacy could so readily slide into madness.

The deadline was several days distant. The invasion continued, but Spirit and the others were able to catch up on some sleep. She hoped that would stabilize her brother.

Then Megan made a public call. Coral, Ebony, and of course

Shelia were with Spirit as they watched Hope receive it. "Hope, for the love of God!"

Megan didn't know how much of the crisis was sham, and Hope couldn't tell her. If Saturn was not bluffed out, the crisis could become all too real. If he broke, and told her—

The tableau held for a brief eternity. Then he turned away from her. Shelia cut off the connection. It was done.

"I remember when you raped Rue," Spirit murmured.

He nodded. Rape was an abomination, but he had been forced by circumstance to do it, and Spirit had witnessed it. What he had just done to Megan was more subtle and more cruel but as necessary. It was surely one of the hardest things he had done, because he loved her and had never before deceived her.

They waited, and the System waited with them. The planet of Jupiter, and probably Saturn also, had paused with bated heartbeat, waiting for the ax to fall—or turn aside.

"Sir."

Spirit saw her brother jump at Shelia's word; perhaps he had not been aware he was dozing. "Um."

"Admiral Khukov."

Now he was fully alert. "On."

Khukov's familiar face appeared. "Will you meet with me, Tyrant Hubris?" he inquired formally in English.

It was evident by his bearing that victory was at hand. Khukov and Hope trusted each other, because of their similar talents, though their motives and loyalties were in many respects quite opposed. "I will, Admiral."

"I will send a boat for you and your sister."

The screen went blank. "Sleep," Hope said. "The crisis has passed."

"Should we make an announcement, sir?" Shelia asked.

He walked over, leaned down, and kissed her on the forehead. "That a meeting has been arranged. No more. Then rest until the ship comes."

Spirit and Ebony departed, suddenly dead tired. It had been a brutal siege, a contest of wills, but victory was at hand. It was good to relax at last.

*

In due course Spirit and Hope, both cleaned and changed, boarded the Saturn shuttle ship. It might seem strange to have the leader of Jupiter so blithely step into the power of Saturn, without even his bodyguard, but, of course, Hope knew Khukov personally, and the whole of the Solar System was hostage to their understanding.

They relaxed and had an excellent meal served by a comely hostess who spoke English. The personnel were uniformly courteous, though they did not speak English. The two guests were permitted free run of the ship.

"Where would you put it?" Hope asked Spirit in Spanish.

"Officer's dayroom," she replied.

He nodded. They rose from their completed meal, went to the region reserved for the ship's captain, and knocked on the bulkhead. In a moment it slid open, and they entered.

Inside stood a pool table, and beyond the table stood Admiral Khukov, cue in hand. Without a word Hope took another cue, oriented on the table, and took the first shot. Spirit took a seat in a comfortable chair and watched. No one seemed surprised; this was the only way a truly private meeting could be arranged. Perhaps even the crew of this shuttle ship had not been aware of Khukov's presence aboard it.

They played, and Khukov beat Hope handily. "Hope, you are out of shape!" he said in Spanish.

Hope replied in Russian. They continued playing. Now they spoke in English, so Spirit could understand. "There will be the usual apparatus, every word and gesture recorded and analyzed from the moment you board the flagship. Speak no secrets there."

"My *brain* is not out of shape, Admiral!"

"When your wife cried 'For the love of God!' and you turned away, Karzhinov knew that nothing would turn the madman aside. He faced the gulf of the holocaust, and his mind broke. We of Saturn know the nature of war on our soil; we fear it deeply. He will retire; his successor is not yet known."

"We, too, know the meaning of losses," Hope said, and Spirit nodded, feeling the pain of what they had experienced in the refugee bubble.

"Madness"

"Two scorpions in a bottle," Hope said.

Khukov smiled briefly. "Would that they were male and female!"

There was a period of silence. Then Hope changed the subject. "Shouldn't you be there, not here?" he asked.

"First I must negotiate a significant agreement, to show that I alone can defuse the crisis."

"What do you need?"

"Your dance with the Premier of Ganymede is very pretty."

"This would be more difficult at light-hours range."

"Yet the game can be played with caution. I cannot say precisely what moves I will need to make, but if the madman responds only to me . . ."

Hope nodded. "And thereafter?"

"What would you have, Hope?"

Hope glanced at Spirit. "Disarmament," she said.

Khukov looked at her, and for a moment she felt the eerie power of his understanding. He nodded. "Yet it must be gradual. First a hold, then failure to replace aging craft."

"Agreed."

They reached across the table and shook hands. Thus was the fate of the Solar System decided.

"I have a gift for you," Khukov said after a moment.

"We did not come prepared for the exchange of gifts," Hope protested.

It did not matter. Soon they separated, so that Khukov could make his way secretly back to his ranks and no one would know where he had been. In due course the shuttle docked at the flagship, and Spirit and Hope were ceremonially ushered aboard. They met formally with Khukov, under the cameras, using translators, he addressing them in Russian, Hope responding in Spanish.

Hope's words were reasonable, but there was a certain glimmer of madness in his expression, and Spirit cautioned him more than once, quietly, as if fearing that he was about to be set off. The Saturn officers present affected unconcern, but they noticed. Yet Hope responded fairly well to Admiral Khukov's direct attention; it was evident that Khukov had a superior touch. This was hardly surprising; it was that touch that had brought him to his present level of power—and would take him that one step beyond. Saturn was safer when his hand was at the helm, especially when dealing with the lunatic Tyrant. That was the point of this particular charade—and there was considerable truth in it.

Then came Khukov's little surprise. As they prepared to depart the flagship he held them one more moment. "Tyrant, allow me to present you with a token of my esteem for you," he said in English.

A young girl, really a child of ten or eleven, approached. She held her left hand up. On the middle finger was a platinum ring, and mounted on the ring was a large amber gem. In fact, it was not merely the color of amber; it was amber itself.

Hope took the child's hand and peered at the amber. It was clear and finely formed, and deep inside it was embedded an insect—a termite. He smiled, taking this as a kind of little joke, for a termite was not a pretty bug. But Spirit perceived something else: this was no ordinary child. There was a curious vacuity about her, a lack of human emotion and expression. Had she been lobotomized? No, her reflexes seemed to be normal, merely uninvoked. Mind-wash? Possibly. Why had such a person been selected to bring the gift, instead of a pretty model?

Spirit distrusted this, though she knew there was no threat to Hope.

She glanced at Khukov, and caught him looking at her. Again she felt that talent, so like Hope's own. It both intrigued and frightened her. This man was now a tacit ally—but what of the occasion when he was not? She smiled as if flirting, to cover her misgiving, and looked away.

"This is an interesting gift," Hope said, glancing up at Khukov. "But it becomes the girl, and I would hesitate to take it from her."

Khukov smiled. "No need, Tyrant."

Spirit caught on. "The girl is the gift," she murmured.

"The girl!"

"As you say, it would not be kind to take her treasure from her," Khukov said. "I know you treat children well, Tyrant, and she is of your culture. You will find her interesting."

Hope was evidently about to protest, but Spirit knew that would not be politic. "Thank you, Admiral Khukov," she said firmly. "We shall see that she is properly treated. What is her name?"

"Amber," he replied, and at that, the girl's eyes widened and her head lifted in recognition.

"Come with us, Amber," Spirit said gently. The girl did not change expression, but she stepped toward Spirit. Evidently she understood. Spirit was bemused by the odd gift, but also by her own reaction to Khukov. The man had perhaps inadvertently shown her his power; were she ever alone with him, he would be able to take her to bed, if he so chose, exactly as Hope could do with any woman who caught his fancy. There was no chance of that happening, but it made her feel uncomfortably vulnerable.

So they returned to the shuttle and to Jupiter, bringing the strange girl with them. The first thing they noted was that Amber was mute. She understood what was said and responded to it, but she did not speak. They had the medical staff examine her and ascertained that she had no congenital or other inhibition; she *could* speak but simply did not.

Amber was older than she seemed. Without her birth record there was no certainty, but physically she was about thirteen, not eleven. She seemed younger because she had not yet developed. This did not seem to be any artificial retardation, just natural variation. Hopie had assumed the physical attributes of maturity by the age of twelve; other girls might delay until age fourteen. The intellectual and social attributes took longer to complete, but of course this could be a lifelong process. Amber was healthy, just a little slow, physically and mentally. Certainly she was no genius.

Why had Khukov given her to Hope? He surely had not done so frivolously. He had to have had excellent reason. They would have to discover that reason.

Spirit set Amber up with Hopie, who had a room with Robertico. Hopie was entitled to a room of her own, but she was generous in this respect; she shared. Robertico was devoted to her and slept quietly when she was near. Amber, though only two years younger than Hopie—possibly only one year—was so obviously better off with company that it seemed best to move her in. The two of them became like sisters, the one highly expressive, the other silent, and Robertico like a baby brother. This allowed Hope and Spirit to proceed with the Tyrant business with minimal distraction, knowing that the gift girl was well cared for.

Hopie found the riddle of Amber as intriguing as Spirit did. She talked with the girl, or rather to her, for Amber never responded in words. Hopie soon became a kind of translator for Amber, ascertaining her preferences and informing others. Amber liked Hispanic food and didn't care for sonic showers; she preferred to wash up with a damp cloth. She always wore the amber ring; the only time she became truly distressed was when the medics tried to remove it for examination. They had finally compromised by examining it on her hand, the radiation showing up her finger bones as well as the interior of the ring, and she had no objection. Hopie wanted to teach her to read, for she seemed not to know how, but Amber just stared blankly at the printed words. She was unable to relate to anything more technical than pictures.

Soon Admiral Khukov was confirmed as Chairman of the Council of Ministers of North Saturn. The result was immediately beneficial to both parties. Saturn abandoned its effort to corrupt Tanamo Base, and the Premier of Ganymede retained his power. Trade, originally limited to sugar, gradually broadened. The mock invasion of Ganymede faded from the media, and no one seemed to question the fact that there were no actual dead from that war. Hope, and therefore Spirit, got on with the complicated business of governing North Jupiter.

There were intractable problems to handle, and no easy solutions. Every proposed reform led to immediate complications, requiring modifications elsewhere in a chain of effects that all too often completed devious circles and came back to knock down the original reforms. It had been easy to see the flaws of the old system, but it turned out to be difficult to fix them. Taxation was an example: nobody wanted to pay, but everyone wanted to receive governmental benefits such as law enforcement, retirement income, medical care, and bubble maintenance. The intangible strengths and weaknesses of the economy determined much of what was feasible, regardless of the competence of the proprietors. The trick was to work out acceptable compromises. It didn't seem to matter whether the administration was liberal, conservative, or radical; the compromises had to be hammered out.

Spirit tackled the problems with a will. This was similar to the administration of a growing battalion in the Navy. This was her element. Hope was the front man, putting his face on the Tyrancy, handling the myriad people involved, but though he had a keen understanding of matters, his heart was not in the dull details. Spirit's heart was; they were not dull to her.

Still, there were special problems. There were attempts to assassinate Hope, some of them clever enough to get past Coral and the secret service. Most of them never came to his attention; Spirit handled them and left him innocent. But some could not be hidden, like the laser beam from a floodlight when he made a public address in Nyork. He had been delayed a few seconds by a trifle—a child had begged for the touch of his hand, and he had obliged—so had approached the lectern late. The very precision of the trap's timing defeated it. He was unharmed, but much aware of the nearness of death. This made him nervous, understandably.

He mentioned this to Spirit. "I am being channeled into the trap of inadequate feedback from the people. Yet, if I don't isolate myself, sooner or later an assassin will catch me. What can I do?"

"I face the same problem myself," she said. "I am now too public a figure to employ my male disguise. There have been more attempts on our lives than I have bothered you with; we are all hostage to our position."

"There has to be an answer," he said.

She quirked a smile. "Go to Q."

It was perhaps a joke, but he took it seriously. He donned a disguise and went to see Reba Ward. She, like all women with whom he had contact, was smitten with him, if not actually in his orbit. She would help him, but he would have to pay her price, and that meant sex.

He returned seeming somewhat shaken, and the girls teased him unmercifully. "Did she teach you anything, Tyrant?" Coral inquired.

"Um." He obviously preferred to avoid the subject.

"Are you limping, sir?" Shelia asked.

He straightened up. "Num."

"I hear those older women can have a lot of experience," Ebony put in.

"Um." He actually seemed to be blushing.

The four women exchanged a meaningful glance. Reba had evidently worked him over well.

Now it was Spirit's turn. "Did she answer your question?"

He spread my hands. "She never spoke!"

They all laughed. Then Shelia tapped her armrest. "She sent a message, sir: There will be an alternate identity created for you."

So he would have not a place but an identity in which to hide. That answer was obvious in retrospect.

But there was another problem he did not yet know about, and Spirit was not at all sure how it should be handled. It was the girl Amber. Hope, with marvelous insight, interviewed her and solved the riddle of her gemstone. It was a mechanism that put her into a spot trance state and changed the language she could fathom. She could understand more languages than most of the others had heard of, but speak only Spanish—when set in that mode. He tuned her to Spanish, and suddenly she was completely communicative. But much of her mystery remained, because she did not fully know her own nature, so could not answer all his questions. In the course of their first full dialogue, the subject of Hopie came up, and Amber naively confided that Hopie blamed herself for Hope's separation from Megan. He hastened to clarify that this was not the case, but had also to clarify that sleeping in the company of a grown person of the opposite gender had a different meaning than what Amber experienced sharing a room with Hopie and Robertico. He was open about his relationships with other women. Amber was silent, assimilating that.

Technically, Amber was a member of the class sometimes called *idiot savants*. Her brain was in effect miswired. The material was there but could not be properly applied to the ordinary concerns of normal folk. Her intelligence, in Spanish, was low-normal; in other languages, she was technically a moron. But she could remember a certain amount of what she heard. That made her extremely useful when Hope was dealing with other planets; he took her along as a nominal servant or clerk, and she picked up on comments that others assumed Hope did not understand.

Coincidentally, Roulette had a dialogue with Hopie, and educated her on the military and pirate way of love, and told her that the one person Hope truly loved was Hopie's mother. Spirit of course could not say anything; Hopie and the Solar System believed that Hope was her father, and her mother anonymous. That was only the half of it. But the two girls surely had an intense exchange of thoughts about romance, love, and sex soon thereafter.

And therein lay the mischief. Amber, as it turned out, was actually fourteen, and though her body was just developing, her emotion was running well ahead. She was already in Hope's orbit, and now he had educated her on the sexual nature of adult interactions. She was suddenly in love with him, and every contact with him intensified her emotion. This was independent of her talent with languages. Hope himself was oblivious; he thought of Amber as a child, and assumed that the intensity of her attention to his words was because of the difficulty she had mastering new concepts. He did not recognize total adoration. He could be quite stupid when his own emotion was engaged, and it was. Amber in certain key ways resembled Helse, and that blinded him. He thought he liked her as the friend of his daughter, and for her linguistic usefulness to him, and he did, but that was hardly the limit of it. The two were together often, and this further strengthened her devotion to him.

Spirit discussed it with Shelia. "What will happen when he catches on?"

Shelia smiled. "We are not jealous of other orbiters."

"You and Coral and Ebony may not be. But what of Hopie?"

Shelia paused. "Suddenly I feel stupid. That aspect never occurred to me. She'll go nova."

"And we can't have that."

"We can't have that," Shelia agreed, knowing that when Hopie novaed, so would Spirit, and Hope. There could be a dangerous chain reaction.

"Can we send one of them away?"

"And break Robertico's heart? They are like two little mothers to him."

"And Hope is like a father to the three of them. But if he connects with Amber—"

"And he will connect, in time," Shelia agreed. "I don't think we can stop it. She is after all a woman-child. We shall have to facilitate it."

"Facilitate it!"

Shelia nodded soberly. "It is the only way. To guide it so that it happens in a way that Hopie can accept, if that is possible."

Spirit didn't like this, but knew Shelia was right. "You have a way in mind?"

"Not yet. Give me a day."

In a day—Shelia was ever prompt in performance—she had it: "A feelie."

"A feelie will hardly substitute for the real thing!" Spirit protested. "Amber loves Hope, not some sexy actor, and Hope likes real women."

"I know," she agreed with half a smile. "But at present Amber does not know what to do with her passion, and Hope does not know she exists as a woman. Let her make a feelie for him: an anonymous female admirer with little experience."

"She can have *no* experience, and be a complete woman with him in an instant."

"Anonymous," Shelia repeated. "So he takes her for a stranger. He will follow up by feelie, because he'll have no other way. They can go as far as they want, and by the time it turns real, maybe Hopie will be ready to accept it."

Spirit considered. "A series of feelie exchanges. That might even prolong the courtship, as it were, giving us more time.

Time is what we need." But then another aspect occurred to her: "But suppose she gives it away early?"

"I will impress on her that it won't work unless she remains anonymous. For one thing, she can present herself as any type of women she wishes. She is not yet grown, so may be conscious of that lack."

"And it will end only when he catches on and names her in the feelie," Spirit said. "I think you've got it, Shel!"

"I hope so. I will get her started."

So it was that Amber made a private feelie, edited by Shelia, and Shelia delivered the anonymous message from a female admirer. It was, Spirit understood, extremely simple, with a glowing man figure resembling Hope approaching a cloaked, veiled woman. He glowed because he was lovable; it was a feelie convention. She was completely anonymous, but obviously the one who loved him. That was all; Hope would have to respond by making his own feelie, and lifting the woman's veil. Then whatever face Amber had chosen would be revealed, but not her own.

Hope did respond. His feelie showed him embracing the veiled woman. That was all.

Over the course of three months, the feelie romance became intense. Shelia quietly apprised Spirit of each stage, and Spirit found herself fascinated in the manner of a person watching a scripted romance. The anonymous woman lifted her veil, and revealed a completely blank face, leaving it to him to define. He defined it as Helse's face. Thereafter they proceeded, at intervals, to kissing, nakedness, and finally sex. Hope was glad to instruct his innocent paramour in the variations of sex, and she was glad to learn; the action became phenomenally hot. And still he did not catch on.

Then, almost a year after the first feelie, Hope was with Amber in a zoo, and there was an assassination attempt, and the two of them had to hide, soaking wet, clinging together, and he recognized her body from the feelie experience.

He braced Shelia, because he knew she had known all along. "Then you know why she wouldn't tell you," she said.

"Yes. I would have cut it off at the outset, before—"

"Before you loved her," she agreed. She didn't make the point that he would have loved her soon regardless. "She needed you—and you needed her."

"But she's a child!"

"Not any more."

"What do I do now?"

"Why, you love her, Hope."

"But she's younger than Hopie!"

"Helse was sixteen," she reminded him.

"Helse was a woman!"

She nodded agreement. The age of the woman had not really changed; Hope's age had. He recognized the validity of the affair. But he knew he had to clear it with Hopie first.

Hopie did not take it well. "Sex? As in the Navy?"

"Yes.

"With *her*?"

"Yes."

"You—she—Daddy, *she's younger than I am!*" Then she blacked his eye. Coral was near, but did not interfere; she knew this was punishment he had to take.

"And what of Megan?" Hopie screamed.

"Your mother and I are separated. She understands."

"She's not my mother! I don't know who my mother is! Sometimes I hate her for being secret—and for making me a bastard! Why did you have to do it, Daddy? What was wrong with your *wife*? You just *had* to—"

"You misunderstand—"

She slammed him in the nose. The blood flowed from a burst blood vessel. "I'm sorry," he said. "If you would talk to Amber—"

"I'll talk to her!" she cried. "You bet I will!"

Only then did Coral come to clean him up. Soon she reported the whole thing to Spirit. "Will it pass?" Spirit asked.

"I think so. Hopie loves him, and Amber."

"That's the problem."

"That's the answer."

She was correct. Hopie braced Amber in a linked feelie session, savagely, but Amber set her back, showing sheer, inchoate, encompassing emotion, such total longing, need, desire, passion, and love that it swept aside all considerations of age, sex, propriety, legality, status, and doubt. Her body might be marginally adult, but her feeling was the essence of womanly abandon.

That ended Hopie's objection. As Coral had said, she did love them both. The two girls embraced, and Amber went from child to lover. No one was more relieved than Spirit. Shelia's ploy had given them time to work it out.

And how would Hopie react when she finally learned the nature of her own genesis? She had cursed Hope for making her a bastard, when it was supportive Aunt Spirit who had done it.

There remained one difficult chore for Hopie to do, however: telling Uncle Thorley. He later messaged Hope, in his eloquent fashion.

I feel it incumbent upon me to advise you of a private interview I had most recently with your adopted daughter, Hopie Hubris. She advised me that you had required her to inform me of a private peccadillo: your passion for a rather young woman in your charge, by name Amber. Now it is your intent to make of this young woman a mistress, she being amenable. The secret passions of any man, I suspect, would embarrass him were they made public. I will keep your secret. I am sure you would do the same for me. Hopie inquired why she had had to be the one to perform this office of notification. "Because, my dear young woman, the Tyrant wished to advise his leading critic in a fashion which could not be doubted that the object of his amorous intention was not yourself."

At that point Hopie fled in chagrin. But at least she understood the rest of it. Had news leaked out of the Tyrant taking a young woman of his household as a mistress, the hostile critics could have raised a ruckus that threatened the Tyrancy itself. But that news would not leak out. Thorley did indeed understand.

But it was time for Hope to get out of the public eye, especially while he was with this particular mistress. Reba Ward had carefully set up a viable alternate identity for him, and now he became Jose Garcia, an ambitious Hispanic who was smart enough but not necessarily patient enough. He had been eased out of his company for being a whistle blower, and was now being given another chance at a new company. He was accompanied by his underage girlfriend. Such liaisons were now approved by the Tyrancy, provided they were verifiably consensual. They would search for natural bubblene bubbles in the atmosphere of Jupiter, hoping to strike it rich with a good discovery.

And, of course, they would indulge in the reality that their feelie romance had emulated. Spirit smiled, thinking about it; Hope had an endless sexual interest in women, and Amber had an endless emotional passion for him. They would work it out.

Meanwhile, Spirit would get on with the effective business of the Tyrancy. She threw herself into it, because she had to remain constantly busy to keep her mind off her desire to have a similarly endless liaison with Thorley. She still got to see him on occasion, but their connections were months apart. It was not nearly enough, but both of them were too prominent to keep many secrets.

CHAPTER 15

Shelia

During Hope's absence, Spirit effectively ran the Tyrancy, and the loyal staff served her. There was no formal declaration, of course; they all knew the situation. Theoretically the Tyrant was nearby, in his office, meeting with a dignitary, seducing a secretary, sleeping—whatever. He did check in regularly, and when his physical appearance was required he put Jose Garcia away for a time and acted as if Hope had never been absent.

Amber maintained similarly private contact with Hopie, who reported that the girl was diliriously happy, had performed sex more ways than she could count, and loved being known as Garcia's ward. Everyone knew what that meant, and she loved having them know. "You must get a man," she told Hopie. But open and expressive as Hopie was on every other subject, she never commented on that aspect of her life. She did not know about Spirit's affair with Thorley, but had evidently learned how to keep a secret when she had to.

Hopie was also active in the reform of education, evidently getting advice from renegades. One little example made the whole office dissolve. Shelia got hold of a sample first grade reader and read it aloud, as if she were a child practicing. "See Dick run. Run run run." She turned the page. "Dick runs to Jane's house. Jane says, 'I'll show you mine if you'll show me yours.' Dick says, 'Great!' Then Jane lifts up her dress. Dick looks. Look, look, look!" She looked up, trying to stifle her mirth. "And that's only the beginning!"

"That girl was always mischief," Ebony said fondly. She and Coral had been like foster parents to Hopie, and loved her little independent ways.

Spirit shook her head. Hopie had certainly reformed the first-grade reader! Her daughter, who had once been so shocked at Hope's relationship with Amber. Surely Thorley had not been responsible for this suggestion; she must have gotten it from Roulette, who was also mischievously motherly to her. "How did Robertico like it?" Robertico was now four, and learning to read.

"He thought it was great!" Shelia said. "He couldn't even handle all the words on the one page, but he wanted to get to the part where Dick showed his. 'See it grow. Big, big, big!' He can hardly wait to be a man!"

Coral and Ebony almost rolled on the floor laughing. "I can't wait for the college edition," Coral said.

Spirit shook her head. If only all the problems of the Tyrancy were like this. But Hopie was a novice at making mischief, compared to Hope.

Jose was Hope's anonymity, but the competence and personal skills of the man could not be denied, and Jose became known in his own right. When a riot developed in Cago Bubble, and the mob elected a spokesman, lo, it was Jose. Spirit was not completely surprised. Now a mob had taken over the mayor's office and was holding him and his staff hostage for city reforms, starting with the Pop-Null program. That was the population control program, necessary because bubble space was limited, as were air, water, food, and the other essential aspects of life support. But the ordinary people wanted the right to breed as freely as they chose.

The Cago administration appealed to the Tyrant, and Spirit took the necessary action. Because the mob had threatened to murder the mayor and his staff if any attempt were made to rescue him, and because it had the power and evident incentive to do it, she acted indirectly. A valve was opened in the hull of the city-bubble, and the Jupiter atmosphere started leaking in. It would take some time for the pressure to rise significantly, but there was horror the moment this was announced. The pressure of the external atmosphere was a terror, and any break in the integrity of the hull was alarming. The valve was filtered, so that no actual poisons entered, but still, the threat was potent.

"The valve will be closed when the mayor of Cago and his staff are released unharmed and the offices vacated without vandalism," the Navy officer in charge of this proceeding announced on the city address system. "By order of the Tyrant, via the Iron Maiden."

That demonstrated the tough-mindedness of the Tyrancy, as was necessary; no one respected an easy authority. But the mob would not readily relent; it had broad public backing. This was when Jose came to the fore. This was not really his choice, Spirit knew; he was simply the natural choice of those who knew him, so he had been unable to decline. People *trusted* him.

Contact was made. The White Bubble connected to the screen in the Mayor of Cago's office. The mayor was shown bound in his chair, and looked somewhat the worse for wear.

"I am Jose Garcia, of Jupiter Bubble," Hope said. "May I speak to the Tyrant, please?"

The clerk at Spirit's end kept a straight face. Of course the average citizen could not call in and be put right through to the Tyrant! "One moment, sir; I will put his secretary on."

Shelia appeared. She, too, kept a straight face, but of course she recognized Hope. "I am Jose Garcia," he repeated. "I have been selected to negotiate for the City of Cago, and if I could perhaps talk to the Tyrant—"

"The Tyrant is not available at the moment," Shelia said smoothly. "However, the Iron Maiden may–"

"Not her!" he said quickly. Everyone knew why: the Tyrant was known to be by far the softer touch. Spirit smiled, unseen.

"Then if you will describe your business further, Mr. Garcia, I will try to determine whether a direct interview is warranted."

"*Señora*, this is important. Twenty people have died, the mayor is held hostage, and the city is under siege by order of the Tyrant. I must talk to him directly!"

One of the mob leaders whispered to him, evidently urging caution. That was a good sign.

"We are aware of the situation in Cago, Mr. Garcia," Shelia said. What a pleasure to see her poise! "I can relay your statement to the Tyrant."

Jose became visibly excited. "More will be killed if something is not done. If the Tyrant cares at all for the common man, as I do . . ."

Shelia didn't respond immediately, taking stock. "Let me check," she said, glancing down at her console. Then: "The Tyrant is tied up in a meeting he cannot leave at the moment, but he is cognizant of the situation in Cago and will negotiate privately through me, if it can be kept brief. Will your party accede to that, Mr. Garcia?"

Jose turned to the mob leaders. "This is the Tyrant's personal secretary," he said. "Is it satisfactory to deal through her?"

The mob leaders exchanged glances. "We care only about results," one said. "If she can deliver—"

"I repeat," Shelia said, "the Iron Maiden is available, and has authority to–"

"The secretary's okay!" a mob leader said. Spirit smiled again. Shelia had such a nice touch.

"The trouble started because of the Pop-Null program," Jose said to Shelia. "The women here want their babies."

"If they get their babies," she replied, "then every other woman on the planet will want hers, and all the ills of overpopulation will return. The Tyrant will not relent on that."

But Jose had to win a point. "Can the schedule for return

be established, so that at least our women know with what they are dealing? The women supported the Tyrant when he sought power, and some reciprocal gesture now—"

Shelia made a show of consulting with her other party. The schedule for the return of babies had already been set but not publicized, pending the appropriate time to announce it.

"The Tyrant agrees that in one year, pending good behavior, permits matching the death rate will be issued in Cago. In two years that will be extended to the nation as a whole."

There was an intake of breath. Surely the women of Cago would eagerly accept that. But Jose pushed for more. "Those errant police must be put on trial and restoration made." Behind him the mob members tensed; he had already gotten them much of what they wanted, and they were concerned that he was pushing too far. They were pawns in his expert manipulation.

"The Tyrant will grant permits for births to match the number of deaths resulting from this crisis," Shelia replied. "An investigation will be made and appropriate action taken."

"But how can we be sure the Tyrant will keep his word?" he demanded. The implied question about the Tyrant's integrity was not good protocol.

"We accept!" a mob leader cried, shouldering Jose aside.

"But no action to be taken against the people in this room!" Jose exclaimed. "Amnesty—"

Shelia smiled grimly. "Amnesty," she agreed. "But I think that if you open your mouth again, Mr. Garcia, the Tyrant may reconsider." Even the mob leaders laughed ruefully.

That ended the occupation of the mayor's office. The mob dispersed peacefully, and the valve was closed, with the other reforms following in due course.

Spirit had been ready to intervene if necessary, exactly as threatened. When the contact broke, she walked to Shelia, bent down, and kissed her. "That's from my brother—and me."

"It's fun being Tyrant for fifteen minutes," Shelia confessed.

But not everything ended well. There was a scandal involving Faith Hubris; she had a lover, and he had used her to obtain illicit appointments. Thorley blew the whistle on it, and they had to act. Hope, distracted by his other business, made the decision to go public before he knew the possible complications, though Shelia had tried to caution him. Faith committed suicide. That was a brutal shock to both Hope and Spirit, but they had to suffer their grief in private. In retrospect, it seemed to have been the first wedge in what was to become known as the Tyrant's Madness.

Spirit did manage to be with Thorley thereafter. "I wish I could assuage your grief," he said. "And to expunge my part in it. I assumed the matter would be handled privately."

"It should have been," she agreed. "But we have so many things going on, we didn't give it proper thought. It's not your fault."

"Still, if I had it to do over, I would choose another avenue. She was a good woman, guilty only of naïveté."

"As were we all!" she agreed emphatically. "All this time, it was my brother's death I feared. It never occurred to me that my sister would be the first to go."

"All this time, it has been *your* demise I feared. I have survived living apart from you; I do not think I could exist without you."

"Spoken like a true married man," she said bitterly. Then, immediately regretting the wound she was inflicting, she reversed. "I didn't mean that!"

"It is nevertheless true. I am a hypocrite. I do love my wife, but—"

She covered his mouth with her fingers. "I know you do. We are caught up in what we should never have started and now can't end. If I could go back—"

"You would unmake your daughter?"

And there went that. "No, of course not. Can we escape in mindless passion for a moment?"

They did that, but it was effective for only that moment before the grief returned.

Then came the hostage situation. A radical fringe group abducted a Jupiter ambassador and held him hostage, demanding release of what it called political prisoners.

"What's the word on those prisoners?" Spirit asked Shelia.

In moments Shelia had the information. "They are common criminals, guilty of assorted crimes including attempted murder. They are slated for terms in deep space. It would not be fair to release them."

"It would not be expedient in any event," Spirit said grimly. "The Tyrancy will not capitulate to terrorist threats."

Shelia sent the Tyrant's response, via the Iron Maiden: no releases. Set the ambassador free unhurt, or there would be repercussions.

The terrorists were not fazed. They sent a holo: A hooded man cutting off one ear of the bound ambassador as he screamed in agony. "Release the prisoners."

Spirit knew this called for stern measures—a demonstration of the Iron Maiden's implacable will. An example had to be made. What would be most effective? She put in a call to QVY: "How do we handle this?"

Reba Ward responded with tough advice. Spirit nodded. It would not be fun, but the alternative would be anarchy.

Within hours close relatives of the terrorists had been quietly taken into custody. Then, under Spirit's direction, the left hands of two of them were cut off. That holo was sent back to the terrorists, together with the hands. Two for one: the Iron Maiden's ratio. Next round, anyone?

It was amazing how quickly the terrorists capitulated. And though that action was not directly publicized, news did leak out. "The Iron Maiden has struck again," Thorley wrote disapprovingly. "Nevertheless, the sympathy of this pundit is limited for fools. What did they expect? The Iron Maiden is notorious. She had a well-earned reputation in the Navy for ruthless nerve, providing the backbone that her more flamboyant brother lacked. But perhaps the operative example was one of the earliest: when she was but a girl of twelve, a pirate raped her sister and cut off the Maiden's own finger to make her brother cooperate. She got a laser pistol and castrated him, then set him adrift alone in a lifecraft. Woe betide he who crosses the Iron Maiden." In the guise of blowing the whistle on another atrocity of the Tyrancy, Thorley was doing the Tyrancy's work, spreading the fear of its enforcer.

And across the planet, and indeed the System, the grim reputation of the Iron Maiden increased. Thorley was one of the few who understood that though Spirit did indeed have the nerve to do what she had to do, she hated the necessity. She cultivated the reputation while privately suffering. Only with Thorley himself could she revel in softness, and that only rarely, because they were both public figures.

It was more than five years before the worst tragedy occurred, but in way it seemed like an instant to Spirit. It started with what was known as Big Iron. The iron companies had grown rich and powerful in fair times and foul, because they controlled the single most vital substance in the System: the power metal, iron. It was the only matter that could be handled magnetically. Without it the mechanized civilization would grind to a halt. The metal was intrinsically inexpensive, but somehow its value magnified by the time it reached the black-hole labs for conversion to contra-terrene iron. The same magnets could handle CT iron, moving it without physical contact with any terrene matter, until the time came for its merging with normal iron and total conversion to energy. Iron furnaces provided the energy for every city bubble to function, including its null-gee shielding. Iron engines propelled the Navy space ships. So far, all things considered, nothing better had been found than iron.

Mars had gotten rich by raising the price of its iron as high as the market would bear, with seeming indifference to the hardships worked on poor planets sorely in need of energy. But it was not the only culprit. The Jupiter iron companies also profited considerably by their handling of Martian iron, because they simply raised their prices to accommodate the higher Mars prices and added a generous margin for profit. More billionaires had been made from iron in the past century than from any other trade.

But the Tyrancy nationalized one of the iron processors, the Planetary Iron Company, or Planico. With that lever, it was forcing Big Iron to moderate its predatory practices, and making a formidable enemy. Soon Big Iron struck back.

The iron companies approached the Tyrant forthrightly: they believed he misunderstood their position, and they wanted to clarify it. Hope did not trust this, but it behooved him to listen, so he agreed to a meeting. This was not a physical meeting, of course; he had learned his lesson from assassination attempts. It was set up with holo: an image of each iron exec was to be projected to the White Bubble, while the actual execs remained in New Wash, close enough so that transmission of the images was virtually instantaneous. This was really just about as good for such meetings as physical presence was, and far safer for Hope.

Thus he was physically present in the Oval Office, along with Shelia and Coral, who confined themselves to the background. Spirit was watching from another chamber, as usual, ready to act if anything went awry. There were seats around the table for six iron execs, and another for Gerald Phist, who also projected in for the occasion. He was the one in charge of industry, including the iron industry, and Hope wanted Gerald to backstop him. He knew the iron magnates would be hurling statistics at him, and he wanted competent refutation at hand.

This setup had the incidental benefit of putting Gerald and Spirit together via a closed circuit. They had been in love when married, and retained considerable feeling for each other. She had long since told him of her relationship with Thorley, knowing that neither he nor Roulette would betray that secret. They had of course caught on that Spirit was the mother, rather than Hope the father, so it was only half a secret for them. So Gerald and Spirit found quiet pleasure in each other's virtual company, while conducting the business of the Tyrancy.

The Iron magnates appeared on schedule. Abruptly the seats were filled, and it looked exactly like a physical meeting. The leaders of Energiron, Spacirco, Rediron, Jupico, Standard Iron, and Abyss Metals. Of course, they sat at similar tables in their own offices, so that when their hands touched the surface, they did not hover above it or penetrate it; they were precisely zeroed in.

"What, gentlemen, is your concern?" Hope inquired evenly.

"We feel that you have underestimated the importance of the profit system," the exec from Standard Iron said. "By forcing us to cut down our margins, you reduce our competitive viability on the System scale. We can no longer expend the same resources for iron exploration that Mars can, and that is not only bad for us, it is bad for Jupiter."

"What's good for Standard Iron is good for Jupiter," Phist murmured sardonically. He was old now and getting crusty, but his mind remained sharp.

The exec grimaced. "Laugh if you will, but there is some truth in that."

"You forget that we nationalized Planico," Hope cut in. "We finally got to the bottom of the iron industry finances. You have been defrauding the public for centuries."

The executive reddened. "That is purely a matter of interpretation! If you insist on defining a reasonable return on investment as—-"

"What you call reason, I'd call piracy," Phist said.

It continued in this vein, with Gerald Phist alertly countering each Big Iron claim. Then there came a garbage unit, trundling along unattended. It was a household robot that had somehow been activated at the wrong time.

The disposer rolled slowly around the table, outside the

ring of chairs, working its way toward Hope. Spirit saw Shelia wheeling to intercept it, simultaneously murmuring into her mike. She was summoning the kitchen staff to come and recover their errant equipment, but meanwhile she would deactivate it herself.

Then several things happened in rapid order. The disposer suddenly clanked and lurched at Hope, its incinerative laser coming into play. "It's remote-controlled!" an exec cried. "Assassination!" another exclaimed.

Coral leapt toward it, her arm moving. "No!" Shelia screamed, jamming her chair right at Hope. But Coral's grenade was already in the air, bound accurately for the disposer. But the disposer, it turned out, was a holo projection. The grenade, which was quite real, was coming at Hope. Still seated in his chair, he could not get away from it in time.

Spirit screamed, but could do nothing. She wasn't physically there. But Shelia was.

Shelia's chair crossed before Hope, crashing into the table. Her right hand reached up and plucked the grenade from the air. She hauled it down to her bosom and hunched over it.

The grenade detonated. Pieces of Shelia and her chair flew outward. Blood spattered floor, table, chairs, ceiling, and Hope. He was half stunned by the concussion, and half blinded by blood, but he was alive. Shelia . . .

Coral was standing there, totally appalled. It had been a fiendishly clever trap that Coral and the others had fallen for. Big Iron had arranged for the Tyrant to be killed by his own bodyguard. Only Shelia had caught on—and taken the grenade for herself. She had foiled the plot.

The assassination had failed, and that of course meant the destruction of Big Iron. The process would take some time, but that industry was effectively dead from that moment. Spirit's immediate concern was Shelia—and Hope. Hope was delirious, and Ebony was caring for him, the only one free and close who could be absolutely trusted. She was putting him through a shower and changing his blood-spattered clothing. She was directing the medics as they treated him. That left Spirit free to focus on Coral.

Coral was in her chamber, laying out a clean mat. She was setting up for *seppuku*, the Saturnian ritual suicide of the warrior class.

"Don't do it!" Spirit pleaded. "We need you!"

But she was adamant. "Had I fathomed the plot, I would not have hurled that grenade," she said. "I failed Hope—and killed my friend."

Spirit could not dissuade her. Only Hope could do that—if he would. She hurried to fetch him.

He was clean and dressed now, walking dazedly with Ebony as she led him by the hand. There was a look in his eye that Shelia recognized: it was the madness. But it was not yet complete. "Hope, it isn't done yet," Spirit said. "We must cut our losses."

"Losses?"

"Coral." She led him to Coral, then backed off with Ebony. It was now Hope's business.

He caught on immediately, for he knew her well. "This is not warranted," he said. "We were all deceived."

"It is not your business to foil plots. It is mine." She gazed at the short sword she had laid out before her. She was kneeling, bare-breasted, on a tarpaulin; she intended to have no blood soil the floor of her room.

"It is your business to safeguard my life. You have not failed."

She turned to him. "Sir, I love you, as she did. Please do me the great honor of acting as my second in this."

That would mean taking the large sword she had, waiting while she used the short sword to disembowel herself, then severing her neck with one swing. This was the honorable and less agonizing way to go, once the guts had been spilled.

"But your job is unfinished," he said. "If you do this now, you leave me undefended."

"There are other bodyguards."

"You are the one I require."

"Sir, I ask you to release me."

"I refuse."

Again she turned to him. "Sir, do you not see the pain I am in? *I failed in my duty and I killed my friend.*"

He knelt before her, straddling her sword. "Woman, do you not see the pain *I* am in?" He gazed into her eyes and let his feeling show. Spirit knew it was the north-northwest wind.

And such was his extraordinary power over Coral that she yielded, even in this extreme of honor. "I apologize for my selfishness. What would you have me do?"

"I would have you join me in vengeance."

She nodded. "We shall wash their bodies."

"We shall wash their bodies," he repeated.

Then he opened his arms to her. She leaned into him, and they hugged each other, sharing their agonies.

And, indeed, the bodies of all the top executives of Big Iron were washed in blood. It was the most brutal vengeance Spirit had seen since the days of the pirates. She was normally the tougher one, but the madness was something else.

Yet it wasn't enough. Spirit, Coral, and Ebony mourned Shelia, and so did many others, but Hope's grief was madness. Only when Spirit read Hope's own account of it, years later, did she appreciate the full extent of it, but the essence was immediately clear. He was mourning Shelia as he once had mourned Helse. In his mind he went to heaven and brought her spirit back, and it occupied the bodies of other women in wheelchairs. He sought them and brought them to the White Bubble and made love to them and released them. They were glad to cooperate; madness it might be, but few woman could deny him ordinarily, and none when he was like this.

He also had a memorial erected in her name, and allocated one billion dollars for the treatment of all who were crippled in the legs. The Shelia Foundation was instituted, dedicated to the study of nerve and limb regeneration, that the crippled of the future might walk again. That was perhaps the single enduring good to come of Shelia's brutal death.

Hope's alternate guise as Jose Garcia continued, and Jose was not mad. He also had the solace of Amber, and that must have helped, though by this time Amber was twenty three and the bloom of her devotion had been well tempered by experience. She had loved Shelia too, but knew that the vengeance taken was out of proportion. She still loved Hope—that never ended for any of his women—but understood that he did have human fallibilities. In short, she could probably live without him, if she had to. Orbits could be distant as well as close.

Meanwhile the Tyrant's evident madness was eroding the heart of the Tyrancy. Jupiter was prospering, but the citizens were increasingly restive. As the behavior of the Tyrant became more bizarre, the Resistance gained strength. It was not that Jupiter chafed under the policies of the Tyrancy; it was that Jupiter feared that too many of the successful policies would be eroded or dismantled. The Tyrant was becoming a loose cannon: a thing without proper anchorage whose random blunderings were a threat to all around him. Yes, he was grief-stricken over the ugly death of his beloved secretary, but where would his pain end? Was there an alternative?

The Resistance had an answer. It sponsored a general strike. It had been years since anything like this had been tried before, and it took some courage, because the Tyrant had acted swiftly and effectively in the past to squelch such efforts. But this one was extremely broadly based; in fact, nearly half of all the employed citizens of North Jupiter participated in it, and a quarter of those in the Latin provinces. Jose Garcia sympathized; he led Jupiter Bubble on strike, granting all workers a holiday for the duration.

This was real mischief for Spirit. She hurt for Shelia's loss in more than one way: no one else had such effective knowledge of the details of governmental management. Things were going wrong in little ways that were all too apt to become big ways. The Resistance strike was a major example: Shelia would have picked up on the signals before it happened, and notified Spirit, and together they would ordinarily have defused it before it broke open. As it was, this was a significant surprise. The Resistance had developed so quietly and peacefully that few people realized the proportions to which it had grown. Probably not all the strikers were members, but this demonstration was enough to paralyze the vital planetary services and too widespread to be amenable to wholesale discipline. It was peaceful but impressive.

Something had to be done, and because this demonstration was obviously well meant, Spirit concluded that it should be met with appropriate restraint. Violent methods, in this case, would alienate a far greater segment of the population than the Tyrancy could afford. What would be both gentle yet effective?

Coral came up with what seemed to be a viable program: Hope would challenge the leader of the Resistance to a contest of some kind, winner take all. Little was known about the leader, except that it was female and savvy, garnering the support of so many women. If he won, the Resistance would be dismantled; if she won, he would retire from the Tyrancy. Spirit herself was against this, but did not object strenuously. She was wary of his madness and thought in her secret heart that might would be better if he did step down.

So the Tyrant made the challenge, and amazingly the leader accepted: Yes, she would meet him in a contest. The terms were acceptable. To the winner would go the management of Jupiter, and to the loser, exile. No blood shed, in either case.

It was necessary to have an intermediary, to arrange the details of the contest. The Resistance leader designated Jose Garcia.

Spirit was elated. "They have played into our hands!" she exclaimed. "They don't know who you are!"

Hope didn't seem so sure, but he agreed it made sense. Jose

was well known and trusted, and this would be a direct avenue to discovery of the anonymous Resistance leader. If it turned out to be Reba Ward of QYV he might well have to kill her, for she would surely recognize him. But if she were someone else, they might indeed be able to negotiate a fair contest. So Jose traveled to Ston, named after a centuries-bygone center of resistance and dance called Charleston, to board a Resistance ship.

And it turned out that the Resistance leader was Megan. She had recognized the madness and recognized Hope long before, and now was acting to take him out of power. She was the one person he could not oppose; the moment she revealed herself to him, Hope was lost. There was no contest; Jose simply returned, went to the White Bubble, was officially closeted privately with the Tyrant for an hour, and emerged to announce that the Tyrant was retiring forthwith. Then he entered a private ship and disappeared from public view.

An hour later Hope Hubris emerged and announced that he was abdicating in favor of his wife, Megan Hubris. He and his sister Spirit would depart Jupiter in exile as soon as an orderly transfer of power could be accomplished.

In the course of the following week, Jose Garcia announced his own retirement, feeling that after negotiating the conclusion of the Tyrancy he had no further need for public life, and he faded from view. Many were disappointed, for he had been an obvious candidate for high office in the new regime. Even Thorley remarked on the regrettable loss of such a fair minded man. He concluded "I must confess to suffering a certain guilty pang of regret for the loss of the Tyrant, also, for he was a marvelously newsworthy figure, and his sister remains a handsome woman." Few understood how sincerely he meant that, or knew what Spirit was feeling as she faced the prospect of being forever separated from her secret lover. She could not show her tears.

Others had to find other placements. Amber returned to

New Wash, alone, where she worked as a translator of recorded transmissions, using the helmet to communicate her renditions. She never commented publicly on her private relationship with the Tyrant or Jose Garcia. She shared a residence with her virtual sister and friend Hopie, who was allowed to retain her post as head of the Department of Education. That was a bit of nepotism the public endorsed, for Hopie had done a decent if sometimes controversial job, and she was legally the daughter of both the former Tyrant and the new administrator, Megan. She represented a tangible bridge between administrations. Their eleven year old virtual brother Robertico joined them there.

Coral, unable to join Hope in exile, accepted a position as a physical therapist with the Shelia Foundation. Ebony joined her there. It was generally known how close they both had been to the living Shelia; they were in this manner remaining as close to her as was possible.

And so Shelia had been not only the central coordinator of the Tyrancy, and perhaps the inadvertent instrument of its demise; she was now the enduring symbol of some of the good the Tyrancy had accomplished. The mascot of the Shelia Foundation was an empty wheelchair, in its way also a symbol of the vacated Tyrancy. Hope in his madness had a vision of Shelia in a heaven populated by folk in wheelchairs; Spirit found that vision comforting, for if heaven existed, Shelia surely belonged there. She was always a good person, and all her associates loved her.

CHAPTER 16

Saturn

Megan headed a brief caretaker government, setting up a framework for restored elections and public representation. She had no interest in power for herself and stepped down the moment the elections produced a new president and Congress. She was called a great woman. She was. Hope loved her, and so did Spirit.

Actually, the Tyrancy had accomplished much of what it could. It had not only balanced the budget, it had paid down the planetary debt. It had instituted adequate medical care for all citizens. It had abolished the drug problem. Crime, both street and corporate, had dropped to record lows. And it had made the press, in all its forms, free; there was no censorship at all. Jupiter had become a beacon of good government, and many of its programs had been emulated elsewhere in the System. So perhaps it was time for the Tyrancy to end. Certainly Spirit was ready for less administration and more adventure in her life, and she liked the prospect of interacting closely with her brother again.

It turned out that a number of planets were interested in providing sanctuary for the exiled former Tyrant of Jupiter. He accepted the most challenging offer. Thus it was that Hope and Spirit Hubris traveled to Saturn to commence what turned out to be perhaps the most remarkable stage of their careers.

Hope was sixty-one and Spirit was fifty-eight, but they might as well have been children again. They faced the presentation screen and gawked at the magnificence of Planet Saturn. The rings were spectacular. Of course the image was enhanced by false color, making it more dramatic, but still it was a wonder. All the colors of the spectrum seemed to be there in the great splay of the rings, and in the roughly spherical body of the planet itself. "Beautiful!" he breathed. "Jupiter's rings hardly compare!"

Spirit murmured agreement. "But nevertheless a sterner environment than we knew on Jupiter," she reminded him. "Their residential band has about eight and a half bars pressure, and their winds are up to quadruple Jupiter's—almost five hundred meters a second."

"A thousand miles an hour," he agreed. Of course such velocities were not directly experienced, because the city-bubbles floated in the wind currents. Survival would be impossible if relative wind velocity of that strength were felt; storms whose winds were only a tenth as strong had been called hurricanes back on ancient Earth, and had wreaked enormous damage.

Hope had just one personal acquaintance at Saturn—but that one was Chairman Khukov, the highest political figure there. He had achieved his dominance at about the time Hope became the Tyrant of Jupiter, and they had worked tacitly together to buttress each other's power and defuse interplanetary tension. Spirit did not really know Khukov, apart from two meetings, but she trusted her brother's judgment.

"Ship under attack," the intercom said. "Secure—"

The voice was cut off by the impact of a strike. The ship shook, and the power blinked. They were not under acceleration at the moment; the normal course was to achieve cruising velocity, then coast to the destination, conserving fuel. The vessel was spinning to provide half gee in that interim.

"Better take evasive action," Spirit muttered. Their careers in space were three decades past, but the reflexes had not been lost.

The ship did not. It drifted along on its original course, not cutting in the drive.

They got out of their harnesses, acting as one. Obviously the ship's captain was a noncombatant, uncertain what to do in battle. That would get them killed promptly enough. He didn't realize that the first thing to do was to put the ship under acceleration, regardless of its course.

They burst into the control chamber. "Get it moving!" Hope barked in Russian.

"But the damage report is not yet in," the pilot protested. He was young, obviously inexperienced: the kind normally used on what was called a milk run, a routine mission. "The captain has not—"

Hope reached down and took the man's laser pistol from his body. He gave it to Spirit. "Get out of that seat," he said. There wasn't time to educate the man in battle procedure.

"But you are passengers! Not even of Saturn—" Then he turned his head and spied the laser bearing on his right eye. He got out of the seat.

Hope jumped into it. The ship's controls were unfamiliar in detail, but he understood the principle well enough. In a moment he had the drive started.

Meanwhile, Spirit was marching the pilot out of the chamber. Hope knew where she was headed. He spoke into the intercom. "Captain, I am assuming temporary command of this vessel," he said in Russian. "Acknowledge, and relay the directive to your crew."

"This is impossible!" the captain sputtered. Spirit heard him on the intercom. She did not know Russian, but the tone gave her the general nature of the man's exclamations. Hope was also speaking Russian, but she knew what he would be saying in a case like this. He was distracting the captain, to give her time to complete her part. Meanwhile she was silently marching the pilot to the captain's office.

It was all coming back: her pirate and Navy experience. She felt a fierce rush of the passion of battle, mixed with the dreadful tension of danger. She loved the one and hated the other, but both came together. She felt more fully alive than she had in some years.

"Captain, we don't have time for debate," Hope said, and she heard him also on the intercom. "I am taking evasive action, but very soon the pirate will reorient and tag us with another shell."

"*This* is piracy!"

"Captain, do you know who I am?"

"No, they did not inform—"

"I am the Tyrant of Jupiter, deposed."

The captain made a gasp of surprise, but it was not entirely because of what Hope had said. Spirit had just entered his office and covered him with the pistol.

"Chamber secured, sir" she said on the intercom. "Orders?"

The captain, realizing that he had no choice, yielded. He agreed to serve the new captain. He gave the information Hope demanded.

It turned out that the ship had been converted for passenger use. It was extremely fast, but had no real weapons. Meanwhile, the attacking ship was showing pirate colors on the communication screen. This was real trouble.

"Spirit," Hope said.

"Have to try chicken," she said in Spanish. If any of the Saturn personnel knew that language, they might still miss the implication. That was the intent. If they caught on, there would be a counterrevolution aboard ship. Chicken was when two foolish kids got into transport bubbles and headed straight for each other. Collision course—and the first to swerve was "chicken." The game had been played in one form or another for centuries, and had accounted for its share of injuries and deaths.

Hope oriented the ship, then jammed up the drive. Suddenly they were accelerating, in the relative framework of the two moving ships, toward the pirate.

It took a moment for the pirate to realize what was happening, for this was completely unexpected. It was like a wounded rabbit charging the pursuing hound. That was the first surprise. Then Hope sprang the second one: he fired the ship's lifeboat at the pirate. It rammed the ship and holed it. The pirates were dead.

Hope and Spirit led a boarding party. They discovered that the pirate crew was of the Middle Kingdom, nominally an ally of the Union of Saturnine Republics. But this seemed to be a frame, intended to implicate an innocent party.

"So we are left with only the mysteries of who is the real assassin, and how the ship spotted us."

"I don't like such mysteries," Spirit said.

"Neither do I. Yet it is like old times."

She smiled. "Like old times."

He put his arm around her, and she melted into him. Those old times had been horrible, but not without their redemptions. They had suffered grievously at the brutal hands of pirates, but had been closer to each other than ever since.

Chairman Khukov was a busy man, but he made time for them. Within an hour of their arrival they found themselves in his private suite. He had aged visibly, with what hair remaining to him turning off-gray, and he had put on weight. They conversed in English, for Spirit did not speak Russian and Khukov's knowledge of Spanish was never advertised. Hope and Khukov trusted each other because each understood the other in a way no other person could. Differences of language or culture or politics became insignificant in the face of this fundamental understanding.

"You know the origin and motivation of the attack?" Hope asked.

"The *nomenklatura*."

They looked blank.

Khukov smiled. "Brace yourselves for a small lecture on Saturnine internal politics. You know that we are theoretically

a classless society, unlike you of the decadent capitalistic planets. But we have classes, and of these the most privileged is the
nomenklatura, the bureaucratic stratum of the Party. Those in
all the key positions of the Party, the military, and the secret
police belong to this hereditary class. *I* belong. They pass themselves off as mere civil servants, but they are the true rulers.
Our society is stultified, because the *nomenklatura* wants no
change; it wants only perpetuation of its own power. This is
your enemy—and mine. I sought to reform our system, to eradi-
cate corruption, to make of Saturn a truly superior power." He
shook his head. "The task was more difficult than I had suspected."

"Infinitely," Hope agreed ruefully. It seemed that the
nomenklatura wanted to stop the reform, and knew that Hope
might be an instrument of reform. Khukov, it turned out, had a
dream: The unification of the species in harmony.

"An excellent dream," Hope agreed wryly. "But difficult to
implement."

He waggled a finger at them. "A dream without substance
is worthless. I have a mechanism, if it can be implemented. Do
you remember how the society of ancient Earth was ready to
explode, to destroy itself by internecine warfare, until the onset
of the gee-shield?"

"That gave man the Solar System," Hope agreed. "The pent-
up energies were released positively by the expansion into the
new frontier, rather than turning destructively upon themselves."

"And now that frontier has been conquered, and the energies are turning destructive again, exactly as before. But with a
new frontier—"

"To divert man's destructive energies," Hope said, beginning to visualize the dream.

"And provide man a common challenge," Spirit added. "But
what could that frontier be?"

Khukov made an expansive gesture. "What else? The galaxy."

"But the gee-shield can hardly do that," Hope said. "Gravity is not much of a problem in interstellar space, so shielding it doesn't make much difference. For that kind of travel, we need sustained thrust that could take us up toward light speed, and even CT drive isn't enough. Even so, it would take a decade or so just to reach the nearest star—where there might not be anything worthwhile for colonization anyway. It's not enough just to get there; there have to be resources to exploit. Just the problem of growing new bubbles to house increasing population—that requires planets like Jupiter and Saturn. The answer always comes out the same: There is no solution in interstellar space."

"Ah, but there *is*," he insisted. "If we can find those suitable stars for energy, and suitable planets for material resources, and get to them. Five, six new systems to start, more when required. We know they exist; our problem is locating them. Reaching them."

"Confirming them," Spirit said. "To make the enormous investment and risk of decades-long travel to them worthwhile."

"But a light-speed drive would make this feasible," he said. "Go, explore, return, report—within our lifetimes, late as our lives are getting. Discovering the galaxy."

"A light-speed drive is a fantasy," Hope said. "A relativistic impossibility. Only radiation does it."

"Just suppose, Tyrant, that there were a breakthrough of this nature. A mechanism to convert a physical object to the equivalent of light, without destroying it. And to restore it to solidity on demand. What then?"

"If a spaceship could be changed to light, travel as a beam, then be solidified at the far reflector—"

"With living things. Human beings, complete city-bubbles, perhaps. Largely self-contained units. But if the city becomes light, time within it becomes infinite, and for the passengers, nonexistent. They could travel four years, and to them it would be not even a moment, no time at all. It would feel like instant matter-transmission. No supplies used, no energy expended, merely a new star beyond."

"Suspended animation," Hope said. "That might make it feasible, indeed." He sighed. "But since there is no such device . . ."

Khukov smiled. "Ah, but there may be. Tests are commencing, and we shall shortly know whether this is a drug dream or reality. If reality—"

"Then it would be worthwhile to seek the political breakthrough," Hope finished. "To get our entire species organized for the great new frontier. For it would have to be done on a System-wide basis, as it was done on an Earth-wide basis before. The new diaspora of mankind."

"The new diaspora," he echoed. "That is the dream."

"When Earth colonized the Solar System," Hope said, "the need was desperate and the leadership inspired. No nation gave up its share of the pie. Thus the political and economic and military situation of Earth was reestablished in the System— with all its problems. We have been flirting with the same disaster as before, on a larger scale."

"But the same solution offers. Except that the galaxy is vast beyond the aspiration of man to fill. It would take a hundred thousand years merely to cross it, and much longer to colonize it. I think we would not soon again see a crisis of confinement."

"The colonization of the galaxy," Hope repeated, feeling Khukov's Dream take hold. "You really believe the challenges can be met?"

"I am prepared to supervise the scientific challenge," he said. "I believe it can be met, if there is cooperation by the other planets. First we must develop a large-scale demonstration project, to prove that it works, and to establish its feasibility in a fashion that all men will believe. That will cost some hundreds of billions of rubles, and I think Saturn could not do it alone. That places it in the camp of the political challenge. If we can unify the planets—"

"Who could do that?" Hope asked, realizing his thrust.

"Who but the Tyrant of Space?"

Hope looked at Spirit. She nodded; she was ready for this. Hope extended his hand to Khukov. Thus began the former Space Tyrant's political and economic service at Saturn. He was given a personal secretary, who of course reported everything to her superiors. Her name was Tasha. She was young and attractive and intelligent and even-tempered. She was amenable to Hope's sexual interest. In short, the ideal secretary.

She was also, as it turned out, a mole: programmed to kill Hope when he had sex with her. She did not know this; it was a buried program. So when Spirit was away, and Hope took Tasha to bed, she caught him in a strangle hold. Only the fact that she wanted him to complete the sexual act before he died gave him time, and only his knowledge of nerve attacks enabled him to escape her. At which point she reverted to her normal state, with no memory of the experience.

Spirit learned about it when she returned. "I accepted her seduction, and she tried to kill me," Hope said simply. "She's a mole—an assassin mole."

This was alarming news. Spirit had never anticipated such a ploy. "And you don't want to eliminate her?" she inquired with raised eyebrow.

Hope explained that Tasha was now a known threat, safer than the unknown threat that might replace her. "But it's dangerous," he concluded. "She still tempts me."

"You always were a fool about women," Spirit said. "Fortunately, they always were bigger fools about you."

"Not this one. If I touch her again I may not survive."

Spirit nodded. "We shall have to get you a woman we can trust. I will ask Megan."

"Megan!"

"She knows your tastes, I suspect."

And so Tasha remained temporarily, while Spirit sent Hope's message to Megan: "Send me a woman."

Meanwhile, they got to work on the corrupt, inefficient Saturn farming system. They decided to introduce some free enterprise, veiled as "progressive socialism." In the guise of eliminating corruption, they deported the agents of the *nomenklatura.* There were soon positive results.

Hope continued to hanker after Tasha, and Spirit knew that they would have to find a safe way for him to have her, before he risked an unsafe way. So Spirit pretended to depart on another business trip, but actually remained close, so she could watch and if necessary intervene. She did not like being a voyeur, but this was necessary.

Hope explained to Tasha that he desired her, but that his taste ran to bondage. She readily agreed, as her normal self had only the desire to please him. They stripped, and he tied her hands and feet to the bedposts. He caressed her, then mounted her sexually. Then it got interesting.

Abruptly Tasha's personality changed. Spirit had expected this, but it was far more dramatic than she had anticipated. Tasha tried to reach for his neck, but could not, and tried to bring up her knees, but could not. "What's this?" she spat.

"This is known as consenting sex," Hope replied, thrusting deeply. Spirit thought of Thorley, and suffered.

"I'm tied!" Tasha exclaimed indignantly. Evidently she had no memory of the activities of her normal self.

"Why, so you are," Hope agreed, nuzzling her right breast.

Her torso bucked. The breast slammed into his face, but of course a weapon like that could do no harm. "I'm glad to have you responding so well," he said, licking her nipple.

She made a sound like an attacking pig, an ugly squeal, and wrenched her nether section violently about. This had the effect of hastening his climax. "Thank you!" he gasped amidst it. Spirit suffered further.

Tasha snapped at his face, but he held his head away and completed his enjoyment of her body.

"I'll kill you!" she hissed.

"With kindness, perhaps," he said, pausing to savor her breast one last time. Then he dismounted. "Thank you for a unique experience."

She spat at him, literally, but even that missed.

Hope cleaned up and dressed, evidently uncertain when it was safe to untie her. Spirit was nervous about that too. They needed to know exactly when the threat abated.

When Tasha saw Hope clothed, her manner changed. "Aren't you going to do it?" she asked.

"I think I am older than I believed," he said regretfully. "You are beautiful, but perhaps another day?"

She shrugged as well as she could in her bonds. "I am disappointed, of course. But I understand."

So they had found a way. But Spirit hoped that Megan would send a safe woman soon.

The enemy was getting impatient. There were other attempts on Hope's life. These were not Tasha's doing; in fact when he was poisoned, she rushed him to the hospital, perhaps saving his life. Still, harm had been done, and that was later to have a dire consequence.

Then Hope acquired an extinct saber toothed tiger. The animal had gotten loose in a biologic facility he was visiting; it might have been another attempt on his life. But he used his special power to tame it, amazing all who saw it happen. Thus Smilo came to join his personal retinue, enhancing his immediate safety and his reputation. Hope had uncanny luck in such matters.

It took six months for the woman Megan chose to arrive. Her name was Fortuna Foundling, more simply called Forta. Khukov was later to dub her "the muddy diamond" with no disrespect intended; he appreciated her value immediately. A good deal faster than Hope did, actually.

Forta was tall and trim and of mixed blood; there were touches of Mongol and Saxon and Negroid derivation in her. Her dark hair was bound back into a bun, and her face was

shadowed by a feminine hat that might have been six or seven
centuries out of date. She wore a suit that was almost military
in its stern cut. She appeared to be in her mid-thirties. She was
definitely no showgirl.

That was not the worst of it. Forta's face was so badly scarred
as to make it hideous. It looked as if she had put her head in the
blast of an accelerating spaceship. Patterns of scars matted her
forehead and cheeks, and the eyebrows were lost in the ruin.
Her ears hardly showed; perhaps they had been cut off. Her
mouth seemed to be little more than a slit amidst the tortured
tissue.

"Childhood accident," she said matter-of-factly, evidently
used to the very kind of stunned reaction Hope was evincing.

Something was wrong. Spirit knew Megan would not play
either a cruel joke or take any kind of obscure vengeance her
husband; neither type of behavior was her way. Virtually all of
his women had been beautiful, herself included; she knew his
taste in that regard. How could she have done this? There had
to be a rationale.

Spirit stepped in. "I am his sister. We have a place for you.
Let's get your baggage."

"This is all," Forta said, hefting her single suitcase.

They went to their rented car. Hope drove while Spirit and
Forta talked. Spirit arranged this, knowing that he needed a
pretext to keep to himself. She had to fathom the rationale, to
find out why Megan had sent this seeming disaster of a female.

"We have been very busy," Spirit said. "We have been reor-
ganizing Saturn industry, and that entails a great deal of research. My brother interviews the personnel, and I see to much
of the implementation. Are you trained in this area?"

"I regret I am not," Forta said. "I do, however, have secre-
tarial skills."

"We already have a secretary," Spirit said. "We really had
not thought of you in that capacity."

"Naturally not," Forta said, smiling. The mystery of this

woman was growing.

"Are you trained in diplomacy?"

"By no means."

Spirit was somewhat at a loss. "Perhaps if you would fill us in on your background."

"Gladly. I was found on Mercury thirty-two years ago, during one of the civil-rights altercations there. My parents may have been killed by the authorities of South Mercury, or merely driven out and prevented from returning. It is possible that I was left for dead, because of the injury done my face. I was picked up by a relief mission and taken to the Amnesty Interplanetary office in Toria. I understand they tried to investigate my background, but of course things are difficult for those of mixed race in that part of the System, and they had no success. So I was christened Fortuna Foundling, being fortunate merely to have survived as a foundling."

"Apartheid," Spirit murmured. "I understand that torture is employed in that region. But why a baby should be subjected to—"

"There is no proof of torture," Forta said. "It could have been a mining accident. The conditions in Mercury's sunside diamond mines—" She shrugged. "I was well cared for by AI. My face healed, but of course they lacked the funds for plastic surgery. I have spent my life with AI; when I became adult I joined as one of their agents. That has been the story of my life, until this point."

"I wonder if there has been a misunderstanding," Spirit said. "We are not engaged in the investigation of human rights. We are on assignment for Chairman Khukov of the Union of Saturnine Republics, being in exile from Jupiter. I should not think that you would care to be connected to this enterprise."

"I did not come as an AI representative," Forta said. "I volunteered as a woman."

Spirit was guarded. "You volunteered—for what?"

"To be your brother's mistress."

There was a silence. Then Hope spoke, not looking at her. "How well do you know me?"

"About as well as any person not of your family or prior staff knows you," Forta said. "I have made a study."

"Then perhaps you know that I do not have relations with strangers."

"True. And you seldom have relations with unpretty women. I intend to be the exception. I think that once you come to know me, you will appreciate my qualities."

"I do not wish to give offense, but—"

"If you care to read me, you will see that I am confident of your eventual satisfaction."

"Show me your power," he murmured under his breath, in the old Navy idiom, with irony.

"Read me," she repeated firmly. It was definitely a challenge.

Hope met that challenge. Spirit took over control of the car, and he spun his seat around to face Forta, who sat in back. He read her, using his talent.

"You are confident," he murmured, perhaps unconsciously. "You believe in yourself. I have known hard women, and talented women, and combinations of the two, but none harder or mere talented than you, except my sister."

That startled Spirit. She did have a scarred face and hands, because of her use of the rocket-propulsion unit to wipe out the pirates. She had never had restorative surgery because she wore her marks with pride. Forta was evidently of this nature, though her scars were far more apparent. But Hope was not looking for an emulation of his sister as a romantic object.

"Strange," Hope said. "You are changing."

Changing?

"Helse," he whispered, amazed.

Spirit had to look. She glanced briefly back. Forta's ravaged face remained, but there was indeed a suggestion of Helse about it, as if the scars covered a fair young Hispanic face. Spirit lacked the ability to read human signals her brother had, but there was definitely something. How could this be?

"Megan," he said, awe in his tone.

Spirit looked again. Now the scars covered the suggestion of Megan. It was apparent that Hope saw the effect much more strongly than Spirit did.

Forta had shown him her power. She was a signal chameleon: She could emulate the facial and body signals of other people. Her talent was, in a fashion, akin to Hope's: she could generate the signals he could read. Thus she could emulate, in a rather subtle but fundamental manner, those people she had studied-and she had studied his two loves. She could be all things to all men, in a fashion.

They reached their apartment, amazed by this manifestation. When Forta unpacked, it turned out that her suitcase contained not a wide variety of clothing but a most versatile array of costumes and masks. These were not crude plastic; they were contour-clinging, lifelike things that could readily be mistaken for living flesh when animated by her expressions. In fact Forta was an accomplished mime: she could don mask and costume and mimic her chosen character so cleverly that the resemblance was startling.

"Do Megan," Hope said.

Forta donned her Megan set, as she called it, and in a moment it was as though Hope's wife entered the chamber. The mask-face, the hair-wig, the walk, the gestures, the subtle body signals—Spirit was shaken despite her comprehension of the device.

Then she spoke—and with Megan's voice, complete with the nuances. "Why, Hope—it is so good to see you again," she said, and extended her arms to him, in exactly the way Megan had done when their marriage was active.

Hope stepped forward and took her in his arms. He kissed her—and did not seem to feel the mask. It looked like a living face, despite their knowledge.

"Can you do me?" Spirit asked.

In moments Forta donned a new mask and wig. "Can you do me?" she inquired, exactly as Spirit had. Hope's jaw dropped.

They stood before a mirror, and Spirit's own jaw dropped. There were two reflections of her, in different clothing. "You look just like me!" she said—and the other image said the same words at the same time. The woman had known exactly how she would react, and emulated it.

Spirit shook her head as Forta removed her mask. "If I had not seen it . . ." she said. "What else can you do?"

"I can also serve as a courier, and as translator."

"You know other languages?"

"Not exactly. I have translation apparatus that facilitates the limited ability I have in that regard."

She demonstrated. She had a pocket multi-tongue language computer, with capsules for the individual languages. An earplug enabled her to hear the ongoing translation in Afrikaans, her native language and the one she thought in. It developed that she had been using the translator for English, though she did speak that language, because it was easier for her to hear words in her own language, then translate her reply, than to deal completely in English.

"English is not your language—yet you have been speaking it," Spirit said.

"I have a prompt," she explained. This was a plug in her other ear, that fed her the words she subvocalized. She demonstrated it in Spanish and Russian.

Spirit had little doubt that this was the most remarkable woman they had encountered. But Hope did not immediately take her as a mistress. His knowledge that she was not the women she emulated cooled his ardor.

Meanwhile, they had a heavy schedule. Forta became part of their party, along with Tasha and Smilo, and was quite useful as an additional secretary, translator, and assistant. Her time would come.

CHAPTER 17

Planets

The heat did not let up; the *nomenklatura* remained deter-mined to eliminate Hope. Khukov reluctantly concluded that they could not safely remain on the planet. If Hope showed his face in public, one of their assassins would go for him first, then if caught would commit suicide, and the body would have no ties to the employer. If he remained in hiding, eventually they would ferret out his location, and send in a bomb. They were no longer interested in being careful; he had to be eliminated, for it was obvious that they were otherwise doomed.

"But you have proven yourself," Khukov said on the pri-vate holophone. It looked just as if he were sitting in their cham-ber. "The procedures you have instituted will carry through to their completion, perhaps more slowly without you, but inevi-tably. You can now be spared for greater things. I want you to negotiate with Rising Sun."

That was Titan, Saturn's greatest moon. In the Solar Sys-tem, Titan was a satellite of Saturn, and this did not accord with their social perspective, any more than their ancestors considered Japan to be an island satellite of the continent of Asia. So they preferred to call themselves the Empire of the Rising Sun.

"Rising Sun," Hope agreed. "But can the Occidental Ty-rant speak for the oriental aspect of Saturn?"

"In many respects, that moon is closer to your planet than

to mine," he reminded them. "Remember, it was Jupiter who occupied it, after System War Two, not Saturn. Now it is an industrial giant in its own right, and we would like to establish better trade relations."

"I'm sure Titan will trade," Hope said. "But it sells finished products, and your interplanetary credit is weak. What can you offer?"

Khukov told them what the USR had to offer. Hope nodded. "I believe I can handle that."

"And it will keep you safely off-planet, while the disturbance here dies down," Khukov concluded.

Thus they undertook their mission as liaison between Saturn and Titan. It promised to be an intriguing challenge.

Titan bore a certain resemblance to their planet of origin, Callisto. Khukov had termed it moon, but as he had noted, the folk of the satellites preferred to call them planets in their own right.

Titan had a substantial atmosphere; its solid surface was completely hidden from exterior view. Critics referred to that atmosphere as solid smog; the natives referred to it as the basic stuff of the origin of life. Certainly it represented a rich chemical environment from which the natives processed many products, and its pressure of one bar (the same as Earth's) facilitated the operation of city-domes in the surface. It was the only planet besides Earth itself whose atmosphere was dominated by nitrogen.

Politically, it was another matter. Titan was colonized by the Japanese of Earth, and they maintained their rivalry and often enmity with huge Saturn. Because Titan's position in space was far superior for the direct launching of ships, Titan's Navy became more formidable than Saturn's. She had turned her energies to commerce—and shortly became a System leader in the construction of merchant ships, and in computerized technology. Titan had beaten its swords into plowshares, and was now stronger as an economic power than it had been as a military power. Jupiter itself imported so much from Titan that it had a sizable trade deficit with that planet.

Their party was transferred in space to a Rising Sun merchant vessel and conveyed to the surface of the planet. This was an interesting experience in its own right. The atmosphere was deep, and developed a brownish hue as they descended. It was not stormy, but very thick; soon it obscured anything that might have been at any distance.

They cruised along a highway that curved around mountains of methane ice, and beside ponds of liquid methane from which methane vapor ascended slowly back into the sky. Brown methane snowflakes drifted down to coat every solid surface. This just happened to be the spot in the System where the temperature was at the "triple point" of methane—where it could exist simultaneously in solid, liquid, and vapor states.

Kyo loomed as a huge dome, girt by many lesser domes. Spirit knew that the main city had more than ten million people, and the region as a population center was much greater. They entered the lock and were treated to another marvelous sight: the oriental splendor of the culture of Rising Sun. Spirit saw a shrine with multileveled upward-curving roofs, diminishing in size as they ascended. There were dwarf trees growing in a special little park. The civilians wore brightly colored sarongs or pajama-type suits, and the petite women had their hair ornately dressed. This was, indeed, the heart of the Orient.

But elsewhere the city was intensely settled, looking quite modern. Evidently the citizens of Rising Sun valued their cultural heritage but did not let it interfere with practical matters.

They were conducted to an elegant apartment complex, where they were abruptly left to their own devices while their hosts prepared for their diplomatic encounter. They enjoyed themselves at the heated pool-sized bath, and had a fancy multicourse banquet. Smilo, released to roam the sealed region of the suite, condescended to tear apart a realistic-looking steak.

His presence, perhaps, was another reason they were being left alone.

Forta did not actually enter the bath; she remained clothed, politely aloof. But Tasha did, and her body was spectacular in the bathing suit. That bothered Spirit, for two reasons: it reminded her that she was no longer in her glamorous twenties, and it provoked desire in Hope. He liked them young and soft and sexy and not too intelligent. Forta was none of these; Tasha was most of them.

Hope grimaced as he sat at the rim and dangled his feet in the water. He was trying to resist temptation, and he had never been good at that. But Spirit could not intervene; this was his private fight, with or without pun.

Tasha swam up. "I will purchase handcuffs," she murmured.

"Thank you, but I do not care to be cuffed," he said.

"For me," she said. "For my hands and feet, and you will have the key."

Oh. The woman was in his orbit, of course. But he demurred. "I am supposed to be through with you," he said. "I have another woman now." He was giving lip service to it, at any rate.

Spirit glanced at Forta, but she seemed unconcerned. Was she so sure of her eventual victory, or masking her woe?

"That is why I must have you soon," Tasha said. "Once you go with her, you will never again go with me." She turned her face to him beseechingly. "Oh, please Tyrant—I want you so much! Bind me, rape me, anything, only take me one more time."

How could he resist? He obviously did desire her, dangerous as she was to desire. "Buy the cuffs," he said.

"Oh, thank you!" she exclaimed, flouncing out of the water to embrace him.

Forta did not react, but Smilo did. He jumped up and growled, forcing Tasha to get quickly clear.

On the following day they were granted a holo interview with the Shogun, the principal dignitary of the planet.

"So good to meet you, Tyrant," he said, lifting his hand in the greeting that was accepted as equivalent to a handshake on such occasions. "I have long admired your management of Jupiter." He glanced to the side. "What a beautiful Smilodon! Have you any of those for export?"

This was a surprise, but Hope picked right up on it. The Shogun really did admire the tiger. "Perhaps a matched pair. Breeders."

"Breeders," the Shogun echoed longingly. Titan had a long history of martial arts, now stifled by the terms of the treaty, and admired superior fighting animals.

Hope signaled Tasha. She nodded and went to their interplanetary phone. It was possible that they would be able to confirm the assignment of a pair of Smilodons before this interview was concluded. Saturn would not want to let them go, but would do so in a case like this. They desperately needed the good graces of the Shogun, and with him, Rising Sun.

The Shogun had been coolly formal. Now he warmed noticeably. He had known Hope as the Tyrant of Jupiter, and was clearly pleased to be interacting with him, despite the changed circumstances. They got down to business.

"Chairman Khukov of Saturn and I share a dream," Hope said. "It is to alleviate economic and political conditions by opening the final frontier to man: that of the colonization of the galaxy."

The Shugun picked right up on the implication. "Therefore no further need for war."

"No need of war," Hope agreed. "How much better it would be to use our resources in the effort to colonize all space. Saturn has raw resources, but lacks proper industrial capacity to exploit them efficiently. This project will be phenomenally expensive, even in the pilot stage."

"But with potentially astronomic rewards."

"True. But at the moment, it is a strain on Saturn's resources. That is why we hope to enlist the participation of others."

"Such as Rising Sun," the Shogun said, "that just happens to have a highly developed industrial base." He did not bother to conceal his keen interest.

"This is true."

"In fact, you seek investors."

"That might be another way of putting it."

"What might Saturn offer, in return for such investment?" The Shogun was of course nobody's patsy.

"Raw iron," Hope said.

The Shogun nodded. "I believe it could be possible to deal." Spirit kept a straight face. Of course it was possible! There was hardly anything Titan needed more than iron, in quantity. This could solve its problem. "But I regret to say that a certain distrust that has existed historically may not be abated immediately."

He was understating the case. The antagonism between Saturn and Titan had been long and bitter. "If there is any way to facilitate understanding and acceptance—"

"There is one whose continued presence would serve to abate skepticism here." He glanced meaningfully at Hope.

Hope was taken aback. "I had it in mind to meet with you, then return—"

"To the hospitality of the *nomenklatura?*"

He had a point. Titan was certainly safer for Hope, and there was indeed a job he could do here, facilitating the organization of the new base.

Hope glanced at Spirit. She nodded. "I would be very pleased to accept your hospitality, if Saturn concurs," he said. "In the interest of forwarding the Dream."

"This may be a dream we shall be pleased to share."

They raised their hands in the gesture of understanding.

The limited treaty between the USR and Rising Sun was considered a diplomatic coup. Shipments of iron ore moved to Titan, and a base was constructed on that planet at a near-record pace, while technicians studied the details of the breakthrough process. Hope interviewed the Rising Sun personnel, weeding out the unfit in his fashion; Saturn retained veto power in this respect, and he was serving Saturn's interest. It was a type of thing he was good at, but since he did not speak Japanese he required Forta's assistance. She translated, using her special equipment, while he judged the technicians' reactions, and it worked well enough. Thus he was making himself useful while also serving the broader purpose of reassuring the Rising Sun public by his presence.

Then when Spirit and Forta were seeing to business on the base, Tasha produced her handcuffs and they went at it. This was foolish of him, but he thought he had taken sufficient precautions. He cuffed her arms and legs to the bed and enjoyed her—but when she changed personalities, the anchorages gave way and suddenly she clamped his body in a tight scissors grip, and hauled his head down. Fortunately Smilo broke out of his cage and chomped her shoulder, rescuing Hope. That was the end of Tasha; she survived, but defected to Titan. In the question of the lady or the tiger, the tiger had won. Spirit was relieved.

Hope was left with Forta, and as time passed he gradually warmed to her. She was a good and competent woman, and available whenever he should choose.

In about two and a half years, the first new ship fitted with the interstellar process was ready for a test flight. They had been working hard to coordinate it, and production had gone well. But would it work outside the laboratory?

Thus it was that Spirit, Forta, Smilo and Hope were conveyed by shuttleship to the orbiting test ship, and given possession. It was small, intended for a crew of three and a passenger load of four, but Smilo's mass qualified him to be all four passengers. This was a public event; the newsships of all the major planets and many minor ones were present. That was why they were testing it personally: to show their confidence in the system, and to make it as much of a media event as was possible.

"Yes, it is a three-light-hour test flight," Hope said, in answer to a query from a reporter on the screen. "From the orbit of Saturn, here, to the orbit of Uranus. We shall be transformed to light, and will then proceed at light speed in the direction the transmitter is aimed, until we are intercepted by the receiver tube at the other end. Three hours to Uranus!"

They knew the System audience would be properly impressed; that trip would ordinarily take three months, by standard travel. In fact, they would arrive there at the same time as the news of their departure did.

"But suppose the alignment is off, and you miss the receiver tube?" the reporter asked.

"Then we go to another star," Hope replied, smiling. It was a joke, but a grim one; that was exactly what would happen. But there would be no receiving tube deep in the galaxy, so they would travel forever, if the computers did not precisely align transmitter and receiver.

Then it went wrong.

An anonymous ship appeared, and fired a cluster of missiles at them. The Saturn battleship protecting them fired back, lasering the missiles. But they fragmented into larger clusters consisting of a few genuine missiles and thousands of decoys that looked just like the missiles. It was impossible to take them all out before they reached the test ship.

Then a new alarm sounded. "Sub alert! Sub alert!"

Spirit whistled. "The nomens are really after us this time!" she said. "They sneaked a sub in under cover of the missile action."

"And we know its target," Hope agreed. "Hang on; I'm taking evasive action."

He spoke figuratively, for they were already strapped in. But it was rough on Smilo, who didn't understand about erratic space maneuvers; his body was thrown back and forth. That couldn't be helped.

The battleship took out the first torpedo, but the sub would simply fire another. They were in real trouble.

"Go for the transmitter!" Spirit said. This was hardly the first time she had faced the prospect of violent death, but Fortuna seemed frightened. She had reason.

Hope caught on instantly; he had always been good under fire. He went for the transmitter, which they had been approaching anyway. Its personnel, cognizant of the situation, would be ready; they would activate it the moment the ship entered it.

The ship plunged into the tube—and out the other side.

"Oh, no!" Spirit breathed. "They didn't transmit us!"

"Look at the environment!" Hope exclaimed. "The light ambiance is only a quarter what it was. This is Uranus orbit!"

"But we didn't take any three hours!" Forta protested.

"We took it," he explained. "We simply weren't aware of it. There is no time at light speed, as far as we're concerned; it's like being in suspended animation."

It had worked! Man could now travel to the stars, with no more apparent time lapse than they had experienced. Mankind could colonize the galaxy!

Now they saw the escort ships of the Uranus nations arriving. They were definitely there.

Uranus was more politically fragmented than was Jupiter or Saturn. It equated to the ancient Europe, and had many languages and cultures, and a turbulent history. A ship bearing the markings of Helvetia, or New Switzerland, came to provide hospitality. But Forta demurred. "I smell a rat."

Hope glanced at her. "You don't like Helvetia?"

"I like it well; I have been here before. But Helvetia has no ships of that class in its Navy.'

"Why not?" he asked. "Historically, on Earth, the region was landbound, but there is no such thing in the System. Helvetia can have any navy it can finance—and it is a rich little nation."

"Isn't that a cruiser?" she persisted. "A ship of war?"

"She's got a point, Hope," Spirit said. "Why should a peaceful nation support a war vessel?"

"They *don't* support any warships," Forta said. "It's policy, not finance. That ship can't be theirs."

"We can verify its credentials in a moment," Hope said, reaching for the communications panel.

Spirit's hand intercepted his. "If that ship is a ringer, it will blast us out of space the moment we try to verify it. Our assassins are fanatics." Forta nodded; she had seen some of those attempts.

"But if we don't go with it, it will realize that we know," Hope said.

"The tube," Forta said tightly. "Will it—?"

"Titan personnel operate that tube," Hope said. "Let's see how smart they are." He spoke casually, but they all knew that they were in trouble.

He touched the communications panel. "Glad to see you, Helvetia," he said, addressing the cruiser. "Bear with me a moment; I want to fetch something at the tube." He cut the drive, going into free-fall, turned the ship about, and accelerated back toward the tube.

The cruiser did not reply. It simply matched their velocity again, performing a similar maneuver and accelerating to compensate for their change. It was not about to let them get away.

The ship headed straight toward the tube. "Minor matter," Hope transmitted to the tube personnel. "You know what I want."

There was a pause. Then the Rising Sun technician came on the screen. "As you wish, Tyrant," he said politely.

"You're going back?" Forta asked. "Suppose it follows?"

"We are gambling on the savvy of the Titans," Spirit said tightly.

"But they can't stop the cruiser from following us!"

"We'll see," Spirit said. But her mouth was going dry. *Did the Titans understand?*

By the time they entered the tube, the cruiser was almost on their tail. They shot through, and out the other side. The cruiser entered right behind, barely squeezing in, and disappeared.

They experienced an abrupt jolt, as though a star had just gone nova behind them. The ship's tail section heated and melted, and the drive cut out. They were boosted forward, but were dead in space. Smilo took another bad fall.

But ships were constructed for exactly this type of acceleration. Their drive was gone, but the hull was intact and cabin power remained on. They had survived.

"What was that?" Forta asked. Her bun of hair had come apart, and she looked disheveled.

"We may have been struck by a laser," Hope said, "or the equivalent."

"Oh—they fired at us!"

"Perhaps," Spirit agreed.

"Where are we?" Forta asked nervously.

"Right where we were," Hope said, checking out the equipment to ascertain whether they retained communication. "The tube did not activate, for us."

"Then where is the other ship?"

He smiled grimly. "That may be difficult to determine. You see, the tube *did* activate for it."

"You mean it's a light beam, on its way to Saturn?"

"It's a light beam," he agreed. Spirit caught his eye, and he said no more.

"So it was transmitted while we were not," Forta said. "But how—"

"The Rising Sun personnel understood our wish," Spirit told her. "Our wish was to be free of pursuit."

"How clever!" Forta said doubtfully.

The face of the Rising Sun technician came on the screen. "Are you satisfied, Tyrant?" he inquired.

"Quite," Hope agreed. "Shall we agree that this matter is finished?"

"Agreed, sir," the tech said.

"We appeared to have suffered some damage," Hope continued. "Possibly from a laser attack. Please request assistance for us."

"A laser," the tech agreed. "We shall see to it, sir." He clicked out.

"Damn good personnel," Spirit murmured.

Rising Sun was forbidden by treaty to produce weapons of war. The light-projection project was considered to be technology of peace, but it had certain difficult philosophical aspects. If a ship was transmitted to another tube, this was a peaceful operation. But suppose a ship was transmitted—and there was no receiving tube? Or the beam of light was deflected on the way? Then there would be no reconversion, and that ship would probably never manifest in solid state again. When that happened, was the tube a weapon instead of a tool?

The Rising Sun personnel had understood. They had let the first ship pass through untransmitted. They had activated the system for the following ship, so that it became light and beamed forward at light speed. The first vessel had blocked its forward path. When it became light, it had struck the physical ship ahead.

That ship was dead. Spirit and Hope knew it, and the personnel of the transmission tube knew it. Forta didn't know it, and perhaps it would be some time before the rest of the System caught on. The tube had just been used as a weapon. Did that put Rising Sun in violation of its treaty? It was a temporary conspiracy of silence.

This had been more of a demonstration than they had planned on—but a most effective one.

Soon they visited Helvetia, after verifying that the cruiser had indeed not been from that nation. They were given excellent lodging, and Hope proceeded with a months-long process of visiting Uranian heads of state, to enlist their support for Saturn's Dream. He was largely successful; it was his genius to persuade people, and the Dream was well worth supporting. But betweentimes he became restive. He needed a woman.

"It is time for you to take over," Spirit told Forta.

"I am sure he will come to me, when he chooses."

"No. I know my brother. He lives for women, but he does not pursue them. They must pursue him."

"This is not my way."

"Therefore the purpose for which you came has been unfulfilled for two years. Take the initiative, woman."

"But—"

"I will depart on an errand. You will become Juana and approach him."

"But Juana is a grandmother."

"Juana at age seventeen. You can do that?"

"Certainly. But—"

"Do it. I will return in two hours."

"If you are sure—"

"*Do* it," Spirit repeated firmly, and departed. She wished she could watch what happened during her absence, but this was not feasible. So she busied herself with inconsequentials, and returned in exactly two hours.

Forta, as young buxom Juana, was sitting on Hope's lap. His head was against her bosom, and her arms were around him. He appeared to be asleep, his face serene.

Spirit nodded and went to her room. The ice had been broken, and Hope had taken Forta as his woman. Not sexually yet, for both were fully clothed, but the acceptance was manifest. That was what counted.

Forta was soon to have another use. The president of Gaul was an old-line warrior whose mind was firmly set. He was not about to be moved by Saturn's new-fangled project, and Gaul would not join without the General's approval. They had to find a way to persuade him.

"I seem to remember that there was one he listened to," Spirit said.

"His daughter," Forta said, having done her research. "But she died five years ago, and after that he stopped caring about any opinion but his own. There is no ameliorating personality around him now."

"His daughter," Spirit said musingly. She glanced at Hope. "They to tend to wrap their fathers around their fingers." Exactly as Hopie did with Hope—and how could Spirit object? The two had an amazing amount in common.

"I could study her," Forta said, speaking of the General's daughter.

Spirit nodded. "If you are willing."

"Megan knew of the Dream," Forta said. "She felt I could help in its realization. I see no ethical problem here, especially considering the alternative."

Hope finally got an interview with the General, and because of the man's attitude about newfangled technology, it was an actual physical meeting, not a holo replication. It was a formality; the General had already made up his mind not to participate in the Dream.

But they had prepared for this. Hope gave Spirit to understand his negative reading, by the slightest nod: thumbs down. She in turn made an unobtrusive signal to Forta, the secretary, who stood at the edge of the room.

Forta turned around a moment, as if suffering an attack of vertigo. She was doing something to herself. Then she turned again, her aspect changed.

The General paused, glancing at her, startled. He got to his feet. Spirit knew that he was seeing a vision of his daughter. Hope read the signals consciously; others did so unconsciously, but they were as persuasive.

Forta spoke in French. She had entirely changed her hair, and she wore one of her masks, so that she resembled a young woman who would have been attractive except for her overly large nose. That nose resembled that of the General. She had become his daughter.

The General looked stricken. He replied in French.

She only gazed at him, shaking her head sadly.

It was as if the General saw a ghost.

"You support this man?" the General asked the ghost.

Forta nodded in a special manner.

"And if I agree?"

Forta approached him, lifted her face, and kissed his cheek. Then she walked slowly out of the room.

For a moment the General stood stunned. Then he strode after her. Spirit and Hope remained where they were, letting this play itself out.

All that the General found in the other room, of course, was the secretary, Forta, who could in no way be mistaken for his daughter. Disgruntled, he returned. "You saw only your secretary?"

Spirit and Hope nodded together, too polite to remark on his erratic behavior. The General's vision had been his alone.

He considered. "Gaul will support your project, Tyrant," he said abruptly.

"Your generosity and foresight are much appreciated," Hope said. "The greatness of Gaul will long be commemorated." They concluded the interview with the usual amenities.

After that success, the others followed more readily. Hope interviewed the Kaiser of Prussia, and the Kings of Bohemia, Lithuania, and Etruria. There was no trouble converting Castile to the Dream; Castile had watched Hope's progress on Jupiter all the way to the top, and had broken relations with Jupiter when he was deposed. It was a real pleasure to be welcomed where Spanish was the natural language. The others soon fell into place.

On Titania, heir to the old Britain, there was another attempt to assassinate Hope. He barely escaped it, with Smilo's help. Spirit hated being under such constant siege, but it was a penalty of Hope's notoriety. One day, she know, an attempt would succeed.

Then they went out to Neptune's moon Triton, to oversee the construction of the main base for interstellar travel. The Dream was proceeding well. Forta assumed the persona of Emerald, Hope's first formal Navy wife before she became Admiral of the full Navy. And Hope turned out to have kidney disease, an evident complication of his poisoning some years before. His body resisted effective treatment. His time was likely to be limited. He had about five years before he ran out of dialysis sites that would not show.

Forta learned how to dialyze him, so he could keep that aspect private. But he needed to bring the remaining planets into the Dream as soon as possible, knowing that there would not be a later chance.

They went to Mars, the home of iron, and Forta manifested as Shelia. She had, she said, a score to settle with Big Iron. Spirit knew that Hope loved all his women, whether they remained alive or dead, but there were ways in which Shelia was the most special of the unofficial mistresses.

She was special in this negotiation too. She made a ghostly appearance, warning Hope of danger. It was well known what part she had played in the Jupiter Iron incident, and its effect on the Tyrant. Hope did not see the ghost, but a bit of the Tyrant's vaunted madness began to show. The Iron magnates hastened to complete the deal.

Thus Hope managed to work out a compromise between Moslem Mars and Jewish Phobos. The elements were in place for the demilitarization of Deimos and the establishment of a major Titan base there, Saturn concurring. Mars iron would be donated and light-shipped to Triton for the Dream project, but the resulting squeeze on the availability of iron would probably triple the value of what remained, making the deal profitable. Phobos would receive a fee of half of one per cent of the value of the shipped iron. That was a formidable value.

Their party went on to Planet Earth, which was now the Nation of India. Forta became Dorian Gray, Hope's mistress during his captivity aboard the submarine. She was dead, but lived again in this fashion, and Hope was evidently satisfied. Spirit marveled anew at Forta's versatility. She was enabling Hope to relive much of his life. Spirit was also intrigued to see what Dorian Gray had been like, get to know her, as it were. She discovered that she rather liked her, though it might simply have been Forta's rendition that made Dorian Gray palatable. Still, it seemed that she had been a lovely young woman caught in a situation, who had done what she had to do. Spirit understood that sort of thing all too well.

They met with the Prime Minister of Earth, who was a woman as tough and politically realistic as the one they had encountered on Phobos. There are not many women in power in the System, but those few were as competent as any man. She wore a colorful toga, looking native, but she addressed them in English, so that Forta did not have to translate. The formal meeting was physical—without holo—and private, with only the two of them. But Hope relayed the essence as soon as he was alone with Spirit and Forta.

"She says Jupiter has not been the same since we departed. She advised me that, though Jupiter's government remains nominally democratic, the predators have moved in. Bad things are happening there."

"Who is really in charge now?" Spirit asked.

"Tocsin."

Spirit shook her head. "So the poison weed grows back."

"She gave me to understand that Earth would not find it amiss if the Tyrancy were to be returned to Jupiter. When Jupiter sneezes, the entire System shudders. She says I was always practical and fair."

"That was the effort," Spirit agreed.

"I reminded her that I represent Saturn now. She firmly reminded me that I represent *humanity* now, and that the project cannot succeed without the participation of Jupiter, and the present powers there will never accede to it. She urged me to reconsider my position."

"Perhaps we were naive to turn our backs on our planet," Spirit said. "We had not reckoned with the sharks."

He shook his head. "The Tyrancy is over. Once all the other planets are part of the Dream, Jupiter will join, as a matter of expediency."

Spirit didn't argue, but she found this news deeply disquieting. Hope continued, advising her of the deal that would be made with Earth: it would provide a hundred thousand qualified test subjects for the new light drive, in return for participation in the Dream.

They also got to tour Earth, the origin planet of mankind. That was a special experience. Here there were actual open-air cities instead of bubbles, mirroring the cultures of the Solar System. And there was yet another attempt to assassinate Hope.

Here, too, they received a most significant caller. "Visitor," Spirit said as she recognized him. "From Jupiter."

"Jupiter isn't speaking to me," Hope reminded her. "Make sure it isn't an assassin."

"No assassin," she said with a smile. Then, to the screen: "Send him in."

Hope was in pajamas, ready for bed, and Dorian Gray was in a flimsy nightie that fairly radiated sex appeal. She jumped up, about to scurry into her room to change clothing and identities.

"As you were," Spirit said. "Robert won't tell."

Their visitor arrived. "My, how you've grown!" Spirit said, stepping out to embrace the visitor. He was a solid, muscular youth in his teens, Hispanic, smiling somewhat foolishly. "Hi, Dad," he said over her shoulder.

"Robertico!"

Dorian Gray dissolved into astonishment and dismay. She sought again to leave, but Hope grabbed her wrist.

Robertico had been eleven; now he was fifteen, and that

seemed to have added most of a foot to his height and fifty pounds to his mass. Hope had never formally adopted him, but he had become part of the family. Hopie had been first his baby-sitter, then his older sister, taking excellent care of him. Of course he was a welcome visitor!

"I come with a message," Robertico said. Then he faltered, staring at Dorian Gray.

Hope smiled. "Dorian Gray, meet my ward Robertico. Robertico, meet your mother."

For he had been the infant son of that woman. Now Dorian Gray had returned, in the only way she could. Of course she was young, in this incarnation, only a few years older than Robertico himself. But that seemed not to matter. She stared at him, knowing what this meant, and he stared at her, seeing his mother for the first time. Then he stepped forward, and she stood, and they flung themselves into each other's arms and wept together.

Spirit felt a tear of her own. Perhaps others would see this as a ludicrous scene, but Dorian Gray was as close to the original as it was possible to be, and Robertico was of her flesh. If ever a man could go back in time and meet his mother as a young woman, this was the occasion.

In due course they got to Robertico's message. "It is this," he said. "'Stay clear of Jupiter.' They do not want you there, and they will execute you if you violate your exile."

They all laughed. This was no news at all.

"Hopie sent me," he continued. "And they let me go, because they knew you would see me. It isn't the same there, now. They mean it; you can't go there."

"But the Triton Project needs the support of Jupiter," Hope said. "It is for the benefit of all mankind."

"They don't care about that. They just don't want you back."

"I wonder why?" Hope asked, as if ignorant.

"My sister told me," Robertico said. "It's because the people would support you. Things were better when you were Tyrant."

"Things always seem better in the past."

"No, Dad, it's true!" he insisted. "There are shortages all the time now, and a lot of police, and anybody who criticizes the government gets arrested and maybe disappears. It's bad!"

"Freedoms are being denied? What does the press have to say about this?"

"The news media are being shut down. They don't dare say anything."

"What about Thorley? Nobody could shut him up."

"He was arrested last year."

"What?" This time both Hope and Spirit were shocked. Indeed they had not been paying attention!

"Well, first it was just house arrest, but when he wouldn't shut up, they came and took him away last month. My sister said you'd want to know about that, even if he did criticize you a lot. She's really upset."

Spirit exchanged a glance with Hope.

They kept it polite, as though they hadn't really reacted to the message. Robertico was there on a limited visa, and had to return promptly. "Tell them I got the message," Hope said as he left.

"Yeah," he agreed darkly. "I'm sorry you can't stop by there. Hopie really wanted to see you."

"Tell her I'll do what I have to do, as I always have."

"And take care of yourself, dear," Dorian Gray said to him, exactly like a mother.

He left. Dorian Gray retired immediately to her room. Spirit knew she had been shaken by the turn her impersonation had taken. She had, for a moment, been a mother, and that was no light thing.

Hope turned to Spirit. "*Now* I am satisfied. You know what to do."

She nodded grimly. "You prepare Forta." Then she went to her own room. Forta wasn't the only one who could do emulations.

She was ready within the hour. She was now in male clothing, and looked like a man. "Give me ten minutes," she said.

Hope nodded. He summoned the hotel staff, and managed to distract the man while Spirit slipped quietly out in the guise of a hotel servitor, escaping undetected. Thus suddenly she was on her way, and no one would know she was gone. Forta would have to cover for her, emulating her as necessary, while Hope's party went on to Planet Venus and planet Mercury, enlisting the governments of North and South Africa. It would surely be a considerable challenge for them to manage without Spirit, but they would rise to it. The need, after all, was dire.

CHAPTER 18

Affair

Spirit, in the guise of Sancho, caught a landbound cab. "Government office," she said tersely.

She arrived at the nearest sub-branch office of the planetary government, and entered the building. "I must speak with the representative."

The clerk questioned her briefly, checked her planetary visitor's pass, then sent her to the local representative's office. "Please, *señor*, what I have to say is most private," she said.

The man was evidently used to complaints. He touched a button on his desk, and the shimmer of privacy surrounded them. "How may I help you, citizen?"

"May I rely on your discretion?"

"If your need is legitimate."

"I am Spirit Hubris, sister of the erstwhile Tyrant. I must depart this planet secretly."

He did not flinch. "You have identification?"

She opened her shirt, showing her bound breasts so that he could see she was female, and from an inner pocket produced her ID card. She had kept herself fit; she had good breasts, and did not want to argue about gender. "I'm traveling incognito."

His mouth quirked as he ran the ID. "You are sixty two? I took you for forty—and male."

"Thank you."

"The Prime Minister will see you now. Please enter the holo

chamber."

She concealed her surprise at this efficiency. "Thank you," she repeated, and entered the chamber.

The wall became a window to the Prime Minister's office. "Hello, Spirit Hubris," she said. "I had supposed your brother had elected not to act at this time."

"He changed his mind."

"You wish assistance returning to Jupiter?"

"I do, thank you."

"We trade with Jupiter and with Saturn. We can put you aboard a merchant vessel of either power."

Spirit considered. "We serve Saturn now. I think I had better consult privately with Chairman Khukov."

"Alone? Physically? Without your brother?"

"This is hardly public business! Hope will continue to travel, and I will seem to be with him. My absence must not be known."

"A Saturn vessel," the prime Minister agreed, understanding. "A car will come for you."

"Thank you."

As Spirit rode in the car, she mused about one trifling aspect of her dialogue with the Prime Minister. The woman had seemed surprised that Spirit should wish to meet with Chairman Khukov alone. Why? Khukov was their employer and most certain ally.

In due course she arrived at Saturn, still traveling as Sancho. A courier ship met her at Scow, and conveyed her to an anonymous residential bubble.

Mikhail Khukov was there, alone. "Spirit Hubris! You have come to me at last."

"We have met before," she said, uncertain of his meaning.

"And you do not know," he said. "I apologize."

"I know that Jupiter is in trouble. I think my brother must take back the Tyrancy. But this can't happen without your support. If you do not wish him to resume power—"

"I would like nothing better. I will do what I can. But meanwhile I must say to you what you may not like."

"There is a price," she said. There was always a price.

"If you wish it."

"I don't understand. We have a choice?"

He faced her squarely. "You understand that my ability is similar to your brother's. That is why I trust him, and he trusts me. We have read each other. We have similar aspirations."

"You share the Dream," she agreed, knowing that this was not his thrust.

"More. I, too, am a man for the women. The more remarkable the woman, the greater my desire."

"Yes, you understand his ways. You provided Hope with a remarkable mistress in Amber."

"You are the most remarkable woman I know."

Suddenly his meaning came clear. "Chairman, I am an old matron!"

"A handsome woman. Even your scars have personality."

"You surely have your choice of fresh young women. You hardly need to bother with–"

"I desired you before we ever met. You were your brother's backbone throughout his military service, and throughout the Tyrancy. Without you, he would never have prospered."

He was on target, to a degree. "But without him, I would never have prospered either. He has the magic."

"And your loyalty becomes you too. If you were mine, you would never betray me."

"I am yours to the extent my brother is. That is why I came to check with you before–"

"I desire you as a mistress."

She paused. "This is the price of your support?"

"If you wish."

There was that oblique response again. "I wish to have your support."

"I wish to have you without buying you. But others would not understand, so if you wish, I will say I bought you."

"You know my pirate and Navy experience. Sex is the least of the price I would pay to support my brother."

"Your love is out of reach. But perhaps not your respect." She contemplated him. "How long?"

"While we associate. As in the Navy: term commitment. Romance not necessary. Not to interfere with your departure when the Tyrancy resumes. Not to be secret, once your brother's purpose is accomplished."

He wanted to be able to say he had the tyrant's sister, and have her agreement. But he would keep the secret of her identity while it counted. Spirit had kept a rein on her personal feeling. Now she let it flow. She was flattered that this remarkable man should desire her sexually despite her age, and desire also to have his passion publicly known. She had been long without a man. This one would do; she was attracted to especially talented men, and Khukov was one. It would not be onerous duty. "Then take me, Navy man."

He smiled. "Not in your present guise."

She laughed, and stripped off her masculine clothing and the binding around her chest. She stepped into him and embraced him. She kissed him. "From Jupiter: surplus Navy tail," she said.

"You understand: I support your brother regardless, for he serves my larger purpose. It is not essential that you do this."

"That does make it easier. But it is not difficult, regardless."

"Thank you."

Then they proceeded to an act of passion that would have done a younger couple credit. Khukov's desire was plainly genuine, and he was indeed the kind of man she preferred: intelligent, powerful, ethical, with a special ability, and, as it turned out, caring.

After the first bout, they cleaned up, and Khukov began giving directives to the Saturn Navy. It would slowly deploy toward Jupiter, but in a manner that did not betray its target. One courier ship would rendezvous with a Jupiter Navy courier for the transfer of liaison personnel, one of which would be an anonymous Hispanic male: Spirit. Then they had another siege of sex. Then they had a good meal. Then more sex, somewhat more drawn out.

"How long since you did it three times in one day?" she asked, impressed.

"Decades. As long as I have been without you."

It really was flattering, and it was no chore to participate. She realized that she had missed the regular sex of the Navy. "Had I known of your interest, I might have made myself available sooner."

"You were married, then committed. I was married. We were at different planets. It was not feasible."

He had desired her when she was with Gerald? He had kept his eye on Hope and his sister a long time!

They spent the night naked in the same bed. She knew this would mean rather constant attention, if not full sex, but she intended to saturate his desire. Indeed, he clasped her as she slept, and in the night she woke to feel him stroking her breast. She let him proceed, lapsing back into sleep. In the morning he slept later than she did; she considered, then stroked him and kissed him, waking him to her interest.

"It is a calculated thing you do," he murmured. "I appreciate that calculation."

"Let it never be said that you found the Iron Maiden insufficient."

"It shall never be said."

They were together a week. Khukov's passion was almost indefatigable, though he was not able to consummate it as often as at first. It seemed not to matter; he was satisfied with her closeness and amenability. Between-times they played chess and pool, and discussed works of literature. There was no pretense of love, merely of mutual interest. His passion for her was clearly greater than hers for him, but that was natural to their genders, and it would not have been possible to fool him anyway. Overall, she enjoyed the experience, and made no effort to conceal her pleasure. She felt two decades younger.

"To have the attention of a independent woman whose interest can not be purchased—this is a thing I have long lacked," he said. "You could be ugly, and it would have appeal. But you are lovely."

"I can endure this kind of criticism."

They laughed and continued. Spirit found it pleasant also that he trusted her, though she knew it was because she was trustworthy. She was not catering to him for his power, but because they had made a mutually beneficial deal.

Then it was time for her to catch the shuttle. "It has been nice," she said.

"It has been paradise."

"Can the shuttle rendezvous again, in a week?"

He looked at her, surprised. "Oh Iron Maiden, I could love you if I allowed it."

She smiled and kissed him once more. "Do not allow it. Just hone your passion, lest I waste my time."

She boarded the shuttle as Sancho. In due course it rendezvoused with the Jupiter shuttle, and that conveyed her to a Jupiter cruiser.

A buxom civilian woman met her at the port. "You will serve my interest, laborer," she said curtly.

Spirit masked her reaction and followed the woman to her cabin. Then, alone, they flung themselves into each other's arms, kissing. "Roulette!" "Spirit!"

"How did you know?"

"Juana told me."

"How did *she* know? This is supposed to be secret."

"Not from Emerald. She has been in touch with Saturn throughout, and when news of your presence came, she gathered the other women. She's on duty elsewhere at the moment, but can see you in two weeks."

"Two weeks is perfect." Then, at leisure, she explained about

Khukov.

"Maybe I could substitute for you," Rue said teasingly. "I'm sure he'd find me more interesting."

"He might indeed! But I'm the one he wants, amazingly."

"Then you will have to give me your brother. He's the one *I* want."

"Hope has another woman now."

"He always has another woman! But I'm a widow, and I want one more crack at him before he dies."

"Before—?"

"Come on, Spirit. If the assassins don't get him, the kidneys will. There's not all that much time."

Spirit shook her head. "Can't any secrets be kept?"

"Not from wives and lovers. No outsiders know."

"All right. If the chance comes, you get him for a while. Now we need to organize."

"His current woman. I have seen her on holo. She's ugly. What's her secret?"

"She's a mime. She uses masks and signals to emulate other women. She is very good."

"She couldn't fool *him*."

"She comes close enough to satisfy him. She emulated Juana at age seventeen, and she can do others."

"Juana at seventeen." Rue pondered that a moment. "Sexually too?"

"Yes."

Rue was intrigued. "Could she do me?"

"I'm sure she could—and will, in due course."

"As I am now?"

"Why not? You remain a sight to stir the male passion."

Rue glanced down at her full figure. "We'll see."

"I presume Emerald retains real Navy power?"

"Potential power. With her husband dead, the edge is gone, but he taught her much. But any use of it could alert Tocsin's men, and they are not incompetent."

"Understood. The strike must be properly timed, and it must be effective. There will be no second chance."

"Meanwhile, we can organize. Do we have a code name?"

Spirit pondered momentarily. "The Affair."

"Mine, yours, and ours." Roulette smiled. "I must return to the Belt so as not to rouse suspicion. But Juana will take over."

"Juana is here?"

"Unofficially. Jupe retirees have staff privileges."

"Staff privileges," Spirit repeated, thinking of Shelia.

Juana was indeed grandmotherly, half again as solid as she had been in youth, smiling and pleasant. "He's coming back?" she asked.

"Yes. With things as they are on Jupiter, we have to act."

"What about Megan?"

That made Spirit pause. "You're right. If she doesn't acquiesce, Hope won't do it. Can we reach her privately?"

"I can, when I return to Jupiter."

"That will do. She regards you as Hope's second wife, and herself as the fifth. She will talk with you. Meanwhile, do you still know the people who know the people?"

"Enough of them. But the wider this gets, the harder it will be to keep it secret."

"Emerald will have to decide who is notified when."

"She can't be here personally yet."

"I know. In a week I must return for Saturn liaison. Then–"

"You have a Saturn man!" Juana exclaimed.

"You want details?"

"I never really liked doing it, but I love hearing about it. Is he a known figure?"

"Chairman Khukov. He's a widower now."

Juana whistled. "You started at the top! How did you ever land him?"

"He desired me. I had not realized. I found it flattering."

"He's like Hope, isn't he?"

Spirit paused. "How do you mean that?"

Juana blushed. "Not that way! I mean, he has the talent to read people. To move them."

Their dialogue continued, as Spirit shared the details of her affair. But now she wondered: Khukov's interest in her was understandable, in retrospect, because she was the sister of a man like himself and had kept herself in physical shape. But she had returned his interest, and truly enjoyed their ardently sexual week. She had thought it was because she respected him, and was flattered by the intense desire of so prominent a man, and she did miss the lost regularity of sex. Could it be, at least in part, because he was a surrogate for her brother? She had never forgotten her lone liaison with Hope, when she was twelve, and she still dreamed of it on occasion. She still loved him in more than a sisterly way. If there were some heaven where a woman could marry any man she chose, she would marry him. That was her abiding secret, even from herself, much of the time. She had been the first girl to fall into his orbit, and not one of them had ever fallen out of it.

She concluded that it was true. She decided to tell Khukov, to be fair to him. She suspected it wouldn't matter to him, but it was a qualification to her side of the relationship.

The week went swiftly, and then she took the return shuttle to the Saturn ship. She broached the matter as soon as she was alone with Khukov: "In fairness, I must say–"

"If my essential likeness to your brother inspires your return passion, I welcome it."

So he had known. "Still, that is an illicit association. My licit ones–"

"One is dead, the other jailed."

Her jaw dropped. "You know?"

"He is a fine man, and now also a widower. When you return to Jupiter, you will marry him, and raise many eyebrows. But for the moment you are mine."

"For the moment," she agreed, bemused.

Their association was less intense than before, but as meaningful. "I still find it hard to appreciate why you should wish to have me instead of a fresher face and body," she said after a satisfying bout.

"Aside from whatever else, you have a wealth of experience that is similar to my own. You are not merely a pretty face." He stroked the scars on her countenance. "If pirates came after me, would you burn yourself to stop them?"

"Yes."

"Because you fear what else would come to power in my absence!" he said, laughing as he read her.

"We agreed: no love," she reminded him.

"But there could have been, in other circumstance."

"In other circumstance."

Meanwhile the Saturn Navy maneuvered seemingly routinely, coincidentally drawing nearer to Jupiter. If the Tyrant asked, it would answer.

"It is a lot of trust you extend, to one who could make real mischief for you if he did not serve your interest," she remarked.

"It is my business to know whom to trust. If Hope Hubris recovers Jupiter he will no longer serve me, but will still serve the Dream."

"That is true." She glanced at him. "May I initiate?"

He read her with that uncanny accuracy. "You are twelve."

She nodded, embarrassed. She had in the course of their more candid dialogues told him details of her other men, and he had understood more than she told.

"A privilege." He feigned sleep. "Helse!" he said, dreaming. "Don't go!" He caught hold of her. She struggled weakly to free herself, then let him draw her in. He tried to kiss her. She turned her face aside, then turned it back and met him squarely. "But I killed you!"

"Do it," she said.

"I love you."

"And I love you." Fifty years, and it remained so clear.

He brought her in close to him, and she felt his hard member. She could draw away, even now, for he would not force her. Instead she found his hand and carried it to her breast. She was Helse, giving him comfort. He kissed her breast, and she arched, responding. Then he mounted her, and she spread her legs, lifting her knees. His member found the place, and nudged inside, slowly, distending the tightness, like a ship docking in a bubble tube. "Helse!" and his pulsing joy erupted.

"Oh Hope, my love!" she breathed, her joy enclosing his, her pulses extending his. The rapture seemed to continue for a brief forever.

Then they fell apart, and she left him sleeping, to clean up by herself. He remained for a time in his dream.

Later, he commented. "How can love be wrong?"

"I fear it can be."

"Speaking for myself: I think I have never had a more fulfilling experience."

"I think Hope and Helse loved with a love that was more than love," she agreed.

"They did what we can not: they spoke of love."

"What we can not."

"Nevertheless, I think I have had of you what you have given no other man."

"Except the first."

He shook his head. "You truly are the Iron Maiden."

"We agreed," she reminded him again.

"Yet if our circumstances should ever change—"

"Then, perhaps," she agreed. It was an oblique, conditional betrothal.

The following week Spirit met with Emerald. Here, too there were fond memories. "That time you flashed your cleft at my husband," Spirit said, laughing.

"Black magic," Emerald agreed.

They kissed each other. Then they got down to business. They knew that no overt moves could be made, but there were some useful covert ones. They devised a system of bottlenecks that would inhibit or prevent certain commands from being carried out efficiently, and the blame would fall on Tocsin's appointees. Only when Hope assumed power, and restored Emerald to command, would full efficiency return. This ploy would work for only a few hours, but that might be sufficient.

Then things went wrong on Planet Mercury. Suddenly Hope Hubris was on the Interplanetary News. He was, it seemed, in a South Mercury prison cell, naked and in bad condition. Somehow someone had bootlegged the holo tape out from under the nose of the controlled press.

Then the face of Spirit came on: Forta, emulating her with uncanny precision. "Oh, Hope!" she exclaimed. "I knew it! They've humiliated you! They've stripped you naked!"

How had this happened? Later Spirit learned that Forta had been abducted, but that Hope had managed to exchange places with her, emulating her while she emulated him and escaped. Then she had become Spirit and made a scene calculated to blow the lid off the tight little dictatorship that was the South Mercury government. They had reversed the ploy with a vengeance.

"And they've tortured you!" Forta-Spirit cried with horror. "Your legs—all scarred and bandaged!"

The scars were from prior loop-sites, and the bandage concealed the present loop. But who would believe that at this moment, when Hope's kidney ailment was not even known? "Beautiful," real-Spirit murmured.

The face of a higher government official appeared, evidently overriding the prior transmissions. "We are being framed!" he exclaimed in English. "We never touched the Tyrant!"

Spirit's visage reappeared. "Then how is my brother locked in your cell, naked and scarred?" she demanded half hysterically. And without giving him a chance to formulate a reply, she continued: "I demand you free him instantly!"

"But we never—" the official protested, obviously at a loss in this abrupt and astonishing turn of events.

"So you refuse!" she said indignantly. "Well, my brother is here as the representative of the Union of Saturnine Republics, and we consider this to be an act of war." Her head turned as she addressed an off-screen party. "Saturn Commander, what is your authority?"

Now the head of a Saturn Navy marshal appeared. "My fleet is at the disposal of the Tyrant, Hope Hubris." Evidently he had been properly briefed, and knew the nature of this ploy, and enjoyed it. "Sir, what are your orders?"

"I seem to have no choice," Hope said with staged regret. "I must assume power in South Mercury. Orient on the major cities, and destroy them if I die."

"Understood, Tyrant," the marshal said with ill-concealed relish.

In this manner Hope came to be the Tyrant of Mercury, in the name of the Triton Project. That was the official reason the Saturn Navy supported him. Forta had performed beautifully, fooling almost everybody.

"I wonder whether your proficient mime emulated you for him, as I emulated him for you?" Khukov inquired innocently.

She bashed him with a soft pillow. "Only in his sleep."

"He has such marvelous dreams."

She put him in a head scissors and threatened to bite off his penis. But he tickled her cleft with his tongue until she had to let him go. They dissolved into ferocious sex, then discussed the ramifications of Hope's Mercury ploy. They both knew that Jupiter was next. But it would take more than the Saturn Navy to handle that.

"Incidentally," she said as a crafted afterthought, "thank you for lending Navy support to my brother."

"You have forgotten that we are allies now?"

"And I thought it was just sex!"

"No, I have no sexual desire for him."

In due course Hope traveled to Ganymede, Saturn's Jupiter satellite. He did it via the light drive, so the Jupiter Navy could not intercept him if it wanted to. Spirit had quietly visited the Premier of Ganymede, preparing the way.

But Tocsin was not passive. He quietly put Hopie Hubris under house arrest. Juana returned with that news, which she had gleaned from Megan. Megan had been uncertain whether she could approve the return of the Tyrancy, but when Hopie was touched, that changed. Megan would not oppose Hope.

But Hope would do nothing if it put Hopie in real danger. He loved her like his own, and Spirit had always known and appreciated that. Hopie had to be rescued. That was the tricky part.

They decided not to tell Hope about Hopie; he had too much else to do. They would get Hopie clear their own way, and with luck Hope would not know until after she was safe.

"Now is your time," Spirit told Roulette. "You must substitute for Forta, so that she can infiltrate the White Bubble and rescue Hopie. I think it is best that Hope not know."

"I must emulate Forta emulating me," Rue said, licking her lips. "I can do that in costume, as it were, but I don't know how to dialyze him."

"You will remain in costume throughout," Spirit said. "You will refuse to step out of character, being typically willful. The Ganymede facilities can dialyze him; the Premier knows what we are up to. Keep him occupied while we do what we have to."

Rue nodded. "That I will do, gladly. And thank you, Spirit."

"Remember, his talent does not work well when his emotions are involved. You should be able to fool him because he does love you in his fashion. If he catches on, he may get chivalrous about Forta, for he prefers to be true to his current woman."

"I know. He was true to me, when I was his. I will do my best."

"I will distract my brother. You must take Forta aside and explain about Hopie. She knows you; she will understand. You

will exchange places with her, and remain with Hope while
Forta departs with me in your guise. If we can fool Hope, we
can fool anyone else."

"I will fool him."

Spirit assumed her Sancho guise, and Roulette donned the
uniform of a Jupiter Navy enlisted person. They went to
Ganymede, and met Hope, Forta, and a third person: Doppie,
on loan from Earth to emulate Spirit when Forta was not available. Spirit updated Hope on her activities for the past months
and told him about the network of interference points that would
paralyze Tocsin's directives. She gave him the names for eleva-
tion to power in the Jupiter Navy, so that he could declare an
immediate and loyal slate. That was vital; he could not prevail
without the firm support of the Navy. The Saturn Navy was
also near, but its support had to be tacit. Meanwhile Roulette
took Forta aside, to acquaint her with relevant details. Few
knew just *how* relevant.

Hope's acuity was less than it had been, because of his ill-
ness, but he made sure to understand the necessary. At last it
was time for them to leave, and for him to undergo dialysis.
Spirit knew that when he came out of that, he would not be
particularly alert; it would be a break-in period for Roulette.

Spirit left with Forta, each in her prior guise. Roulette remained behind. Hope was bound to have a remarkable time, in
the next few days.

They went to Jupiter. Juana acquainted them with connections supporting Hope, even among the service personnel of
the White Bubble. Forta assumed the identity of a female guard
who was to be in charge of a very special prisoner: Hopie. She
could not rescue Hopie, or even tell her what was up; they
needed to act only when Tocsin did. So she learned the ways of
the White Bubble staff, and served competently in her trusted
capacity. Everything hinged on her performance when the crisis came.

Spirit retreated to a private bubble. Now all she could do

was observe, hoping that no serious glitch occurred. It was up to Hope, and Forta, and the Jupiter and Saturn Navies.

The ships of the Jupiter Navy moved into place about Ganymede—and warships of Saturn appeared in Jupiter space. Abruptly there was a planetary crisis, for both these maneuvers were technically acts of war. Spirit knew that Hope had to act, without knowing whether Spirit had completed her preparations.

Tocsin made a public broadcast, declaring a blockade. Then a new signal overrode it: Hope Hubris on a pirate broadcast. "Hello, people of Jupiter," he said in English. "I am Hope Hubris, your former Tyrant. I was exiled five years ago, but now I have returned to resume the government of Jupiter." He paused, glancing back. Roulette's face was there.

There was a delay of several seconds, because Ganymede was three light seconds out from Jupiter. He was waiting for the public reaction. Then Hope spoke again, smiling. "I see you remember me." Music played as a background to his voice. "You also know that your current government has descended rapidly into corruption and incompetence. Industrial efficiency has declined. The planetary debt is rising. Freedom of the press has been curtailed. In fact, the leading critic of my day, Thorley, *is now in prison.*" This time he paused for a full ten seconds to let the reaction come.

Rue was watching Hope, sending out signals of wonder and joy. The monitor of the number of sets tuned in to Hope's broadcast was rising rapidly; he had started on a preemptive basis, but now they were seeking him.

Spirit knew that Tocsin would be barking orders between curses. Hope had only a few more minutes before he got cut off; he had to make them count.

"I was deposed by my wife, Megan. I have known many women, and some have been beautiful." He glanced across at Rue. The rest of her was now being picked up, and she was bare breasted. In six seconds the response would go crazy! Hope had always been a good showman. "But the one I most truly respect is my wife, and she is the one I still heed." He peered into the holo as if searching for a particular person, while the sound did indeed go crazy, on its delayed response to Roulette. "Megan! Are you on?"

The seconds passed, and abruptly the sound abated, as if every watcher were holding his breath. Then Hope's wife did indeed appear, hardly even seeming surprised. She was now past seventy, but still a handsome woman. "Megan," Hope said to her. "Do you still oppose—"

Tocsin cut in. "Mrs. Hubris. You cannot allow this dictator to return!"

Now Hope was silent too, along with Jupiter, awaiting her reaction.

Megan turned her gaze on Tocsin, her ancient enemy. She said no word. Then she turned her back on him.

The holo cut off. Tocsin's technicians had established their intercept, and Hope's broadcast could no longer get through. But it had been enough. Megan would not oppose him—and the people of Jupiter knew it.

Spirit relaxed, for the present. The appearance of the Saturn ships had nullified Tocsin's siege of Ganymede; the Jupiter Navy was now outgunned in this region of space. Ploy and counterploy; it was not the first time this had occurred here. But now the Saturn ships were spreading out to menace Jupiter itself. That was the muscle behind the takeover of the planet; Hope's words were merely the declaration of intent, while Saturn was the mechanism. The Triton Project needed the resources of Jupiter, and Tocsin had made it plain that the present government would never join.

How had the Saturn ships been able to spread without molestation? That was where Spirit's advance work had come in. The interference points. Naturally Tocsin had ordered action, but somehow the task forces had gone astray. Orders had been confused, and foul-ups had occurred. Not one Jupiter ship had fired on a Saturn ship. That was part of what had kept Tocsin occupied during the interim; he had realized that the Jupiter Navy had been partially subverted.

But the true balance of terror lay with the subs. Largely invisible, the subs of each planet surrounded the other, ready to fire their missiles and lasers and blast the enemy cities out of atmosphere or space. The System had lived for centuries under that threat, and no one liked it, but there had been no way to escape it. Until now. That was another reason that the Triton Project was so important. It was why this terrible risk was necessary.

A day later, Hope broadcast again, the technicians having nullified Tocsin's jamming. "This is the Tyrant, again. As I explained yesterday, the government of Jupiter has been corrupted. I charge Tocsin with treason against the planet of Jupiter, and I require him to step down and turn himself in for justice. How say you, Tocsin?"

Tocsin, thus challenged, came on. But he seemed neither astonished nor dismayed. "Tyrant, you think you have won," he rasped. "But you've lost. You think your friend on Saturn supports you, but he doesn't."

"He supports me," Hope asserted. "I am acting as the representative of the Triton Project, and will govern Jupiter as a supporting planet, not as a conquest of Saturn."

"You fool, he doesn't support you because he *can't* support you!" Tocsin shouted. "Because he is dead!"

Spirit stared at the screen. What was this?

"Chairman Khukov was assassinated this morning."

Spirit was stricken. She knew immediately that Tocsin had conspired with the *nomenklatura* to do it, timing his fell strike as precisely as Hope had timed his own action. At one stroke, Tocsin had deprived her of her lover, Hope of the vital support of Saturn, and the System of the Dream.

Tocsin watched Hope in silence, a cruel smile playing about his homely face. He was savoring this moment of victory over the man who had deposed him once and threatened to do so again. All Jupiter was watching.

What could they do? Spirit had prepared for Tocsin's threat to Hopie, but she had underestimated the man. He had struck in more than one direction.

Then she realized that Forta was in the White Bubble, and armed. She would know what to do about Tocsin. She would assassinate him. It might not restore the Dream, but it would punish the man who had destroyed it.

But Hope had another answer. "Saturn fleet! Chairman Khukov is dead. He supported me; I still support him. I am doing what he wanted to be done. I am assuming direct command of the fleet. You will answer to me exactly as you have been doing." He did not *ask* the commanders of that fleet, he simply *told* them, not giving them the chance to think about it. Probably Roulette, the pirate lass, had told him what he had to do.

Could this work? Spirit watched the screen, hoping.

"Jupiter Navy," Hope said next. "I am similarly assuming command over you. I hereby depose your present admirals, and elevate those of my choosing. Specifically, Admiral Lundgren is retired as of this instant, and Admiral Emerald Mondy restored to that command."

"You can't do that!" Tocsin protested. "You have no base! No authority!"

Hope ignored him. He continued to name particular admirals for retirement and restoration, drawing on the names Spirit had provided. "You will cooperate with the Saturn Navy to safeguard the planet of Jupiter from attack. My aide, Roulette Phist, will provide the details of the transition and assignment."

"Countermand!" Tocsin exclaimed, realizing what Hope was doing. "There is no legal basis for this action!"

Spirit smiled grimly. They were way beyond legalities at this point.

"I am not basing this on legality, but on power," Hope said.

"The officers of the Jupiter Navy know what is best for the Navy, and the people of Jupiter know what is best for Jupiter. Participation in the Triton Project is best." Then he launched into the major aspect of his presentation. "As many of you already know, Chairman Khukov of Saturn had a Dream. He shared it with me, and I am sharing it with, you. It is the Dream of peace and prosperity for all men. It is the abolition of oppression, restriction, and hunger." He continued, making the point: lightspeed expansion into the galaxy would solve most of mankind's problems. "Are you with me, people of Jupiter?"

The response was huge: the people were with him. Despite the recent censorship, they had known what was happening elsewhere in the system, and how Jupiter was being left behind. They wanted the Dream.

"It's a lie!" Tocsin shouted. "He's just making it up so as to seize power for himself!"

Hope was ready for that. He dropped his pants, showing his scarred legs. "I have only a few years to live, because my sites are running out; when I can no longer be dialyzed, I shall die. I have no further use for power, other than to forward the Dream."

Tocsin threatened to use the Jupiter subs to attack Saturn. Hope was ready for that too. "People of Saturn, I, Hope Hubris, the Tyrant, am assuming the office vacated by my friend Khukov, who is dead. My purpose is to stabilize the government of North Saturn and bring the assassins to justice. The fleets of Jupiter and Saturn support me, and I am preventing the Jupiter subs from attacking the planet. In the interim I appoint Khukov's most trusted deputy to maintain the present government on a standby basis, until my return to Saturn." He named the deputy; he was a competent and loyal man who did not aspire to power for himself.

Spirit knew that Hope's power over these planets was being constructed largely on bluff and imagination, but it seemed to be working. In this moment of crisis, they had no better figure to turn to. It was the special magic he had with any audience.

They knew they could trust him to do as he promised, and he promised justice and the Dream. It was an easy compromise to make.

But Tocsin was not yet finished. Indeed, he seemed to have recovered his bravado. "I have a little ace in the hole here, Hubris," he said nastily. "You don't dare order this dome destroyed." And he played his ace: Hopie, captive. She was now a woman of thirty, pretty enough, with her dark hair flowing about her face.

"Don't do it, Daddy," Hopie said. "Don't let him have his way. I can die if I have to."

"You don't respond, Tyrant?" Tocsin inquired. "Then I will encourage you. Surrender yourself for arrest, or I will have this woman dispatched before your eyes. Guard!"

And at that a female guard stepped up, carrying a laser pistol. Slowly the woman raised her pistol, until it pointed at Hopie's head.

Hope looked—and Spirit saw the glint in his eye as he recognized Forta, and understood. "Give your order, hemorrhoid," he said.

And Forta's pistol pointed at Toxin. She could take him out before any other guard could rescue him. She put her free hand to her face and drew off her mask, revealing her scarred features.

Tocsin stared at her. Now he knew he had lost. He was not the suicidal type; he always made the best deal he could, in whatever circumstances existed. "Exile," he said.

"Granted," Hope said.

Thus simply did the crisis end. Hope was Tyrant again.

The first thing Spirit did was go to the prison to release Thorley. No one challenged her. Everyone knew that the old order was returning, and that she spoke for the Tyrant. Why the Iron Maiden would want to free the Tyrant's leading critic was her own business. Oh, yes—because the Tyrant believed in free speech, even for those who chastised him. That had been absent in recent years.

Thorley stood as she entered his cell. He looked older, and not merely in age. The stifling of the press had been destroying him more than the imprisonment. She plunged into his embrace, avidly kissing him. "You knew I'd come for you, troglodyte."

"I knew," he agreed. "But I feared for you. And for others."

"Fear no more. Just write your expose." She kissed him again. "After you take me to your apartment."

"But others will see! They will know!"

"Let them know! I love you."

He gazed at her in wonder. "It can be open now?"

"Don't you believe in freedom of expression?"

"Not when it pointlessly hurts those I love. There is such a thing as privacy."

"Let this be public. All except–"

"I understand."

They went to his apartment, and it was much as it had been thirty five years before. They were both old, but there was, as he would later put it, a mighty store of passion to expiate.

Forta, Spirit and Hopie went to Ganymede to join Hope. He hugged each in turn, then reverted to immediacies. "Why didn't you tell me about Roulette?"

Hopie caught on. "Forta emulates your former wives?"

"Something like that," he admitted, embarrassed.

"And you lacked time to cover your body when the broadcast started?" Spirit asked Rue with a smile.

"I didn't want anyone disconnecting early,"

"Nobody on the planet disconnected!" Spirit agreed.

It was the end of the affair, in more than one sense.

CHAPTER 19

Fifteen Women

The following three years were busy ones, as Spirit organized the renewed Tyrancy and kept the mechanics of the Dream operating. Hope, under doctor's orders to relax, was satisfied to be the figurehead. He wrote most of the final volume of his memoirs, directing that all of them go to his daughter at his death. Hopie had an education coming!

In those three years there was full production of another breakthrough: self-receiving light-travel units. With Jupiter participating, technology was advancing rapidly. This meant that a slow physical ship did not have to take decades or centuries to reach a new settlement region and set up a receiver; the lightship itself could translate to physical form and set up the new bubbles. Colonization of far reaches would still take time, of course, for space was huge, but the process could start immediately. To the colonists, translation from the local System to that of a far star would seem instant, though many years would have passed.

Hopie was much involved in this effort, and she roped in Robertico and Amber. Hopie was also assuming more of the likeness of Hope, in little mannerisms and talents. She had known Hope all her life, of course, and admired his ways (with certain limited exceptions), but this was more than mere imitation. She sometimes had visions, and on occasion seemed to be able to read people. She was of course related to him by blood, if not the way she supposed; something could have been passed along. Thorley, now a widower, remarked on it also.

Spirit went with Hope and Forta to review the Triton Project. She had been in close touch with it all along, of course, but Hope had not. As their ship approached Triton she saw and appreciated his amazement. The project had started as a single dome on the planet. Now it was a monstrous complex spreading from crater to crater. Projection tubes orbited it, not one or two, but hundreds. As they drew near, the size of them became apparent: each greater in diameter than any ship they had known in the Navy. What monstrous vessels were they designed to accommodate?

Then, in closer orbit, they spied those vessels: colony ships of a scale hardly imagined before. Even after allowing for necessary supplies for a decade or so, including construction equipment for planetary sites, each ship looked big enough to handle tens of thousands of colonists. Yet these were not the major vessels; the big ones were bubbles, to be projected entire, with up to a million residents each. Those were being outfitted in the atmosphere of Neptune. No wonder this project was expensive!

Hope shook his head, bemused by what was being wrought. "If only Khukov could have seen this," he murmured.

Spirit squeezed Hope's scarred arm, signaling her understanding. Her life, too, was merged in this project. She had done the actual organizational work to make it come to pass. She also had been closer to Khukov than many others knew. She had not loved him, but had come to care for him, and his untimely death still pained her. She had of course told Thorley, and he had understood. He knew about illicit romance.

Hope glanced at her. They had been apart much of the time in recent years, as she traveled to Jupiter and the inner planets, handling the myriad executive details of the organization of man's effort of colonization. She was sixty-five now, and believed she looked it. She had not bothered with the treatments and cosmetics that retarded the semblance of aging, and the faint pattern of scars on her face had become more pronounced.

Then he was kissing her. She had not known he was going to do it. She was kissing back; she had not known she would do that, either. She felt as if she were twelve again. Then he drew away, and looked away, and she neither moved nor spoke. They still shared a secret: their continuing muted passion for each other.

Forta was gazing ahead, looking at Triton and the massive complex of the project on its surface. "You left your kidneys here," she murmured. She did not comment on the kiss. And Spirit wondered again: did Forta emulate Spirit for Hope on occasion? She had done it to conceal Spirit's absence, but did she also do it in bed? It was a question Spirit could not ask. It sent her into a daydream: could she do what Roulette had done, and substitute herself for Forta's emulation of her, so that Hope did not know? What would happen then?

But now they were landing, and her daydream was left incomplete. It was unrealistic anyway; surely Forta would emulate Spirit as she had been in her twenties, not her sixties. Spirit could not emulate that herself.

Then they parted. Spirit had special business to handle on Triton, while Hope and Forta went to South Saturn to enlist its participation in the Dream. There was a problem: the Rings of Saturn were needed as a staging area for South Saturn supplies, and the two governments were hostile to each other. Some reconciliation had to be accomplished, but neither side would yield any power to the other. This was the kind of challenge Hope was good at solving; could he do it again? She followed his effort via the news releases.

Hope managed to talk the two parties into what he termed a decision of fate: each would choose a champion, and the two champions would meet in combat, and the winner would decide the issue. The Middle Kingdom selected a finely trained warrior, perhaps the ranking martial artist of the System. But Wan was smarter than that. It selected a young woman, the fairest flower of her age, stunningly beautiful, skilled in the creative and performing arts and of an endearing disposition. Any man would welcome her as his bride, and probably would do anything for the mere favor of her smile.

The Premier of the Middle Kingdom wanted to abort the contest, but feared losing face. Especially if it seemed that South Saturn was afraid to risk its champion against a mere girl. Also, news leaked to the public, together with a holo photo of the girl, and suddenly the imagination of the nation was caught up in the notion of their virile hero having total access to such a creature while they watched. Let him use her, then win the contest by escaping. So it proceeded. They used a honeymoon bubble: an enclosure with supplies for two for one week, rather luxuriously appointed, and a single jet-powered space suit. Only one could escape it; the other would die, one way or another. The two were placed within it unconscious, their memories washed; then the watch began. For almost every part of the bubble was covered by concealed holo cameras.

Both nations—and indeed, the rest of the System—became riveted to the saga of King and Wan as it played itself out, that week. The two became lovers, of course, and their lovemaking was enjoyed by virtually the whole of the System. Then, realizing that they could not both escape, they made a mutual suicide pact, to occur on the day the food ran out, two days thereafter. He would use the largest sword to decapitate her cleanly, then stab himself through the heart. Their blood would mingle, and they would travel together to the afterlife.

Now the public will became urgent: save the lovers. Abort the contest. Make them instead the Prince and Princess of the local Titan Project mission. But all the provinces of the Middle Kingdom had to ratify the compromise—and one refused. This was Laya, where Tocsin had gone in exile.

Thus it was that Hope went on one more special mission:

to Laya, to persuade it to agree. He went with Forta, emulating Spirit. Spirit herself remained out of sight; it was not generally known that she had not been with her brother all the time. Smilo was also with them.

And then, suddenly, the horrifying news came: Tyrant Hope Hubris and the Iron Maiden and tiger were dead.

But Spirit was already on the way to Saturn, rendezvousing with Hopie. Reba Ward had known before the news was released, and sent an urgent private call to her and Hopie.

"Secret message from the Middle Kingdom?" Spirit inquired as they traveled.

"From Laya," Hopie said. "Reba said the common folk there like the Tyrant; he worshipped at their shrine. But they could not help him."

But Reba's call had come before any such message could have arrived. It was her business to know things, and she made a specialty of Hope, but there was something eerie about this. Spirit let that pass, and invoked her resources to ascertain exactly what had happened on the mountain retreat in Laya. It was an ugly scene, but she controlled her grief and rage. She had a job to do before she could mourn.

It was hours before a party came to the place where Hope and Forta lay, in snow on a mountain, and it was no rescue operation. Their bodies were locked together, his face against her breast. They were dumped unceremoniously on a sled and brought to a holo unit. "The Tyrant and his evil sister are dead!" they exclaimed for the camera, and broadcast the picture to the System. "They fell down the mountain, and we could not reach them in time."

"Daddy!" Hopie cried in anguish as she saw the cruel picture.

Now it was Spirit's turn. "Here is the first lie," she said on the planetary holo. "I am not dead. It is the Tyrant's secretary who died with him, garbed as me."

Astonished, the men of the city of Hasa went to Forta. Her

mask came away. Their chagrin was apparent.

"And the second lie," Spirit continued resolutely. "It was no accident. The Panchen sent his robot snow monster to throw them down. See, there is the wreckage of the machine in the background." And, indeed, the guilty robot was there.

"And the third lie," Spirit said. "The rescue party did not try to come promptly. They could have reached any point in that park in minutes, had they wanted to. Instead they prevented the common folk of the city from coming."

Now her face set into hard lines. "Hasa murdered my brother," she said. "What does Laya say to that?"

Laya's answer was grim.

Spirit could not rest; she had to contact the Triton Project personnel, to secure loyalty to the new order. The Dream would continue, but only if grasped before a vacuum at the top let it come apart. It was Hopie who went to claim the bodies. But her ship was barred by police bubbles of Laya. "First there is business we must do," they informed her.

And while they barred her entry, the people of Laya rose up as one, their car-bubbles massing against the city of Hasa. They covered it with the cannon of a cruiser, forcing entry even as the common folk of the city charged the locks and opened them. Then, armed, the people stormed in, making prisoners of the authorities and all who had supported them. There was little love for the Panchen beyond the city, and now he had given the people the pretext to rebel.

"Now watch what we do," the rebel leader announced on the holo. "The Tyrant will be avenged."

An automatic lock was set up, and the first prisoner was fired out into the atmosphere of Saturn. His body was pulped inward by the tremendous pressure of the atmosphere, as it fell toward even greater pressure. It was followed immediately by the second prisoner, and then a stream of them, at one-second intervals. A line of bodies was forming, streaming steadily down

from Hasa: the Panchen's supporters. The broadcast was relent-
less.

It was four hours before Hopie got into the city and reached
the lock. "Stop it! Stop it!" she cried.

The carnage was stopped at last—but almost fifteen thousand had been executed. The people of Laya had made known
their sentiment and saved face for their province. Face did not
come cheap, in the Middle Kingdom.

The veto of Laya was reversed, and the lives of the Prince
and Princess were saved. But the Tyrant was dead, and Forta,
and Smilo the tiger as well.

They returned to Jupiter, where a considerable service was
held for the Tyrant. It was held at the Shelia Foundation, and
broadcast System wide. Hope's surviving wives and other women
were there, united in grief and memory. There was no apparent
jealousy between them. That had always been the case with
those in his orbit; each understood the feeling of the others.

The ceremony was carefully choreographed, and was as
much show as reality, but Spirit found herself nevertheless caught
up in it. The key element was the Tasting of the Ashes, performed by all of Hope's significant women, or their stand-ins.
Hope's body and that of Smilo Tiger had been cremated, ground
to a fine powder, and set out in a basin the shape of the planet
Saturn, the rings contiguous with the main planet: the site of
his death.

Thorley was the master of ceremonies. "We are gathered
here to honor and pay our final respects to Hope Hubris, otherwise known as the Tyrant of Space," he announced grandly. "I
am Thorley, his most persistent critic. Thus I am here for this
final critique. Though I opposed his politics and policies for the
main part, I have always sustained a sincere respect for the man
himself, and believe I understood him in a special way. For one
thing, I am in love with his sister." There was a collective gasp
of surprise; this had not been known beyond a very select group.
Spirit felt herself blushing as all eyes turned on her, but she

nodded, acknowledging the association. It was a relief to have it out at last.

"Here with me is the Tyrant's daughter Hopie Hubris. She was adopted, but is generally believed to be his illegitimate child by an anonymous Saxon. Certainly she favors him." Thorley turned to Hopie, who stepped up to stand beside him. "And certainly she loved him."

Spirit saw the tears course down Hopie's face. She did favor Hope, and did love him. She was the closest to him of those not among the Fifteen.

"There will be other events elsewhere; this one is confined to his special women. Those he loved." Thorley paused, looking around at the vast assembly of women. He was one of only two men at this particular affair. "Of course all women were special to him, and he to them. But these were the ones who knew him in an especially intimate way." There was a murmur of understanding; they knew what he meant. The Tyrant had been notorious for his appreciation of women, and almost every woman he had encountered in any capacity had felt special in his presence.

"The ashes of Hope Hubris and his tiger companion are here. Each person will pay her respects as I call out her name. When this is done, there will be an orderly procession for the others present, until the ashes are gone. All of you will get to share the essence of the Tyrant, in due course." He paused again, then commenced the names. "Helse Hubris, his first wife, deceased at age sixteen, here represented by her second cousin thrice removed, named in her honor. Helse."

Music played. A young Hispanic woman walked out. There was another murmur, for not only did she appear to be sixteen, she wore a patchwork dress of exactly the kind legend said the original had worn the day she married and died. On an ordinary day she might have been average or pretty, but in this context she was verging on beautiful. Spirit was astonished at the likeness; she was the only person here who had actually known Helse, and this girl did favor her. In fact the similarity was painful; Spirit had loved Helse too, in her fashion, and never quite gotten over her loss. Helse had taught her to play the part of a boy—and to be a woman. To appreciate both the romantic and practical uses of sex. O *Helse*!

She came to the basin of ashes, hesitated, then licked her forefinger, touched it to the basin, lifted a thin film of powder, and put the finger in her mouth. Applause broke out; Helse had partaken of the Tyrant, making him one with her.

The girl stood as if about to faint, an expression of awe on her face. Then Thorley stepped forward and took her elbow, guiding her to a dais behind the basin. He left her standing at its edge. She faced the throng as he returned to his station. Now it could be seen that her face was wet with tears. She was not the original Helse, but she was overwhelmed by the significance of the moment. So were the watching women; many of them were crying similarly. Never had love seemed so young or tragic.

"Spirit Hubris, his sister, The Iron Maiden." The music played again, this time her song: "I know where I'm going, and I know who's going with me; I know who I love, but the dear knows who I'll marry." For much of her life she had been nicknamed "The Dear" by those who suspected how deep her love for her brother really was. There was another murmur, this time of surprise, as she walked to the basin. But this, too, was a relief; another dark secret had been abated. She was, indeed, one of Hope's women, in the special sense. She touched her finger to the powder and licked it off, partaking of her brother.

Suddenly she felt his presence beside her, almost tangibly. She dared not look, for fear the presence would dissipate. "It must not end here, my sister, my love," he told her, and kissed her on the cheek. She thrilled to his touch, as always. He was the dreamer, she the practical one, but he had always been her dream.

"My brother, my love," she murmured. Then it struck her

with full force: her brother was dead. She had been too busy to allow her private feelings rein, but now they governed.

A hand took her elbow. It was Thorley, guiding her to the dais. That was just as well, because she could not see her own way there. She was blinded by tears. She leaned for a moment against his shoulder. "He's gone," she said. "He was so much a part of me, all my life. I lived for him. How can I live without him?"

"You must, for the sake of the Dream," he replied. "That all he lived and worked for be not lost."

"Of course." That was so obvious, once enunciated.

She found herself standing beside Helse. Then she was hugging Helse, and their tears were mixing. Fifty five years had peeled away, and she was there in the bubble with her first woman friend. "He was my first love," she sobbed.

"Mine too," Helse sobbed in response. And of course it was more than true. "I mean, I know I'm not really *her*, but somehow–"

"You are her," Spirit reassured her. "That's the way it was, with him. Helse came back to him in the form of other women, to help him do what he needed to do. Now he needs to die. Helse is with you."

"Yes!" she agreed gratefully. Then: "That was how it was with you?"

"I was twelve," Spirit said. "Helse made me a woman, for him. But I loved him too."

"Of course. When I tasted the ashes, I—I felt him enter me. I mean–"

"Not merely in the mouth," Spirit said. "You are a woman."

"I am a woman. First with him."

Spirit nodded. The girl had experienced an orgasm as she tasted Hope's ashes. It was understandable. "He made many women. None ever truly loved elsewhere, after him. We refer to them as orbiting him."

"I'm in orbit," Helse agreed.

"Juana Moreno, his first military roommate/wife, the Used Maiden," Thorley announced, and the music was "Early one Morning," with the refrain "Oh don't deceive me, Oh never leave me, how could you use a poor maiden so?" For Hope had lived with her without marrying her; enlisted personnel could not marry. The nickname was humorous, but she loved it.

Spirit tried to blink her eyes clear. Through the wash of tears it seemed that Juana was sixteen again, the lovely girl Hope had been put with when each of them had had trouble with the introduction to the Navy Tail. Hope had not wanted to sully the memory of Helse by being intimate with any other woman, and gentle Juana had been raped by pirates and afraid of sex. They had worked it out, but only after coming to mutual understanding. She had been his loyal supporter from that point on, and Spirit had always liked her.

Juana arrived at the dais, and her face too was wet. Spirit embraced her and kissed her. "You were good for him," she said.

"Thank you."

Then Helse hugged her too. "Are you in orbit?" she asked.

"Oh yes, dear! Always." Juana glanced at Spirit, catching on to the transformation the girl had experienced. "Some of us loved elsewhere, and married, but we never left Hope's orbit."

"Or he ours," Spirit said.

Juana nodded. "That time he was hallucinating, and I took him on—I think he knew it was me."

Helse was perplexed. "He wasn't supposed to?"

"He was an officer then. I was enlisted."

"Oh. But he still loved you."

"Always," Juana repeated. "He loved all of us, in his way. But he was loyal to his current woman, whichever one that might be."

"Emerald Sheller, his first full military wife, the Rising Moon." Now the music was "For the pikes must be together, with the rising of the moon." Emerald walked forth, now seventy but retaining military bearing. She tasted the ashes, was overcome, and was guided to the dais. Her face was as wet as any. "Damn it, I thought I was over that," she muttered as she joined them.

"You're a woman," Juana said, smiling sympathetically. "Always in orbit." Then they all hugged her.

"Roulette Phist, his pirate wife, The Ravished." The music played her song "Rue." Roulette, in her late 50's, remained a stunningly proportioned woman, and she had dressed the part. But she too was overcome when she tasted the ashes. She too had to be led to the dais.

"He's there!" she exclaimed. "He made me cry."

"He made you cry," Spirit agreed. Rue had sworn never to cry for another man, and as far as Spirit knew, she hadn't.

"Megan Hubris, his final wife," Thorley announced, and there was new music. She was seventy five, still a stately woman, her hair turning gray. The throng broke into a cheer; they knew her as the best of women, and the erstwhile leader of the resistance that temporarily overthrew the Tyrancy. She too tasted the ashes, and seemed about to faint.

Thorley caught her and steadied her, and guided her to the dais. "Oh, dear," she said. "I did not mean to make a spectacle of myself."

"He touched you," Spirit said.

"He touched me. Now he is gone, and I think I do not wish to continue."

"But you must," Helse said. "You were his truest love."

Megan looked at the girl, and suddenly Spirit saw the likeness of their faces. It was as if the one were the grandmother of the other. That likeness had caused Hope to seek Megan, after he lost Helse. It had been a foolish pursuit, but he had never relented, and in the end had brought her into his orbit too.

"Not as true as the rest of you," Megan said. "I opposed him."

"'I could not love you half as much, loved I not honor more,'"

Emerald said, quoting. "You loved honor more. He always respected that. He loved you best."

"I had to separate from him, but I could endure as long as I knew he was all right. But now he is dead, and my life has no further meaning."

"But the Dream continues," Spirit said. "You must live to see the Dream realized."

"And you remain," Megan agreed. "And Hopie. You are correct; I must endure. But it is so empty without him."

"Oh, yes!" Helse breathed.

"Come cry with us," Juana said. "It is what we have in common."

Megan considered. "I believe I will." Then they clustered around her, and all of them cried again.

"Shelia," Thorley announced. This time a woman in a wheelchair came forth—and she did bear a passing resemblance to Shelia. "Represented by her niece, who loved the Tyrant during his madness."

"Her niece?" Megan asked, surprised.

"Her sister's daughter," Spirit said. "She suffered a similar accident, but Shelia's example gave her courage. When Shelia died, she came to apply for her position, and I would have hired her, but his madness was upon him. Instead of interviewing her, he loved her and let her go. Then the Tyrancy ended. She went to work for the Shelia Foundation, and has benefited by it. Now it is a decade later, and she has her chance. She will work for me."

"Of course," Megan said. She had known about the "staff privileges" and had never seemed to resent them. She had known the three staff women well, and respected them, as they respected her.

The wheelchair arrived. "Welcome, Shelia," Megan said, and bent down to kiss the woman.

"Thank you, Megan." She, too, was crying. "When I tasted the ashes—"

"We know," Helse said.

"I was you, when he took me the first time," Shelia said. "And I was Shelia when he took me again, just now."

"We were all Helse, at first," Megan agreed.

"Coral," Thorley announced. "The Tyrant's bodyguard."

"And lover," Megan said. "I would have let her have him earlier, had there been a way. She had such a good body."

Now Spirit was surprised. "You thought he wanted her body rather than yours?"

"I thought he deserved it. I—was older, and too reserved. It was not fair to him. But he would not stray, while we were together."

Coral arrived at the dais. "I killed you," she said to Shelia. "But he would not let me join you in death."

"Nor should you have," Shelia said. "It was an accident."

"And I was not there to protect him, and he died."

"None of us could protect him, in the end," Roulette said.

Then Ebony joined them, and Amber. The girl seemed hesitant, but the others welcomed her. "We all understand," Juana said.

"I couldn't help myself," Amber said. "I was young, and he–"

"Age is irrelevant," Megan said. "He was the planet, we the satellites."

"But he didn't pursue me. I pursued him. I sent him feelies."

"Honey, he didn't pursue nobody but Megan," Ebony said. "We were all hot for him from the start. To be a woman was to want him, and if he agreed, you were his."

"I was his," Amber agreed.

"Dorian Gray," Thorley announced. "Represented by her son Robertico." There was a wash of laughter through the crowd, to have a man as one of the wives. But it was a laugh of understanding, not derision. He was the closest relative, and this was his right.

It occurred to Spirit that Dorian Gray should have come

before the three staff members, because Hope had been intimate with her first. But of course they had known him more than a decade before they became his lovers. It was a judgment call.

Robertico tasted the ashes, and joined the group on the dais. "She was my mother," he said simply. "But I like to think of him as my father, and Hopie as my sister." He glanced at Amber. "And you, Amber."

Amber embraced him. "Little brother," she said. "You were always my family, when I finally had a family."

"Reba Ward, mentor and mistress," Thorley announced.

There was another judgment call! The woman of QYV had associated with Hope for thirty years, usually indirectly, and of course had fallen into his orbit. She had been instrumental in forwarding his military and political career, but had had sex with him only once. But yes, she counted.

"Tasha, the mole." No one had any secrets, for this occasion. Hope's Saturn attractive secretary walked out to taste the ashes.

"Doppie, assistant on the inner planets."

As far as Spirit knew, Doppie had never had sex with Hope. She had substituted for Spirit, emulating her during her absence, serving as secretary, and that was all. But perhaps she had managed to be with him, or had said that she had, to qualify for this occasion. Did it matter?

"Fortuna Foundling, the muddy diamond, represented by another anonymous orphan from Amnesty Interplanetary." And the final woman came forth, looking ordinary until she tasted the ashes. Then she transformed, as all of them had, and a patina of scars seemed to form on her face. She joined them, and she did resemble Forta.

"Hello, Megan," she said, as if greeting an old friend. "Hello, Spirit. I am glad I could be with you, this moment."

"You were his last," Spirit said.

"Yes, I died with him. But he loved all of us."

"And you emulated the others of us," Emerald said, "So that he could be with us again even if we could not be with him physically."

"Yes. He did not like being apart from you. Any of you. But at the end he did accept me, also."

"You certainly deserved it," Megan said, and the others nodded agreement.

Tasha was looking at Forta. "I knew you. Before he took you."

"Yes." Forta smiled. "The manacles."

"It was the only way."

This continued eerie. How had the new Forta known about that aspect? But Spirit realized that such things were on the comprehensive record.

"Now the fifteen who wifed the Tyrant are united," Thorley concluded. "Their dialogue is their own. The rest of you will form a line for the tasting, and depart. Thereafter others may come if they wish, men included, until the ashes are gone. Then this ceremony will be ended, with the Tyrant made a part of all of you. He loved all of you."

They watched the line form. There was no pushing; it was completely orderly. Each woman came to the bowl, dipped her finger, and put it to her mouth as she moved on. As far as Spirit could tell, all of them were weeping—and all of them assumed expressions of awe as they tasted. The Tyrant was with them.

Thorley and Hopie left their station, and walked slowly across to join the group on the dais. Her hand was on his arm, acceding to his courtly manner. To Spirit's eye, they made a nice couple. How was it that it wasn't obvious to everyone that they were father and daughter?

"We are excused at this point," Spirit said to the others. "But I hope we can remain together for a time. There is so much I want to hear from the rest of you—about my brother."

"There is a restaurant that oversees this square, in my building," Shelia said. "Shall we go there, and talk?"

"Yes!" Helse said, for all of them.

Thorley and Hopie arrived. "May we join you ladies?" he inquired with a wink at Robertico to show that he recognized the non-literality of that case. "I believe it is Hopie's birthday, and it would be difficult to imagine a more compatible group to share it with."

"Your birthday!" Ebony said. "Yes it is! We forgot."

"If I may ask—how old?" Tasha asked. "I remember your letters to him. He liked them so well."

"I'm thirty four today," Hopie said, blushing as if half that age.

"We were thinking of going to the restaurant," Spirit said, flicking her gaze toward the Shelia Foundation building.

"Of course."

They went to the restaurant, and indeed it had a broad window providing a panoramic view of the line of women. They sat at a semicircular table, seventeen of them facing each other and the scene below. The line of women outside seemed end-less.

"How did he die?" Helse asked. "I don't wish to cause pain to others, but it is a thing I must know."

"Of course, dear," Megan said. "We all want to know."

"I have researched this in detail," Reba said. "I have his itinerary throughout. Forta assumed the aspect of Spirit so that others would not know that Spirit was busy elsewhere." She glanced at both of them. "Hope insisted on seeing the Panchen of Laya, despite the urgent plea of the Premier of the Middle Kingdom. He was sure the Panchen would not be so foolish as to have them killed, because that would bring the wrath of the System upon that kingdom."

"It did," Emerald said grimly.

"And its own people," Rue said. "They knew what to do."

"So Hope and Forta went to Laya alone," Reba continued. "They arrived at Hasa, the Forbidden City, where they were not welcomed. They commandeered a vehicle for themselves and the tiger." Reba smiled. "People remember the tiger; this facilitated the tracking. They paused to pay homage to a shrine of the Buddha. Hope said he had always wanted to be like Asoka, and mentioned the four great truths Buddha spoke of: existence is suffering, the origin of suffering is desire, suffering ceases when desire ceases, and the way to reach the end of desire was to follow the Eightfold Path. The people there were impressed. Then they took the footpath up the mountain to find the Panshin. They obtained heavy clothing for the cold, and left Smilo part way up, as he was old and not a cold-weather tiger. It was a difficult climb for Hope, because of his ailment, but Forta helped him. At the top they were attacked by a robot in the shape of a white snow monster. They overcame it, but in the process fell down the steep slope. They tumbled to the base. Hope's clothing had been shredded, his dialysis loop was severed, and Forta's leg was broken. They could have been saved at that point, but were not. Bleeding and dying, they slowly froze to death while waiting for a rescue that did not come."

There was horrified silence. Then Forta spoke. "When I tasted the ashes, I suffered a vision of that scene. I was in the form of Spirit, and I held him to my breast, trying to keep him warm. He addressed me as Spirit, and spoke of the baby. I did not understand but he was insistent that I had given it to him. Then we sang their songs of the Worried Man and The Dear. We rehearsed the Eightfold Path. I tried to tell him that we would be rescued, but he said no, that Helse was coming for him. Then I felt the spirit of Helse join me, and I held him as he died. He was with her at the end. And I was with her too." She paused, for she was weeping. "I could not save him."

There was silence again. Spirit knew that what Reba had said was research—but what way was there to account for Forta's words? *The real Forta had not known about the origin of the baby.* That was why she was perplexed when Hope mentioned it. She was emulating Spirit, but was not Spirit. This Forta was emulating the original Forta, complete with her ignorance.

"Of course it was just a vision," Forta said. "Perhaps I got carried away."

"It was a true vision," Spirit said. "This is how he died."

"You did bring him a baby," Megan said. She glanced at Hopie. "That baby became mine."

"Of course," Spirit agreed, hoping that Hopie would not catch on. Yet was there a continuing point to that secret, now that Thorley's wife was dead? Hope had kept it loyally, accepting decades of condemnation, to protect his sister's secret liaison. But that secret was no longer necessary.

The dialogue continued, as the others spoke of their intimate moments with the Tyrant, and these were also eerily accurate. There were things that only Spirit now knew, yet others mentioned them. Even Robertico told of details of his mother's relationship that Hope had told only to Spirit and she had told no one. Hope really had come to them with the ashes.

The only ones who did not speak were Thorley and Hopie. Perhaps that was just as well.

CHAPTER 20

Dream

A few days after the memorial service, Reba Ward delivered Hope's five autobiographical manuscripts to Hopie, as she had agreed to do. Hopie, evidently astonished to learn of their existence, disappeared into them for several months. Spirit dreaded to imagine what the straight-laced young woman thought of them. She had always been somewhat diffident about, if not openly hostile to, Hope's peccadilloes, choosing not to understand the way he needed women. But she did love him, and did relate to him in special ways. Some very special ways.

So Spirit focused on getting the restored Tyrancy in order, and on finding and placing superior personnel for the Triton Project, and guiding South Saturn toward acceptable details of compromise for their participation in it. King and Wan were intelligent and sensible and meant well, but untrained in project management, so they came to Spirit for advice, and she helped by putting them in direct touch with the most competent personnel she knew of.

But it was more than that. "Please, we are doers, rather than directors," King told her. The two had come in person to plead their case, and he was a dynamic young man, and she a stunningly lovely young woman. "We want to participate."

"I am not sure I understand."

"We want to go to space," Wan said simply.

"But there is need for you here! You are cultural icons, the symbols of the unity of South Saturn and the Rings, known to all the System."

"That, too," he said. "We would like to achieve some privacy, as we thought we had when we met."

"And to bear and raise children," Wan added. "Not in a fishbowl."

Spirit considered. Hope had thrived on notoriety, but Spirit had always preferred some isolation from public awareness. She had lost that, with the death of the Tyrant, and missed it. Her romance with Thorley was the current subject of endless media exposes, and extravagant conjectures, making his position difficult too. She realized belatedly that they would have been better off keeping the secret longer. Public scrutiny was hell on romance. "I understand. I would like to go too. But the penalty of responsibility is to suffer degradation or loss of private wishes."

"Perhaps a lesser responsibility," King suggested. "Something necessary, but less public."

"A small hop," Wan agreed. "To go, and return when it is done."

Spirit shook her head. "We must either remain in the Solar System, or go out many light years. There are no small hops. Even a mission to Alpha Centuri would require four years to travel, and longer to make a viable bubble colony."

"Not necessarily," King said.

"You have a way to travel faster than light?"

"A shorter distance. Nemesis is within half a light year."

"Nemesis!"

"We have talked with our people," Wan said. "They approve the Triton Project, but are wary of untested one-way journeys to space. A colony by the dark star offers a fair test of the technology, close enough to return and report before the long-range ships go out. It would be reassuring."

Spirit considered that. This smart young couple had a truly intriguing idea. South Saturn was not the only region wary of untested one-way travel. A close test project could be emotionally as well as technically useful. Also, this could be perhaps the ideal launching-pad to galactic space, because Nemesis was the System's richest lode of matter, more massive than the rest of the planets and moons and fragments combined. There was a plan to set up mining and construction operations there, but it had been deferred pending availability of equipment and personnel to operate what would necessarily be a huge and dangerous enterprise, largely isolated from the rest of humanity.

She looked at them. It was clear that they understood the significance of this project, and were volunteering for it. Their participation could advance the schedule considerably.

Spirit nodded. "I believe there would be no objection elsewhere if South Saturn and the Rings wish to sponsor a model Nemesis project and make the information obtained available to all others."

"We shall attend to it," King said, clearly pleased. "And participate ourselves, so that all will know that it is viable."

"Thank you," Wan said, and came to kiss Spirit. Her beauty and personal magnetism were such as to make even an old woman thrill to her touch.

It seemed but a brief time before Hopie came, though it was not. "You are my mother," she said.

So she had at last caught on, as was perhaps inevitable after the mention during the Tyrant's memorial service. Spirit found herself holding her daughter, and crying. "So he finally told you, Hopie," she said, thinking of Forta's vision.

"He wrote it in his manuscript," she said. "I never suspected, before."

Hope could have done that, though it surprised Spirit. "Because you are so like him. You inherited so many of his ways."

"Then who is my biologic father?"

There was the other shoe. She deserved to know. "Thorley."

"Thorley," she repeated, her mind almost visibly sifting significant files.

"You know how he saved Megan, suffering injury himself, and Hope told me to take care of him."

"You really took care of him!"

Spirit smiled ruefully. "I really did, dear. We could not marry, but I could not give up the baby. So I brought it to Megan, and she—she was, *is* a great woman." Spirit was crying again. Hopie held her, as Spirit had held Hopie in her infancy, and now the secret between them was gone. "I got to keep you, in my fashion."

"And that's how Megan repaid Thorley for saving her life," Hopie said.

"Oh, it was so much more than that! Megan loves you, dear."

"I know. I could not have had a better mother than Megan, or a better father than Hope Hubris, and I will not deny them now. But how much my new knowledge of my natural parentage adds to my life! The times Thorley was with us, as when he joined our expedition to Saturn when Daddy was Governor of Sunshine. And sending me to him for advice on Education. That's why Daddy let him do that!"

"Yes, in part. Thorley loves you too."

Hopie digested that. "Must this remain secret?"

"That is for you to decide. I may marry Thorley. We can no longer be hurt by your origin. Do what is right for you."

"Aunt Spirit—" Hopie faltered, embarrassed. "Spirit, your story must be told!"

"Hopie, I have never written personal things down; only my brother did that. Now I am the Tyrant, carrying on in his stead; I have no time for such a narrative."

"Then tell me, and I shall write it for you!" she said. "There is so much that you alone know, that will otherwise be lost with you."

"But the time, even for that—"

"In snatches," she pleaded. "At odd moments, when you are free. Tell me, or dictate briefly for a tape that I can transcribe. I can fill in the context from his narrative. All the details he omitted, because you took care of them—"

Spirit shook her head. "Hopie, it just isn't feasible! You have no idea how busy I—"

"*It cannot end here, my sister, my love!*"

Spirit stared at her daughter, startled. That had been Hope's voice issuing from her, just as Spirit had heard it when she tasted the ashes. Hopie *did* identify with him.

What choice did she have? Spirit bowed her head. "As you wish, as ever, my brother, my love," she whispered, and there was comfort in that capitulation.

Now the full story would be out, as Hopie made her inexorable way through Spirit's private life. It was time to deal with Thorley.

She went to see him. "Something has come up?" he inquired, for it was not one of their scheduled trysts.

"Yes. Hopie knows."

"Does she accept?"

"Yes. She means to write my biography. The System will know our secrets."

He laughed. "I will stand revealed as a philandering hypocrite, by my own illegitimate daughter. It is perhaps a fitting finish for the Tyrant's leading critic. Hope Hubris is surely laughing. I hope she is kind to us."

"He's not laughing," she said. "He visits Hopie, and sometimes speaks through her mouth."

"She is a victim of mass hysteria. She has a special problem dealing with his death."

"So do I." But she had not come for this. "Thorley, I want to marry you now."

He considered. "Are we then to assume legal responsibility for what we have done?"

"Yes. Isn't it time?"

"It is time," he agreed. "But I trust you will still be my lover."

"Your *only* lover," she agreed firmly.

They were formally married in a civil ceremony, Hopie attending. They moved in together, but continued their separate public personae: Spirit as current Tyrant of Jupiter, Thorley as the leading critic of the restored Tyrancy. "We do not discuss politics in the bedroom," Thorley reported in a column. But others remarked with some humor that surely the Tyrant had had his vengeance on his critic by chaining him to the Iron Maiden. He came to be known as the Chained Man.

There was a holo session with King and Wan: "We are getting the hardware, but not the software, as it were," King said. "The ships are assigned, but only half filled. We need face personnel."

"Need what?"

"People of stature, of high visibility or notoriety, to attract the masses. Most are already committed to other projects, and the colonists are signing with them. Nemesis is a dark star; there will not be much light, and folk don't like that. They need further inducement to join."

"But notoriety is a thing of the moment," Spirit protested. "It is fickle. In a decade there will be an entire pantheon of other notables."

"This is the moment," Wan said.

Spirit sighed. They had a point. "I will see what I can do."

"Thank you."

How was she going to find "face" personnel? Virtually all the evocative figures had been taken. The ships did need to be filled, or the project would falter. In the restored semi-democratic framework, complements could not simply be assigned; they had to volunteer. That meant attractive names, for an otherwise unattractive mission.

Hopie came again. Spirit could not deny her, and did not want to. "I can't call you 'Mom,'" she said. "Megan will always be that."

"Of course. She raised you and gave you her name." A thing

Spirit would forever appreciate. What could be more fitting that to have her daughter's surname be Hubris?

"But I want to be with you, Spirit. And with Thorley. I want my lost family back."

"Oh, Hopie, it is too late to have that. You have your own adult life to make now."

"I still want it. I want to be with you and Thorley. Amber and Robertico want it too."

"But they aren't–"

"I was adopted. They were virtually adopted. We grew up together for a decade, and have not separated since. We think of ourselves as siblings. We all use Hubris as our surname."

"You want to seem to be a family?"

"We *are* family, in ways that count. We want to be together."

"I don't think I understand."

"You have married Thorley. Take us in."

"Hopie, none of you are children any more!"

"And you are old. So there isn't a lot of time. But we can have a few years together, if we do it now."

Spirit was about to protest again. But two things stopped her. First, she found this crazy idea strangely appealing. She had never had a family, formally, and realized that she missed it. Hopie *was* her daughter, and it would be wonderful to be truly together with her as family members. She knew Thorley would want it too; he had always had to mask his sincere appreciation of the Tyrant's daughter, lest it be misunderstood—or, worse, understood. Second, she suddenly realized that there was a way. "How would you like to go with us to Nemesis?"

Hopie stared at her. "You're going there?"

"If you do. They need participants of notoriety, to attract a full complement of colonists. I think the five of us could help. It would be somewhat isolated, in terms of the Solar System, but we could return in perhaps two years once the colony is fairly established."

"Or go from there to deep space, once the technology has

proved itself. And we would be together, away from the cyno-
sure."

"We would be workers. The colonies can't afford slackers."

Hopie nodded. "I like it. Let me check with the others."

Thus readily was the decision made. They would go halfway to space—and be a family. It seemed fitting.

It was another year before the Nemesis Project was ready to
depart, but it did have a full complement. Hopie, Amber, and
Robertico were all active recruiters, holding responsible positions and working hard. Spirit gradually shifted her duties to
competent and incorruptible leaders, so that the Tyrancy would
become an oligarchy—a government by a few. That would not
be perfect, but nothing was. With luck it would hold long enough
to get mankind safely into space and established at several stars.
The long-range effort, of course, would not be realized for centuries, because it would take the colony ships that long to reach
their destinations, even at light speed. But once they were fairly
started, there would be no stopping the program, even if the
solar System itself defaulted. Like the original Earth, it would
no longer be crucial.

Hopie came through to a degree that surprised Spirit. "All
the Fifteen are coming," she reported.

"Hope's women?" Spirit asked, amazed. "The ones who
tasted the ashes?"

"Yes. Once Daddy possessed them, they want to remain
together. Even Mom." She meant Megan. "They understand
each other in a way few others do. It was what Thorley calls a
numinous experience."

"Numinous?"

"Mysterious, almost supernatural or religious, arousing feelings of honor, duty, loyalty and such," Hopie said, evidently
quoting a dictionary definition. "Hope Hubris came to them in
love, and possessed them again."

Indeed, Spirit had seen it happen, and experienced similar

herself. "Numinous," she agreed. "But how is it you understand this, when you did not taste the ashes?"

"I didn't need to. Hope was already with me."

"With you?"

Hopie looked her in the eye. "My sister, my love," she repeated in Hope's voice. And in that moment, it was Hope's face Spirit saw.

Thorley called it mass hysteria. But he had not tasted the ashes, or seen Hopie like this. *Hope was indeed with her.* "My brother, my love," Spirit repeated, understanding how all of the fifteen would join. Even Megan. How could they leave the Tyrant?

The colony ship was actually a bubble, a small city of about fifty thousand, with all the amenities. Its light was internally generated from contra-terrene iron. They would have to mine to get more iron, which meant capturing planetoids at first. Touching the surface of Nemesis would be extremely difficult even with gravity shielding, for it was a small dead star. Instead they would orbit it, and try to draw from its relatively small heat for their purposes. Then they would see about establishing a robot base on it. It was generally agreed that if they could establish a viable colony by Nemesis, they could do it anywhere.

There was a formal ceremony of departure from the Saturn Rings. Then the bubble moved slowly to the giant transmission tube, where it was stabilized and oriented. Though the light craft were self-receiving, that did not mean that it was done by the personnel aboard them; it was set at the time of transmission. It was precisely calibrated to solidify them near Nemesis, at orbital velocity. They would have to build a new transmission tube at the other end, before any return could be made, and that one would be much smaller. The main bubble would never return.

The moment came. Their nuclear family, Thorley, Spirit, Hopie, Amber, and Robertico held hands. The other women were aboard, forming similar groups. They all knew that this could be instant oblivion, if anything went wrong, so there was some nervousness. There was sand in space that could interfere with the light-phase transmission by fuzzing essential parts. But Spirit could not think of a better way to end, if that was what it was to be.

Hopie looked at her. "It is not the end," she said in Hope's voice.

Thorley was startled. "For a moment I thought the Tyrant was speaking."

"He was, dear," Spirit said, privately pleased by his surprise.

"Numinously," Amber agreed.

Then came the announcement: "Transmission completed." They were there, almost five light months distant, and it had seemed like an instant.

"We made it!" Hopie exclaimed, and hugged Spirit, and then the others.

"We have, as you so quaintly put it, made it," Thorley agreed. "Now comes the real challenge: establishing a viable colony."

They gazed at the monitor. There was the great somber sphere of Nemesis, the so-called dark star. Actually it was a brown dwarf, a burned-out remnant too small to implode into a neutron star, but far more massive than any other planet. They were establishing their orbit around it.

There were four additional city-sized bubblene bubbles, empty shells. Each consisted of two halves suitable when paired for independent space bubbles, or individually as planetary domes. Two had to be halved, landed, secured, sealed, gravity-shielded, and filled in several respects: pressurized with breathable air, set up with buildings and parks, and staffed with living people. The other two would be sealed, pressurized, illuminated, and established in separate orbits, to be used as farms.

As it turned out, in the course of careful investigation, Nemesis was smaller and less dense than believed. It would after all be possible to plant domes directly on its surface, and set up direct mining operations. That was a huge break for the project.

For the Nemesis Colony was to be the main launching pad for the effort of galactic colonization. The original bubble would remain in orbit, spinning to generate effective internal gravity. The four halves would be set on the surface of Nemesis and shielded to reduce the effective gravity to about a hundredth of the planetary surface, so that human beings could live there. These would be the mining and construction centers, drawing on the huge mineral resources of the planet.

The work started immediately. All of the "Fifteen Women" were by definition supervisors, there to direct and encourage the workers. The mere presence of any of them served to enhance morale, and they had to maintain the special personal quality required. They were representatives of the Tyrant, partaking of his magic.

Though the fifteen—and Thorley and Hopie—were scattered during the artificial days, they came together often, sharing their spot experiences and simply appreciating each other's company. "Do you know," Megan said to Spirit, "I had supposed my life was over, when Hope died, but you were correct: there remains much to live for. This is a worthwhile enterprise."

"Yes, it is the implementation of Chairman Khukov's, and Hope's dream also. Yet I am sorry in a way to be stealing your daughter."

"*Our* daughter. She remains much with us. I always valued your association too, Spirit." Megan paused thoughtfully. "Do you know, Robertico is no blood relation, yet he reminds me increasingly of Hope at a young age. I did not know Hope then, of course, but there are mannerisms."

"Hopie and Amber virtually raised him," Spirit said. "He had close contact with Hope throughout his early years."

"Of course. But I did come to know Hope well, and there is a remarkable affinity apart from familiarity. I do not mean in training; Robertico is a fine engineer, while Hope was more of a military man. But there are other alignments."

"Now that you mention it," Spirit said, "Helse Two seems remarkably close to Helse One as I knew her. Of course she is distantly related. Still–"

"I am told she resembles me as I appeared at that age, eighteen," Megan said. "Physically."

"I think she does. You were beautiful." Then Spirit caught herself. "I do not mean that you are not now–"

Megan smiled tolerantly. "I believe the soul of Hope really has touched us all."

Spirit could only agree.

The work continued. They landed the first half-shell on Nemesis, then the second, and sealed them. Special robot crews went down to begin the work of pressurization and to establish the gee-shields. One of the empty bubbles was also sealed and pressurized, and a living crew entered to set up the lights and hydroponics. Things were proceeding well enough.

Then Robertico and Helse Two came to Spirit, obviously distressed. "We have been working together," he said. "We think we should be reassigned."

"Reassigned? That can readily be done. You don't have to work together if you don't want to."

Helse actually scuffled her feet. She was a lovely young woman, but what had seemed so mature when Spirit was twelve now seemed very young. "That's not really it."

"Oh, you mean you would prefer some other placement— both of you."

"Not exactly," Robertico said.

"I'm not sure I understand your problem."

"We are two—two aspects of Hope's women," he said. "We honor that role. Yet–"

"And you have played it well," Spirit said. "Megan and I were remarking on the manner the two of you remind us of Hope and Helse One when they knew each other."

"That's the problem," Helse said. "We are not real. Not really related, I mean. We're emulations. We have roles we must not violate." She looked miserable.

Suddenly Spirit caught on. "You're attracted to each other!" Both bowed their heads, ashamed.

Spirit considered. They were trying to be true to the roles they were playing, but interpersonal attraction was getting in the way. Was that wrong? Her own experience with Thorley suggested that it wasn't. "Give me a day to consult with the others."

"We thought you should know," Robertico said.

"Before anything happened," Helse added.

"Cool it for one day. We'll have a decision."

But they didn't leave yet. "Could we—before that decision–" Robertico said.

"Could we at least kiss?" Helse asked.

"In the circumstance, I think it best that you not kiss."

They didn't argue. They departed gloomily.

Spirit got on it. "Thorley, you're relatively objective. Robertico and Helse Two want to step out of their roles. They're attracted to each other. Will you and Hopie arrange a meeting of the Fifteen?" That meant that it would be by his authority, and Hopie would locate and tell each woman what was up.

"This is a problem?"

"It is to them."

"Would it not be simpler merely to inform them that their concern is groundless?"

"I think they need parental blessing, as it were."

"Then I will chair the meeting, and perhaps make a preliminary statement."

Spirit called King and Wan. "We have a problem of identity," she said. "Robertico and Helse Two represent two of my brother's women, but have feelings for each other."

"The Tyrant died, that we might live," King said. "We value his feelings in death as in life."

"He has possessed Robertico," Wan said. "Of course he loves Helse."

"But the roles–"

"We too have roles," King said. "But we understand young love. There is no necessary conflict." He smiled at Wan. Their own young love had ended a major conflict.

"Let Hope and Helse love again," Wan said.

Spirit was gratified. If the leaders of the Nemesis Project did not object, who else would? "Thank you."

The assembly occurred later that day. They gathered in a private meeting room. Robertico and Helse were present, sitting apart from each other. "We have learned that two of your number have feelings for each other that do not fit their roles," Thorley said. "I propose to put the matter to a vote of the thirteen others, as this may be a precedent. Do you wish to continue the roles you played at the Tyrant's funeral, or to abate them in favor of individual lives?" He looked around, then fixed on Megan.

"Public roles are not necessarily identical to private roles," Megan said. She looked at Reba Ward.

"It has been two years since the Tyrant's death," Reba said. "There is little further need for roles."

"Roles can change," Forta said.

"Who can deny young love?" Juana asked.

"May I speak?" Hopie asked.

The others exchanged glances. "Speak," Shelia said from her wheelchair.

Hopie looked at Spirit. "You knew Hope and Helse One. Is this like that?"

Spirit thought about that long-ago association. It was hidden at first, because Helse had to pretend to be a boy, but it would not be denied. Robertico and Helse Two did seem similar in essence. "Yes."

There was silence.

"I now call the vote," Thorley said. "All in favor of new

roles kindly so signify."

Megan lifted her hand. Roulette and Emerald raised theirs. Juana and Spirit nodded. Then the others followed suit.

"The motion is carried thirteen to nothing," Thorley announced. He looked at Robertico and Helse Two. "Now you may kiss."

They stared at him. "You mean it's all right?" Robertico asked, amazed.

"Indubitably. Your new roles are to emulate the kind of young love the originals found. They were in a small bubble, seeking salvation at a new planet. You are in a big bubble, seeking salvation at a new system. This time we trust there will be no pirates. I am sure the spirit of Hope Hubris wishes you well."

"He does," Hopie said with Hope's voice.

"Can I be a bridesmaid?" Amber asked. The others laughed; she was already seeing the two as marrying. But surely they would.

"And I'll be Maid of Honor," Hopie said. "Remember, we're your sisters, Robertico." She looked at Helse Two. "And you will be our sister in law. Part of the family."

The girl's eyes were shining. "I will be Helse Hubris."

Spirit tried to maintain her composure, but her tears were already flowing. It was so *right*.

Thorley made a grand gesture. "Let the new order commence. Love and be loved, openly, and accomplish great things."

Robertico and Helse Two approached each other. They embraced and kissed, tenderly. The new order commenced.

EDITORIAL EPILOG

The life story of Spirit Hubris, the Iron Maiden, is not yet ended, but I chose to end the biography here for several reasons. For one thing, there has been too much of death already; I prefer to leave this narrative upbeat, to the extent possible. It seems fitting that it conclude with the re-enactment of the romance of Hope and Helse, with the prospect of a far more positive continuation this time. This is indeed the way my father Hope would have wanted it—in fact, *does* want it. He lost the first great love of his life, but can recover it in this manner. Robertico and Helse Two will see the Dreams of the original Beautiful Dreamer Lieutenant Repro, and Khukov, and Hope himself, to their fair completion. They will bring their children into those Dreams as citizens of the galaxy.

But there is a rather more practical reason, too. That is that the death of Spirit Hubris can not be known at this time. For she, along with the rest of us, will be going on the next mission: from Nemesis to the galaxy. That is, to an unnamed, numbered star approximately fifty light years distant that has a family of planets. The light transmission technology has been proven, and the colonization of galactic space is commencing. We mean to be part of that—the Fifteen, and their associates, and the personnel of the Nemesis project. We have labored in darkness for two years, and now are ready for the sight of our own colony star. The folk of Nemesis have worked together, and believe in their competence to do it again, this time for real, as it were. So the bases on Nemesis will remain, and the orbiting farm bubbles, buttressed by further bubbles from Sol, but the origin city-bubble will restock and ship out. That's the problem.

Think of the time element: to us, the transmission will seem instant, but it will be fifty years. A return message will take another fifty years. *It will be a full century before news of our colony reaches the Solar System.* So if the system is to have Spirit's biography, it can not be complete. It must end with her departure from the System. It may be that our beam will pass through a meteor shower in deep space and be disrupted, so that we never materialize at our star. Or we may be completely successful. But no one remaining at the Solar System will know, either way. Only their descendants. Spirit's life to this point is all that can be made available.

Meanwhile we have indeed been becoming a family, Thorley, Spirit, and I, together with Robertico and Amber when they wish to participate. We do family things together, and discuss things other than politics, getting more comfortable with each other. It is quietly pleasant, between the chronic emergencies of the colony construction work. I think Spirit appreciates it too, though she has difficulty unbending enough to say so. The iron fades slowly from the maiden.

And so we prepare to go, together as a family and as a wider family of the rest of the Fifteen. This volume will be the final one to be done by this editor, at least for this System. There remains one question that perhaps should be addressed. I am the daughter of the Tyrant, by whatever convention, and related to him by blood. At times I seem to have close rapport with him, such as when I completed his final volume. I sometimes shared his visions when he was alive. Taken as a whole, he was considered at times to be mad. Now he visits me on occasion; I feel his presence, and speak with his voice. Thorley considers it to be hysteria, but he does not know the range and depth of what I experience. Have I inherited Hope's madness?

I rather think I have. That pleases me.

AUTHOR'S NOTE

I'm getting older. At this writing I am 65 and on Medicare, and suffering from what answers the description of shingles: a pain in my left side, just over the ribs, that is quiescent except when I aggravate it, such as by coughing, sneezing, running, lifting, exercising, or rising from a chair. Shingles is a complication of chicken pox: the one strikes early in life, the other late. It's one of the herpes family, and it hides for decades until the body's immune system relaxes, then comes out to aggravate a nerve. I had it four years ago, in my right upper jaw, and it made my teeth so cold sensitive that I could not eat or drink anything cold; in fact I had to heat water to brush my teeth, because room-temperature was painful. I understood at that time that I would not get it again, but elsewhere read that there can be repeat episodes. It has been about two weeks now, and it is slowly, reluctantly easing. Could be something else, I suppose, but I didn't strain anything or do anything extraordinary; it just started slowly and built up for three days, giving me a small hint of hell. Meanwhile I am uncomfortably aware that several other genre writers I knew and interacted with, like Roger Zelazny and John Brunner, are dead. I am comparatively well off. Age, with all its complications, is certainly better than the alternative. But the game as I knew it is ending; the old order passes.

But apart from the complications of age and nostalgia, I'm not slowing down much. I'm still writing, and involved in other significant projects. I don't expect ever to retire; I'm a self-employed workaholic, so don't have to. But I am making a

conscious effort to catch up on things that I want to have done
before I kick the bucket, and this novel is one such. In fact it
derives from the confluence of two of my life projects. The first
is to get all of my 115-and-counting books into print by republishing all those that have gone out of print, so that any readers
who want them all can have them; and the second is to make it
possible for every other writer or hopeful writer to do the same.

In 1997 I heard from one John Feldcamp, whose ambition
was to set up a publishing facility that would enable anyone to
be published. I told him that I liked the idea, but thought he
didn't know what he was getting into. But as our dialogue developed, he satisfied me that he did know, and was quite serious. Thus I became an investor in XLIBRIS, and learned through
experience about the perils of venture and angel capitalization.
Venture capital pays for things like Internet Dot.com startups,
and if they don't go bust and lose all the money, they may become powerful new forces and repay their investors many times
over. I'm not sure what the ratio of successes to failures is, but I
suspect it is small; more investments are lost than gained. It's
really a very pricey gamble. So why does anyone do it? Because
the few that do pay off may be so rewarding as to make up for a
number of losses elsewhere. That is, a venture capitalist might
invest in ten startup companies, and eight might fail, one might
break even, and one would become a success, repaying twenty
times the investment. Thus, taken as a whole, the investor might
double his money in a fairly short period. Angel investment is
even more so, because that's the one that invests in what the
venture capitalists pass up as too risky. Now I'm not a gambler;
I won't buy a lottery ticket. I won't even match pennies. I was
raised as a Quaker (The Religious Society of Friends), and though
I did not join that religion, a number of its precepts rubbed off
on me, anti-gambling among them. Another is doing well by
doing good—trying to invest money in socially responsible ways
that are also good business. So my wife and I invested in Xlibris
not in the wild hope of making a lot of money—we really don't

need more money at this stage in life—but in the hope of enabling all the writers of the world to realize their dreams of being published and read. I figured it was 50-50 that we would lose our money, but we had to give it a try, just in case we might in this manner forever change the face of publishing for the better. That was a dream worth gambling on. So we became in effect an angel investor. This was a considerable education, and at times it seemed rather like a roller coaster ride, with no assurance that the track would continue beyond the next bend. At one point it seemed that we had doubled our money; a day later it seemed that we had lost it, with the company on the verge of collapse. So we doubled our investment, to enable the company to continue, and thereafter things improved. After another bad scare or two Xlibris obtained major venture capital investment, and was on track to become perhaps the dominant force in this type of publishing. Chances are that every writer *will* be able to publish, and that our investment will prove to be very good. It is nice when doing good does mean doing well.

So now I am republishing my back novels at Xlibris, and by the time I am done I expect to be the single largest author there, as it were, with fifty or more titles. But it's a job, because we have to scan the old books into the computer, and proofread them, and I had to write author's notes for them, and send them in, and proofread the galleys, and ponder new covers, and so on. If I set out to proofread every novel I have had published, it would take me perhaps two years, without doing any original writing in that time. So this will be somewhat spaced out. I started with the Bio of a Space Tyrant series, and as I went through each novel I made notes, character lists, timeline, and whatever else I needed to keep it all straight. Then, because the material was now organized and fresh in mind, I wrote the concluding novel. This one. So it has a certain significance. You might say that in order to do this project, I had to help set up a publishing services company, and republish the five prior novels. Only when I had done those things was I ready for *The Iron Maiden*. Eventually this novel, too, should be republished at Xlibris, but first I'll try to give it its chance at Parnassus, the conventional publishing establishment, because that's where the money is. Some critics profess to be horrified by the discovery that I write for money, as if that's not true of every commercial writer. If a writer can't earn his living through his writing, he will not remain a writer long unless he is independently wealthy. Except via the agency of companies like Xlibris, where writers publish more for the love of it than for money.

Now for *Iron Maiden* itself. It was a challenge to do a novel that is in a sense a sequel to a complete prior series. I had to cover existing material accurately, without making a collection of excerpts. Spirit Hubris's whole life was tied in with that of her brother Hope; she was always dedicated to his interests. If I skipped her interactions with Hope, I would leave most of her life a blank. If I included them all, it would become merely the same story seen through another viewpoint. So I compromised by including most of them, but abbreviated or summarized, and interspersing them with Spirit's own private thoughts and events that were not shown before. My effort was to make a separate story that could be read and understood by readers who had not read the original series, and that would also add significant material for readers who were familiar with the others. It may be that some will read this novel first, then go on to the prior novels; if so, I hope they discover things there that were not fully developed here. It may be that some who read the series when the novels were first published will find pleasant reminders in this novel. I hope so.

I wrote and adapted the first 88,000 words (of about 140,000) in July and August 1999, then had to break off to work on a movie project with a deadline, *Princess Rose*. When that was done I had to move on to the Xanth novel *Swell Foop*, also on a deadline. Then I took two months to catch up on backlogged reading and other chores, such as my participation as a member of the board of directors of Xlibris. Then in February I returned to write the last 50,000 words of *Iron Maiden*, and finished it in March, 2000. I don't like interrupting projects this way, but my career is a constant weighing of projects, and I work on those that require it, when they need it, rather than on those I might prefer. This comes under the heading of commercial writing: the project I did because I felt it was time for it had to wait on the paying projects. I'm used to it.

I receive huge reader input for my Xanth series, as fans suggest puns, characters, and stories, but very little for my other projects. That's all right; I have more notions of my own than I will use in my lifetime. But on occasion other novels are affected, and that happened here. Marisol Ramos maintains a web site devoted to my works; my own hipiers.com has a link to it. She is of Hispanic descent, and caught an error of mine in the Space Tyrant series: since Halfcal is supposed to derive from Haiti, how can the refugees be Hispanic when Haiti is not? So I scrambled for the explanation, as given in this novel: they are at the fringe, in a territory that changed hands. So now I'm covered, thanks to Marisol. I hate to make significant mistakes, and that might have been a disastrous one.

As I read the first novels, after a lapse of about fifteen years, I must say I was impressed by their quality. I feel that the Space Tyrant series is some of my best writing. Commercially it paled compared to my fantasy, but commercial success is not the same as quality. Neither is critical success, incidentally. Both commercial and critical success are functions of a complex of forces, and merit is only one of those forces, and probably not the main one. So my judgments of my own work (and that of others) are independent of sales or ratings. But to be specific: do I feel Space Tyrant is superior writing to Xanth? Yes. That does not mean I think Xanth is bad, just that it's a different type that happens to appeal to a larger audience. So Xanth is more commercial. As for critical ratings—Space Tyrant garnered some of the lowest. I think that's a reflection on the inadequacy of the critics rather than the series. Ideally, reviewing and criticism are good and necessary things, but in practice they can be degraded to the point of uselessness. I think that's too bad. So my opinion is only my own—but that is the one I value most. I am glad to have these books available again, and the series complete.

So do I plan to write any more Space Tyrant novels? No. I feel that this novel catches up some loose ends and completes the story of the Tyrant. The exploration and human colonization of the galaxy will be left to other hands.

This Author's Note was written in March, 2000.

Printed in the United States
29612LVS00004B/20

9 781401 043964